WHAT WAS A NICE JEWISH GIRL FROM HARVARD LAW SCHOOL DOING IN A CASE LIKE THIS?

A case of the most sordid kind of sex, captured in scandalous, graphic detail on video.

A case of savage murder, with the finger of guilt pointing in an unthinkable direction.

A case of an intricate web of evil that ran from the mansions of the rich to the penthouses of the powerful, and from the shady side of St. Louis riverboat gambling to neon-lit Las Vegas sin strips.

A case where old high school classmates brought back bad memories and caused new headaches and heartaches, and a sweet little sister turned out to have a great big nasty secret.

Rachel Gold didn't ask for ~~~~ she couldn't drop it—as she set o~~~~ the things they never taugh~~~~

"Delicious ... ~~~~ it."
—*St. Louis Post-Dispatch*

"A compelling read packed with clever plot twists and memorable players."
—Judith Kelman, author of *Someone's Watching*

THE RACHEL GOLD MYSTERY SERIES
BY MICHAEL A. KAHN

☐ **FIRM AMBITIONS A Rachel Gold Mystery.** Attorney Rachel Gold didn't expect her very last divorce case to land her at a chic health club full of rich, bored wives who find Andros, its fitness trainer, irresistible. Unfortunately for the love-starved ladies, he's the one who dies, suddenly of cyanide-laced vitamins.
(179617—$5.99)

☐ **DEATH BENEFITS A Rachel Gold Mystery.** Savvy, sharp Chicago attorney Rachel Gold has been hired to clear a hefty but controversial insurance claim following the messy suicide of one of the firm's managing partners. Rachel discovers that the conservative partner was into some peculiar cases as well as a sexy paralegal. Even more shocking, he may have located a legendary Aztec treasure linked to a chain of grisly deaths that spans the centuries.
(176871—$4.99)

☐ **GRAVE DESIGNS A Rachel Gold Mystery.** When one of Abbott & Windsor's senior partners, Graham Anderson Marshall III, succumbs to heart failure and leaves behind a wacky codicil to his will: $40,000 to maintain a grave in a pet cemetery for "Canaan", the staid law firm asks savvy Chicago attorney Rachel Gold to discover what Marshall really buried in Wagging Tail Estates—since he never did own a pet. (402936—$4.99)

*Prices slightly higher in Canada

Buy them at your local bookstore or use this convenient coupon for ordering.

PENGUIN USA
P.O. Box 999 — Dept. #17109
Bergenfield, New Jersey 07621

Please send me the books I have checked above.
I am enclosing $_____ (please add $2.00 to cover postage and handling). Send check or money order (no cash or C.O.D.'s) or charge by Mastercard or VISA (with a $15.00 minimum). Prices and numbers are subject to change without notice.

Card #_____ Exp. Date _____
Signature_____
Name_____
Address_____
City _____ State _____ Zip Code _____

For faster service when ordering by credit card call **1-800-253-6476**

Allow a minimum of 4-6 weeks for delivery. This offer is subject to change without notice.

FIRM AMBITIONS

A RACHEL GOLD MYSTERY

MICHAEL A. KAHN

AN ONYX BOOK

ONYX
Published by the Penguin Group
Penguin Books USA Inc., 375 Hudson Street,
New York, New York 10014, U.S.A.
Penguin Books Ltd, 27 Wrights Lane,
London W8 5TZ, England
Penguin Books Australia Ltd, Ringwood,
Victoria, Australia
Penguin Books Canada Ltd, 10 Alcorn Avenue,
Toronto, Ontario, Canada M4V 3B2
Penguin Books (N.Z.) Ltd, 182–190 Wairau Road,
Auckland 10, New Zealand

Penguin Books Ltd, Registered Offices:
Harmondsworth, Middlesex, England

Published by Onyx, an imprint of Dutton Signet,
a division of Penguin Books USA Inc.
Previously published in a Dutton edition.

First Onyx Printing, September, 1995
10 9 8 7 6 5 4 3 2 1

Copyright © Michael A. Kahn, 1994
All rights reserved

 REGISTERED TRADEMARK—MARCA REGISTRADA

Printed in the United States of America

Without limiting the rights under copyright reserved above, no part of this
publication may be reproduced, stored in or introduced into a retrieval system,
or transmitted, in any form, or by any means (electronic, mechanical, photo-
copying, recording, or otherwise), without the prior written permission of both
the copyright owner and the above publisher of this book.

PUBLISHER'S NOTE
This is a work of fiction. Names, characters, places, and incidents either are
the products of the author's imagination or are used fictitiously, and any resemblance to actual persons, living or dead, events, or locales is entirely co-
incidental.

BOOKS ARE AVAILABLE AT QUANTITY DISCOUNTS WHEN USED TO PROMOTE PRODUCTS
OR SERVICES. FOR INFORMATION PLEASE WRITE TO PREMIUM MARKETING DIVISION,
PENGUIN BOOKS USA INC., 375 HUDSON STREET, NEW YORK, NEW YORK 10014.

If you purchased this book without a cover you should be aware that this book
is stolen property. It was reported as "unsold and destroyed" to the publisher
and neither the author nor the publisher has received any payment for this
"stripped book."

For my special, wonderful Hanna

1

CHAPTER

Despite the allegations in the petition, fellatio is no longer included on Missouri's list of infamous crimes against nature. It remains, however, "deviate sexual intercourse," which the criminal code defines as "any sexual act involving the genitals of one person and the mouth or tongue of another." The code calls it a class A misdemeanor. Vicki MacDonald calls it a Big Mac with Special Sauce.

Over the course of her two-year relationship with Stanley Webster, Vicki had 204 Big Macs. She kept track in her general ledger. Under the final settlement decree, the Estate of Stanley Webster paid her an amount equal to $1,715.69 per Big Mac. You could build a franchise on numbers like that. And with a few more fees like the one Vicki paid me, I could almost get used to the peculiar path my legal career seemed to be following since I had moved back home to St. Louis from Chicago.

Vicki MacDonald had been the very first client to walk into my St. Louis law office, which was on the first floor of a converted Victorian mansion in the Central West End. She was, as the host of the old *What's My Line* would put it, self-employed in the service industry. She had been referred to me by a Chicago client who practiced the same trade in the Windy City.

Vicki earned a handsome living through her mastery of certain physical skills and her understanding of the keys to success in any service industry. Unlike her physician clients, she made house calls. Unlike her attorney clients, she came to your office. Unlike her CPA clients, she took Visa and MasterCard. (The $549.99 charge showed up on the monthly statement under something called Professional Relief Systems, Inc.) And unlike most of her clients, Vicki brought genuine ability *and* enthusiasm to her craft: she was good at what she did, and she clearly enjoyed doing it.

As a result, Vicki was weathering the recession quite nicely when Stanley Webster died in a freak airplane crash outside Detroit. Although the stock of Webster Industries fell seven points in heavy trading the following day, it bounced back by the end of the week and was actually up a point and a half when the market opened on the day of his funeral. In short, things seemed to be returning to normal.

And then the fourth codicil to Stanley Webster's will was revealed. In it, Stanley bequeathed to Vicki MacDonald enough stock in Webster Industries to entitle her to a position on the board of directors. Under the rules of the Securities and Exchange Commission, that sort of transaction is known as a material event requiring public disclosure.

When Rosalind Webster, former president of the St. Louis Symphony Society and current member of the Washington University board of trustees, learned of her late husband's codicil, she did what any wealthy widow would do in response to that sort of material event: she instructed her lawyers to obliterate it. Specifically, she hired three vicious and expensive St. Louis litigators—barracudas with Rolexes—and told them to do whatever needed to be done to nullify the codicil and destroy "that blow-job bimbo."

Vicki MacDonald was no bimbo. That was obvious when she arrived at my office, grim and determined. She had brought along the petition delivered to her by Rosalind Webster's attorneys. It was the so-called hammer draft—designed to make the other side crater at the prospect of having such a lawsuit filed. The hammer draft alleged that the stock bequest should be invalidated on the ground that Vicki had already been "vastly and unconscionably overcompensated for her infamous crimes against nature, as more fully detailed on the decedent's monthly Visa statements attached as Group Exhibit A." Highlighted in yellow on those Visa statements were 112 charges over the past eighteen months to Professional Relief Systems, Inc., each for $549.99, for a total of $61,598.88.

It was a nasty ploy by Rosalind Webster's lawyers—especially the part about the monthly Visa statements, since they knew that Vicki would realize that public disclosure of the Visa statements would give a prosecutor an easy road map for a quick prostitution conviction. The ploy, especially the risk of criminal prosecution, would have worked against most people. Vicki MacDonald was not most people.

"I really liked Stanley," she told me that first day in my office, "and he liked me. He treated me special. We had fun together. I'm not some floozy his wife's lawyers can force back under a rock. I've thought it over, Rachel. I don't want you to get me on the board of directors, and I don't want to get into an alley fight over the stock. You know what I want? Two things. First, I want you to make her lawyers start pissing in short jerks. Second, I want you to make that bitch back down and apologize."

So that's what I did.

I started by upping the ante: I sent Rosalind Webster's lawyers a draft response to the hammer draft. My best buddy Benny Goldberg called it the "Yo' Mama Answer." Among other things, it attached as Exhibit C an excerpt from Vicki's journal quoting Stanley Webster's graphic and disgusted descriptions of a few of Rosalind Bingsley Webster's rather unusual sexual preferences, which included, among other things, an occasional "golden shower."

Four days later, one of Rosalind's lawyers—the middle barracuda—called to suggest that it might make sense for the parties to explore an amicable resolution of their differences before anyone rushed off to court.

I told him that my client was not in an amicable mood. "Nevertheless," I said nonchalantly, "cooperation isn't out of the question. For example, it might make sense for us to coordinate a joint press conference at the outset of the lawsuit. By the way, Ron, I'm willing to recommend to my client that we consent to having the photographs filed under seal. Of course, I can't promise that Vicki will agree, but she might."

"Which, uh, photographs would those be?"

"Of your client. The golden-shower shots."

He called six times over the next twenty-four hours. I took the sixth call after having my secretary put him on hold for ten minutes. His voice sounded a full octave higher since our prior conversation, and his speech mannerisms did indeed suggest a man with blockage in the urinary tract. I laid out my settlement demands. Miss Manners herself would have been pleased with the tone and substance of his response. Two days later we signed the settlement agreement: Vicki surrendered her claim to the stock in exchange for (1) a cash payment of $350,000 and (2) a notarized written apology from Rosalind Bingsley Webster.

Little did I know that the Big Mac case was the beginning of my descent into that level of domestic hell known as divorce law. Vicki sent me the next divorce—one of the CPA clients. Three others came through the door based on what they had heard through the divorce-case grapevine. Vicki's lucrative settlement seemed to have catapulted me onto the St. Louis short list of prospective lawyers for high-stakes, bad-blood divorces. It was a list I had no desire to be on. Although the fees were lavish, my daily sorties into the war zone of crumbled marriages, shrill emotions, revenge schemes, and creepy lawyers became increasingly oppressive. The practice of law just wasn't fun anymore.

So when June Greisedick came along I decided that she would be my last. June was a farmer's wife from Jefferson County. Her husband Bob's idea of carnal bliss was to sit naked on the edge of the bed while Big Sal licked his nether parts. Big Sal was a purebred tricolor collie. All in all, it was a vision of the American farmer somewhat at odds with the Jeffersonian ideal. I proceeded to file what I assume is the only divorce case in America in which the correspondent has papers from the American Kennel Club. It was, to say the least, an unusual case for a nice Jewish girl from Harvard Law School. My only consolation was that I would never handle another divorce case.

* * *

Never say never, I reminded myself, as I sat behind my desk and watched Eileen Landau reapply her lipstick. She was a friend of my sister Ann, and Ann had begged me to see her.

Eileen checked her lipstick in the mirror of her compact, dropped the compact back into her Louis Vuitton bag, and looked up at me. "And another thing," she said with a shudder. "He sheds."

"Your husband?" I asked uncertainly as a vision of a tricolor collie in heat flashed through my mind.

She nodded in disgust.

I stared down at my hands and sighed. A dull mechanic's lien case sounded good about now.

"Eileen, I'm not quite sure I'm following you."

"He's physically repulsive," she said. "When's the last time you saw Tommy?"

I had a vague memory of Tommy Landau from a summer evening many years ago, maybe all the way back to high school: a long-haired rich guy revving the engine of his Jeep convertible as he waited for the light to change. There was a smirk on his face as he turned toward the car I was in. He was wearing wraparound sunglasses and smoking a cigarette. The light changed and he roared off with a screech of the tires.

"I don't know," I said. "Maybe ten or fifteen years."

"I bet he's put on fifty pounds since then," Eileen said. "And he keeps getting hairier. After we have sex and he finally rolls off of me—he's always got to be on top, you know—half the time he falls asleep up there as soon as he comes, which usually takes thirty seconds max, and then I have to shove him off me—anyway, after he rolls off I go right into my bathroom, turn on the light, and stand in front of the mirror. It takes me half an hour to pick all the hairs off my body. It's totally gross."

The phone rang. My secretary answered it on the second ring. Maybe it was a new client with a really boring insurance coverage dispute. Better yet, a property tax appeal.

"Have you tried marriage counseling?" I asked, hoping for an escape route.

"Rachel, I don't want marriage counseling. I don't want this marriage. I've spent the last fifteen years of my life married to Tommy Landau. I'm sick of him. That's why I'm here. I don't want to be his wife anymore."

I studied my newest client. The Eileen Landau seated across the desk from me in no way resembled the Eileen Cohen who had graduated from University City High School eight years ahead of me. Back then her nose was hooked, her breasts were small, her hair was brown, her teeth were crooked, and she wore glasses. Back then she was treasurer of the student council. Now she was a homecoming queen. Plastic surgery, orthodontia, an expensive hairdresser, and tinted contact lenses had converted Eileen Cohen into a striking red-head with high, round breasts, a small retroussé nose, and capped white teeth. She was wearing the mandatory daytime shopping outfit for the wealthy ladies of Ladue: a white tennis dress, a diamond tennis bracelet, and a diamond pendant.

Like the Jaguar she drove, Eileen Landau looked expensive to maintain. She hadn't always been that way. Her father—Sid Cohen—owned Cohen's Drugs, a gloomy little pharmacy with trusses and prosthetic devices and sun-faded posters in the front window. Cohen's Drugs was sandwiched between a kosher deli and a dry cleaner in a strip shopping center in University City across the street from the small Orthodox synagogue where Eileen had been confirmed in a dress sewn by her mother.

That was many years ago, long before Sid Cohen's daughter married into one of the oldest and most prestigious Germanic Jewish families in St. Louis. She had adapted quite nicely to the ways and means of the Jewish country-club set. Indeed, Eileen Landau seemed more of a Landau than her husband, Tommy, who was something of a black sheep in a family whose name adorned a building and a professorship at the Washington University School of Law, an elementary school in north St. Louis, and an endowment fund at Temple Emmanuel.

Tommy Landau was the son of a prominent St. Louis attorney and the grandson of a judge on the Missouri Court of Appeals. Tommy Landau, however, hadn't even graduated from college. As I recalled, he was expelled in the aftermath of some sort of date-rape scandal at his fraternity. From there, he moved into drugs—first as a consumer, then as a retailer. By the time he was arrested on drug charges in his mid-twenties, he was allegedly dealing cocaine to the yuppie stockbrokers, bankers, and lawyers he'd met during his formative years at the St. Louis Country Day School. After Tommy beat the drug charges, he moved into a field more receptive to his talents and tendencies: he became a real estate developer. He currently owned a dozen strip shopping centers throughout metropolitan St. Louis and southern Illinois.

"When did it start going bad?" I asked.

"When I heard him say, 'Celtics by six.' "

"I'm not following you."

"Everything I needed to know about our marriage I learned on my wedding night," she said with a sad shake of her head. "When we got to our hotel room, I ordered champagne and caviar from room service and went into the bathroom to put on my nightgown. I bought it especially for our first night. I so wanted it to be romantic—a typical young bride, I guess. What did I know? All I'd been up to then was a kindergarten teacher. When I came out of the bathroom, he was on the phone and had the TV and the radio on. You know why?"

"No."

She rolled her eyes. "We got married in the middle of the NBA playoffs. He had one game on the tube and another one on the radio. I came out of the bathroom just in time to hear him place a five-thousand-dollar bet with his bookie. Five thousand dollars. 'Celtics by six.' Those were the first words I heard. He looked up when I walked out of the bathroom, but I could tell he didn't even notice me or the nightgown. 'Be with you in a moment, babe,' he said, and then he placed another bet."

I winced. "You must have been so disappointed."

"It was a nightmare. The West Coast games were still going when I fell asleep. We never even made love that night."

"Does he still bet on sports?"

"All the time. He dropped eighty thousand dollars on the Super Bowl last year. He missed half of our son's bar mitzvah because he was out in the hallway at a pay phone placing bets on college basketball games."

I gave her a sympathetic look. "That's awful."

She nodded. "I've always come second in his life. He's a

workaholic, and when he's not at work he's either watching sports or placing bets. When my son Brandon was in first grade the art teacher had each of the children make a wall hanging using words of wisdom that one of their parents had taught them. You know, 'Love your neighbors,' 'Be nice to animals,' something normal. Do you know what Brandon chose? 'Dogs at home.' "

"Huh?"

"It's one of Tommy's betting guides. If the teams seem evenly matched, then bet on the underdog when they're playing at home. 'Dogs at home.' Can you believe it? Now that Brandon is in junior high, he wants to go on a safari with his father. Kill a gazelle. Isn't that touching?"

"A real safari?"

"Tommy goes to this game reserve in South Africa every summer. He brings back a trophy each time. Usually a stuffed head mounted on a board. You should see the family room. Even worse, you should see his office. He's got a mounted cow's head in there."

"An African cow?"

"No. An American cow." She snorted in disgust. "Isn't that sick?"

"Your husband hunts dairy cows?"

"No. That one was an accident. He goes deer hunting somewhere in southern Illinois every fall. Two years ago he shot a cow by mistake. He thought it was so funny he had the head stuffed and mounted." She shuddered. "I can't stand that man, Rachel."

I leaned back in my chair and looked at Eileen. Tommy Landau sounded like a real creep. Despite my prior vows, I could sense my litigator's pulse quicken ever so slightly at the thought of going into battle against him. "Does he know you're here today?" I asked her.

"No."

"Have you told him you want a divorce?"

She took a deep breath and exhaled. "Not yet."

"Why not?"

"Because I wanted to meet with you before I told him."

"What made you finally decide to divorce him?"

She tilted her head as she pondered the question. "I guess it started when they stole my ballerina over Christmas."

"Who?"

"Burglars. They broke into our house while we were down at Sanibel. It was a totally professional job. They got in and got out without setting off the alarm. They took the usual stuff: color TV, stereo, the kids' Apple computer, a couple paintings. Tommy's parents called us the day after it happened. We came home the next day." She closed her eyes for a moment. "The whole time I kept praying, 'Please let my ballerina be there.' "

"What kind of ballerina?"

"She's one of those beautiful Lladro porcelain figurines. I bought her in Chicago a few years ago." She looked at me and sighed. "Oh, Rachel, she was so gorgeous, so graceful. She's seated on the floor and slipping on one of her ballet shoes. I put her in the sunroom, which is where I have my coffee every morning after the kids go to school. Just looking at her made me feel better."

"They stole her?"

She nodded sadly. "I was upset for weeks. It drove Tommy crazy. When he couldn't stand it anymore he contacted a Lladro dealer in New York and had another one sent by overnight courier. But it was never the same. In fact, it was actually kind of worse."

"Why?"

"I looked at the new ballerina, which looked almost exactly like the old one, and it made me realize what a pathetic person I'd become. When I was little I used to dream of becoming someone special when I grew up. Like a ballerina. Well, I obviously hadn't. But surely I could do more in my life than stare at a porcelain copy of a porcelain copy of a little girl's fantasy."

She paused to stub out her cigarette. I waited.

"Everything seemed to come together on my fortieth birthday in February," she said. "I remember looking at myself in the mirror that night while I stood there picking his hairs off my body. I said to myself, Eileen, you're never going to be that ballerina, but you still have half your life ahead of you. You've followed all the rules. You did your homework. You got good grades. You stopped at all red lights. You always sent a thank-you card. When's it supposed to be your turn?" She paused, with an expression of fierce determination. "That's when I decided. Now. It's my turn now."

"Is he seeing someone?"

She nodded grimly and checked her watch. "Probably as we speak."

"Who?"

She shrugged. "No one special. It never is. Tommy's the king of the quickies. You know those motels where they rent rooms by the hour? Tommy needs a place where they rent by the minute."

"What about you? Are you seeing someone special?"

She smiled with undisguised carnal pleasure. "Definitely."

"Tell me about him."

"He's thirty years old and he's gorgeous. He's totally different from Tommy." She leaned forward and raised her eyebrows in a lascivious manner. "Especially in the bedroom."

"Oh?" I said with a smile.

"Let me tell you, Rachel, that man is hung like a bull, and he can last as long as I need. I've had more orgasms in an hour with Andros than I've had in a year with my husband."

"Andros?" I asked with surprise. "You mean the aerobics guy?"

Eileen nodded proudly.

I'd been hearing about Andros for months from my sister Ann. He was the crown prince of St. Louis exercise instructors. He had a place called Firm Ambitions in the Plaza Frontenac shopping mall, where he conducted aerobics and exercise classes a few hours each day. He also did personal workout sessions at the homes of dozens of clients, who were, for the most part, wealthy women between the ages of thirty-five and fifty-five.

I was especially intrigued because I would be seeing Eileen's lover in action for the first time that night. Ann was an Andros fanatic. After dinner she was taking me to his high-impact aerobics class at Firm Ambitions.

"Do you think your husband suspects anything?" I asked.

"No. Andros and I are very careful about the whens and the wheres."

"What if he found out?"

She laughed bitterly. "He'd kill me. He'd view it as a breach of our understanding."

"Which is what?"

"I get the furs and the designer clothes and the Jag and two weeks at LaCosta every February. He gets the safaris and the gambling and the sport fucking. Meanwhile, I stay pure and raise the kids. Screwing Andros isn't part of that deal."

I asked her some questions about Tommy Landau's finances. As I expected, she knew very little beyond what Tommy told her, and Tommy told her very little. Over the past couple years she had glanced at a few of their financial statements when his lawyers had her sign various documents in connection with refinancings of some of his shopping centers. As she recalled, the assets on the financial statements included numerous limited partnerships, and the liabilities included millions of dollars in loans. From various overheard phone conversations at home, she had the sense that some of his shopping centers were having financial problems.

I explained that we would need to hire a good forensic accountant to help make sense of her husband's real estate holdings in order to be sure that she got her fair share of the property division. I concluded the meeting by describing the sequence of events from the filing of the petition to the date the judge issued the final order of dissolution.

"Who's Tommy likely to hire?" I asked.

"Hard to say. Maybe his father, if that firm does divorce work. If not, maybe Charles Kimball."

"*The* Charles Kimball?" I asked, impressed.

She nodded. "They go way back. All the way to when Tommy got kicked out of college."

"Did Kimball represent him in the rape trial?"

She nodded. "And in the cocaine case. Got him off both times. Tommy's pretty loyal to him."

"With good reason," I said as I walked her to the door. "Well, we'll find out soon enough. Drop those documents off tomorrow, if you can. Especially the tax returns. We'll plan to meet next week before I file the petition."

After Eileen left I dictated the notes of our meeting and asked my secretary to set up a new divorce file. *Your last di-*

vorce file, I told myself as I took a sip of coffee. The property issues were going to be dull and complex, especially the valuation of Tommy Landau's equity positions in each of his strip shopping centers. But, I reminded myself, dull wasn't necessarily bad. The case of *Landau v. Landau* would be a peaceful change after several months of Big Macs and Big Sals. And the Andros angle at least added a tinge of excitement. Maybe. *Don't get your hopes up,* I cautioned myself. *The only reason you agreed to take this case was that Ann begged you to.*

I nodded in resignation. How could I say no to my sister?

I should have, of course. But I didn't realize that until much later. Neither did Ann. And by the time we both did, it was far too late.

2

CHAPTER

I stared uncertainly at the plate in front of me. "What kind of Jewish mother are you?" I finally asked.

"It's good for you," my mother said as she joined me at the kitchen table.

"You used to make me brisket and kasha with shells."

"Not anymore. Too much fat and cholesterol. And anyway, brisket before an exercise class? It'll sit like lead in your stomach."

I looked down at the plate again. "What is this, Mom?"

"My own concoction."

"Does it have a name."

"Not yet. Try it."

I did. "Not bad," I said with a surprised smile. "This is tofu?"

"With red peppers and onions."

"And mushrooms?"

"Right."

I took another taste. "Ginger?"

She nodded proudly. "Fresh."

"What gives it the color?"

"Soy sauce."

I nodded approvingly. "It's pretty good, Mom."

She gave me a maternal smile. "What did I tell you, sweetie?"

"You'd better keep this recipe a secret, though. Otherwise," I said with a wink, "you'll get drummed out of the temple sisterhood."

"You'd be surprised what Yiddishe mamas are eating these days." She checked her watch. "When is Ann picking you up?"

"Five after seven."

"I have fruit compote. You have enough time. How about some herbal tea?"

"Sure." *Life back home,* I said to myself with a contented sigh.

Back when I left home for college fourteen years ago I vowed that I would never return to St. Louis. Then again, I also vowed that I would never become a lawyer. In the familiar words of some pundit—perhaps Yogi Berra, himself a native St. Louisan—never say never.

At the start of freshman year of college, my two role models were Rosie in *The African Queen* and Albert Schweitzer in Gabon. I planned to become a Jewish Katherine Hepburn, M.D.—heading down the Yulanga River with a stethoscope and a doctor's bag and Robert Redford cast in the role of my Charlie Allnut. Those plans changed junior year in a course called organic chemistry. So it goes.

When I graduated from law school I moved to Chicago and joined Abbott & Windsor, the third-oldest and second-largest law firm in the Midwest. After a few years in that pinstriped sweatshop I left LaSalle Street to open my own office on West Washington Avenue. Several years later, business was doing just fine at the Law Offices of Rachel Gold. Indeed, I was so busy that I was starting to think about hiring an associate and a paralegal to help out.

And then my father died. Suddenly. Of a massive coronary occlusion. The day after Thanksgiving.

My mother found him on the kitchen floor that morning. I was up in the bedroom at the time, putting on my jogging shoes—I had come home for the long holiday weekend. Somehow I knew that my father was dead the moment I heard my mother moan, "Oh, no."

I remember dashing downstairs, one shoe on, the other in my hand. My mother was kneeling next to my father, who was facedown on the floor. The sports section of the *Post-Dispatch* was clutched in his left hand, his reading glasses were hanging from one ear. The mug of coffee on the kitchen table was cold. So was my father. The paramedics told us that he'd been dead for more than an hour when my mother found him.

That was the worst part—that no one was with my father when death jumped him from behind, throttling down so fiercely that he couldn't even cry out for help. He struggled alone, no one there to hold him as he died. That vision haunts me still.

I moved back home in January. Literally back home—into the house and into the bedroom where I grew up. My mother didn't want to live alone in the house. I agreed to stay with her while I looked for a permanent place to live and she decided whether to move in with her sister, my Aunt Becky, in a townhouse near the Jewish Community Center off Lindbergh.

Although my mother and I were in our fourth month of what we both knew was only a temporary arrangement, we were certainly getting along better than the last time we lived together under that roof. We divided up the chores, took turns making dinner, and otherwise tried to live as much like normal housemates as a mother and her recently returned adult daughter can.

"After you get back from this class," my mother said as we sipped our tea, "I want you to tell me what you think of this Andros."

"Ann thinks he walks on water."

"I know."

I looked at my mother. "Am I missing something?"

She pursed her lips and looked at me. "Just tell me what you think of him," she said quietly.

"Okay. Do you know anything about his background?"

"There was a profile of him in the Everyday section about two years ago," she said, her brows furrowing in concentration.

I leaned back to listen. If there was a newspaper article, my mother would have read it and remembered it. She reads two newspapers cover to cover and has a near-photographic memory for everything she reads. Although she came to the United States from Lithuania when she was three and was never able to finish high school because she had to support her family after her mother died, she is one of the smartest and best-informed people I have ever known. While she has no patience for fiction ("With all my real problem," she tells me, "who's got time to worry over pretend ones?"), she devours her newspapers and news magazines. Don't ever play her in Trivial Pursuit.

"He's an immigrant from some country in the Middle East," my mother said. "Saudi Arabia, I think. Or maybe Iraq. After he moved here he got his start in one of those health-club chains."

"Vic Tanny?"

She shook her head. "No. It's the one with that pretty Olympic swimmer, what's her name? Gateway. Gateway Health Clubs. That's where he started. He got to be their most popular aerobics teacher, and then he went off on his own."

We heard the front door open. "Anyone home?" my sister called.

"In here, doll baby," my mother answered.

Ann came in and gave my mother a kiss.

People say that I'm my mother's daughter and Ann takes after our father. We both have my mother's high cheekbones, but Ann inherited our father's broad nose, bowed upper lip, and dark blue eyes. Although she and I are almost exactly my mother's height, Ann is a little stocky, like our father. She inherited his straight hair, too, which I used to pine for back when I was a teenager. Every night before bed in high school I would wrap my hair tight around an empty orange juice can in an effort to get rid of the curls—an effort doomed in the St. Louis humidity. Now, however, both of us have dark curls—mine compliments of my mother's genes, along with the red highlights, Ann's compliments of her stylist at Jon 'N Company, who perms in the curls and paints in the blond highlights every six weeks.

"You almost ready?" Ann said to me.

I stood up. "All set."

She looked at my outfit and raised her eyebrows. "Okay," she said with just a touch of disdain.

We were quite a contrast. My sister was in a hot pink spandex bodysuit with an emerald thong bikini bottom stretched over the spandex. She looked like a cast member from *Barbarella*. I definitely did not. Assuming that the principal focus of an aerobics class would be the aerobics part, I had actually dressed for exercise.

My mother walked with us to the door. "What about my silver dress with the beads?" she asked Ann. "I just got it back from the cleaners."

Ann mulled it over for a moment and nodded. "Perfect. I'll pick it up when I drop Rachel off after class."

Ann and her husband, Richie the orthodontist, were leaving in a week for their annual four-day trip to Las Vegas. She needed an extra outfit for Barry Manilow. Ann and Richie always go to Las Vegas with the same two couples, and Ann schedules their trip each year to coincide with Barry Manilow's appearance at the Dunes—a fact that continues to make me wonder whether we could possibly have come from the same gene pool.

"Thanks for seeing Ellen today," Ann said on the drive to Plaza Frontenac.

"No problem."

"She told me she feels a hundred percent better already."

"It helps to talk to a lawyer. You feel like you've shifted some of the burden to another person."

"He's such a shit."

"I barely know him."

"He's been cheating on her for years. I don't know why she waited as long as she did."

I remained silent. I had to. The conversation was edging into the realm of attorney-client communications.

"So is there another man?" she asked. "God, for her sake I hope there is." She glanced over at me.

"You'll have to ask her."

"Come on," she prodded. "I'm your sister."

"And she's my client." I shrugged helplessly. "You know

how it works, Ann. What she tells me is privileged. I can't tell even you."

She glanced over and smiled. "Is it someone I know?"

"Ann," I warned.

"Okay, okay."

"I hate to say it," Ann said as she turned into the shopping center parking area, "but I think she married him for the money. Or for his name."

"It's usually not that simple," I said.

She snorted. "What other possible reason could there be?"

I shrugged. "From what I've seen, people get married for reasons they rarely understand at the time."

We found a parking place on the front lot of Plaza Frontenac. She turned off the engine and looked over at me with a grin.

"What?" I finally asked.

"It's not Steve Rosenthal, is it?"

I shook my head with feigned irritation. "For God's sake, Ann."

She rolled her eyes. Okay, okay."

"Silicon Valley."

That's what Ann calls the high-impact aerobics class at Firm Ambitions. The reasons—large matched pairs of them—were obvious throughout the room, especially when the women (including my sister) were on their backs doing warm-ups.

All four walls were mirrored. I watched as the women checked their hair in the mirror or applied lipstick. Many were wearing heavy makeup. All were wearing high-fashion spandex exercise outfits. I looked completely out of place in my sweatpants, T-shirt, gym socks, and 100-percent natural (i.e., gravity-friendly) breasts.

As I stretched from side to side I spotted a familiar face across the room. It took me a moment to attach a name to the face.

"Oh, God," I said to Ann. "Is that Chrissy O'Conner?"

Ann squinted to see and shook her head. "Not Chrissy anymore. Chris*tine*. Christine Maxwell. *The* Christine Maxwell. Of Maxwell Associates. How do you know her?"

"She was two years ahead of me in high school. She was in charge of the homecoming dance. I was just a lowly sophomore on the decorations committee."

"You don't sound like one of her fans."

"I'm not." I studied Christine from across the room. She was a tall redhead—taller than me—with the fierce look of an avant-garde fashion model. She had straight red hair cut short and held in place with a sweatband. With what I admit was uncharitable pleasure, I noted her battleship hips and sagging rear.

"She's kind of a bitch," Ann said.

At precisely seven-thirty the music started. A Janet Jackson number blared out of the huge speakers that were set on raised platforms in the front corners of the room. The women formed into rows facing the mirrored front wall and started doing stretching exercises. Within seconds all of them were moving in sync. I found a spot between Ann and a platinum blonde with a tush to die for and pneumatic boobs.

"How do you know her?" I asked Ann as I tried to coordinate my stretching with the rest of the class.

"Christine? Mainly from class. I've tried to be friendly, but she's a real snob. One of those society types. Always in the *Ladue News* and Berger's column."

"What did you say her company's called?"

"Maxwell Associates."

"What is it?"

"Something with investments, I think, or insurance."

The music continued to build in volume as Janet Jackson faded into the Miami Sound Machine. It felt as if the bass guitar was in my rib cage. There was a raised stage in front. To the side of the stage was a red door set into the mirrored wall. As the music reached a crescendo, the door burst open and Andros leaped onstage.

"Ladies," he yelled as the music paused, "it's show time!"

He was a striking figure—bronzed skin, a strong, angular face, a cleft chin, and a thick mane of shoulder-length jet-black hair combed straight back and held in a small ponytail. The drums pounded as he leaped high, punched his fist into the air, and shouted, "Let's get busy!"

We got busy and stayed busy for forty minutes. It was definitely show time for our instructor. He was wearing a body mike—the music was so loud he couldn't have been heard otherwise. He strutted back and forth in front of us like some hybrid of Mick Jagger and Richard Simmons, exhorting us and prodding us and verbally abusing us. His aerobics outfit was part of the show: a scarlet muscle shirt and matching bikini briefs over black tights. He had a muscular torso, narrow hips, and tight, round buns. The scarlet briefs accentuated the body part that Eileen Landau had compared to a bull's. Based on the visible evidence, she hadn't exaggerated much.

I did my best to keep up with his exercise pace, and was pleased to discover that I was in better condition than most of the women in the class. By the time the session ended, my lungs were burning and sweat blurred my vision.

"That's a wrap, darlings," Andros shouted as the last chords of M. C. Hammer's "Too Legit to Quit" rap faded out.

Panting, I walked over to where I had left my towel by the wall. My legs felt wobbly.

I was sitting on the floor cross-legged and wiping my face with the towel when Andros came over. He positioned himself directly in front of me. His arms were crossed over his chest and his legs were slightly apart. He was standing so close that I had to crane my head up to see his face.

"You and Ann are family, no?" he said. He had a slight foreign accent. I hadn't noticed it when the music was on. Greek? Turkish? I couldn't quite place it.

"We're sisters."

"You are very good," he said sternly. He had dark blue eyes and long black eyelashes.

"Thank you," I answered, not knowing how else to respond.

He held out a hand. "Stand up."

I stood up without his help. He stepped back and crossed his arms. With a look somewhere between clinician and swinger, he studied me from head to foot. I shifted uncomfortably.

"Your triceps," he finally said, frowning.

I couldn't keep a straight face. "What about them?"

"I can shape them. I can make you magnificent."

I laughed. "Come on," I said, feeling myself blush.

He shook his head impatiently. "Your body is a gift from God." He stared into my eyes. "I can help you attain the perfection God intended for you."

It was hard to take him seriously. He seemed so much sexier—and taller—up there on his stage, strutting around and shouting commands and showing off his tight little buns. As a pin-up, he was definitely a hunk, a suitable Mr. March for the "Men of Aerobics" Calendar. But down here in person, hustling business and feeding me lines, he seemed more of a small-time con artist.

I could see why Eileen Landau might pick him for a one-night stand, or even a short bout of revenge sex. But the way Eileen talked, it sounded like she was having a real affair with this guy. I couldn't see it. But then again, I hadn't spent the last fifteen years of my life picking Tommy Landau's chest hairs off my body.

Andros started pitching his personal workout program to me. I interrupted his spiel, explaining politely but firmly that I really wasn't interested. As I moved away, several other women crowded around him with questions about their fitness routines. They giggled and flirted as they asked him questions and listened wide-eyed to his answers. When Ann and I left a few minutes later he was still surrounded by women.

"Well," Ann said as we walked through the mall toward the parking lot, "what did you think?"

"It's a good workout," I said, intentionally answering the question she hadn't asked.

"Not the aerobics. I mean Andros. Isn't he gorgeous?"

I shrugged. "He's okay."

"He's okay? Come on, Rachel! Doesn't that little tush make your mouth water?"

"It's cute," I agreed.

"How about that package up front?"

We walked in silence for a moment. "He's just not my type," I finally said.

"Oh, yes." There was an edge in her voice. "I forgot. He's not an intellectual."

"That's got nothing to do with it, Ann."

"Rachel, honey, the last thing to worry with a guy like that is the size of his brain."

The phrase "Rachel, honey" was the warning signal. It meant that we were headed toward a fight, sinking into that familiar La Brea Tar Pit of our relationship.

I tried to slog toward firm ground. "Come on, Ann. That's not what I said. He's just not my type."

"Which means what?"

We had reached the parking lot. Ann turned to face me.

I tried to gauge where the tar pit ended and firm land began. "He's too smooth. Too . . . coiffed. And . . ."

"And what?"

I shrugged. "A little slimy."

Ann shook her head in angry amazement. "Slimy?" I was now up to my knees in tar. "You think he's slimy? I see. He's too good for *you* but he's just right for me, huh?"

"Come on, Ann. I never said that. I don't think he's your type either. He just struck me as the kind of guy who preys on rich women, a gigolo."

"A gigolo? I can't believe you, Rachel. I bring you to *my* exercise class, a place that's special for *me*, a place I want to share with my *only* sister, and what do you do? You dump all over me and the people I care about."

I was sinking deeper. "Ann, I didn't—"

"Just forget it," she said as she spun around and stomped off.

I stood there watching her stomp down the row of cars.

Again, I moaned.

I thought back to when Ann and I were in elementary school, back before we moved into a bigger house with separate bedrooms. I had felt closer to her than I have ever felt to anyone since. We slept in the same bed, bathed in the same bath, walked to and from school together, invented our own secret clubs, protected each other from our parents. I can close my eyes and still recall the smell of her breath in the morning. We once had our own private language. Now we often seemed to need a translator. ("What your sister really means to say is . . .")

Off in the distance, I could see her unlock her car door. She got in and slammed the door shut. A moment later I heard her car engine rev as the rear lights came on. With my shoulders slumped, I turned to find my car.

"Oh, damn," I said aloud as I remembered how I'd gotten there. I turned back as Ann pulled her Suburban alongside me. She was staring straight ahead.

We drove home in silence.

"Ann," I started as she pulled into the driveway, "he's definitely cute. It's just—"

"Forget it," she interrupted as she turned off the engine and opened her door. "We're different. That's all. Forget it."

My mother was ironing in the den. There was an Italian opera on the television.

"Hi, Mom," I said with forced cheerfulness. "Phew, that's a real workout."

In the five seconds it took her to put down the iron and look at her two daughters, she had sized up the situation and decided that tonight it was best to let the parties cool down on their own instead of initiating multilateral peace talks. She gave Ann the dress and a container of fruit compote for her family and walked her to the door while I waited in the den.

"So?" my mother said when she returned.

I shrugged. "I don't know."

"What did you fight about?"

"Andros, I think."

"What about him?"

"I'm not sure. Ann thinks he's a hunk. I thought he was so-so. Maybe she was thinking of fixing me up or something. I don't know."

"Did she talk to him afterward."

"No."

"Did you know he comes to her house for workouts?"

"That's the fad these days, Mom. It's part of his business. These exercise people make house calls. After class he even tried to hustle me for that stuff. If you had gone, he'd have done the same to you."

"What's he like?"

"He's a good-looking guy. Dark, nice body, great eyes. Maybe thirty. He's a hustler."

She shook her head and frowned. "I don't like hustlers."

"Mom, I wouldn't worry about Ann and him. I happen to know for a fact that he's in the middle of a wild love affair with another."

"Oh?"

I nodded.

"I still don't like it," she said.

Twenty minutes later I was pulling back the covers and getting into bed. I set the alarm and reached up to turn off the reading light. As I did I paused to look around. My bedroom looked the same as it had the day I left for college. The red-and-white Cardinals banner over the dresser ("1967 World Champions"), the Billie Jean King poster over the desk, the multicolored scented candle on the nightstand, the psychedelic Eric Clapton poster on the back of the door, the large peace sign glued to the headboard. The only decorating touch I'd added since moving back were the two framed 5×7 photographs on my nightstand. I found them when I went down to my father's office to clean out his desk and personal belongings. They were in the top drawer of his desk. One was from high school, with me in my U City cheerleader outfit; the other was at my law school graduation, with me in a black gown and mortarboard. In both pictures, my father is standing next to me beaming with pride. Now his gentle smile is the first thing I see in the morning and the last thing I see at night.

"Good night, Daddy," I whispered as I turned out the light.

3

CHAPTER

The phone started ringing as I came in the front door lugging the bag of softball equipment in one hand and my purse and briefcase in the other. I dropped the equipment bag, ran into the kitchen, and reached the phone before the answering machine clicked on.

"Hello," I said, panting from the exertion of carrying the heavy bag of equipment from the car to the house.

"How are you, Rachel?"

Not again, I groaned to myself as I put my purse and briefcase on the counter. "I'm fine, Andros."

It had been almost two weeks since his aerobics class, and he had called me at least ten times, sometimes at home, sometimes at the office, urging me to enroll in a series of personal workout sessions that he would be happy to conduct at my house. At first I thought it was just a pickup gambit—I could almost feel him trying to smolder through the phone line. But eventually I realized it was just part of the sales shtick. He was the personal-exercise equivalent of one of those demoniacally persistent life insurance salesmen. At the end of the last week, refusing to take ten separate nos for an answer, Andros had mailed me an appointment card stating that he would come by my house at 3:00 P.M. on Wednesday to give me a free personal fitness session. I received the note on Saturday.

I tried to call him the day I got it, and then again on Monday. It was now Tuesday.

"Rachel, my assistant, Kimmi, tells me you've been trying to reach me."

"I have. Look, I have *no* interest in a personal fitness session, and even if I did—which, believe me, *I definitely do not, I promise*—I work during the day. I'm not interested and I just don't have the time."

"But what could be a more important use of your time than to fine-tune that magnificent body?"

My mother had the call-waiting feature on her phone, and it started making that clicking signal. "Hold on," I told Andros. "I have another call." I depressed the cut-off button once. "Hello?"

"Tell your mother's cat I'm running late." It was my pal Benny Goldberg.

"Where are you?" We had left the softball practice at the same time.

"Well, I decided to drop by Wolfie's on the way over to your house."

"Oh, Benny. For what?"

"Just a nibble."

"Define nibble."

"Just a sampling of some of the basic food groups."

"Which ones?"

"Meat, vegetable, and dairy."

"Specifically?"

"A Big Daddy with extra grilled onions and a chocolate shake."

"Benny," I said with disapproval, "I thought you had a hot date for dinner."

"Hey, Rachel, that's later. This is now. Gotta keep the furnace stoked."

"You stoke enough in your digestive tract to run a Bessemer steel operation down there. If you don't watch out you're going to end up on Oprah."

"Funny you should mention her. I'm already scheduled on a panel next week: Big Men Who Turn Women into Love Slaves."

"Are you sure it's not Big Men Who Need Lobotomies?"

"Very funny. Listen, I'll be there in ten minutes, but that's not why I called. As long as I'm at Wolfie's, I thought I'd bring Ozzie a treat. Can he eat frozen custard?"

I smiled. Ozzie was my golden retriever. Benny was taking care of him temporarily. "Sure. But just a small cone. I've got to get off. I have Andros on the other line."

"Again? Tell that oily putz if he doesn't leave you alone I'm going to haul his sorry ass outside and beat him like a rented mule."

"A rented mule?" I was laughing. "See you soon, Benny. Bye." I clicked back to the other line. "Andros?"

"Rachel, you say you don't have time to devote—"

"I don't. Period. I get my exercise jogging. That's plenty."

"Oh, Rachel, when I think of the punishment that jogging inflicts on your supple legs and hips, I get tears in my eyes."

"Don't. I'm canceling tomorrow's personal fitness session. I appreciate the offer, but I'm not interested."

"I don't understand how can you pass up my offer to—"

"I just did," I snapped, and then immediately felt a tinge of remorse for being so abrupt. "I'll tell you what," I said. "Do you still have that aerobics class on Wednesday nights?"

"I do."

"I'll go to it tomorrow night, but *only* if you promise to leave me alone and never call me again. Okay?"

There was a long pause. I heard him sigh. "With great sadness, I promise."

As I went back to the front hall to get the bag of softball equipment I heard my mother's car pull up the driveway. I waited until she came in the house.

"Hello, sweetie pie," she said as she gave me a kiss.

"Good day?"

"Good enough. Are Benny and Ozzie here yet?"

"Benny's running late. They'll be here soon. Where's Gitel?"

My mother looked beyond my shoulder and smiled. "There's my little princess. Come here, young lady." I turned around to see the cat promenade down the stairs from the second floor. She gave me a withering glance as she passed by. The feeling was mutual.

Gitel was the reason Ozzie and I were separated. Ozzie was

a Valentine's Day gift from a former boyfriend named Howard Stein who now is a gynecologist in San Diego. He was six weeks old at the time. Ozzie, that is, although Howard often seemed to hover around that age emotionally. Howard and I didn't last to Ozzie's first birthday. Ozzie and I celebrated our seventh Valentine's Day together this past February—which says something about dogs, and probably men, too.

Gitel, on the other hand, is a Persian with more than a touch of the Ayatollah in her. While she tolerated having me around the house, she declared a *jihad* on Ozzie the Infidel the day we moved in. She made his life miserable during the forty-eight hours he spent there, poor thing. He'd been living with Benny ever since, and I was starting to feel guilty about the arrangement.

Benny is my best friend and soul mate. We started off together as junior associates in the Chicago offices of Abbott & Windsor. A couple years after I left Abbott & Windsor, he left to teach law at De Paul. Last December, he was offered a faculty position at Washington University's School of Law. I told him he was an idiot not to accept the offer. Although I had pretty much decided by then to move back to St. Louis, I still meant what I told him. Benny took the job and moved to St. Louis two months before I did. Now he jokingly claims that the whole thing was a ploy to find Ozzie a home in St. Louis.

Meanwhile, I was missing Ozzie terribly. With my work and other commitments, I wasn't able to see him anywhere near often enough. So Benny and I had decided to try our hand at matchmaking after softball practice.

"I didn't have time to pick up any food," I told my mother as I lifted the bag of softball equipment. "I'll take you out to dinner after Benny leaves."

"Don't be silly. I've got stuffed cabbage in the refrigerator." She now made her stuffed cabbage with ground turkey meat. "It'll take a minute to heat it up."

"Mom, it's my turn tonight, and I'm taking us out to dinner."

I took the duffel bag of softball equipment down the stairs to the basement and lugged it into one of the back storage rooms. Our basement had terrified and tantalized me as a child. A creaky wooden staircase with handrails on either side descended into what seemed, at least back then, a haunted house of blue pilot lights, spiderwebs in the corners of low ceilings, and camphor-scented clothing hanging in garment bags like cadavers. Each of the three prior owners had expanded the house, and each time a new foundation had added yet another basement hallway and set of storage rooms. I spent hours as a child back in that maze of little rooms beyond the staircase, poking around and opening up and peering into the foot lockers and storage boxes in each room. In fact, I knew my way around so well that even now, so many years later, I didn't need a light to find my way back to the storage room.

As I stashed the bag of equipment in the corner of the room and turned to go, my foot bumped against something. Reaching overhead, I found the pull string and turned on the light. I stared down at my father's battered shoe-shine kit. I smiled as I kneeled beside it. Father's Day. Back when we were in elementary school, Ann and I would sneak down to the basement early on that special Sunday morning, unload the black Kiwi polish and the brushes and the rags from that wooden shoeshine box, and shine our daddy's shoes. Then we'd carry them proudly into our parents' bedroom with shouts of "Happy Father's Day!" And now, more than twenty years later, I opened that same battered box. There was still a tin of Kiwi polish inside the box, along with a worn-out brush and a couple of stiff rags stained black. The black polish inside the Kiwi tin was dried and cracked. My eyes watered as I closed the lid.

I must have been in the basement much longer than I realized, because as I came up the stairs I heard Benny's voice. I reached the top stair and opened the door to the kitchen.

"I cannot believe this," I said in amazement.

Benny was at the kitchen table with my mother. There was a steaming bowl of stuffed cabbage in front of them. He gave me a big smile. "Hey, gorgeous."

He was wearing baggy khaki slacks, black Converse Chuck Taylor high-tops, and a red T-shirt with the white-lettered message PLEASE HELP ME—I AM AN ENDOMORPH. His black curly hair was at least a month overdue for a trim.

"Mom," I said in exasperation, "he has a dinner date tonight, and he's already had a grilled Polish sausage and milkshake on the way over here."

She waved her hand dismissively. "He'll have room," she said. "The boy has capacity."

"Extra protein," he said. "I might need my strength tonight."

"Oh?" I asked, eyebrows raised.

"Some women seek me out because of my charm, others because of my devilish good looks, and a few for my expertise in, shall we say, certain rare techniques perfected in the boudoirs of the Far East. My companion for this evening, however, at least according to rumor, places a high premium on sheer physical endurance. That means that tonight, God willing, I may need some extra lead in my pencil." He turned to my mother. "And anyway, who could pass up Sarah Gold's stuffed cabbage?"

My mother smiled.

Benny Goldberg was fat and crude and gluttonous and vulgar. He was also brilliant and funny and thoughtful and ferociously loyal. I loved him like the brother I never had.

"So," I said, "how're the matchmakers doing?"

"This boy is a *meshuggener*," my mother said.

"Your mother thinks I'm a pervert," Benny said with a grin.

"So do most people," I replied as I turned to her. "What did he suggest?"

She shook her head, smiling against her will. "Crotchless panties."

I glanced at Benny. "For the cat?"

He shrugged, running his thick fingers through his hair. "Well, an outfit like that would certainly put me in a conciliatory mood."

"Ozzie's already in a conciliatory mood," I said. "The problem is that damn cat."

"Rachel," my mother warned, "don't talk like that about my little Gitel."

At the sound of her name, Gitel materialized at the kitchen door. In a haughty manner, she padded across the room and jumped into my mother's lap. As my mother kissed her on the head, Gitel gave me a smug look.

"Well," I said wearily, "I guess it's time. I'll go get Ozzie."
I looked at Benny. "Is he in your car?"

Benny nodded. "The door's unlocked."

As I stepped out onto the front porch, Ozzie started barking and jumping between the front and back seats of Benny's car. He was scrabbling against the car door as I opened it.

"Hey, Oz," I said happily. "How you doing, pal? How you doing?"

He jumped up, placing his paws on my shoulders, and started licking my face. I laughed as I rubbed his head and scratched him behind his ears and gave him a hug. He sat down in front of me, his tail flopping wildly, and barked three times. Then he jumped up again and licked my cheek.

"I know, I know. I miss you, too, Oz. We're going to see if Gitel will let you move in this time."

"Don't get your hopes up," Benny said. He was coming down the front walk. "Did you see the look that fucking cat gave you? In cat talk, I think it meant 'Don't even think about it, bitch.' "

I nodded with resignation. "I know. If this doesn't work, I'm going to have to find a place to live."

"What's your mom think of that?"

"It'll be hard. On both of us. But we both know it's got to happen sooner or later. She's got her life, and I'm starting to feel like an old maid."

"An old maid? What are you talking about, woman? You're a total babe."

"Benny, look at the facts. I'm thirty-two, I'm single, and I'm living at home with my mother. And my mother's cat. This is not normal. I've got to get my act together."

"Jesus, Rachel, you've got your act more together than anyone I know. Come on, let's see if Ozzie and Gitel want to get it on."

We started up the walk.

"And then this divorce case." I shook my head glumly.

"Your sister's friend?"

"I should never have taken it."

"Not another Tommy turd?"

"No, thank God."

A week ago I'd filed the petition for dissolution of marriage in the case of *In re the Marriage of Thomas A. and Eileen Beth Landau.* I filed the day after Eileen dropped the news on Tommy. She told him on Sunday afternoon when he returned from eighteen holes at Briarcliff Country Club. The children were at her parents' house at the time. She told him she had packed most of his things and wanted him out of the house by dinnertime. She had feared that he might become violent; at the very least, she expected screams and curses. At my insistence, the Ladue police were on standby, so that if anything happened they could respond quickly.

But Tommy seemed to take the news in an eerily passive way. He nodded, tugged at his mustache, and told her he'd get his stuff. He was upstairs finishing packing when Eileen left to go to her parents' house. He was gone when she returned with the children after dinner. She had expected to find a note from him. He didn't leave a note. He did, however, leave a message, which she discovered when she got ready for bed that night: an enormous fresh turd nestled in her lingerie drawer. God, I hate divorce cases.

"No," I said to Benny, "not another Tommy turd. Almost as bad. His attorneys filed their appearance today."

"His father's firm?"

I nodded. We were on the porch. "I expected them. I even sent a courtesy copy of the petition to his father. But when I received the respondent's entry of appearance today, there were *two* signature blocks on the court form: one for the firm of Landau, Mitchell & McCray and the other for—you ready for this?—Abbott & Windsor."

Benny looked at me with surprise. "In a divorce case? Who signed the appearance?"

"L. Debevoise Fletcher."

"Deb Fletcher? Oh, shit," he groaned.

I nodded grimly. "Exactly my reaction."

L. Debevoise Fletcher had moved to St. Louis a year before to head up Abbott & Windsor's beleaguered branch office after the suicide of its first managing partner (Stoddard Anderson) and the hushed resignation of its second (Reed St. Germain). In an effort to stop further erosion, the executive committee of Abbott & Windsor decided to send one of its own to head up the St. Louis office.

According to my friends at A&W, Deb Fletcher had actually volunteered. Most assumed that he wanted a change of scenery in the aftermath of his extraordinarily bitter divorce from Tricia Fletcher. She had been his second wife—the so-called trophy wife. By the end of the divorce trial, however, she had a few trophies of her own, including, went the joke around Abbott & Windsor, Fletcher's bank accounts and testicles.

"So now I not only have a complete jerk for an adversary," I said to Benny, "but one who has a personal incentive to turn someone else's divorce into a nightmare."

"And don't forget your delightful personal history with that dickhead."

"I know. It's going to be an awful experience."

"Well, if anyone can handle that pompous sack of shit, it's you."

Ozzie nudged my hand. I kneeled down beside him and scratched his forehead. "Okay, Oz," I said as I kissed him on the forehead. "Get psyched."

Poor Ozzie. Gitel greeted him in the foyer with back arched, hair on end, hissing and spitting. Ozzie practically clawed his way through the screen door trying to get back out of the house.

I had an extra key to Benny's place, so while he headed off for his dinner date with the stamina sultana, I drove Ozzie back to his temporary quarters. On the way over we stopped at a park to play fetch.

When I got back home there was a message from Ann.

"It's about the claims adjuster," my mother explained.

During her long weekend in Las Vegas, burglars broke into my sister's house after first disconnecting the alarm system. The police were called by a neighbor who, unable to sleep, had gone for a walk at two in the morning and noticed movement in my sister's house. The burglars were gone by the time the squad cars arrived. The police called the alarm company to find out whom to contact. I was the first name on the list and got the call at three in the morning. I went over to her house and told the detectives not to disturb Ann and Richie, who still had two days left on their holiday. I hung around the house to help them put together a preliminary inventory of stolen items, which included Ann's silver, Richie's baseball card collection (appraised for close to $20,000, including Sandy Koufax and Lou Brock rookie cards), all of the video and stereo equipment in their "home entertainment center," two paintings, three pairs of Richie's shoes, and all of his X-rated videos.

I filed the initial notice of claim with Richie and Ann's insurance company and had them file a supplementary claim when they returned from Vegas. Although the insurance company seemed to be acting responsibly, there were a few legal hurdles that I was helping Ann and Richie get over. I returned Ann's call, listened to her questions, and offered some advice on how to deal with the claims adjuster. "If he still has a problem," I told her, "give him my number and tell him to call me."

"Okay. Thanks, Rachel."

"Sure. Hey, you want me to give you a ride tomorrow night?"

"What's tomorrow?"

"Firm Ambitions. The aerobics class."

Her tone quickly shifted. "As far as I'm concerned, that bastard can go straight to hell."

I paused, startled by her bitterness. "I assume that means no," I said.

"It means hell no," she snapped.

"What happened with Andros?"

"It's not worth talking about."

"Tell me what happened," I said.

"Nothing. Just forget it."

I asked my mother the same question before I went to bed. She shook her head. "Ann hasn't told me a thing."

"That's odd," I said. "The guy has been calling me practically every day for two weeks, and he's never even hinted there was a problem with Ann."

"As far as I'm concerned," my mother said firmly, "if she's done with him and that class, that's fine by me."

I went anyway. The rest of Silicon Valley was in position doing stretching exercises when I arrived at 7:20 P.M. The class was supposed to start promptly at 7:30. According to

Ann, Andros was obsessed with punctuality. As the rare late-comer learned, his rage over tardiness was dreadful to behold.

So we all knew something was wrong when 7:30 P.M. came and went without the usual warm-up music. By 7:40, people were getting agitated. At 7:55, a flustered temporary receptionist came in to announce that the class had been canceled. She offered no explanation.

The explanation arrived the following morning on the front page of the *St. Louis Post-Dispatch,* beneath the headline

AEROBICS INSTRUCTOR FOUND DEAD;
POLICE SUSPECT FOUL PLAY

The article stated that Ishmar al-Modalleem, a Saudi national better known in St. Louis by his professional name, Andros, had been found naked and dead the prior afternoon in a hotel room in the St. Louis suburb of Clayton. According to the article, he had spent several years with the Gateway Health & Racquet Clubs before leaving to open Firm Ambitions. While police had not yet received the autopsy results, the preliminary evidence, according to the article, "strongly suggested that his death was caused by poison."

I read the story twice and put the newspaper down. I took a sip of coffee as I stared out the breakfast-room window. I glanced down again at the headline with a queasy feeling.

4

CHAPTER

An hour later, I was flipping through the deposition exhibits in one of my trademark cases and glancing at my scribbled outline as I asked the court reporter to swear the witness. We were seated around a conference table in one of the downtown firms. The deposition ended just before noon. I met a friend for lunch at the Media Club and headed back to my office around one-thirty.

"Mrs. Landau's in there," my secretary told me as I walked through the front door.

I paused. "Eileen?"

"She called here five times this morning. I told her you'd be back after lunch. She's been waiting in your office for an hour."

"What's wrong?"

"She wouldn't say." My secretary leaned forward and lowered her voice. "She seems upset."

She was. Frantic, to be more precise. Eileen was pacing back and forth in my office, a cigarette in her mouth. The room was thick with smoke. There were eight stubbed-out butts in the ashtray, each with a peach lipstick stain on the end of the filter.

"Eileen," I said softly, "I heard about Andros. I'm sorry."

She spun toward me, her eyes wild. "I was there."

"Where?"

"When he died." She took a long drag on her cigarette. Her hand was unsteady. "My God, it was dreadful."

"Sit down, Eileen. Can I get you some coffee?"

"No more. I'm totally wired. I must have had three pots already. I couldn't sleep last night." She crossed her legs, uncrossed them, changed positions in the chair, crossed them again.

"Tell me about it," I said gently.

She took a deep breath and exhaled. "It was horrible. Absolutely, totally horrible."

"The papers said he died in a hotel room."

She nodded. "We'd met there before. Several times. He called the day before yesterday. He said he had a personal fitness cancellation for Wednesday afternoon. I told him I'd meet him at the room at three o'clock."

"Did he show up?"

"Oh, yes. We made love. Twice. It was fantastic." She took a drag on her cigarette and turned to blow smoke toward the window. Her cigarette hand was shaking.

I waited for her to continue.

"What happened?" I finally asked.

She shook her head distractedly. "I showered. Then Andros showered. I heard him singing in the shower as I put on my clothes. By the time he turned off the shower, I was dressed and putting on my makeup. And then . . ." She stopped and stubbed out her cigarette. I waited. She stared at the ashtray.

"And then?" I prompted.

She took a deep breath and exhaled. "He came staggering out of the bathroom. He was naked. He looked sick. His skin was gray. He wasn't breathing right. I had him sit down on the edge of the bed. He said he was nauseous. I told him to take a few deep breaths. I went into the bathroom to put on my eye liner." She looked at me with a helpless gesture. "I thought he just had an upset stomach. A moment later I heard him fall off the bed. I ran to him. He was on his side." She shook her head. "God, it was gruesome. His whole body was shaking. He was making these gagging noises. I bent over him. He was frothing at the mouth. Literally frothing, Rachel. Stuff was bubbling out of his mouth. I thought he was having a heart attack. I called the front desk. I told them to get an ambulance. When I got off the phone—he wasn't moving, he wasn't breathing. Then something happened to his insides, because suddenly all this—I couldn't believe it—all this shit and piss came out of him. I knew he was dead."

"Oh, Eileen. What a nightmare."

She nodded as she lit another cigarette. Leaning back in her chair, she took a deep drag and exhaled through her nostrils. "That's when I really freaked. I knew there would be police. He was dead. There was nothing more I could do. I knew I had to get out of there before the ambulance arrived. I grabbed the pictures, stuffed them into his Lands' End attaché—"

"What pictures?"

She paused and looked me straight in the eyes. She took another drag on the cigarette. "Of us."

I nodded. "Go on."

"The pictures were on the nightstand. So was the camera. I stuffed them into his attaché. I grabbed my purse and grabbed his bag and got out of there as fast as I could."

"Have you called the police?"

She gave me a look of disbelief. "Are you kidding? No one knows I was there."

"What about the hotel people?"

"I always pay cash in advance. I never use my real name."

"Does Tommy know?"

She laughed—a quick, manic bark. "Tommy? Are you crazy? That's all I need."

"Eileen, according to the article the police are already suspicious about his death. They think he was poisoned. They'll have autopsy results soon. If he didn't die of natural causes—and that sure didn't sound like a heart attack—there's going to be a major homicide investigation. Count on it. He was practically a celebrity. That'll put extra pressure on the police. It's better if you come forward now."

"Jesus Christ, Rachel, I didn't kill him," she said with outrage.

"That's not my point, Eileen. Look, the autopsy is going to show that he had sex just before he died. You probably left something in the room—maybe your lipstick or mascara, certainly your fingerprints, probably strands of your hair. It'll be a lot easier on you if you come forward now instead of letting them track you down on their own. I know how these things play out. I can arrange it for you with the police. You can tell them what you saw and—"

"Forget it," she interrupted impatiently. "I tell the police today and then read about myself in the newspaper tomorrow. No, thanks. I'm not about to become some scandal slut. And anyway, I didn't leave my lipstick there. I didn't leave anything there. And I've never been fingerprinted in my life."

"Eileen, you're not thinking straight."

"I'm thinking very straight. I've been thinking very straight and very hard about this very subject and about nothing else since I got home last night. I know how these things work, Rachel. I know what kind of people are in the media. They're vultures. No, vultures wait till you're dead. They're parasites. They feed on live flesh. I saw what they did to Tommy on his drug charges. Here's a simple question: Can you guarantee that my name won't appear in the newspaper if I come forward?"

"Well, I can't guarantee it."

"That's the answer, then. I'm not going to have my children read about this. I'm not going to have them teased at school." She paused to take another drag on her cigarette. "Do you know what the first Sunday of next month is?"

"No," I admitted, conceding defeat. You can give a client advice, but you can't make them take it.

"It's CSL Night."

"Oh," I said, trying to put a little enthusiasm into my voice.

CSL Night. Short for Cocktails over St. Louis Night. It's an annual fund-raising event put on by the Women's Auxiliary of the Mount Sinai Hospital of St. Louis. For $1,000, you can join the Jewish glitterati of St. Louis on a voyage to nowhere, i.e., a black-tie evening featuring cocktails and a motion-picture premiere aboard a specially chartered Lockheed L-1011 jet that departs St. Louis at 8:00 P.M., circles southern Illinois for four hours, and returns to St. Louis at midnight. For the Jewish country-club set of St. Louis, it is *the* social event of the season, which the Women's Auxiliary thoughtfully times to coincide with the opening of the spring fashion season. I am told that when the hospital's president announces during cocktails how they plan to spend the money raised on that year's flight, the passengers—or at least some of the sober ones within earshot—feel a warm glow.

"I'm chairman of CSL this year," Eileen explained. "I've been planning for the event the whole year. We're having John Goodman *and* John Landis for the premiere of their new movie. There are a lot of people counting on me, Rachel. Important people. Look, Andros is dead. There's nothing I can do for him. This event is important to me. It's where my life's at these days. It's where my future is. I'm not going to have some sleazy sex scandal ruin it for me."

Nothing I could say would change her mind. Maybe she'd get lucky. I doubted it. The Clayton police weren't the Keystone Kops.

"Okay," I said with a sigh. "Let's talk about what you should do if the police call."

I took her through the usual police techniques and the response she should make to each question they asked. "Understand?" I repeated.

"Yes, yes, yes," she said. " 'I want to talk to my lawyer before I answer that,' " she recited.

"Good."

Eileen reached under her chair and handed me a canvas attaché. "Speaking of my lawyer, I want you to keep this for me."

"What is this?" I asked, although I had guessed the moment she pulled it out.

"His briefcase. The one I took from the hotel room. I want you to keep it until the investigation is over."

I set the Lands' End attaché on the edge of my desk, where it seemed to spontaneously generate a series of ethical issues worthy of a law school exam.

"Eileen, this is—"

"Look, Rachel, if someone really killed him, they certainly didn't use anything in that bag. Believe me, nothing in that bag could hurt him. But the two pictures in there could ruin me. I admit I was stupid. All I wanted were the damn pictures, but I panicked and took the whole goddamn bag. Now I'm stuck. I can't exactly sneak it back into the room, right?"

I stared at the attaché. It sat there like fresh roadkill. This truly had become the divorce case from hell. "I have a safe in here," I finally said.

"God bless you, Rachel. You have no idea . . ."

I held up my hand to stop her. "I'll keep it there for now. No promises about the future."

"I understand." She reached across the desk and grabbed my hand with both of hers. "Thanks."

A fierce spring thunderstorm was raging outside my office window. Cars were creeping down the street, their windshield wipers flailing at sheets of water. The rain came in waves, thundering across the roofs, clattering along the streets. Raindrops bounced off the asphalt like shotgun pellets. The office lights flickered. I glanced at the bulky safe in the corner.

Eileen had left almost immediately after I locked the attaché in the safe. An hour later, alone in my office, still feeling used, I had looked dully up as my secretary poked her head in to say good night. The sky was already dark by then, and the wind was blowing. The first crash of thunder sounded five minutes later, followed by the rain.

I stared at the safe.

Although she said nothing in that attaché killed him, I told myself, *how can you be sure of that unless you look?*

But, I interrupted, *it's really none of your business what's in that attaché.*

Are you crazy? I answered. *How about when the police get involved? What if there's evidence of a crime in there?*

Eventually, I won the argument. Closing the blinds, I opened the safe. Placing the attaché on my desk, I unzipped it and removed the contents, one by one, writing them down as I did:

1. one yellow legal pad (blank);
2. three blue felt-tip pens (medium point—0.5 mm);
3. three microcassette audiotapes (Leuwenhaupt Model 5400), each with a title written on the stick-on label:

   - "Dance Routine";
   - "Low-Impact Workout";
   - "High-Impact Routine w/Jazz Steps";

4. one calculator (Texas Instruments 2000G);
5. a handwritten outline of an article on breathing exercises that Andros was apparently planning to write for an aerobics magazine called *Fitness 2000*;
6. a Polaroid Impulse camera;
7. a vibrator (battery-operated);
8. a French tickler (I think); and
9. the two photographs that had caused me to inherit the bag.

I studied the photographs. Eileen was the star of both. In one, she was alone, "posed" on her back on the bed, her legs wide apart, her right hand pressing the tip of the vibrator into her vagina. In the other, she was licking an erect penis (presumably attached to Andros). The second picture was off-center and slanted, as if Andros had taken it by holding the camera out to the side and snapping the shot. Both pictures were in focus, and Eileen was clearly identifiable in each one.

I could understand why Eileen hadn't wanted the police to have those pictures. But I couldn't understand why she had wanted Andros to have them in the first place. He seemed precisely the type who would collect pictures of his conquests the way others might collect hunting trophies. And like most mementos, his pictures looked like they existed to be displayed. I wouldn't have been surprised if Andros's trophy case included explicit shots from other affairs.

For Eileen's sake, I hoped the two shots she had taken from the hotel room were the only such pictures he had ever taken of her. I wasn't optimistic.

5

CHAPTER

By 12:25 A.M. I knew it was going to be a rotten day.

Twelve twenty-five, I said to myself as I turned in bed and stared at the alarm clock. *That's not so bad. If I fall asleep in five minutes, I'll still get six hours of sleep.*

The next time I checked, it was ten minutes after one.

No problem, I assured myself. *I can still get more than five hours of sleep.*

I tried breathing slowly. I tried breathing deeply. I tried breathing through my nose. I tried breathing through my mouth. At 2:45 A.M. I turned the alarm clock toward the wall and told myself that all I really needed was three and a half good hours of sleep. I revised the estimate to three hours at 3:10. The next thing I knew the alarm was ringing and it was 6:30.

The same thing happens to me every night before a trial or an appellate argument. I get in bed after telling myself how important it is to get a good night's sleep—which for me is the best way to ensure that I won't get a good night's sleep.

But this time my insomnia was due to more than nerves. I had a loser. A fascinating loser, but a loser nevertheless. My client was an elderly man who had lost his life savings in an investment partnership that owned, according to the prospectus, a huge quantity of frozen semen collected from several prized Brangus bulls, including 200,000 "straws" of semen (surely the least appetizing unit of measurement ever coined) from a blue-ribbon stud named Lucille's Grand Slam. But when the bottom fell out of the show cattle market and the bank foreclosed on its collateral, it discovered a distressing lack of congruence between the descriptions of the collateral contained in the security agreements and the actual collateral contained in the storage freezers. Even in a depressed market, a bucket of Grand Slam's *liqueur de vivre* had real value. Two hundred thousand "straws" of frozen milk, however, did not.

My client had come to me with a judgment for $380,000 against the general partner of the partnership. Unfortunately, the general partner had a negative net worth. I struggled with the appellate brief for weeks, trying to find a way to break into the corporate fortress and get at the folks with the money. I even went to the extreme of citing a line of California decisions. Benny Goldberg warned, "Hey, trying to get a Missouri court to buy a California precedent is like trying to get June Cleaver to buy a set of gold nipple rings." By the time oral argument ended that morning, it seemed obvious that the three appellate judges weren't in a buying mood either.

As I trudged out of the courtroom and down the hall, I heard someone call, "Miss Gold!" I turned. It was one of the assistant court clerks. "Your secretary called, Miss Gold. She needs to talk to you right away."

I returned the call from a pay phone down the hall. "What's up?"

"You need to get right over to the Clayton police headquarters. Mrs. Landau called from there an hour ago."

"Eileen? She called from the police station?"

"She left the number."

"Damn. Is this about Andros?"

"I think so. The police asked her to come down for questioning."

"Call her back. Tell her I'll be there as soon as I can. Tell her not to talk to anyone until I get there."

The first person I saw at the police station was L. Debevoise Fletcher.

"Well, well, well," he said with a big, hearty smile. "The

lovely Rachel Gold." He held out a huge paw. "Delightful to see you, dear."

We shook hands. His face became solemn and he covered my hand with his other one. "I am terribly sorry about your father, Rachel." There wasn't a trace of sympathy in his slate-gray eyes.

"Thank you, Deb," I said.

Deb Fletcher was, as usual, outfitted for the part he had so adeptly played throughout most of his legal career: the role of "show" partner. He definitely *looked* the part: tall, tanned, thinning brown hair tinged with gray, a London-tailored suit. His teeth were capped, his voice was deep and booming, his hands were huge, and his brain was small. Like most litigation show partners, Deb Fletcher kept a pair of tortoiseshell reading glasses in the inside pocket of his suit jacket. The glasses were pure stage prop, as I personally witnessed several times during my days at Abbott & Windsor in Chicago. When a judge asked him a tough question during oral argument, he would remove the glasses from his pocket and pensively chew on one of the ends, thereby creating the impression that he was actually familiar enough with the facts and the law not only to understand the question but to formulate an intelligent response thereto.

In fact, Fletcher was rarely well prepared on any of his cases. He brought to the practice of law a lethal combination of mental sloth and sixty-watt intellect. Nevertheless, he had parlayed stellar family connections, a patina of charm, and a sixth sense for even the subtlest of shifts within the Abbott & Windsor hierarchy into a lucrative career in the law. And given that 95 percent of all significant commercial lawsuits settle before trial, the huge gaps in Fletcher's mental armor could be concealed behind a phalanx of brilliant young attorneys whose job it was to get him ready for show time.

To put it mildly, Deb Fletcher and I did not get along. On my first day as a lawyer, fresh out of law school, I had received my first assignment from L. Debevoise Fletcher. One day later, when I returned to his corner office to ask a question about the assignment, Fletcher gave me my first partner's-arm-around-the-waist. Two weeks later, as we were walking down the hallway in the federal courts building,

Fletcher gave me my first and my last partner's-pat-on-the-tush. It took a moment to overcome the shock and react to what he had just done.

"Mr. Fletcher—"

"Please, Rachel," he had interrupted, "call me Deb." And then he placed his hand on my shoulder to give me a friendly squeeze.

I had shrugged out from under his hand and turned to face him. "Don't do that, sir." My voice quavered from a combination of fury and fear. After all, I was a first-year associate and he was not only a corner-office partner but a member of the firm's executive committee. "If you ever touch me again," I warned, "I'll take you to court and make you sorry you did, so help me God."

The only thing worse than our three-block walk back to the office from the courthouse was the elevator ride up to the Abbott & Windsor offices. For all fifty-one floors it was just the two of us in that little room. The ride seemed as long as an Apollo moon shot. Although we never worked together during the rest of my years at Abbott & Windsor, Deb Fletcher always took the time to write down a few corrosive observations about me for the annual associate reviews each spring. The partner who conducted my review told me each year, "With one notable exception, Miss Gold, you seem to have many admirers and supporters among the partners."

And now, standing in the lobby of the police station, I looked up at the notable exception and asked, "What are you doing here, Deb?"

"The police wanted to talk to young Thomas. I stayed here with him while his father arranged for appropriate criminal counsel. As you may recall, criminal law is not my area of expertise."

I resisted the temptation. Instead, I asked, "Tommy's a suspect?"

"I don't believe he is anymore. However, I fear that the same can't be said for Eileen Landau."

"Where is she?"

He chuckled in a patronizing way. "I believe she is with her attorney."

"*I'm* her attorney."

"And I'm sure you'll do a fine job for her in the dissolution proceeding. However," he said with a condescending smile, "as we both know, criminal law is hardly your métier." He mispronounced it *ME-dee-er.* "When Thomas no longer needed the services of a criminal defense specialist, his father arranged for the retainer to be applied to Mrs. Landau's representation."

"So Tommy's criminal lawyer is now representing Eileen?" I asked incredulously. "That's outrageous. I want to see her immediately."

I pushed by him and walked up to the desk sergeant. Deb Fletcher strolled over as I demanded to see my client. I was infuriated by the presumptuousness of Fletcher and the Landau males.

"There's hardly anything sinister going on here, Rachel," Fletcher said after the sergeant told me he would send someone to fetch Eileen. "The Landau family hires only the best."

"How humble of you."

"Now, now, Rachel," he said with an avuncular chuckle, "I doubt whether even you would quibble with the qualifications of Charlie Kimball."

It made me pause a beat. "Charles Kimball is going to represent Eileen?"

"If you and your client will allow me to, Miss Gold," said a familiar gravelly voice from behind me. It was a voice I had last heard in a lecture hall at Harvard Law School.

I turned to find Charles Kimball smiling at me. Next to him stood a flustered Eileen Landau.

Kimball reached out to shake my hand. "Charles Kimball, Miss Gold. I am delighted to meet you at last."

I reached for his hand, trying to act like an adult, trying to mask my awe. Ever since I had heard him speak at a memorial service for Martin Luther King back when I was in sixth grade, Charles Kimball had been in the lawyers' wing of my pantheon of heroes, right up there with Clarence Darrow, William Kunstler, Thurgood Marshall, and Ruth Bader Ginsburg.

Now in his mid-sixties, he still had radiance and he still looked damned good. He had dark green eyes, that trademark dimple in the center of a strong chin, and the same unruly mane of hair. Back when I heard him speak at the Dr. King memorial service, the hair was black and hung down to his shoulders. He still wore it brushed straight back, but now it ended at his shirt collar, and now it was gray. The gold medallion was long gone, and—I noted by quickly glancing down—so were the cowboy boots, replaced by shiny cordovan Bass Weejuns.

"Actually," I said as I shook his hand, "we've met before."

"Good God," he responded with mock dismay, "this must be the first sign of senility. While I may forget an occasional face or name, I take pride in my perfect recall of two things in life. One is the federal rules of evidence. The other is the face of every beautiful woman I have ever met."

I shook my head good-naturedly. "No wonder you do so well before women jurors."

He put his hand over his heart. "Do I detect a skeptic? Wait ..." He studied my face for a moment, and then he smiled. "Harvard Law School, right?"

"Right," I said, still skeptical. After all, Deb Fletcher could have told him a little about me.

He had his hand on his chin. "About ten years ago, I believe. You asked me a question after my lecture."

I was stunned. "That's remarkable," I said.

His eyes twinkled. "I told you I don't forget."

"Which reminds me," I said, trying to get us back to the topic at hand, "I need to talk to Eileen."

Deb Fletcher, who had been observing our conversation, jumped in. "Charlie, I told Rachel that you'd be handling this matter for Mrs. Landau."

Kimball held up his hand to Deb. "Well, I think that's a decision for Rachel and her client to make, Deb, not us." He looked at me with a friendly smile. "There's a small conference room down the hall on the right. Eileen and I were back there when you arrived." He turned to Eileen. "Why don't you and Rachel go on back and talk it over. I'll wait out here."

Eileen and I walked back to the conference room. It was small and cramped, with three metal chairs and a metal table. "He's a terrific lawyer," I told her after I closed the door.

She pulled a chair up to one side of the table and sat down. "Tommy thinks he walks on water."

I sat across from her. "How 'bout you?"

She shrugged. "I like him. But I like you, too."

"Eileen, if you can get Charles Kimball to defend you, do it. He's one of the finest criminal defense lawyers in the country. He can handle the criminal side, and I'll take care of the divorce side."

"You're sure?"

"Definitely. This isn't a popularity contest. I'm not a criminal defense lawyer. Charles Kimball is. I can work with him. Now tell me what's going on here."

"It's horrible, Rachel," she said, lighting a cigarette. "They know I was in that room with him."

"How'd they find out?"

She shook her head in displeasure. "I'm so stupid. One of the hotel security guards remembered my car was in the parking lot."

"How did he remember it?"

"He saw it there."

"There must be dozens of cars in there."

"Not dozens of red Corvettes with my vanity plate?"

"What's your vanity plate say?"

" 'EILEEN-L.' "

I smiled. "Well, I guess that would tend to narrow it down."

"One of the girls at the front desk recognized me, too. A couple weeks ago my picture was in Jerry Berger's column. She remembered."

"Have you talked to the police yet?"

"No. I did exactly what you told me to do. And when Mr. Kimball arrived, he wouldn't let me talk to them either. He met with the detective for a while, then he asked me some questions about the death, and then he went back to talk to the detective some more."

"And that's all?"

"So far. He said we should wait until you got here."

"Let me go talk to him. Wait here." I looked at her and shook my head in puzzlement. "I can't believe that they really think you're a suspect."

She reached across and grabbed my arm. "Rachel, there's

some vile little man from the *Post-Dispatch* hanging around out there. Don't let him find out why I'm here."

I gently patted her hand. "I'll see what I can do." She released her grip and I stood up.

"And Rachel . . ."

I turned at the door. "Yes?"

She looked distressed. "They have more pictures."

"Of you?"

She nodded, her lips quivering.

As I walked through the lobby of the police station, I spotted Charles Kimball on the sidewalk outside. He was deep in conversation with Deb Fletcher, his arms crossed over his chest. Standing next to Fletcher was a heavyset man in tight gray slacks and a white crew-neck sweater. The sweater was snug enough around the chest to show the outline of a pack of cigarettes in the breast pocket. He looked vaguely familiar.

Kimball spotted me as I pushed open the glass door and stepped out into the glare of the midday sun. He waved me over. "Well?" he asked when I reached him.

"We need to talk," I said. "Alone."

"Of course." Kimball turned to the other two. "Gentlemen."

The heavyset guy was staring at me. "This her lawyer?"

"That's her," Deb Fletcher said.

"I apologize," Kimball said. "I didn't realize you two hadn't met. Tommy, this is Rachel Gold. Rachel, this is Tommy Landau."

Eileen was right. He'd really put on weight since I had last seen him. Indeed, he looked as if someone had inserted an air hose into his midriff and inflated him to about 30 percent over the recommended pressure. But there was nothing soft or cuddly about this Michelin Tire Man. Tommy Landau had a thick neck and meaty hands. He wore his straight brown hair combed at an angle across his forehead. He had dark, squinty eyes, a full walrus mustache, and a thick porcine nose. His eyebrows joined along the ridge at the bridge of his nose. If you dressed him in a white full-length apron, put a cleaver in his hand, and posed him stiffly behind a meat counter,

Tommy Landau could pass for a south St. Louis German butcher in one of those nineteenth-century daguerreotypes.

"Hello, Tommy," I said coolly.

"Your client's got a lot of nerve," he said. His voice was flat and slightly hoarse.

"Pardon?" I said with a touch of annoyance.

He snorted as he shook his head. "She sues *me* for divorce, and all the while she's fucking that scumbag camel jockey."

I turned to Fletcher. "Control your client, Deb."

Fletcher chuckled. "What can I say, Rachel? My client's got feelings."

"Genital warts, too, according to his wife. Tell him to save his speeches for the witness stand." I turned to Kimball, pointedly ignoring Tommy Landau. "Can we go somewhere to talk?"

He gave me a conspiratorial wink and turned to the other two. "Gentlemen, we'll finish our discussion later."

Kimball moved through the police with the easy assurance of a man on familiar turf. He greeted clerks and officers by name as we passed them in the hallways, and each gave him a smile and a hello in return. He ushered me into an empty office. I sat behind the desk and he stood near the door as he filled me in on what he had learned about the status of the homicide investigation.

"Cyanide?" I repeated when he finished.

Kimball nodded. "I'll have the police get you a copy of the autopsy report."

"How was he poisoned?"

"Through his daily vitamins. Apparently, he carried around a big bottle of the damned things. A real potpourri of pills and capsules and tablets—megavitamins, calcium tablets, powdered seaweed, flower pollen, powdered egg protein, mineral supplements, amino acid capsules. He took several different ones each day." He gave a bemused chuckle. "Supposed to keep him healthy, make him live longer. The police found the bottle in the hotel bathroom. It had fallen behind the toilet. According to the inventory, there were twenty-nine capsules in the bottle, along with various pills and tablets. The lab report showed that twenty-one of the twenty-nine capsules were filled with powdered sodium cyanide."

"How many did he swallow?"

"Just one, but one was enough to kill five men."

I leaned back and crossed my arms. "Is Eileen really a suspect?"

Kimball squinted and shook his head. "Not much of one. I spent twenty minutes with Detective Israel. He's the homicide dick on the case. Frankly, I think the police are more peeved with Eileen than suspicious."

"Peeved?"

"Based on the evidence, Andros clearly had a visitor in that hotel room. When the police figured out that Eileen was the one—indeed, that Eileen and Andros were having an affair—Poncho was furious that she hadn't come forward on her own."

"Who's Poncho?"

"That's Detective Israel. His first name is Bernard. But except when he's on the witness stand, most folks call him Poncho. In any event, he's cooled off. He's been running down other leads."

"And Tommy's a suspect, too?"

"Again, not much of one. That's my sense. Frankly," he said with a wry shake of his head, "I am a little surprised. In a pill-tampering case, one would think Tommy would be more of a suspect than his wife, at least at the outset."

"Why?"

"Because of Tommy's prior experience—or, more precisely, his alleged prior experience—in the, shall we say, pharmacological area."

"But where's his motive?"

"The oldest in the book, Rachel: the jealous husband."

"Tommy knew?"

Kimball raised his eyebrows and shrugged. "Attorney-client privilege."

I nodded. "If you're relying on that privilege, Charles, how can you represent Eileen when the police still suspect Tommy? You have a conflict of interest."

"I agree, Rachel. For that reason, I've given her no legal advice and have told her to confide nothing in me. I've merely shielded her until you arrived. Although I hope neither will be charged, I certainly cannot file an appearance on behalf of Eileen until, if, and when the police confirm that her husband is no longer a suspect."

"Fair enough. What made the police so sure she was having an affair with Andros?"

"The autopsy report revealed that he had sex shortly before he died. In addition, the medical examiner recovered several pubic hairs from his body that were not his. Witnesses placed Eileen in the hotel, and probably in the room, at the time he died. For that reason, the police were already considering a warrant for a medical examination of Eileen. But that was before they searched his apartment last night."

"What did they find?"

Kimball studied me. "Wait here, Rachel," he said as he placed his hand on the doorknob. "Let me see if Poncho will let you see it."

Kimball returned a few minutes later with Detective Israel. I had assumed Detective Bernard Israel was Jewish, and perhaps he was. When I heard his nickname, I thought perhaps he was a Sephardic Jew, and perhaps he was. But he certainly didn't look Jewish. Bernie "Poncho" Israel was black as coal and built like an offensive tackle. He seemed to fill up the doorway. He was holding what looked like a photo album.

"Rachel, allow me to introduce Detective Israel."

"Hello, Detective," I said as we shook hands. "Nice to meet you."

"Same here, Miss Gold." He had a Fu Manchu mustache and sad eyes.

"Call me Rachel."

He smiled. "And call me Poncho. Charlie said you'd like to see this." He held out the photo album.

I took it from him and set it on the table. "You found it in his apartment?"

Poncho nodded. "We've already checked it for fingerprints. They all belong to Andros. As you will see, it's clearly his album."

"It's an album full of suspects," Kimball said. "I should think it will keep Poncho and his posse busy for quite some time."

I looked down at the album cover. I knew what was inside,

but was reluctant to open it with the two of them watching me. I looked up. They both got the hint.

"I'm down the hall to the left," Detective Israel said as he backed out of the room. "Just drop it off when you're through."

I nodded.

"If it's okay with you," Charles Kimball said to me, "I'll go bring Eileen up to date while you look through the album. I think Poncho may let her go home after she answers a few questions. I'll check back here before she talks to him." He closed the door behind him.

I opened the album.

It was not the type that Mom, Dad, Junior, and Sis leafed through while seated before the fireplace in a Hallmark Christmas card scene. There were close to thirty pages of Polaroid photographs neatly mounted in the album. Eileen was the star of three pages near the front—ten color shots of her in total. The photos left absolutely no doubt about the nature of her relationship with Andros. She was naked in every shot but one, and in that one she was wearing black panties and a black pushup bra. In most of the shots she was alone and posed in classic homemade porno positions: on her hands and knees with her legs spread wide; looking over her shoulder; licking a nipple; squeezing her breasts; etc. In two pictures, she and Andros were together. The shots were off-center, as if he had placed the camera on a chair facing the scene, set the timer, and joined her for the pose. In one she was kneeling on the carpet in front of him and licking his semierect penis; in the other she was on top of him, her back arched as his hands squeezed her breasts. In both pictures Andros was staring dully into the camera, detached from the performance.

I slowly flipped through the photo album. Page after page of women. Each posing for him the same ways Eileen had posed. I studied the faces. I recognized several women from the aerobics class. Here was one I had stood next to the night the aerobics class was canceled. I think someone had called her Judy. Or Julie. When the class was canceled, she had called home using a cellular phone she took out of her purse. I had heard her talk to one of her kids about piano lessons. Here she was in the album, leaning back in a chair, her legs wide apart and hooked over the chair arms, her fingers pulling herself even farther apart. I looked for Christine Maxwell but didn't find any pictures of her.

I grew more and more depressed as I slowly turned each page and saw yet another naked woman frozen in an explicit pose under the plastic covering. It reminded me of that musty room in the Field Museum of Natural History in Chicago—the room with display case after display case of dead butterflies skewered on pins. For the sake of these women, I just hoped Andros hadn't shown his butterfly collection to anyone.

I was so disheartened that I didn't even recognize her pictures at first.

"Oh, no," I groaned when I realized who it was. "That bastard."

6

CHAPTER

"Oh, no," Ann groaned. "That bastard."

We were alone in my mother's living room, just the two of us. I had tried to reach Ann when I got back to my office from the police station. I left a message on her machine that I needed to see her as soon as possible. Between her carpools and other commitments, Ann couldn't come over until after her daughter's dance class, which ended at 8:00 P.M.

By the time Ann got to the house, however, I was even more disoriented. That was because she arrived twenty minutes after my mother left.

With a state court judge.

On a date.

Her first since my father had died.

My mother broke the news just a few minutes before her date arrived. I had been sitting alone in the den trying to decide how to break the news to Ann when my mother walked in, fastening one of her earrings.

"Don't sit in the dark, sweetie," she said as she walked over to the lamp. She fastened the earring and turned on the light.

I looked up. It took a moment to come out of my reverie and notice how pretty she looked. "You look great, Mom."

She shrugged. "Halfway decent."

She was wearing a burgundy wool jersey cardigan over a

white ribbed cotton turtleneck sweater. The cardigan was un-buttoned. Below she had on black, high-waisted, stretch stir-rup pants with a black patent-leather belt.

"You going out?"

She nodded. Her smile seemed almost too buoyant.

"Where you going?"

"Miniature golf."

I was surprised. "Miniature golf?"

She blushed. "Miniature golf."

"With Aunt Becky?" Her sister Becky was also a widow.

"Not with Becky." She paused, as if choosing her words carefully. "I'm going with a man."

It took a moment for it to register. "You mean a date?"

"A date."

"Really?"

"Maybe you know him. He's a judge."

"A judge? You're going out on a date with a judge?"

"Rachel, sweetie, relax. He's not married. His wife died of cancer a couple years ago. He seems like a nice man."

"Where did you meet him?" My emotions were swirling.

"At the store." My Aunt Becky owned a gift and card shop in Clayton, and my mother helped her run it. "He came in last week looking for a birthday gift for his secretary. And . . ." She shrugged and smiled.

I forced a smile. "That's nice."

The doorbell chimes sounded. We looked at each other, momentarily flustered. When my dates rang the doorbell in high school, my mother would send me upstairs before she answered the door. She would usher my date into the living room and give him the once-over. What was proper etiquette when the man at the door was going out on a date with your fifty-six-year-old mother?

She took control of the situation. Smoothing her cardigan, she said, "I look okay?"

"Beautiful. Which judge?"

"Maury Bernstein." She turned toward the door.

Tex Bernstein? He had been the judge in one of my divorce cases. *My mother is going out on a date with Tex Bernstein?*

His Honor stepped into the foyer with one hand behind his back. Sure enough, he was wearing snakeskin boots and a string tie. "Howdy, Sarah," he said in that unmistakable twang. He brought his hand out from behind and handed her a long-stem red rose. "This here's for you."

Good move, I conceded. I'm a total sucker for flowers. Still dazed, I smiled as I watched my mother take the rose from him.

"Thank you, Maury," Mother said. "It's lovely." She turned toward me. "This is my eldest daughter, Rachel. She's a law-yer from Harvard. Rachel, do you know Maury Bernstein?"

"She most certainly does," he said, stepping over to shake my hands. "Mighty fine to see you, Counselor." Tex gave me a radiant smile. He had large protruding ears and a bulbous nose. His bald head was gleaming, as if he had stopped on the way over to have it waxed and buffed.

"Hi, Judge," I said, still slightly dazed. *My mother is going out on a date with Tex Bernstein?*

"Come on, Rachel," he said, pretending to be peeved. "In your mama's house I'm jes' plain ole Maury."

The three of us struggled through a few minutes of overly animated small talk. I noted a fresh shaving nick on his chin and the scent of Old Spice after-shave lotion. I was pleased that he had shaved a second time that day for my mother, but I was also aware that my father's brand had been Mennen.

Maury turned to my mother. "Well, Sarah? Ready to saddle up and hit the trail?"

My mother gave me a kiss. "I'll see you later, sweetie."

"Bye, Mom. Goodbye . . . Maury. Have fun."

I walked back into the den shaking my head in bewilder-ment. *Judge Bernstein.* All the lawyers called him Tex. Be-hind his back, of course. Maury Bernstein was born and raised in a small town in the bootheel of Missouri. He came to St. Louis for law school, landed a job as an insurance claims adjuster after graduation, got active in Democratic pol-itics, paid his dues, and eventually ascended to the bench. At that point, depending upon your view of the man, Maury Bernstein either dropped all pretense or became all pretense. Regardless, he traded in his wing-tips for boots, installed a Remington bronze sculpture in his chambers, put up a framed *Lonesome Dove* poster, hung a ten-gallon hat on the peg by the door, and became St. Louis County's first Yiddishe cowboy circuit judge.

There's nothing "wrong" with him, I told myself as I heard his car pull way. *After all, he's got a reputation as a hardworking, honest judge. Not particularly bright. Actually,* I admitted as I recalled the last motion I argued before him, *sort of dense.*

But don't forget, I reminded myself, *he brought your mother a red rose.*

It was hard enough dealing with my mother going out on a date. Going out with a judge, however, made it seem even stranger. And having that judge be Tex Bernstein made it surreal. Back when I was ten, I was in the supermarket with my mother one day and saw my third-grade teacher selecting a head of lettuce in the produce section. Up until that very moment it hadn't even occurred to me that my teacher had an existence outside the school. Same with Tex Bernstein. Now he was on a date with my mother.

And then Ann arrived.

I told her about Mom's date. She seemed only mildly curious, but that was probably because she was much more concerned about why I was so anxious to see her. So I told her.

"I feel like such a fool," she said, more to herself than me.

I didn't say anything. I was keenly aware that I was the big sister. She was sitting on the couch across from me, her head turned toward the fireplace, her arms crossed in front of her chest, her legs pressed together. She frowned at the fireplace. "I feel like one of those sluts back in high school. A total loser."

I wanted to say something comforting, but it seemed that anything I could say would only make it worse. In the Gold family mythology, I was the smart one and Ann was the flighty one. Back when I was little, my mother put me to bed every night with fairy tales about college and medical school. "Someday you'll be somebody," she would whisper as she kissed me good night. "Not a doormat like your poor father. 'Dr. Gold,' they'll all say. 'Please help us, Dr. Gold.' " Ann was allowed to be the girl of the family, the one my mother sent to the Barbizon School of Modeling. She went through high school with a C average and dropped out of the University of Missouri after her sophomore year to marry her ZBT boyfriend, who was graduating that year.

"Ann," I said gently, "you're probably going to be contacted by the police. I assume they'll talk to every woman in his photo album."

She looked at me with a frown. "What?"

"I said the police are going to talk to every woman in his photo album."

She nodded dully and turned back toward the fireplace. "Is Eileen in there, too?" she asked without looking at me.

"Yes."

She shook her head in resignation. "Who else?"

"I don't know any other names. I recognized some from the aerobics class."

"God, how many girls are in there?"

"A lot," I said.

"What's a lot?"

"Twenty. Maybe thirty."

She looked at me. "All the same?"

"What do you mean?"

"Naked. Posed like hookers. Squeezing their tits. Sucking his cock."

I nodded.

She squeezed her eyes closed for a moment and took a deep breath. "And now the police have them." She looked at me and shook her head. "Talk about humiliation—a bunch of cops drooling over those pictures. Jesus Christ."

I moved over to the couch. I took her hand and held it in both of mine.

After a while she sighed. "I really did it this time, huh?" She looked at me. We shared a pair of sad smiles.

"Look for the silver lining," I said. "That's what Dad always told us."

"There's no silver lining here."

"Well," I finally said with a sheepish look, "all things considered, I'd rather be you than Andros right now."

"I guess," she said with a reluctant smile.

"And I'd rather be you than Eileen Landau, too."

"Was she really there when he died?"

I nodded.

She shuddered. "Death by cyanide. Totally gruesome."

"That's the way it sounded."

"Was Christine Maxwell in the album?"

"I didn't see her in there. Why?"

She shrugged. "Just curious. Are you going to the funeral tomorrow morning?"

"Probably. Benny wants to go, too."

She smiled. "Benny? God, that'll be perfect for him."

I nodded. "He told me he felt himself, quote, duty bound as a warm, sensitive New Age man to be available at the funeral home to succor any woman looking for consolation, close quote."

"Succor, eh?" It made her laugh. "Sounds like Benny thinks he might get lucky."

"Probably. Hey, you want some tea?"

"I need something stronger than that."

"How about grain alcohol and an IV tube."

She smiled. "It's a deal."

I stood up. "Come on in the kitchen."

Ann took another sip of wine. "I was so upset when I found out Eileen was having an affair with him."

"How did you find out?"

"Debbie told me."

"When?"

"One night in Las Vegas. We were up in the room alone. The men were down in the casino and Janet was off getting a massage. Debbie had no idea about Andros and me. None. She's just a gossip. She was telling me about her lunch date with Eileen at the Ritz the day before we all left for Vegas. Eileen had started off telling her about the divorce. They got to talking about husbands, about men, you know, the usual. That's when Eileen told her about her affair with Andros. She swore Debbie to secrecy. She told Debbie that she was meeting him in a hotel room after lunch that day. Oh, Rachel, I was totally devastated. What made it even worse was that I knew exactly what I had done the day before we left for Vegas. I had spent the morning in bed with that goddamn son of a bitch. Can you believe it? He screwed me in the morning and screwed her in the afternoon. I bed he fed us both the same line of bullshit."

"Did you say anything to Debbie?"

Ann shrugged helplessly. "What was I going to say? I was dying inside, but I didn't let on. When she went to the bathroom I poured myself a glass of vodka, downed it in three gulps, and vowed that I'd never have anything to do with that bastard ever again." She closed her eyes and shook her head. "That's why this stuff with the photo album is such a nightmare. It's like having someone dig up a corpse right after I buried it."

I nodded sympathetically, although the lawyer side of my brain was clicking away. "So you were still seeing him back when you took me to his class."

"Oh, yeah. We were in the middle of a hot and heavy love affair, or so I thought. He was probably screwing three other girls from the class at the same time. Jesus Christ."

She finished her wine and poured another glass. I took a sip of tea and watched her. "He didn't seem your type," I finally said.

She gave me a sharp look. "And what's my type?" There was an edge in her voice.

I shrugged. "I kind of thought Richie was your type."

"Well," she said with a glum smile, "Andros certainly wasn't Richie. That's for sure."

"When did you start seeing him?"

She leaned back in her chair and brushed back a lock of curly hair. "Three weeks after Dad died," she said.

I waited, sipping my tea.

She had a wistful look. "I started thinking about having an affair the week we sat *shiva* at my house. Isn't that terrible?"

Sitting *shiva* is the Jewish version of an Irish wake, except it begins after the funeral, lasts for seven days, and is held in the home of one of the family members.

"Death triggers strange thoughts," I said.

Ann frowned as she tried to remember. "Actually, I probably started thinking about it at the end of the funeral service. Richie was one of the pallbearers." She stared at her wineglass. "I remember it so clearly. I was watching him carry Dad's casket out. All of a sudden I realized how much Richie and I were like Dad and Mom. I don't mean that he acts like Dad, or even looks that much like him, which he doesn't. It was just that—I don't know, it sort of struck me how much our marriage was like Mom and Dad's. 'My God,' I said to myself as I sat in that chapel, 'we're going to be just like them.' "

She took a sip of wine. "Let's face it, Rachel, Mom and Dad didn't exactly have the most exciting marriage in the world. I mean, Dad was sweet and all, but you're got to admit, he wasn't Warren Beatty." She sighed. "Dad was more like—well, he was like Richie: predictable, reliable, predictable, dependable." She leaned back in her chair. "Totally predictable."

I reached across the table and placed my hand over hers.

She closed her eyes. "Sometimes when I'm with Richie I feel like I'm living in the middle of a rerun that I've already seen a thousand times. When we go out to a restaurant, I know exactly what he's going to order—everything from the Bud Light and shrimp cocktail at the start to the cup of decaf with Sweet 'n Low at the end." She opened her eyes and shook her head sadly. "It's the same when we make love. I know every single thing he's going to do, from the way he turns on his side toward me when we get into bed until he falls asleep. Everything. I know when he's going to touch my boobs. I even know which one. Everything. We've been doing it the same way for ten years. Not just sex. Everything in our relationship. You know what I felt like sometimes?"

"What?" Ann hadn't talked to me this way in years.

"Like the train in that children's book I used to read to the kids when they were little." She paused for another sip of wine. "This little locomotive goes back and forth over the same tracks, day in and day out for years and years, until one day she decides she has to break loose."

"And what happens?"

"She has fun at first, running through the meadows, smelling flowers, playing tag with the butterflies. But then she realizes that it's more complicated than flowers and tag. She gets scared, she gets in trouble, she almost gets destroyed. In the end, she flees back to that old familiar track. She hugs the track, just as grateful as can be. She promises that she'll never ever leave that railroad track again for the rest of her life."

"What an appalling story," I said.

Ann nodded. "I thought it was totally depressing, but the kids loved it. They made me read that book over and over again. I got so sick of it I threw it out one night after they were in bed." She sighed. "They'll probably turn out just like Richie. He'll never leave the track. Anyway, that's what I was thinking while I watched Richie in his boring blue suit help carry out the casket. I guess that's when I started thinking about Andros."

"But it must have been thrilling for you at first."

"Oh, yes. Believe me, that man was nothing like Richie. He was an animal. Anytime, anywhere, he was always ready. He had a perpetual hard-on." She giggled lecherously. "I don't think Richie and I have made love anywhere but in our bed for at least five years." She shook her head in disappointment, her smile gone. "Not anywhere but *my* side of the bed. But with Andros, I don't think we made love in a bed even half the time. He used to come over to the house on Monday mornings for a personal fitness session. It was some session. We did it in every room in the house. In the shower, against a wall, in the car, in the backyard, you name it. We did things I'd never done before." She blushed at the memory. "I was like a drug addict. If I didn't get my Andros fix every couple of days I'd start to have withdrawal pains."

"How did you handle the rest of your life?"

She rolled her eyes. "My life turned into a soap opera. I wanted him all to myself. I started thinking insane things, like leaving Richie for him. I thought I loved him. I made him tell me he loved me. Like a fool, I believed it. Then I found out he was screwing Eileen at the same time he was telling me he loved me. I couldn't believe it. At first I was in shock." She shook her head. "I was so naive, Rachel. I went crazy. I wanted to kill him. I mean it."

"Did you confront him?"

"Not to his face. I sent him a really nasty letter. That was the last contact I had with him."

"What did you say in the letter?" I asked, the lawyer side of my brain going on red alert.

"I don't remember," she said. "I wrote the letter, drove right over to the post office, and mailed it. I was seething."

"Where did you mail it?"

"What do you mean?"

"To what address?"

"His home address. Why?"

"I'm just thinking of the homicide investigation. They're going to match your name to your pictures in the album. If he saved that letter, it could make the police suspicious."

"I don't think he saved *that* letter, Rachel. I sure wouldn't if I got something like that in the mail."

"Keep your fingers crossed."

She checked her watch. "Listen, I better get home."

We both stood up.

"Thanks for listening to me," she said with a sad smile.

I pushed a curl off her forehead. "I love you, Ann."

We hugged.

"When's Mom supposed to come home?" she asked as we walked to the front door arm in arm.

"She didn't say. They're playing miniature golf. I bet they go somewhere for pie and coffee afterward. That's a mom sort of thing. They'll probably be home by eleven."

"Weird, huh?" Ann said with a smile. "You waiting up for Mom to come home on a date."

I nodded. "Weird."

She opened the door and paused. "Richie doesn't know," she said softly. "He would be so hurt. Now that I look back on what I did, I think I must have been totally crazy. How could I have allowed myself to risk everything just for a fling with that slimeball?"

"Richie may never find out," I said. "But if he does, it won't be the end of the world. He's part of what drove you to Andros. You deserve more in your marriage, Ann. Regardless of whether he finds out, you're going to have to find a way to help him understand what you're going through."

"Richie? Are you kidding? He'd never understand. He's the kind of guy who wouldn't have an affair even if I ordered him to." She gave me a kiss on my cheek. "But I'm not going to worry about it. If the police call, they call. I'll let you know. Thanks, Rachel. I love you."

"I love you, too, Ann."

* * *

When I got into bed at twenty to twelve my mother still wasn't home. I tried to read a chapter of *Emma* but my eyes started smarting after two pages. I was feeling my three hours of sleep the night before.

As I clicked off the reading lamp and set my alarm, I thought back to Ann's parting comment about Richie. In her determination to turn him into my father she had blinded herself to some of his qualities. I had held my tongue.

Unlike Ann, I had been suspicious of Richie's fidelity from the start. He confirmed those suspicions six years ago at a big New Year's Eve party he and Ann threw. Around one in the morning I had walked into their kitchen for a beer. I didn't realize Richie had followed me in. As I reached into the refrigerator, he grasped me by the hips and jammed his crotch against my rear. I was so startled that at first I thought he was joking. But then he turned me around and backed me up against the built-in Amana microwave oven. "God, you have magnificent incisors," he groaned as he tried to stab his thick tongue into my mouth. I had to conk him on the head three times with the beer can, splattering foam on their new hardwood floor, before he loosened his grip enough for me to shove him away.

We've pretended that that little incident never occurred. Nevertheless, as far as I am concerned, any man who would try to French-kiss his wife's sister in his wife's own kitchen is someone who, contrary to Ann's belief, might fool around even without an order to do so from his wife.

I glanced over at the clock. Ten to twelve. Last night I had been trying to get to sleep. Tonight I was trying to stay awake.

As I lay there, Gitel the cat walked into the room and stopped by my bed. She stared at me, her eyes phosphorescent, the white of her fur almost electric. I turned on my side and watched. She crouched slightly, and then she jumped onto the bed. She sat on her haunches, studying me.

"Good evening, Gitel," I said with a hint of reproach in my voice, but after a moment I gave in and scratched her behind her ear. She purred. Then, wonder of wonders, she curled up against me and closed her eyes, her head resting on her paws. This was the second time for us in under a week. Maybe there was still hope for Ozzie.

Thinking about Ann and Richie made me think about the kind of guys I seemed to fall for. Starting back in junior high and moving up to my latest ex, a heartless heart surgeon at Barnes Hospital, only one of my boyfriends had been anything like my father. He was a pediatrics resident who had begged me to marry him and move back home to Cleveland after he finished his residency. I had been a second-year associate at Abbott & Windsor in Chicago, and I ultimately told him no, explaining that I wasn't "ready" for that kind of "commitment"—cop-out language if there ever was. I was still in my Young Professional Woman phase back then. There were dragons to slay and scores to even. A lot of women of my generation went through that phase, until we started to notice that the men we were trying to emulate didn't seem all that happy with their own careers or with what those careers had done to their lives.

Perhaps there was some truth in what I told that sweet boyfriend from Cleveland—I really hadn't been "ready" back then. But, I conceded to myself as I scratched behind Gitel's ears, there was also the fact that he was, like Richie and like my father, predictable. There was nothing exciting about him. Nothing dangerous. And like Richie and like my father, he shared little in common with the other men I had dated over the years. Almost to a one, they were strong-willed and, ultimately, not very nice.

Ann had married a man just like our father. Had I been trying to avoid that kind of man, to avoid the kind of relationship that my mother had with my father? Was I selecting men that I couldn't dominate the way my mother dominated my father, men that wouldn't be congenial enough to give in on every important issue, the way my father always gave in to my mother?

As I turned on my side in bed, losing my struggle against sleep, I couldn't decide whether I had made a genuine discovery about myself or had become a living, breathing C+ term paper in Psych 101. Maybe I just happened to be the kind of woman who found Butch Cassidy a whole lot more attractive than the stolid menfolk in the posse that eventually killed him.

CHAPTER

7

"Whoa," Benny said reverently. "Mine eyes have seen the glory."

"Where?"

"Ten o'clock. Blue dress. No bra. Praise the Lord."

She was a platinum blonde. I studied her as she paused in the aisle to our left, three rows down from us. She looked like this year's poster girl for the American Society of Plastic Surgeons. Her high round breasts didn't merely defy gravity; they were completely oblivious to it. I recognized her from the aerobics class. She had not been in the photo album.

Benny placed his hand over his heart. "I believe I am experiencing what the Catholic Church describes as an epiphany."

"Oh? Is that a Torah in your tabernacle or are you just glad to see her?"

Benny turned to me with a solemn expression. "Now, now, Rachel. As the good Lord is my witness, so long as I have a face, that woman will have a place to sit."

Benny and I were in the back row of the mortuary chapel. We had arrived early and passed by the open coffin while the chapel was still empty. I had been surprised to see that Andros was dressed in a black-and-silver Nike warm-up outfit.

"Tacky," Benny had said with a shake of his head as we

took our seats in the empty back row of the chapel. "He's going to feel like a total putz when he shows up on Judgment Day in that silly costume."

The other early arrival had been Poncho Israel. He came in just after we took our seats. He walked by the coffin up front and settled into a seat in the back row on the other side of the chapel. He had looked over and acknowledged me with a friendly nod.

"How 'bout this babe?" Benny asked, gesturing toward the right aisle. "She in the album?"

There were several women in the line of mourners slowly moving down the aisle. "Which one?"

"The redhead in the double-breasted jacket."

"Oh, no. Not her."

"You know her?"

I nodded. "Her name is Christine Maxwell." She was wearing a conservative double-breasted glen-plaid suit jacket with a matching knee-length skirt and a black silk blouse. Her short red hair was parted on the side and combed back behind her ears.

"Is she a lawyer?"

I watched as she moved down the aisle toward the front. "No. According to Ann, she's some sort of insurance agent or financial adviser."

"Married?"

"Don't know. But she's not for you, Benny."

"How do you know that? When it comes to tall redheads with long legs, I can be very tolerant.

"She's not. Trust me."

She moved slowly past the open coffin and followed the path to the aisle against the far wall. As she started up the aisle, looking for a seat, a dark-haired man in the second row stood up and gestured her over. He pointed to a space next to him.

"Her husband?" Benny asked.

I watched her move down the row toward the man. He had a dark mustache, a deep tan, and a gold band on his ring finger along with big pinkie rings on each pinkie. He was wearing an expensive-looking green suit with no back vent. When she reached him, he put a hand on her shoulder and she kissed him quickly on the cheek. "I don't think so," I said. They seemed more like business colleagues than husband and wife.

I checked my watch. The funeral was scheduled to start in ten minutes. The chapel was already half full, and the line of people waiting to pay their last respects stretched to the back of the chapel. Most were female. Several were dabbing at their eyes or wiping their nose with a handkerchief.

I heard someone's pager start beeping. Poncho stood up and clicked it off as he left the chapel.

"So how was Sarah's big date?" Benny asked.

"She got home after midnight."

"Sounds to me like Sarah and Tex played more than one round of miniature golf."

"Don't start, Benny. No golf jokes."

"Not even one about Hizzoner's putts?"

"I'm warning you, Goldberg."

"My, my, my. Aren't we touchy today."

"Benny, she's my mother."

"Hey, Rachel, lighten up. Give your mom some slack. She looks pretty good for her age. Hell, she looks pretty good, period. She's not even sixty. She's entitled to have some fun."

"I've known my mother for thirty-two years, okay? This is her first date since I was born. The first time she's gone out with any man but my father. Life goes on. I know that. She's going to start dating. I know that. That's the way it should be. That's what I tell myself. But no jokes, okay?"

Benny put his arm around my shoulder. "Sorry, pal."

After a moment I turned to him with a sheepish smile. "I'll say one thing, though: Tex Bernstein is not exactly one of the Chippendale dancers." My thoughts drifted. "But then again," I added quietly, "neither was my father."

Benny squeezed my shoulder.

The organist came to the end of the song—"Climb Every Mountain," I think it was—and then there was silence, broken only by a muffled sob or the blowing of a nose.

An elderly man walked in a side door to the left of the coffin and slowly climbed the three stairs to the podium. He was extremely tall and slightly stooped. Placing his hands on the podium, he looked out at us and smiled. When he first appeared, I thought for a moment that he might be a family member. He clearly wasn't. He had the gaunt, Anglo-Saxon look of a bank teller from a Charles Dickens novel: long face, high forehead, limp hair, beaked nose, protruding ears, large Adam's apple.

"My name is Alfred Mellon," he said in a kindly voice as he withdrew a folded piece of paper from the inside pocket of his suit jacket. "I've been asked to say a few words about a young man who worked in my pharmacy his first year in America. I knew him as Ishmar al-Modalleem."

Mellon paused as he unfolded the paper and smoothed it on the podium. He put on his reading glasses, took a deep breath, and exhaled slowly. "Many of you are here today," he read, "because Andros touched you in a special way."

A woman three rows in front of us started to sob. Benny smothered a laugh.

"He knew how to fill that private space within each of you," Mellon continued. "To fill it in the way only he could— with good and wonderful feelings."

Benny snickered. "Can you believe this knucklehead?" he whispered.

"Shush," I told him, struggling to keep a straight face.

"I know," Mellon continued. "Because he filled that special space inside me, too."

"Oh, God."

"Shush."

Mellon's eulogy moved on to other equally infelicitous metaphors, groped around without success for a unifying theme to the deceased's life, and eventually ended on a poem that had all the power and resonance of a store-bought sympathy card. When he finally took off his reading glasses and left the stage, many of the women in the audience were crying.

Next up was a swarthy little man in a blue leisure suit. He spoke for a few minutes in a thick, guttural accent. I couldn't decipher most of his speech. Whatever he said, it certainly moved him. His voice kept cracking, and he had to stop twice to blow his nose.

He was followed by a plump man with basset-hound eyes. He was either the funeral director or a minister of unclear de-

nomination. I couldn't tell which during the short time it took
him to read two psalms, recite a prayer, and signal the pallbearers. I noted with interest that the dark-haired man next to
Christine stood and took up a position alongside the casket.
As the organ music swelled, the pallbearers carried the casket
out the side door to the waiting hearse.

Benny and I joined the crowd that was moving slowly up
the aisles and out of the chapel. As we stepped into the
sunlight, I saw Poncho Israel standing off to the side. He gestured for me to come over.

"Wait here a sec," I told Benny.

I walked over to Poncho. His eyes looked even more mel-
ancholy than usual. "What's up?" I asked.

"Rachel, we just took your sister into custody. We've given
her her rights. She refuses to say anything until you're there
with her."

"Ann?" I said, confused. "What did you arrest her for?"

"Murder."

"Are you serious?"

He nodded. "I'm afraid so."

"There must be a mistake."

"I don't think so."

"Who?"

"Pardon?"

"Who did my sister supposedly kill?"

He gestured toward the chapel. "The man they just loaded
into that hearse."

"I can't believe this, Poncho. You actually think my sister
killed Andros?"

He nodded solemnly.

"And you think you have evidence to support that?"

He nodded again.

"What?" I demanded. "What evidence?"

"Let's go down to the station, Rachel. We can talk there."

"It can be used to clean silver," I suggested, remembering the
blurb on the label.

"Uncle Harry," Ann said dully.

We were alone in the attorney-client room at the police station, seated on opposite sides of the metal table. I had ex-

pected Ann to be a wreck. Maybe she was inside, but outwardly she seemed wooden, almost eerily so. She had her hands flat on the table.

"Uncle Harry?" I said. Our Uncle Harry had died of lung cancer five years ago. He had owned a small jewelry store in University City.

She shrugged. "Maybe."

"Come on, Ann. I know this is hard on you, but it's important to try to remember this stuff now. Concentrate. Did Uncle Harry give you a can of cyanide?"

She tried to concentrate. "Possibly," she said.

"Why?"

"When he closed his store," she said without inflection, almost mechanically. "After Aunt Rose died. He had a lot of stuff left. He didn't have anywhere to keep it. Richie let him put his stuff in a storage closet in the basement. It was mostly old-fashioned watches and fountain pens and totally out-of-date costume jewelry. I think he put a box of chemicals down there, too."

I stood up and walked over to the window. There were bars on it. "What makes you think he put a box of chemicals down there?"

She shrugged. "I just do."

Be patient, I reminded myself. I took a breath and exhaled slowly. "Did you ever look in the box, Ann?"

"I don't remember."

"Then how do you know it had chemicals in it?"

She thought it over. "I think Uncle Harry said something while I helped him put his stuff in the basement. He put a box up on the top shelf. He told me to make sure the kids kept away from the box. I think he said there were chemicals in there that he used to clean and fix watches and rings."

I came back and sat down. I placed my hands on top of hers. "The cyanide that the police found was in a red can. Does that sound familiar?"

She frowned. "Red? I don't know."

"It's a quart-sized container, with one of those lids you have to pry off with a screwdriver, like a paint can. The brand name is Vigor."

"I'm sorry, Rachel. I don't remember."

Detective Poncho Israel had shown me the container before I went in to meet with Ann. The red label, emblazoned with skull-and-crossbones symbols, had given me the creeps:

VIGOR
Sodium Cyanide
Eggs
CL-520
Used by all jewelers for cleaning jewelry, silverware, watch and clock movements.

Poison B UN 1689

Notice: This product is for sale for professional use only. Not for sale for household use or use by nonprofessionals.

DANGER!
POISON!

KEEP OUT OF REACH OF CHILDREN

This product is HIGHLY TOXIC. Very small quantities, when in contact with acid, give off deadly fumes.

Very small quantities, if swallowed, cause death in seconds.

Use with extreme caution! Use only in well ventilated area. Wash hands after use.

STORE OUT OF REACH OF CHILDREN!

The label described the contents as "sodium cyanide eggs," and that's exactly what they looked like: small white bird's eggs. There were four eggs left. I had asked Poncho how much it would take to kill a man. He pointed to the layer of white powder in the bottom of the can. It looked like confectioner's sugar. He told me that if I moistened my fingers, pressed them into the powder at the bottom of the can, and licked them off, I would be dead in five minutes.

"Listen carefully," I told Ann. "We're not going to say anything about Uncle Harry to the police. Not yet. If we're lucky, there'll be another can of cyanide in Uncle Harry's box."

"Lucky?"

"It makes it easier to argue that someone set you up, that someone planted that can of cyanide. That stuff is hard to buy. If there *already* was a can in Uncle Harry's box, there'd be no reason for you to go through all the trouble of trying to buy another can. It helps show that you were set up."

She was staring at me, barely listening. Suddenly her face contorted in anguish. "Do you believe me, Rachel?"

I squeezed her hands. "Yes. But we have to convince the others—the police, the bail judge, maybe the prosecutor." *And*, I said to myself, *a jury, God forbid.*

Her eyes went dull again. "Ask Richie. Maybe he'll know what's in the box."

I didn't tell Ann what else the police had found in the white powder at the bottom of the can of cyanide: one half of a yellow capsule. It was the same make as the eleven yellow capsules in Andros's pill bottle that were filled with cyanide powder. That news could wait until after I had a chance to see what Uncle Harry had put in the box.

"I can't remember what I wrote in that letter," Ann said. "Did I really threaten to hurt him?"

She was referring to the angry letter she'd sent to Andros. It was postmarked the day she got back from Las Vegas. From what I had been able to piece together in my ride to the police station with Poncho Israel, the discovery of that letter in Andros's apartment had changed Ann's status in the homicide investigation from photo album curiosity to possible suspect.

"Not specifically," I told her as I opened my briefcase. "Detective Israel made a copy for me."

I handed her the photocopy of her letter. Although it was unsigned, it was on her personalized stationery and was clearly in her handwriting: *I absolutely cannot* BELIEVE *you could be such a* TOTAL HEARTLESS JERK. *I am not one of your bimbos,* MISTER! *Forget it! You are SO TACKY! I will not ALLOW you to USE me ... or anyone else, buster!!*

* * *

Ann read through it twice, nodding darkly. "He really was a bastard. Whenever I think of that horrible photo album, that's when I say to myself that that creep got exactly what he deserved."

I pointed to the last sentence of her letter. "That's what the police are focused on. They think it's a threat."

"It probably was, but not a physical threat, for God's sake. I may not be the Gold girl who went to Harvard Law School but I'm not dumb enough to send a death threat on my own stationery." She handed me back the photocopy. "That's all?"

I paused a moment. "No."

She looked at me, her eyes narrowing. "What else?"

"A real threat."

"A letter?"

"More like a note. Like one of those kidnap ransom notes—you know, with cutout letters and words arranged in a message and pasted onto a piece of cardboard."

She looked surprised. "What did it say?"

"Your basic threat. That he had violated the trust of too many women, that he was a cold heartless jerk—that's a direct quote. I warned him that his days were numbered."

She frowned curiously. "Why didn't he call the police when he got it?"

"I don't know."

"When did he receive it?"

"The police don't know. They found it in the trash can under the sink. They haven't been able to find an envelope for it, so they don't have a postmark."

"So he could have received it anytime." She made a dismissive gesture. "It could be a year old."

"No, Ann," I said with a worried shake of my head. "It's not more than a month old."

She gave me a puzzled look. "How do they know that?"

Although I believed my sister, I watched her face carefully as I told her. "When the police searched your house, they found last month's *Harper's Bazaar* and *Cosmopolitan* between the mattress and the box springs in the master bedroom."

She looked bewildered. "What?"

"They're yours," I said, "or at least the *Bazaar* is. It has your mailing label on it."

"But what was it doing under my mattress?"

"That's what they asked."

She still looked confused. "Go on," she said.

"There are four pages missing from the *Bazaar* and four missing from the *Cosmo*."

"So?"

I paused. "None of this is ringing a bell?"

"No," she said with irritation. "Of course not. I've never put any magazine under any mattress. Maybe it was the maid. Or one of the kids. I don't know. What's the big deal with the missing pages? Maybe there were recipes on them, or some of those reply cards for mail-order catalogues."

I shook my head. "According to Detective Israel, the words and letters on those missing pages match the words and letters pasted on the death threat."

She tilted her head. "Huh?"

I continued, "The police obtained complete copies of both magazines. They compared the words and letters in the death threat with words and letters on the pages missing from your issues." I paused. "Detective Israel says they're a perfect match."

Ann sat back in her chair as it sank in. For the first time, she looked scared. "Who would do this to me?" she asked quietly.

I came around the table and sat next to her. "I'll find out," I said, putting my arm around her shoulder. "I promise, Ann." I squeezed her shoulder. "I promise."

8

CHAPTER

The judge set Ann's bond at $50,000. Richie was in the court-room with us. He had the dazed look of an accident victim as I helped him fill out the bond forms. I told Ann I would come by the next morning after her kids were off to school. She and Richie seemed in shock as they left.

I caught up with Detective Israel in the hall.

"You called earlier," he said. "What's up?"

"I want to go over to Firm Ambitions and look around."

He raised his eyebrows. "When?"

"Today. The sooner the better."

He tugged at his mustache. "Well ..." he drawled in a doubtful tone.

"Come on, Poncho, she's my sister."

He sighed. "Okay. I'll send someone over with a key."

I smiled. "Thanks."

"No problem. Say, do you know how to use a computer?"

"Sure. Why?"

"There's one on the premises. You can look through the computer files. We've already made a copy of everything on the hard drive."

"Good."

"If you need anything else after today, ask for Detective Green, Curt Green. I'll be out of town for the next couple days. Going on a fishing trip with my son. Curt's covering for me."

"Have fun."

"I sure hope to. Oh, by the way, Rachel, did you ever cancel your personal fitness session with Andros?"

I hesitated. "I didn't realize I had one."

He tugged at one side of his Fu Manchu mustache. "He has you listed on his appointment calendar for three that afternoon."

"What afternoon?"

"The afternoon he died."

"Oh, right," I said as I recalled my efforts to cancel it. "He made that appointment, not me."

"Come again?"

"I went to one of his workouts at Firm Ambitions a few weeks back. He started pestering me to sign up for his personal fitness sessions. I wasn't interested. I kept turning him down, and then, out of the blue, he sent me a postcard confirming an appointment. I canceled it. Why?"

He shrugged. "Andros died around four o'clock. If you hadn't canceled your session, the odds are he would have been with you when he died."

"That's weird," I finally said.

We rode the elevator down together and said goodbye in the lobby. I called my mother from a pay phone. She was waiting at Ann's house with the two children.

"They should be there in a few minutes," I told her.

"So?"

"Not good."

"How bad?"

"Bad enough."

"Who would do such a thing to Ann?"

"I don't know, Mom. Neither does she."

"When's the trial?"

"That won't be for months."

"Months? Why months?"

"It's how the system works. But I'm hoping she won't ever have to go to trial. First thing we do is hire a good private investigator. I've got some names. I'll start making the calls later this afternoon."

"Later?"

"I'm going over to Firm Ambitions now. Detective Israel agreed to let me look around the space. He's sending someone over to let me in. I want to get there right away, before he changes his mind. I'll start calling around for investigators when I get back to the office."

"Good."

"I'm thinking of talking to Charles Kimball."

"Who's that?"

"A criminal lawyer. One of the best."

"What do we need him for?"

"For Ann, Mom."

"She's got you."

"Mom, I'm not an expert in criminal law. He is. He's a first-rate lawyer."

"So are you. We don't need a stranger. This is family. You should do it."

"I don't think that's a good idea, Mom," I said patiently.

"Of course it's a good idea," my mother answered firmly. "You're her sister. How could anyone represent her better than her own sister?"

"Mother, you don't understand. Doctors don't treat their own family members."

"Don't talk to me about doctors, those gonifs. Especially heart surgeons. But you're not a doctor. You're a lawyer. A great one. And she's your sister."

"Okay, Mom," I said wearily. As I had learned by the age of thirteen, it is pointless to argue with my mother once she makes up her mind about something. About anything. She immediately becomes impervious to logic, empirical data, rational argument, and all other forms of persuasion, whether the subject is the merits of capital punishment ("Don't talk nonsense to me about rehabilitation. What if, God forbid, that animal killed me? Then what, Miss Smarty-Pants Liberal? You're going to teach him how to make hand puppets?") to the demerits of some guy I was dating ("Don't ask me how I know. A mother knows these things. This one is not going to be a good provider"). The best—indeed, the only—way to get my mother to change her mind was to let her calm down and then have someone else raise the issue. Such as Tex. I smiled. I could have Tex do it. She might listen to a judge explain why it isn't wise for a criminal defendant to be represented by her sister.

"We'll talk later, Mom. I love you."

Poncho Israel sent a female officer over to Firm Ambitions to unlock the door. She showed me how to lock up on my way out and told me she'd stop by in a few hours to make sure everything was okay.

The layout of the Firm Ambitions space was simple and functional. The glass entrance doors opened into a reception area not unlike a physician's waiting room, complete with magazine racks and a sliding window cut into the wall between the waiting area and the receptionist's desk within. Unlike a doctor's office, however, the walls had framed Nike "Just Do It" posters instead of Norman Rockwell prints and the magazine racks held the latest copies of various aerobics, exercise, and beauty magazines instead of stale issues of *Family Health* and *Ranger Rick*.

A set of swinging café doors led from the waiting room to the interior space. There was a receptionist cubicle on the left, with an IBM personal computer and telephone on the desk, a set of filing cabinets in the back, and a small Canon photocopier. Directly ahead was a short hallway leading to the dance studio. To the right was another short hallway leading to the women's and the men's changing areas. To the left, beyond the receptionist cubicle, was a door leading into Andros's office. I poked my head into the dance studio and the two changing rooms. All three areas were empty.

Andros's office was surprisingly small and dull. There was a cheap table desk with nothing on it but a telephone, a pad of paper, a dozen sharpened pencils in a green cup, and a Rolodex. There was a couch—his casting couch?—against the wall facing the desk. Against the wall beyond the couch was a mini-refrigerator. I crouched down to open it. There were a dozen or so cans of Bluebird brand grapefruit juice and several eight-ounce cartons of lemon yogurt. Beyond the refrigerator was a private bathroom with a shower. Next to the bathroom was a closet. On hangers inside the closet were several aerobics outfits, a loud yellow sports jacket, and a Reebok sweatshirt.

On the credenza behind the desk was a Sony boom box and a portable color television. Strewn across the credenza were several CDs—Paula Abdul, Michael Jackson, C+C Music Factory, the Pointer Sisters, Miami Sound Machine, En Vogue. There was nothing noteworthy in the credenza drawers other than a box of condoms and a tube of K-Y jelly in the bottom drawer.

On the wall above the credenza were two framed 8x10 black-and-white photographs. In the first picture I immediately recognized former heavyweight boxing champion Mike Tyson. Dressed in a tuxedo and grinning broadly, he was in the center of the group of people posed for the camera. Standing next to him was Andros, who was wearing a casual sports jacket over a shirt unbuttoned halfway to his navel. Tyson was half a head taller than Andros and had one of his huge arms draped around the smaller man's shoulder. I leaned closer. Standing next to Andros was that dark-haired man from the funeral who had gestured to Christine Maxwell, the one with the deep tan and black mustache. He looked like a middle-aged, huskier version of Olympic swimmer Mark Spitz. The fourth person in the photograph, standing to the left of Tyson, was a slender woman with long, coal-black hair parted in the middle. She had sharp Mediterranean features and a sad smile. She looked familiar, but I couldn't place her. In the background was the insignia for the MGM Grand in Las Vegas.

Andros was also in the other 8x10 glossy. It was another group shot, but this time the celebrity in the middle was Donald Trump. Andros and Trump were shaking hands as they both smiled stiffly at the camera, posed in what looked like a huge hotel lobby. The words TRUMP PALACE were engraved in the marble floor at their feet. The dark-haired man from the funeral was in this shot, too. And so was another familiar face: Christine Maxwell. This time the dark-haired man was positioned to the left of the celebrity. Christine was standing to the right of Andros. She was wearing a low-cut sequined dress and smiling at the camera, her hand resting gently on Andros's shoulder.

I looked back and forth between the two framed photos. And then it clicked. Now I remembered where I had seen the black-haired woman in the Mike Tyson photo. I leaned forward and studied her face to make sure. It was definitely her. I took the Mike Tyson photo off the wall, carefully removed it from the frame, and went down the hall to the copy machine. After adjusting the darkness level several times, I was able to make a fairly clear copy of the photograph.

I hung the framed picture back on the wall and put the photocopy in my briefcase. I looked again at the other picture—the one with Donald Trump and Christine Maxwell. As I turned to leave I glanced at the Rolodex on his desk. Leaning over, I flipped through the M's and found the card for Christine Maxwell:

MAXWELL, CHRISTINE O.
MAXWELL ASSOCIATES
(Insurance)

The card listed her home and work addresses and phone numbers. I jotted them down on my legal pad.

I walked back to the reception desk, pulled up the chair, and flicked on the computer. As it booted up, I checked the desk drawers: nothing but standard office supplies. Paper clips, note pads, pens, stamps. The computer terminal beeped. The screen displayed the menu, which included word-processing software, an appointment calendar, and an accounting program.

I started with the appointment calendar and browsed backward through the days and weeks. The calendar entries included his regularly scheduled aerobics and jazz dance classes at Firm Ambitions and the personal workout sessions at the homes of his clients. He had three or four personal workout sessions most days. I flipped back to the day he died. Sure enough, for 3:00 P.M. it showed a session with Rachel Gold at my home address. I kept flipping back. Eileen Landau had a regular session at her home at 2:00 P.M. every Tuesday and Thursday. I found my sister's last appointment, which was the day before her trip to Las Vegas. On a hunch, I entered a search command for the name Maxwell. Sure enough,

Christine Maxwell had been a regular Wednesday and Saturday personal workout client for more than a year. Curiously, however, her last session had been almost three months ago. I leaned over and turned on the printer. After some fiddling around in the calendar program, I figured out how to print out the last six months of his appointments. If his killer was a jilted lover or jealous husband, her name would likely appear on the calendar.

As the calendar pages began advancing out of the printer, I switched to the word-processing program and found the directory. There was nothing that looked exceptional. Mostly client form letters: confirming an appointment, describing a new program, enclosing a bill. There was a press release file. There was an advertisement file. There was a general file of approximately fifty business letters (most one-pagers) to various individuals and companies. When the printer finished the appointment calendar, I had it print off the entire collection of business letters.

As the printer clicked and whirred, I browsed through the accounting program. It included a general ledger, a checkbook ledger, a list of accounts receivable, a list of accounts payable, and various form invoices. I skimmed through the accounts receivable data base. Based upon the names and the zip codes, the accounts were mostly women from the affluent suburbs. I printed the list.

I browsed through the accounts payable data base. It included the past three years. There were all the usual payables: the electric company, Southwestern Bell, the landlord, the cleaning service, the water company, the copier machine service. Then there were the oddball vendors: magazine subscriptions, an after-hours telephone answering service, several athletic apparel suppliers, something called Mound City Mini-Storage. Mound City Mini-Storage? I called up the file onto the screen. Firm Ambitions had paid a quarterly fee to Mound City Mini-Storage for the entire three-year period covered by the computer files. The mailing address for Mound City Mini-Storage was in the North County area out near Lambert–St. Louis International Airport. I printed off the page showing the payment history, account number, and address. I looked for a Maxwell Associates accounts payable file and didn't find one.

I printed off a list of the names of all accounts payable for the last two years and scanned through the rest of the files on the computer.

Satisfied that there was nothing else that seemed worth investigating, I turned off the computer and swiveled my chair toward the filing cabinets. As in every case I had ever worked on, there were lots of documents to review. And as in every such case, the key evidence was buried somewhere in those documents.

Two hours later I closed the last file drawer and stretched my sore back. I had several pages of notes and at least as many pages of photocopies from the file drawers. I carried the materials into Andros's office and sat down on his couch to review them. As I leafed through the notes and photocopies, I made a list of items that might be worth a deeper look. My list included:

1. Capital Investments of Missouri, Inc.;
2. Landau, Mitchell & McCray;
3. Mound City Mini-Storage; and
4. Southwestern Mutual Life Insurance Company of Texas.

I checked my watch. Three-twenty. Benny was supposed to meet me at my office at four-thirty. That gave me enough time to call around for an investigator before he got there, which was good, because Benny and I had a lot to talk about.

9

CHAPTER

"Just as well," Benny said as I hung up. "Guy sounds like a dork."

"How can you say that? You've never even met him."

"Nudger? Alo Nudger? What kind of guy has a name like that?" He turned to Ozzie and rubbed his head. "Am I right, boychik?"

Ozzie whacked his tail against the side of my desk. He was clearly loving his time with Benny. It almost made me jealous.

"Nudger has a good reputation," I said.

"Unlike most of my girlfriends."

"Look, if we were still in Chicago, I'd hire Vic. But we're not in Chicago, and she's not going to be effective down here. I talked to three criminal lawyers this morning, and Nudger was on each one's short list."

"Okay, okay," he said reluctantly. "How long is this noble paladin going to be out of town?"

"The doughnut guy said two more weeks."

Benny gave me a dubious look. "Doughnut guy? What the fuck is a doughnut guy?"

I grinned sheepishly. "I think his office is above a dough-nut shop. The guy who runs the shop answers the phone when Nudger's out. His name is Danny."

"Above a doughnut shop, eh? And this is the *shmegegge* you're going to hire to save your sister?"

I looked down at my list of names. "Damn," I sighed as I crossed off Nudger's name. "I'm meeting with Ann tomorrow morning. I wanted to at least have a name for her. Something to pick up her spirits some."

We were in my office—Benny, Ozzie, and me. Benny lived within walking distance of my office. Even back before this craziness with Andros, it was not unusual for him to drop by around dinnertime, often with Ozzie, to drag me off to eat at some new restaurant he'd discovered.

"What do you need an investigator to do?" Benny asked.

"Look at records."

"What kind?"

"All kinds. The case against Ann is entirely circumstantial, right?"

"Right," he said with a nod.

"If they can accuse her with that kind of evidence, maybe we can find someone *else* to accuse with other circumstantial evidence. I've got some of my own leads to run down, but I can't do that *and* dig through the records. Mom wants to help, and that's fine. I'll give her copies of some of the stuff I printed off the computer at Firm Ambitions. She can try to match up names and dates, maybe even run down some items on microfilm at the library. But there are limits to what she can do, especially with legal records and court filings. That's why I need an investigator, especially one who's good with documents."

"Such as?"

"Court records, for example. Did Andros have any legal problems? Did he ever get sued? Did he have financial problems? Was he ever married? Is there a vindictive former wife? Are there any angry ex-husbands out there who blame him for wrecking a marriage? I need someone who knows how to dig through court files for answers to those questions. And then there's his company."

"That aerobics place?"

I nodded. "Peculiar stuff. I found some of the corporate records in the files out there. According to what I saw, the sole shareholder of Firm Ambitions is something called Capital Investments of Missouri, Inc. What is it? Who owns it? Who are the officers? Who's the registered agent? The Missouri secretary of state's office ought to have some of that information." I shrugged. "Things like that. I need someone good to poke around in court files, corporate files, real estate records—browse around, look for leads, run them down."

"Hey," Benny said with a grin, "you remember *Bottles & Cans* boot camp?"

I smiled. "Sure."

Benny and I had both worked on *In re Bottles & Cans* when we were associates at Abbott & Windsor in Chicago. It was—and remains—the largest civil lawsuit in American legal history. At last count, there are eighty-seven plaintiffs and 102 defendants. The plaintiffs' documents are stored in three warehouses in Cedar Rapids, Iowa; the defendants' documents are in two warehouses out near the Dallas–Fort Worth airport. As junior associates assigned to the case, Benny and I had each spent the mandatory four months at one of those warehouses, seated in a cubicle reviewing documents, twelve hours a day, six days a week. It was known as the *Bottles & Cans* boot camp.

"Shit," Benny said with a wave of his hand. "If I can survive the boot camp, I can handle these records."

He was right, of course. Back when we were both young associates at Abbott & Windsor, many of the firm's nonlitigators viewed Benny as an obnoxious Jew whose continued survival at their staid WASP firm seemed inexplicable unless one presumed that he possessed negatives featuring members of the firm's management committee and several docile sheep. But that was most definitely not the view of the litigation partners on the *Bottles & Cans* team, who considered Benny one of their MVPs. Not only could Benny put together a brilliant research memorandum on a labyrinthine procedural issue in under twenty-four hours, he could then board a plane, fly to Cedar Rapids, and spend sixteen hours the next day seated in a warehouse cubicle reviewing, evaluating, and digesting thousands and thousands of documents. I personally witnessed him inspect documents for nine solid hours without anything other than two bathroom breaks. It earned him the nickname Iron Butt. In short, if anyone had the patience and fortitude to search for an evidentiary needle in a haystack of documents, it was Benny.

"It could take days," I warned.

"So? I've got plenty of time. I'm a law school professor, for chrissakes. It's not like I have a real job."

"I don't know, Benny. I just can't ask you to do all that."

"You don't have to. I'm volunteering. You'd be doing me a favor. I desperately need an excuse."

"Excuse for what?"

"Ray Hellman is out for at least another month."

Raymond Hellman was a professor of law at Washington University. A week ago he'd had open-heart surgery.

"So?"

"Someone has to cover his courses. The dean's looking for volunteers. He approached me yesterday." Benny rolled his eyes. "You know what he wants me to teach?"

"What?"

"How about a Mr. Rogers' Neighborhood hint?" He gave me a saccharine smile and gently said, "Rachel, can you say 'couch'?"

I frowned. "Couch?" And then it clicked. "Oh, God, are you serious?"

Benny nodded bleakly.

Many years ago, a law school professor named George J. Couch wrote a twenty-six-volume treatise called *Cyclopedia of Insurance Law*. Long considered the Talmud of insurance law, it is known within the legal community as *Couch on Insurance*—a title almost as weird as *Beard on Bread* and one that makes you wish that sociologist Gustav Hamm had published a monograph on the New York town of Rye.

Benny and I loathed insurance cases.

"It's even worse than you think," Benny said. "He wants me to teach a third-year seminar on advanced insurance law. Can you imagine the dorks and weenies who'd spend the last semester of law school in a seminar on *advanced* insurance law?"

I made a gagging noise. "What did you tell the dean?"

"I told him that, all things considered, I'd rather give circus bears blow jobs."

I shook my head. "Oh, Benny, you didn't."

"I sure as hell did. But I also told him I thought I might have some other significant time commitments. So far, all I have is my expert-witness gig, which, by the way, looks like it's going forward."

"Really," I said, pleased for him. Benny had been retained as an expert witness on certain antitrust issues by the plaintiffs in a major trial scheduled to begin in Chicago in a week or so.

"Yep," he said. "But that's still seven to ten days off. I need other time commitments. So how about giving me one?"

"Well," I said, feigning reluctance, "there's going to be some broken hearts over at the Barnum & Bailey bear cage."

"C'est le cirque," he said with a shrug. "Where do I start, boss?"

"With Andros, I guess. See what you can find in the criminal records."

He reached for a fresh legal pad. "Okay. And what was the name of the shareholder of Firm Ambitions?"

I checked my notes. "Capital Investments of Missouri, Inc. Here's some others for you. Landau, Mitchell & McCray. The Landau is Harris Landau, Tommy's father. They represented Firm Ambitions in the negotiations over the lease."

"No kidding?"

"There's a whole file on the lease. I don't think Tommy's father is personally involved in the representation, though. At least I didn't see any correspondence or phone message slips in the file with his name. But keep an eye out for the firm."

"I will."

"See what you can find out about Southwestern Mutual Life Insurance Company of Texas." I waited until Benny finished writing down the name. "This one's more of a hunch. Firm Ambitions had a $75,000 line of credit with the First State Bank of Hazelwood. I looked through the loan file. There are copies of financial statements in there for Firm Ambitions, along with its tax returns for the last couple years. As far as I can tell, Firm Ambitions is showing a life insurance policy as an asset on its books."

Benny looked up with a puzzled expression. "A life insurance policy?"

I nodded. "It was definitely deducting the premiums as a business expense. I'll bet it was a policy on Andros."

"Ah, one of those key-man policies?"

"That's my thought. And if it is, maybe you can find out who the beneficiary is. It would sure give us another person to talk to."

Benny looked at his notes. "The policy was issued by this Southwestern Mutual Life Insurance outfit?"

"That's my guess. The accounts payable files listed two insurance companies: Southwestern Mutual Life and Omaha Fire and Casualty Company. I assume the latter wrote the general liability policy for the business."

Benny nodded. "Any other leads?"

I skimmed through my notes. I looked at Benny while I pondered the two 8x10 pictures I had seen in Andros's office.

"What?" Benny asked.

"Well, when you're poking around in the court files," I said, "keep your eyes open for anything having to do with gambling or gambling debts."

He raised his eyebrows. "Really?"

I shrugged. "Just a wild guess. Let me show you something." I found my photocopy of the 8x10 glossy. "Take a look at this."

He took it from me. "Mike Tyson, eh?" he said with surprise. He leaned closer to study the picture. "Hey, isn't that the guy from the funeral?"

"It is. Andros had two framed pictures in his office. This is a copy of one. The other has Donald Trump in it. Both pictures were taken in casinos. See?" I pointed to the MGM Grand insignia. "Las Vegas. The one with Trump was taken in the Trump Palace. I don't know much about casino life, but what kind of guy gets Donald Trump to pose with him in Trump's casino?"

Benny leaned back and crossed his arms. "You think Andros was a high roller?"

I shrugged. "It sure seems possible."

"Interesting." Benny scratched his neck. "Very interesting. You start running up big gambling debts and all of a sudden you're going to start running into a whole different breed of debt collectors."

I nodded. "That was my thought, too. It's another lead."

"I'll start in on the court records first thing tomorrow."

"Thanks."

He waved his hand in dismissal. "No problem."

"I mean it, Benny. Thanks."

"Hey, thank you and thank Ann. You two have rescued me from a semester of insurance law."

"Our pleasure," I said as I stood up. On the way out of my office I kissed him on the cheek. "I'm buying tonight."

He grunted his acquiescence.

I knew, and he knew I knew, that his volunteering to be an investigator had very little to do with wanting to avoid teaching an insurance law seminar and very much to do with wanting to help my sister out, but—like most guys—he'd just get uncomfortable if I made a mushy scene over it.

"Guys don't emote," he had once explained when I tried to get him to share his feelings about a girlfriend who had just dumped him.

"Then what *do* guys do?" I had asked.

"When something like this happens, we go to a Bulls game and shout a lot and get shit-faced." As luck would have it, the Bulls had been in town that night, so Benny and I went to the Bulls game and we shouted a lot and we got shit-faced. Benny threw up in the parking lot and I drove him home and fell asleep in his easy chair and woke up the next morning with an awful hangover and felt ineffably sad, and Benny woke up with a mild hangover and felt great, and that's when I concluded that men and women are actually members of two separate species.

The phone started ringing as I was closing the office door. I paused, my hand on the doorknob, as the answering machine clicked on after the third ring and the tape recording of my secretary's voice told the caller to leave a message after the beep.

Beep.

"Hello, Rachel," a familiar, hearty voice said. "Deb Fletcher here."

I looked over my shoulder at Benny and rolled my eyes.

"It's, uh, quarter to seven," Fletcher continued. "I've been meaning to call you ever since we ran into one another down at the police station. I thought it might be worthwhile to toss around some ways to resolve this divorce thing without any, well, without any adverse publicity. Of course, back then I thought Eileen was the only gal we'd be concerned about whose pictures were in that A-rab's photo album. Well, I just heard about your sister. Understand she'd got her pictures in there too."

"How did he find that out?" I said in outrage.

"Hell," Fletcher continued, "I sure hope you're not in that album, too. Wouldn't that be something?" He chuckled. "Anyway, in light of your client's, shall we say, compromising positions, I think we've got ourselves a bit more of a level playing field here. As you know, a court can consider the conduct of the parties during the marriage when deciding how to divide up the marital property, if you get my drift. Anyway, I think this might be a real good time to get the property settlement wrapped up, before Tommy and I have to amend our answer and start airing your gal's dirty linen. You file something like that, it becomes a public document. One of those nosy reporters gets ahold of it, and shit, it's in the damn papers. So run this by your client. See if she's in a mood to settle this thing. By the way, Tommy tells me Eileen has a big charitable do in a couple of weeks. I understand she's been working on it the whole year. I'd just hate for the damn media to ruin that special day for her. I'll be in New York tomorrow, but I'll be back in the office on Monday. Let's talk."

There was a click and then a dial tone and then silence.

"That bastard," I muttered.

Benny walked over to the answering machine, pushed the eject button, and removed the tape cassette. "Where does she keep the fresh ones?" he asked, holding the cassette.

"In the top desk drawer."

Benny found one and put it into the machine.

"He is truly a despicable human being," I said.

"And a moron, too. Here," he said as he tossed the cassette to me.

I caught it and gave him a puzzled look.

Benny shook his head in anger. "If you're going to blackmail someone, you don't do it into a fucking tape recorder. That dumb fuck doesn't realize he just stepped on his own dick. Level playing field? Shit," he said with another shake of his head. "Hang on to that cassette. If that miserable sack of shit starts giving you *any* trouble, you just play that tape for him. And then you know what you do?"

"What?"

"Hand him the fucking code of professional responsibility. While he reads it, sit back and listen to the most beautiful sound an opposing lawyer can ever hear."

"Which is what?" I was grinning.

"The sound of your opponent's testicles ascending into his pelvic cavity."

10

CHAPTER

Ann's arrest made page three of the morning's *Post-Dispatch*, beneath the headline

LADUE WOMAN CHARGED IN FATAL POISONING OF EXERCISE GURU

Fortunately, there was no mention of the photo album or her romantic involvement with Andros. But that would all come out—every last juicy, humiliating detail—if her case went to trial. I'd been the plaintiff's lawyer in one such case—a sexual-harassment lawsuit in Chicago—and I knew that Ann's trial would attract the trash weeklies and "sweeps week" local TV news producers the way fresh chum attracts hungry sharks. Even if we could overcome the state's circumstantial case—a big if so far—there was no way Ann could avoid a media feeding frenzy. Unless we could find a way to avoid a trial altogether.

Avoid the trial.

That was our principal goal, I reminded myself as I pulled into the driveway of Ann's English Tudor home. Ann was in the kitchen, seated on a bar stool at the counter talking on the portable telephone. She gave me a wan smile as she put her hand over the mouthpiece. "It's Mom." She pointed to the counter. "There's fresh coffee in the pot. Those are blueberry muffins."

I filled a mug with coffee. Leaning against the refrigerator, I took a sip of coffee and studied my little sister. Everything was back in place—her hair, her clothes, her makeup, her kitchen. The breakfast dishes were already in the dishwasher, the countertops were spotless, the floor was swept clean. Fresh coffee in the pot, fresh blueberry muffins arranged on a platter, a roast defrosting in the sink. Although there were bags under her eyes, Ann was coping. Between yesterday afternoon and this morning she'd somehow found a way to tap her inner strength. My little sister had inherited more from my mother than high cheekbones.

"Gotta go, Mom," she said. "Rachel just got here. I'll call you later. I love you." She clicked off the phone and looked over at me.

"Hi," I said.

She gave me a weary sigh. "Hi."

"Kids at school?"

"Yep."

"Is Richie at the office?"

"Yes," she said, her shoulders sagging. "Thank God."

"Bad?"

Ann nodded glumly. "You know Richie—he's not a big one for sharing feelings. Something personal comes up between us, he grabs the remote, hits the power button, and turns to ESPN. Well, last night he was mainlining ESPN. I feel like shit every time I look at him." She paused, her lips quivering. "He doesn't deserve this."

I came over to her side of the table. "Neither do you, Ann."

She looked down. "More than him."

I put my hand on her arm. "Ann, someone set you up."

She pulled her arm away and shook her head. "Rachel, I was the one who had the affair, not him. No one set that up. I did that all by myself. And look at what's happened to me, to Richie, to my poor children. My God." She stopped, her eyes filled with tears. I squeezed her arm. She took a deep breath and frowned, determined to continue. "I tried to talk to Richie about it," she said, with a defeated shake of her head, "just like you said. But he won't let me. All he says is 'That's okay, hon, that's okay.' I can't stand it. I want him to scream at me. I want him to start breaking dishes. I mean, if he was the one who'd cheated on me, if he was the one whose name was in the newspaper, I'd be coming after him with a rolling pin." She was breathing hard, her voice shaking. "He hasn't even raised his voice. All I get is 'That's okay, hon, that's okay.' "

I gave her a hug. "It's going to take time, Ann."

"At this point, I don't know." She got up and took her coffee mug to the sink. She stopped at the sink and turned toward me with a frown. "Hey, why aren't you at work?"

"We have to see what's in Uncle Harry's box."

"Oh, yeah." She put her mug in the sink. "Let's go take a look."

We went down to the basement and got the box down off the top shelf of the storage closet. I opened the box and removed the chemical containers one by one.

"Darn," I said when we were through. There was no cyanide.

"I'm still not following you."

"Sodium cyanide is extremely difficult to buy in pure form," I explained as I closed the box. I reached up and put it back on the top shelf. "In fact," I said as I turned to her, "I doubt whether you would even be able to buy it. At least in pure form."

Ann gave me a quizzical look. "That's good, right?"

I nodded. "Normally. Because the prosecution has to explain how an ordinary person like you got hold of a container of that stuff in the first place. That's where Uncle Harry's box of chemicals comes in. It's the perfect explanation for them: you didn't need to go out and find any cyanide because you already had a can of it in the basement."

She frowned in puzzlement. "But I didn't."

"That's the point," I said as we started up the stairs to her kitchen. "The prosecutor can explain away the difficulties you would have had to overcome to get a can of cyanide by telling the jury that the cyanide the police found in your basement must have come from Uncle Harry's box. You see, for us it would have been better if we found a container of cyanide in the box. Then there would be *two* containers—the one the police found and the one in Uncle Harry's box. It would tend to show that you were set up." I turned to her at the top of the stairs. "If you already had a container in Uncle Harry's chemical box, why would you have gone to the trouble of getting a second container?"

Ann followed me into the kitchen. "Wait a minute," she said. "I bet Richie could get his hands on a container of it. He uses a bunch of different chemicals in his practice. I'll call him now."

It was my turn to frown. "I'm not following you."

Ann walked over to the coffeepot and poured herself another mug. She gave me a conspiratorial wink. "You said if there had been some cyanide in Uncle Harry's box, it would help make it look like I was set up. Right? Well, let's put some cyanide in there."

"No," I said firmly.

Ann tilted her head in surprise. "What do you mean, no?"

"No way." I shook my head. "I don't like it."

Ann gave me a look of disbelief. "Come on, Rachel, they've charged me with murder. Don't be such a Girl Scout."

"Being a Girl Scout has nothing to do with it. It's not worth the risk."

"What risk?"

"Of having your credibility destroyed on the witness stand. Even assuming you could find an old container of cyanide—and it would have to be an old one to match the dates of the other chemicals in that box—even assuming that, *and* assuming that the police don't give you a lie detector test the moment they hear about the container, very few witnesses are good liars. Trust me on that." I refilled my coffee mug and joined her at the kitchen table. "Ann, a decent lawyer can sense when a witness is lying and knows how to expose it on cross-examination. The case against you is entirely circumstantial. That means the jury's going to start off on your side. But it also means that they'll turn on you if you betray their trust. I can't let you take that risk. Adding the cyanide adds too many variables, too much risk. Trust me on this. We'll stick to the truth."

"The truth?" She shook her head in dismay. "That's all?"

I shook my head earnestly. "My goal is to get you out of this *before* trial."

"But how?"

"By doing what the police should be doing. Now that they have you, they're going to treat the case as solved, which means they've stopped looking for suspects. We've just got to keep looking. I've already found a few promising leads. I've got Benny checking out others. We're making progress. I promise we are, Ann. Which reminds me." I stood up. "I want to show you something."

The phone rang while I got my briefcase in the front hall. "Here," Ann said, handing me the receiver when I returned. "It's for you."

I took the phone. "Hello?"

"Rachel, Charles Kimball, returning your call."

I had tried to reach him earlier that morning and had given his secretary my office number and Ann's number.

We exchanged the usual opening pleasantries and then I got to the point. "Charles, I want to meet with you. I want to talk about my sister's situation."

Ann looked up from her coffee mug in surprise. I nodded at her.

"Certainly," Kimball answered without any hesitation.

I had my pocket calendar open on the counter. "The sooner the better. How about today?"

"Let's see. No, I'm afraid today doesn't look good. I have appointments the rest of the morning and a sentencing in federal court at two-thirty. I have to be back in my office by four to prepare a client for an appearance before a grand jury tomorrow morning."

"Any time tomorrow afternoon?"

"Hmmm, I'm afraid that won't work either. I'm booked on the eight-A.M. flight to New York. I'll be up there the rest of the week. Can this wait until next week?"

"I guess it'll have to," I said, disappointed.

"I have an idea. Why not join me for dinner this evening? We can talk about it then."

"Dinner?" I said unsurely.

"I can rearrange my plans for the evening."

"I don't want to put you to that trouble."

"I can assure you, Rachel, it is no trouble at all. I would much rather dine with you, and the sooner we talk about your sister's situation the better. How does Tony's sound? His veal goes perfect with homicides."

I laughed. "That sounds wonderful."

"I'll call Vince and see if he can set us up in a private corner. Shall we say seven-thirty?"

"I'll see you then, Charles."

When I hung up, Ann asked, "Who was that?"

"Charles Kimball."

"The lawyer?"

I nodded.

She looked at me uncertainly. "Why do you want to talk to him about my situation?"

"Well," I said carefully, "I want to run some thoughts by him. A couple strategy points. Maybe see if he'd like to help out. If we can't get the charges dropped before trial, we're going to need a good criminal lawyer at trial, and we're going to need to get that lawyer on board as soon as possible. Charles Kimball is one of the best criminal defense attorneys."

"But you'd still be my lawyer?" There was a hint of anxiety in her voice.

"Of course," I assured her. "It's just that we're going to need a specialist to help us." I reached for my briefcase, eager to change the subject. "Take a look at this picture." I pulled out the photocopy of the 8 x 10 glossy, the one with Mike Tyson and Andros in the middle. "This guy was at the funeral yesterday." I pointed at the dark-haired man with the tan and mustache who stood to the right of Andros. "Do you know who he is?"

Ann took one look and nodded in disapproval. "Don't ask Richie about him."

"Who is he?"

"Nick the Greek." She made a face. "A real creep."

"What's he do?"

"Now? He's got some sort of gambling business. I think he's an owner of that new riverboat casino on the east side. But he used to be a dentist."

"A dentist?" I looked down at his picture. A dentist? It seemed incongruous. "Is that how Richie knows him?"

She nodded darkly. "It was a real scandal. About six years ago. You were still in Chicago."

"What did he do?"

"His female patients, that's what." She snorted in outrage. "Several women, and a couple high school girls, too. A real sleaze. He'd give the women laughing gas. Once they were high, he'd slip off their panties, unzip his fly, and fill one extra cavity, if you know what I mean."

"He got caught?"

"His nurse figured out what was going on. She complained to the dental board. Richie was on the board back then. In fact, he headed up the investigation. They found two female patients who were willing to testify. They held a hearing and voted to suspend him indefinitely." She shook her head in revulsion. "There were criminal charges, too. Rape, I think. He ended up pleading guilty to something and surrendering his license."

"Did he do any time?"

"I don't think so. He ended up filing for bankruptcy, though, after about thirty of his female patients filed a big lawsuit against him."

"I take it Richie doesn't like him."

"I guess so," she said with a shrug. "But it's more like Nick can't stand Richie. I think he must blame Richie for screwing up his dental career, as if he didn't do it to himself. We ran into him at the Zoofari ball last year." Ann's eyes widened at the memory. "Believe me, Rachel, if looks could kill, Richie would be dead."

"And now this guy owns a riverboat casino?"

"Part owner, I think. After he declared bankruptcy, you didn't hear anything about him. He just sort of disappeared. Then about three years ago he started showing up in gossip columns as some sort of gambling promoter. You know, those three-or-four-day gambling junkets to Las Vegas and Atlantic City." She pointed at the 8 x 10. "This is probably one of them. He was sort of like a casino travel agent. Still is, I think. Except his specialty is down in the Caribbean."

"What do you mean?"

Ann shrugged. "I guess they have casinos down there. San Juan, Freeport, places like that. He puts together junkets, or at least he used to. Anyway, I read in Berger's column about a month back that he's going to be one of the owners of that new riverboat, the *Cajun Belle*."

"What's his full name?"

"Kazankis. Nick Kazankis."

"Did Andros ever mention him to you?"

She thought it over. "I don't think so."

I stared at the photograph. "Did Andros ever talk to you about his gambling?"

"Not much. He knew that Richie and I went to Las Vegas every year. He told me he went, too. He used to joke about how we should try to schedule our trips out there for the same time so I could sneak up to his room."

"What did he say about his own gambling?"

Ann frowned, trying to remember. "He liked craps. He told me the odds were better at craps than blackjack. He said he'd teach me someday. He never did." She thought for a moment and shook her head. "That's about all I remember."

"How about gambling debts? Did he ever mention any?"

"I don't think so. Why?"

I pointed at Andros in the picture. "There he is, out there in Las Vegas with Nick the Greek. Someone with real pull got Mike Tyson to pose for that picture. From what you say, it sounds like that someone was Nick. It's always possible that Nick was a good friend of Andros, and did it because they're friends. After all, he was one of the pallbearers. But maybe he did it because Andros was a heavy hitter. They do things like that for heavy hitters—comp them on suites and meals and hookers, get their pictures taken with celebrities, things like that. If Andros was a heavy hitter, he was probably a heavy loser once in a while. Maybe too heavy. From what I've heard, running up big debts out there can be hazardous to your health."

Ann stared at the picture, trying to recall. "It doesn't ring a bell," she finally said. "I don't remember him even mentioning gambling debts."

I pointed to the woman standing to the left of Mike Tyson in the photograph, the slender woman with the sad smile, sharp features, and long black hair parted in the middle. "Is that Nick's wife?" I asked.

Ann nodded. "Sheila."

"You know her?"

"Not really. She used to go to Firm Ambitions. She stopped going maybe six months ago. Sometimes I see her at the supermarket. She's very shy. People say she's sweet, though. Kind of a homebody. Poor thing stayed by his side through that whole laughing-gas scandal and the investigation and the bankruptcy."

"You say she stopped going to Firm Ambitions six months ago?"

"About that time."

"Any reason?"

"No idea," Ann said. "She just stopped. Why?"

I looked down at Sheila in the picture, and then I looked up at Ann. "She's in the photo album."

"Sheila?" Ann looked down at the picture and shook her head sadly. "God, her, too."

I stared at Sheila's face in the 8 x 10 glossy. It was definitely the same sad smile I'd seen in the photo album. "There was another picture in his office," I said as I looked up at Ann. "Another celebrity shot."

"Who?"

"Donald Trump."

"No kidding?"

I nodded. "Trump, Andros, and Nick. No Sheila, though. Guess who the woman in that picture was?"

"Marla Maples?"

"Christine Maxwell."

Ann raised her eyebrows. "Really?"

I nodded. "In a slinky dress. She was standing next to Andros with her hand on his back."

Ann leaned forward, her eyes animated. "Was she in the album, too?"

I shook my head. "Is Christine still married?"

"Oh, no. He's dead. She killed him."

"She killed her husband?"

"Well, not like murder. It was more of an accident. Down at the Lake of the Ozarks. They were out water skiing. She was driving their boat and he was skiing. He fell and she brought the boat around to pick him up. Something got stuck or jammed in the motor, and the boat ran right over him." She winced. "The propeller cracked his head open. I think he died immediately."

"It was ruled an accident?"

Ann nodded. "I think she sued the boat company."

A lawsuit meant court records and possibly press coverage. I made a mental note to pass that lead on to Benny and my mother. "Who was her husband?" I asked Ann.

"Ronald Maxwell. He was one of those playboy types. Polo at St. Louis Country Club, stuff like that. He came from old money. His family had a brokerage house. I think he was a stockbroker there when she married him. A couple years later they sold the company for millions to one of the biggies."

"How long has he been dead?" I asked.

"Maybe five years."

I gestured toward the 8 x 10. "So she was probably single when this was taken."

"Probably."

"Is she still?"

Ann nodded. "She's got a boyfriend, though. His name is Sandberg, I think. He's the head of some company in town. They're one of those power couples. It seems like once a month the *Ladue News* runs a picture of them together at some fundraiser."

"What's his company?"

"I can't remember. Wait." She stood up and started toward the door from the kitchen to the garage. "I've got some old issues of the *Ladue News* in the recycling bag. Let me check."

I rinsed my cup out in the sink while I waited for her. It was nearly eleven o'clock. I had one more stop to make on my way to the office that morning.

"Here they are," Ann said as she came back into the kitchen with a copy of the *Ladue News*. She placed it on the counter, opened to a two-page spread on a black-tie fund-raising benefit for the St. Louis Art Museum. The short article, headlined A PICTURE-PERFECT EVENING, was accompanied by several black-and-white photographs taken at the event. In one of them, Christine stood next to a good-looking man in a white dinner jacket. He vaguely resembled James Caan. The caption beneath the photo read: "Shep Sandberg, CEO of Midwest Refinishing Co., with his lady friend Christine Maxwell."

"Can I take that picture?" I asked her.

"Sure." She closed the issue and handed it to me. "Why?"

I shrugged. "We have to look at every possible connection to Andros. According to his appointment calendar, Christine was one of his regular personal workout clients for at least a year. She stopped going to him about three months ago. Just because she wasn't in his photo album doesn't mean he wasn't sleeping with her, too. If so, maybe we have a jealous boyfriend."

Ann glanced over at my copy of the 8 x 10 glossy of Mike Tyson, Andros, Nick Kazankis, and Sheila Kazankis. "Or maybe a jealous husband."

I nodded as I reached for the 8 x 10. I paused before putting it back in my briefcase, paused to study Sheila's face again. Sheila Kazankis had been the star of the single most explicit and unerotic Polaroid in the entire photo album: posed naked on the carpet, her legs pulled back and spread wide apart as her fingers pulled her vagina open. When I had come across it in the album, I had sat back with a start. The camera flash had dyed the shades and patterns of genital pink into lurid steaks of red, so that at first it looked like a textbook photograph of an appalling knife wound. That initial shock made me linger over the Polaroid. Her sad smile had burned itself into my memory. It was the same smile in the 8 x 10 glossy.

I glanced at her husband in the 8 x 10, and then at Andros. They seemed like three pieces to a puzzle—three pieces that just might snap together if I could figure out how to get them correctly aligned.

11

CHAPTER

In addition to Andros, Firm Ambitions listed one other employee: Kimmi Buckner. Kimmi's title was Administrative Assistant. She lived in Dogtown, which was just a short detour off Highway 40 on the way to my office that morning after I left Ann.

Kimmi.

I envisioned a perky little blonde with perky little boobs and a perky little tush.

Names and titles can be misleading, as was clear the moment she opened the door to her little bungalow. There was nothing in the least bit perky about Kimmi Buckner, or any part of her. Indeed, she exuded a total absence of perk. Words like "sprightly" and "chipper" fit Kimmi Buckner the way a thong swimsuit fits an elephant. And like an elephant, Kimmi Buckner was large and lethargic.

I introduced myself and told her I wanted to ask her a few questions about her ex-boss.

She shrugged. "Well," she said sullenly, "I guess you might as well come in."

She lumbered into the tiny living room. There was a battered La-Z-Boy recliner against one wall and a color television against the opposite wall. Above the La-Z-Boy was a framed painting of Jesus Christ with eyes rolling heavenward and a framed photograph of Pope John Paul II. Against the side wall was a rickety couch upholstered in orange corduroy. In the corner between the couch and the La-Z-Boy was a TV tray with three empty crumpled thirty-two-ounce bags of M&M's. The television was tuned to *The Price Is Right,* and as I walked into the room the announcer hollered, "Ruthie Eppingham ... COME O-O-O-O-O-O-O DOWN!"

Kimmi winced as she lowered herself into the La-Z-Boy. "About a year," she said in answer to my question.

"Who was there before you?"

She frowned in thought. "Linda Somebody-or-other. I never met her. Her old man got transferred somewhere. Alabama, I think."

I leaned against the doorjamb. "What were your duties?"

She sighed listlessly, her eyes shifting back and forth between me and the television as she spoke. "I answered the phone. I sent out the bills. I opened the mail. I paid the bills. I deposited the checks. I typed his letters. I scheduled his appointments. I kept the business running." She snorted angrily. "All that for seven damn dollars an hour."

"Did you ever hear about anyone threatening him?"

She stared at me, her eyes narrowing. "Not exactly," she said with a shake of her head. "But those girls were disgusting. Like dogs in heat around him. It made you want to puke. Threats? No, but some of those girls were desperate." She grunted. "They'd call me three, four times a day, some of them, asking where he was, who was he with, when would he be back, why hadn't he called them, was I sure I gave him their message?" She shook her head angrily. "Disgusting. Sometimes it was their husbands would call, checking up on their old ladies."

"Do you remember who?"

"Are you crazy? Half the time the callers wouldn't even tell me who they were. They'd kind of hem and haw around and sort of ask if I knew where he was or knew whether Mrs. So-and-So had an appointment with him and if so where that appointment was." She squinted at me. "Let me tell you something, lady: if there's a heaven up there, Andros ain't in it by a long shot. You know what he was?"

"No, ma'am."

Her face flushed with rage. "He was an unrepentant fornicator. He'll burn in hell." She looked around the room, her eyes darting back and forth, as her breathing slowed to normal. The television caught her attention, and she fixed on it.

"You don't remember any names?" I asked.

She looked at me with a frown. "Names of what?"

"The husbands. The ones who called?"

"Nah."

She was distracted by something on the game show. I waited until the commercial break, studying her as she watched her show, trying to figure out how she fit in.

"Did you know he had a bottle of vitamins?" I asked.

She snickered. "Sure. I had to order half the crap he took—seaweed, crushed eggshells, weird-sounding stuff."

"Where did he keep the bottle?"

She gave an impatient sigh. "The police asked me the same thing. I'll tell you the same as I told them. When he had his classes and stuff in the building, he'd leave it right on the desk in his office. When he left, he took the bottle with him." She paused, and her stare turned cold. "Lady, if someone wanted to stick poison in there, it wouldn't have been hard. You'd just have to duck in there while he was running one of his classes, dump out some of those pills, and pop in the poison ones."

"But they'd have to get past you."

She snorted. "Big deal. We didn't exactly have airport security in there, if you know what I mean. Those gals were in and out of that office all day long. Let me tell you something, he did more in that office than talk on the phone, if you get my drift." She shook her head in distaste. "I didn't like that place. I'm glad I'm done with that job."

"So he took the bottle with him when he left?"

"Oh, yeah. He had to." She rolled her eyes in derision. "Eight, four, and ten," she recited. "That was his motto. Eight, four, and ten."

"I don't understand."

"Eight in the morning, four in the afternoon, ten at night. That's when he took those damn pills. He had a whole system. He took certain ones in the morning, others in the afternoon, others at night. He made sure he had that bottle handy when it was time to take his pills."

I kept my tone neutral. "It sounds like you don't think much of him."

She shrugged. "I didn't spend a whole lot of time thinking about him. I got the job through one of those temporary secretary outfits. Most of my bosses have been jerks. He was worse than some, better than others. I guess I'm not jumping for joy that he's dead, but I sure ain't in mourning for him."

The commercial break ended and the announcer commanded someone else to COME O-O-O-O-O-O-N DOWN! At the next break I gave her my card and asked her to call me if she remembered the names of any of the men or women who had called her about the whereabouts of Andros or any of his clients. She put my card on the table by the crumpled M&M bags. I thanked her for her time and said goodbye. As I backed out through the front door, Kimmi Buckner was staring slack-jawed at the television.

I got to my office shortly before eleven. After reviewing the mail, returning the morning's phone calls, and dictating several deposition notices in one of my copyright cases, I tried calling Sheila Kazankis. Although the telephone directory had no listing under Kazankis, I was able to find her number in one of the lists I'd printed out of the Firm Ambitions computer.

A businesslike female voice answered. "The Kazankis residence."

"Mrs. Kazankis, please."

"May I tell her who this is?"

"Certainly. I'm Rachel Gold."

"And you are?"

"I'm an attorney."

"Just a moment, Miss Gold." There was a pause, and then the same voice returned. "What is the nature of your call, Miss Gold?"

I was starting to get irritated. "It's a personal matter."

"What *sort* of personal matter, Miss Gold?" Her tone was icy.

"I don't believe that's any of your business. Now would you please put Mrs. Kazankis on the phone?"

"I'm afraid I can't do that, Miss Gold. Good day." And she hung up.

I stared at the receiver in disbelief. Glancing down at my notes, I saw the next name on my list: Christine Maxwell. Reluctantly, I dialed her number.

"Maxwell Associates," a cheerful female voice announced.

"Ms. Maxwell, please."

"And whom may I say is calling?"

I told her. A moment later a different, deeper female voice came on. "Ms. Maxwell's office." This voice had a two-pack-a-day rasp to it.

"This is Rachel Gold. Can I talk to her?" I was getting fed up with the gauntlet.

She put me on hold and left me there for a full minute—a long time when you're on hold—and came back on the line. "She'll be right with you, Miss Gold."

A moment later, Christine came on the line. "Hello, Rachel. How are you?" There was forced friendliness in her voice, a layer of warmth one millimeter thick.

"I'm fine, Chrissy. Yourself?"

We spent a few minutes pretending we were actually interested in each other's lives, and then I got to the point. "I need to talk to you for a few minutes. Would you have some time this afternoon? I could come by your office around four."

She hesitated. "Business?" she asked.

"No. Andros."

Her voice went dead. "What about him?"

"Everything about him. Whatever you can tell me."

She paused. "I'm afraid I'm busy this afternoon." There was no trace of regret in her voice.

"Fine. Is there a good time tomorrow?"

"Why do you want to talk to me about him?"

"Because you knew him."

"So did a lot of people," she said, irritated.

"I'm talking to a lot of people. You're one of them."

Another pause. "I have a busy day tomorrow."

"So do I," I said. "But I'll work around your schedule. All I'm asking for is fifteen minutes." I tried to keep my voice congenial. "Take a look at your schedule, Chrissy, see if you can find a hole in it tomorrow, and call me back this afternoon. I'll make myself available when it's convenient for you."

"I'm very busy tomorrow."

"As I said, so am I. But I'll make room. Give me a call. Goodbye, Chrissy." I hung up.

A few minutes later, I left to meet Benny and my mother for lunch. On the way out, I gave my secretary the telephone number for Sheila Kazankis. I told her to tell the woman who answered the phone to give Sheila a message to call me after lunch. Maybe she'd have better luck getting through than I had.

"Who goes first?" I asked after the waitress refilled my coffee mug and set a long-neck bottle of Budweiser in front of Benny.

"Wait," he said. "Here comes Sarah."

I turned just as my mother arrived at our booth. We were having lunch at Blueberry Hill, which just so happens to be the finest bar and grill in America. It has a first-rate jukebox (which was actually playing "Blueberry Hill" at the moment), an entire room of dart boards, an awesome hamburger, and a cavelike dance room in the basement named in honor of Elvis.

I scooted over to make room for my mother. "Hi, Mom."

"Hello, sweetie." She slid in and looked up at the waitress. "I'll take a cup of coffee, honey."

My mother scanned the menu while the waitress went to fetch her coffee. When she returned with the steaming mug, my mother ordered a salad.

"A salad?" Benny said when the waitress left. "At Blueberry Hill you order a salad?"

"What?" she responded, not giving an inch. "I should order blueberry pie?"

I put an arm around my mother's shoulder. "Don't pay attention to him, Mom. I think a salad is the only thing on the menu he didn't order this time."

"Hey," he protested, "I just taught a two-hour seminar on the fucking Hart-Scott-Rodino Act. I'm in dire need of replenishment."

I gave Benny an exasperated look. I'd been bugging him

for years to cut down on his intake of fatty foods. "Benny, I'd call a quarter-pound chili dog, a large bowl of chili, and a large order of fries more than just a pit stop."

"Enough with the food," my mother said. "Let's hear what you found this morning. First, Rachel."

I told them about Uncle Harry's box of chemicals and Ann's identification of Nick and Sheila Kazankis in the 8 x 10 glossy and my unsuccessful attempt to talk to Sheila on the phone. I described my interview of Kimmi Buckner and my efforts to get a meeting with Christine Maxwell.

"Is that the one who ran over her husband in the lake?" my mother asked.

"What's this?" Benny asked avidly.

I told him the story Ann had told me that morning.

"Sliced open his head with a propeller blade," Benny said with a grimace. "Ouch. I hate when that happens."

I turned to my mother. "Ann said there was a big lawsuit over it."

She nodded. "I remember reading about it. I'm going to the library this afternoon. I'll find it on microfilm."

"How's the Widow Maxwell doing these days?" Benny asked.

"She's got her company and a new boyfriend," I said. "Ann showed me his picture in the *Ladue News*. In fact," I said as I reached into my briefcase to pull out the issue, "here he is."

I opened the paper to the spread on the Art Museum function and handed it to Benny. He looked at the picture, nodded, and handed the paper to my mother. She read the caption and frowned.

"What?" I asked.

"His company's been in the news."

"Sandberg's company?" I asked.

My mother nodded. "Midwest Refinishing. I recognize the name." She leaned back, trying to remember. "A couple months ago. Something with pollution. I'll find the article when I'm at the library."

The waitress brought Benny another beer and told us our food would be right out.

"So?" I said as I turned to Benny. "What have you found?"

"A little here and there," he said. "Where do you want to start?"

"With the company. What do you have on Firm Ambitions?"

"You were on target," he said. "The sole shareholder of Firm Ambitions is Capital Investments of Missouri, Inc."

"Which is what?" I asked.

"Good question. It's a Missouri corporation. According to the Missouri secretary of state's office, it's current on its taxes and in good standing."

"What does it do?"

"Apparently nothing but own Firm Ambitions."

"Does it have any officers?"

"Only one: Ishmar al-Modalleem. He's president and secretary."

"Who?" my mother asked.

"Andros," I told her. I looked at Benny. "Is he the only director, too?"

"No," Benny said. "There are three. Andros, Harris Landau, and Betty Russell."

"Is Harris Tommy Landau's father?" my mother asked.

Benny nodded. "His firm, Landau, Mitchell & McCray, did the corporation formation work."

"Who's Betty Russell?"

"Harris Landau's former secretary."

"The lawyer and his secretary," I said. "Not unusual."

"What's not unusual?" my mother asked.

"To have the lawyer and even a secretary from the firm named as directors for the client," I said to my mother. "Especially for a real small company." I looked at Benny. "Where's his secretary these days?"

"Dead."

"When?"

"Six months ago. Ovarian cancer. In her fifties."

"How in the world did you find all that out?" I asked.

Benny smiled proudly. "Makes you tingle all over, doesn't it?"

"Are there any shareholders besides Andros?" I asked.

"He isn't a shareholder."

I sat back, surprised. "Who is?"

Benny smiled. "You ready for this? Capital Investments of Missouri is a wholly owned subsidiary of Capital Investments of Illinois."

"Which is what?" I asked.

"A wholly owned subsidiary of Capital Investments of Vermont."

"You're kidding," I said.

"Nope. By the time I got to Vermont it was lunchtime. I'll call the Vermont secretary of state's office after lunch."

I shook my head. "All those parent companies—that's weird. Did you find out anything else about them?"

"Not yet."

"What was a big shot like Harris Landau doing representing a pisher like Andros?" my mother asked.

Benny turned his palms up. "Don't know. My guess is that he did it as a favor to some heavy hitter who referred Andros to the firm."

"You find out anything else?" I asked.

"You were right about the insurance policy."

"Life insurance?"

"Yep. A key-man policy."

"How much?"

"One million dollars."

I whistled. "Beneficiary?"

"I'm working on that one."

"How so?"

"I've been sweet-talking someone named Marge down in the Houston underwriting department of the insurance company. She said that the original beneficiary was Capital Investments of Missouri but that her records show that there was a change of beneficiary put through last year. She's trying to track it down."

I leaned over and kissed him on the cheek. "Isn't this guy incredible, Mom?"

My mother nodded, her forehead wrinkled in thought. "You should ask this Marge who the agent was. If it's someone in St. Louis, we could talk to him."

"Good point, Mom."

The waitress arrived. My mother watched in awe as she

started unloading Benny's order. "My God, you weren't kidding."

I shook my head. "One more item and she'd need a forklift."

Benny looked at my mother and me with raised eyebrows. He gestured toward his food. "May I be the first to advise you lovely ladies that I will soon be consuming a chili dog *and* a large bowl of chili—both of which are loaded—indeed, gorged—with kidney beans. Within an hour my colon will be celebrating Mardi Gras. Mock me now, ladies, and I will be sure to put you both on the parade route."

While Benny dug into his huge lunch, I told them about my plans for the afternoon, which included a visit to Mound City Mini-Storage.

"Why go there?" my mother asked.

"According to the business records, Firm Ambitions rented storage space there. Maybe there's nothing in the space but old files, but you never know."

Just then our waitress came over to the table. "Excuse me," she said. "Is your name Rachel Gold?"

I looked up in surprise. "What is it?"

"Your secretary is on the phone. She needs to talk to you."

I followed her to the bar, where the bartender held out the phone.

"I'm sorry, Rachel," my secretary said, "but this man on the phone insists that I call you. He said you'd be very disappointed if you didn't get to talk to him. I said you were at a lunch meeting at Blueberry Hill but he insisted."

"Who is he?"

"I'm not sure. He told me to tell you his name is Nick the Greek."

I felt my stomach tighten. "He's still on the phone?"

"Yes. Shall I patch him in?"

"Okay."

There was a click, and then my secretary said, "Go ahead, sir."

"Rachel?" He had a deep, honey-coated voice.

"Yes?"

"This is Nick Kazankis." It was an FM disk jockey voice. "Sorry to interrupt your lunch, but I wanted to make sure we touched base before I left town. My flight's in two hours. We should talk before then."

"About what?"

He chuckled. "Andros, of course. What I can tell you about him will be far more germane than what Sheila can."

"How do you know that."

He chuckled again. "Well, I suppose I don't. I suppose I'm making an assumption. I'm assuming you're looking for information that might be germane to the charges against your sister. If so, then we should talk. If, however, you're trying to find out how big his cock was, well, I can't help you there, and I'm going to have to ask you to seek that kind of information from someone other than my wife. It's your choice, of course, but you're going to have to make it fast. My flight is to Miami, where I change planes for Freeport. I'm going to be difficult to reach for a few days."

I thought it over. "Okay, where's your office?"

"Across the river."

"In Illinois?" I reached into my purse for a pen. "How do I get there?"

"No need to worry about that. I've already sent a limo and driver. They should be there any minute."

12

CHAPTER

The stretch limo featured a wet bar, a television, a stereo system, copies of the day's *Wall Street Journal, Chicago Tribune,* and *New York Times,* a personal computer, a facsimile machine, and enough open space for a game of lacrosse. It had the desired effect: I peered out the window as we crossed over the Mississippi River into Illinois, trying to spot our destination, which I assumed would be a cross between the Taj Mahal and Tara.

It wasn't, at least not on the outside. We turned into a nondescript strip shopping center just off the road near Granite City and pulled up to a three-story office building at the far end of the shopping center. Parked in front of the building was a red Infiniti J30 with an Illinois vanity plate that read NICK K.

The limo driver got out on his side of the limo, came around the side, and opened my door. It was then that I noticed that he had, in addition to freshly pressed gray livery and shiny black shoes, a cauliflower ear and a Cicero accent.

"Mr. K's office is on da second floor," he said, gesturing with his thumb. "I'll wait right here for ya, madam."

"Thank you, Jeeves."

The building lobby was clean, but the elevator was out of order. The building directory listed him simply as KAZANKIS, N.—#203. No business name or other identification. I took the stairs with no Taj Mahal expectations. The only identification on the door to 203 was the word KAZANKIS in gold press-on letters.

The small reception area inside was a bit more upscale, with comfortable chairs, fresh flowers in a fluted glass vase, and current issues of *Newsweek, Fortune,* and *Vanity Fair* on the coffee table. The receptionist was a gorgeous honey blonde with a friendly smile. She was typing at her computer terminal when I walked in. I told her my name and she buzzed her boss on the intercom. She talked to him a moment, gave me a dazzling smile, and told me he'd be free in a few minutes. I declined her offer of coffee or a soft drink. I took a seat on the couch while she resumed her typing after putting back on a set of earphones that looked like the type the airlines pass out on longer flights. At first I thought she was listening to music, but then realized that the earphones were attached to a microcassette transcriber on the desk near her computer. It was similar to the device my secretary used for transcribing dictation tapes.

As I waited, I stood to look at the brightly colored framed posters on the walls. Each featured a gambling casino in the Caribbean. Behind the couch was one poster with the garish Princess Casino, a huge Moorish palace in Freeport, and another of El Centro in San Juan. On the other walls were several I'd never heard of before: Casino Maho in St. Maarten, Casino Troi-Ilets in Martinique, St. James Club in Antigua, Gosier-les-Bains in Guadeloupe. The posters surrounded the room, creating a heady swirl of tropical colors and beaming faces and shining roulette wheels and beautiful women. Taken together, they created one of those exotic worlds where you expect to find James Bond himself, in a black tuxedo, smiling roguishly across the chemin-de-fer table at a scowling Ernst Blofeld.

"Oh, Miss Gold," the receptionist trilled, "you can go on in. Nickie's ready for you."

Nickie? I repeated as I opened the inner door and, to my surprise, stepped into the Taj Mahal.

"Come in, Rachel," Nick Kazankis said as he stood up and came toward me.

I looked around. "Wow."

It was a spectacular office—lots of chrome and glass and white leather. There was a Persian rug over a parquet wood floor. A dramatic cathedral ceiling rose two stories overhead, punctuated with skylights that were covered with stained glass. The sunlight streaming through the stained glass splashed reds and greens and blues on the white walls. The sounds of Dave Brubeck's "Take Five" cascaded through the room from hidden speakers.

There was no desk or formal office seating arrangement. In one corner a large white leather couch and matching love seat were arranged in front of a fireplace. Directly above the fireplace were five huge built-in color televisions, each tuned to a different station, all with the sound muted. In another area of the room was a chrome-and-glass conference table with eight chairs. On the wall above the conference table there was a grainy black-and-white blowup of what looked like a news photograph. In the photo an enraged Nick Kazankis was standing on the sidewalk outside a building and in the process of slamming a Channel 5 minicam to the ground while a young male reporter with a microphone ducked out of the way.

"Sorry to keep you waiting," Nick said as he extended his hand to shake mine. "I was trapped on one of those never-ending conference calls. Come sit down, Rachel. Let's talk."

I followed him to the couch-and-love-seat area. He took the couch and I took the love seat. A large framed portrait of Sheila Kazankis hung over the couch directly behind him. From a distance at the funeral, Nick Kazankis had reminded me of a pumped-up Mark Spitz. But up close in his throne room, he seemed more like a tough Arab sheikh dressed for cocktails at the country club. His deeply tanned skin looked leathery. He had dark eyes, a strong nose, and thick, jet-black hair combed straight back. He was wearing a yellow madras short-sleeved shirt, green twill slacks, boat shoes, and no socks. The top three buttons of his shirt were open, exposing a forest of black hair and a gold cross. The slacks were snug, especially around the crotch area, revealing, indeed emphasizing, that he—as the expression goes—dressed to the right.

He glanced at his gold Rolex. "We have less than thirty

minutes," he said with a charming but carnivorous smile. "Why don't we skip the preliminaries and get started?"

"Fine with me," I said.

"You're trying to help your sister. You think she's innocent."

I shook my head. "I *know* she's innocent."

"Fair enough," he said with a chuckle. "You know she's innocent. For her sake, let's hope you're right. You want to find who killed him."

"And who set her up."

He nodded. "Presumably the same person. You're looking for likely suspects, right? And his photo album seems like a good place to start."

I was genuinely surprised. "How do you know about that album?"

He shrugged good-naturedly. "In my line of business, Rachel, it's important to have current and accurate information."

"Speaking of which," I said with an inquisitive expression, "what exactly is your line of business, Nick?"

"Gaming. The world of chance." He made a dismissive gesture, as if the subject bored him. "But back to your situation. You looked through his photo album, you happened to come across poor Sheila with a mouthful of cock, somehow you learned who her husband is, and suddenly"—he snapped his fingers—"you made the connection: gambling. Gambling debts and a jealous husband." He leaned back with a predatory grin. "Am I right? Of course I am." He reached over and pushed the intercom button on his telephone. "Sally, dear, bring in our account statements for Andros." He crossed his arms over his chest and arched his thick eyebrows. "Why play cat and mouse, like in one of those silly whodunits? I don't have much time, and you need to get off the wrong track and find the right one. Did he fuck my wife?" He frowned and nodded his head. "I'm afraid so. Did I get angry? You're goddam right I did. Did I consider killing the little bastard? Maybe. Would I do it by poison?" He looked up and smiled. "Come on over, Sally."

His secretary came in carrying a large maroon ledger book. She was wearing a short red leather skirt and matching red pumps, neither of which had been visible behind her prim reception desk. She had tanned dancer's legs.

"Did you find Andros?" Nick asked.

She gave him a three-hundred-watt smile. "Right here, Nickie." She opened the ledger book and set it on the coffee table facing him.

"Thanks, doll," he said to her as she turned to go. "Wait a sec, Sally."

She turned back.

"Rachel and I were just talking about jealous husbands," he said. "Let's say I found out some guy was doing Sheila, and let's say I decided to kill him. Would I do it with poison?"

Sally smiled and shook her head. "I don't think so."

"How would I do it?"

"With your bare hands, right?"

Nick glanced at me with a proud smile. "This woman knows me." He looked back at Sally. "And then what would I do when he was dead?"

She blushed. "Oh, Nickie."

"You can tell Rachel."

She giggled. "You'd cut off his weenie."

"And?"

"And stick it in his mouth."

He gave her a proud wink. "On the money, doll. Now go get ready."

I had watched the performance with a skeptical eye. It could have been scripted in advance for my benefit, although why he would bother wasn't clear.

After Sally left the room his smile faded. He rubbed his chin thoughtfully and shook his head. "I probably wouldn't cut it off. Hard to say. But no poison. Definitely no poison."

"But would you try to set up my sister?" I asked.

"Your sister?" he said with an astounded laugh. "Why would I ever do that?"

"Her husband," I said without a smile.

"You mean little Richie?" he said. The disdain in his voice was unmistakable. "That's ancient history, Rachel. As far as I'm concerned, little Richie is just a pathetic, second-rate toady."

"That doesn't sound like ancient emotions."

He gave me a patronizing look. "Little Richie isn't even a blip on my radar screen." He glanced down at the open page of the ledger book and scanned the rows of penciled numbers. "Okay," he said as he turned the ledger book toward me. "In my business I need to keep track of certain debts."

"Debts to you?"

"Some to me. Mostly debts to others, especially my casino clients." He pointed to one column of numbers. "That's the account for what he owed me."

It was a running ledger, with dates and amounts going back several years. It showed a high debt of $14,500 about two years ago and a low of $2,500 about nine months ago. The last entry was dated two weeks before his death.

"So he died owing you five thousand, two hundred and fifty dollars?"

Kazankis nodded. "Tough luck for both of us. He would have been good for it."

I pointed at the other columns. "What are these?"

He took me through them one by one. All were casino accounts, including one in Las Vegas, one in Atlantic City, and two in the Caribbean. Excluding the $5,250 he owed Kazankis, Andros died owing a total gambling debt of $13,500, divided fairly evenly among the four casinos. According to the ledger, his total casino debts had fluctuated over the past eighteen months from a high of roughly $50,000 to a low of $3,000, which put him somewhere south of high roller and north of chump change.

I looked up at Kazankis with a frown. "This means?" I asked.

"It wasn't gambling," he stated decisively. He motioned toward the open page and shook his head. "You don't get killed for those debts. You don't even get a broken leg."

I sat back and studied him. "Do you still do those junkets down to the Caribbean?"

"Sure. I'm hooking up with one leaving today."

"What's the level of betting your junketeers do down there?"

He tilted his head from side to side as he thought it over. "Varies."

"More than ten grand?"

He laughed. "They sure as hell better. Most are up in the fifty-to-a-hundred-grand range, some more than that."

I pointed at the columns of numbers in the ledger book. "But not Andros."

He smiled in acknowledgment. "You're right. He was an exception."

"Why?"

"He used to work for me."

"Gambling?"

"No. Exercise."

Now I was really confused. "What do you mean?"

"I own the company that's the general partner in Gateway Health & Racquet Clubs. We have three locations—one off Lindbergh near Highway 40, one in Chesterfield, and one here on the east side. I gave Andros his start in the aerobics business. He worked for me before he went on his own. He liked to gamble. Since he was willing to help run the junkets and be my gofer down there, I brought him along several times."

"What about Christine Maxwell?"

He gave me a puzzled look. "What about her?"

"Is she a gambler?"

He was far too smooth to show anything beyond simple confusion. "Why?" he asked.

"Andros had a photo in his office of you, Andros, Donald Trump, and Christine Maxwell."

And now he put down the confusion card and turned over the next reaction in his deck: innocent recollection. "Ah, I remember. That was up in Atlantic City. You're right. I forgot Chrissy was there, too. It wasn't a junket, though. Andros and I were up there for a health club convention. I can't remember why Chrissy was there. But back to your question, I don't know whether Chrissy's a gambler." He checked his watch. "I hope this has helped. If you have more questions, give me a buzz when I get back. I'll only be gone four days."

"What's going on, Nick?"

"Pardon?"

"Why'd you bring me over here? Why are you telling me all this personal information?"

He stood up and stretched his arms. "I've already told you

why. I assumed that these were the questions you'd eventually get around to wanting answered. I decided to speed up the process."

"But why?"

He gave me a tolerant smile. "So you'd start looking somewhere else."

"Where else?"

He walked over to the fireplace and turned toward me. There was no longer any amusement in his face. "*Anywhere* else. I don't care." He paused, solemnly weighing his words. "My wife is not a strong woman. Sheila has many fears and anxieties. They eat her up inside. Literally. Certain things bother her more than they bother most people. Especially unexpected encounters." His eyes narrowed. "You were about to become an unexpected encounter. That would have upset her, and when my wife is upset, I become upset. I decided that if I could fill in the gaps and answer your questions, there would be no need to upset her. That's why I invited you over here." He lowered his voice and intensified his stare. "You see, Rachel, I don't want my wife to be upset."

It was more of a warning than a statement, and it seemed to invite a response. I decided not to make one. We studied each other for a moment. I stood up and put my notes back in my briefcase. "You've been helpful," I said calmly. "Have a good trip."

As my stretch limo pulled away for the trip back across the Mississippi, I turned back in time to see Nick and Sally come out of the building. Each wore sunglasses and each had a carry-on flight bag slung over a shoulder. As Nick leaned over to open the trunk of the red Infiniti, Sally patted him on the rump. He looked back at her with a lecherous grin.

I leaned back in my seat, pulled out my legal pad, and tried to sift through what he had told me.

13
CHAPTER

Mound City Mini-Storage is located beneath one of the flight paths into Lambert–St. Louis International Airport. As I pulled up to the entrance, a TWA 727 in its final approach roared past overhead, flaps down and landing gear deployed. Directly outside my window at eye level was one of those black cardkey security devices mounted on a metal pole. In the center of the device was a slot with the words INSERT MAGNETIC CARD HERE engraved above it. Below it was a call button and a speaker box. I reached out and pushed the call button.

Nothing happened. Staring at the speaker box, I felt as if I was in the drive-thru lane at the ultimate no-frills hamburger joint. I pushed the call button again.

I looked around as I waited. The steel entrance gate was motorized and set on tracks. The entire perimeter of Mound City Mini-Storage was surrounded by heavy-duty chain-link fence topped with barbed wire. Inside the fence were three long low aluminum buildings. Each was bright orange and looked like a cross between an army barracks and a forty-car garage. There was a smaller building off to the side and closer to the entrance gate. The sign in front identified it as the main office.

The chain-link fence began to vibrate as another jet approached. This one was a jumbo—an American Airlines 747. The dark shadow of the plane rushed across the orange metal roofs and asphalt driveways of the Mound City Mini-Storage premises. As the jet disappeared over the bunkers surrounding the airport runways, I pushed the call button again.

There was a burst of static. "What is this that you want?" a voice crackled, the words spewed out so quickly that it took a moment for my brain to parse them.

"I need to talk to the manager."

"Who is this?"

"I'm an attorney. I need to talk to the manager."

"Whatisthisabout?"

"Pardon?"

"What is this about?"

"I'll explain it when I see the manager."

"This is the day manager." The voice had a foreign accent that I couldn't place. "What is this that you want?"

"Let me in and I'll tell you."

I waited, staring at the speaker box on the cardkey stand. After thirty seconds or so, there was an electronic buzz from near the steel gate, followed by a metallic click. The gate started to slide open. As I drove slowly through the opening, a short, dark-complected man came out of the door of the office. He vigorously waved me over to where he was standing. I pulled my car into the space in front of the office.

He was all smiles as I got out of the car and introduced myself. He had thick horn-rimmed sunglasses, a white short-sleeved shirt, a fat orange tie that was way too short, and wrinkled black slacks. He told me his name, which sounded like Dan or Zan or Van. From his accent and complexion I guessed that he was Pakistani or Indian.

"It's Dan?" I asked.

"No, no." He shook his head rapidly, still grinning. "Not 'Dan.' 'Dan.' You see? It's 'Dan.' Not 'Dan,' but 'Dan.' Yes?"

"Right," I said without much conviction. Every "Dan" had sounded exactly the same.

"Good, good," he said, bobbing his head.

Dan-not-Dan was maybe an inch or two shorter than me, which would have put him about five feet five, although it was hard to tell for sure because of the way he nervously bobbed his head and shoulders.

"Is it that you need a space?" he asked as he jammed his left hand in the front pocket of his pants and started fiercely jangling what sounded like $500 in change.

"No, I need to talk to you about someone else's space."

"Someone else?" he repeated uncertainly, still jangling the change.

"Let's go in your office," I suggested. "I can explain."

He squinted at me, his head bobbing, and then said, "Okay, lady."

I followed him into the office.

As those who regularly do it will attest, nine-tenths of getting access to where you're not supposed to be is to act like you're supposed to have access. I did the nine-tenths part, and Dan-not-Dan's boss added the final tenth by not being available when Dan-not-Dan tried to get him on the telephone. When he hung up, even more jittery than before, I removed my Missouri Bar membership card from my wallet, put on my Joe Friday face, and slid the card across the desk to him. "It's okay," I told him. "I'm a Missouri attorney."

He frowned as he studied the card. I waited. His knees were clapping together beneath the desk, the pocket change jangling.

"Okay," he finally said, handing back the card. "Firm Ambitions it is, yes?"

I nodded gravely.

He turned toward the computer terminal and typed in various sets of instructions, hitting the transmit key after each set. Finally, the screen went blank for a moment, and then three columns of numbers appeared. I leaned forward and squinted:

11346782	02-08	21:08
11346782	02-14	02:12
11346781	02-20	23:12
11346782	02-21	22:56
11346781	02-22	01:43
11246781	03-06	01:17
11246780	03-09	11:46
11246781	03-10	01:08
11246782	03-18	23:41

The numbers filled the screen.

Dan-not-Dan gave a puzzled grunt and pushed the PAGE DOWN key. Another three columns of numbers filled the screen:

```
11346780    04-02    12:21
11346782    04-04    02:57
11346781    04-12    22:29
11346781    04-16    03:34
11346780    04-19    12:13
11246780    04-22    21:23
11246782    04-25    03:23
11246781    04-25    23:02
11236780    04-31    01:19
```

Dan-not-Dan gave another puzzled grunt.

"What?" I asked.

He shook his head rapidly. "Very strange this is."

"What's it mean?"

"Wait," he said, walking over to a file drawer. He pulled it open and flipped through the folders until he found the one he was looking for. He lifted it out and studied the first page. "Okay," he mumbled. "So three there are."

"What are?"

He looked up and squinted toward me. "Three cards. Is not usual this."

"I'm not following you."

He walked back to the terminal screen and pointed to the first column of numbers. "Card number," he said. "This is card number. It is the case with most customers, Miss Gold, that there is one card only. For some it is true that there are two cards, yes. Here this is the case that there are three cards. This is not usual."

I studied the terminal screen:

```
11346780    04-02    12:21
11346782    04-04    02:57
11346781    04-12    22:29
11346781    04-16    03:34
11346780    04-19    12:13
```

11246780	04-22	21:23
11246782	04-25	03:23
11246781	04-25	23:02
11236780	04-30	01:19

"So every time a customer inserts his card into that box at the front gate the computer records this information?"

"You are correct in this."

"And the column on the left has the cardkey number."

"You are correct in this."

"What are the other two columns?"

He pointed to the middle column. "This is for to record the day and the month." He slid his finger over to the third column. "And this is for to record the time of the insertion."

I stared at the screen as I nonchalantly removed a yellow legal pad from my briefcase. "Okay. So the bottom row means that someone with card number 11236780 opened the gate at one-nineteen on the morning of April 30."

He nodded his head rapidly. "You are correct in this."

I copied down the information on the screen, writing as quickly as I could, just in case Dan-not-Dan decided to turn off the computer.

"This is not routine," he said. "Very not routine."

"Pardon?" I was barely paying attention as I scribbled down the columns of numbers.

"The times are not the times that are routine. Not many persons come most of the time late at night."

I paused to study the terminal screen. He was right. The times recorded were mostly between 10:00 P.M. and 3:00 A.M.

"I'll need to see that storage space," I said with as official a tone of voice as I could muster.

Dan-not-Dan looked at me with uncertainty.

"Just routine," I assured him. "Obviously, I won't disturb anything in there."

"This I do not know," he said.

I gave him a firm but sympathetic look. "It'll be better if you cooperate."

He frowned as he thought it over. "Well, this is something that if we do it it is okay if we only do it for a few minutes, yes?"

"You're absolutely right," I said, standing up. "Let's do it for a few minutes."

I followed him out to the door to the Firm Ambitions storage space, which was located about halfway down the left side of the center building. Dan-not-Dan used his body to shield my view as he punched in the combination to the electronic lock. There was a click. He reached down, grabbed the handle of the sliding door, and pulled it up.

"Okay, Miss Gold. For just a few minutes, yes?"

"Right."

"Then please to hurry."

I stepped inside the storage room, which was roughly the size of a one-car garage. It was nearly empty. On the cement floor in one corner was a Macintosh computer with a cracked screen. Against a side wall were a pair of Bose speakers that looked brand-new. In another corner was a shattered Panasonic VCR that looked as if it had been dropped onto the floor and kicked to the side. On the ground next to the VCR was a baseball card facedown. I kneeled down and turned it over. It was an old Lou Brock card—so old that he was in a Chicago Cubs uniform. The card was hardly in mint condition. It looked like someone had stepped on it—there was a smudge from a footprint across Brock's face, and the edge of the card was bent. I found the copyright information on the back: Topps 1962. The text and statistics on the back confirmed what I had guessed: this was Lou Brock's rookie card. I glanced back at Dan-not-Dan. He had his back to me, his arms crossed, his right foot tapping rapidly. I slipped the baseball card into my briefcase and pulled out my yellow legal pad. I went back to the Macintosh computer and copied down the serial number. I did the same with the Bose speakers and the Panasonic VCR.

"This is most certainly time enough, Miss Gold," he said to me. "I must tell you that I am completely starting to feel most uncomfortable. Now has come the time that we must go."

I was kneeling by the VCR when he spoke, the legal pad balanced on my knees. "Sure," I told him as I stood up.

And that's when I saw it.

"Just a sec," I said.

On the floor in the corner near the door was a porcelain

ballerina without a head. I turned and surveyed the storage space. The head wasn't anywhere inside the storage area. I stared at the broken figurine, my mind racing for the connection. She was in a seated position, slipping on one of her ballet shoes.

"Really, Miss Gold, I must tell you that I am continuing to feel most uncomfortable."

I smiled at him. "You've been most helpful, Dan."

"Not 'Dan,' Miss Gold. 'Dan.' "

14
CHAPTER

I got back to the office at five-thirty, just in time to get my phone messages before my secretary left for the day. Along with the usual calls from clients, court clerks, and opposing counsel in various lawsuits, there was a call from Benny Goldberg and one from Charles Kimball. Benny left a message that he would meet me at my house around six-thirty to tell me what he had found. Kimball's message was that Tony's was completely booked by a private party so he had made dinner reservations at Dominic's and would come by the house to pick me up at seven forty-five. His choice in restaurants was impeccable: of the many wonderful restaurants on "the Hill," as the St. Louis Italian neighborhood is known, Dominic's was my favorite. I was also pleased that he was going to pick me up instead of having me meet him at the restaurant. After all my running around that day, some old-fashioned chivalry sounded just right.

I was feeling kind of grungy, especially after Mound City Mini-Storage. I wanted to get home, shower, and change before Benny got there so that I could give him plenty of time without having to worry about getting ready for Kimball. I sat on the edge of my desk, opened my briefcase, and quickly sorted through my printouts and notes from Firm Ambitions, Nick Kazankis, and Mound City Mini-Storage. There were plenty of things for Benny and me to talk over.

I held up the Lou Brock baseball card and pursed my lips in thought. My brother-in-law would know. He went to a dozen card shows every year. I checked my watch. Five forty-five. He might still be at his West County office, especially with the way he was avoiding my sister. I reached for the phone and dialed his office number.

I glanced at my watch again. *Three minutes,* I said to myself, *and you can still be home by six-fifteen. Plenty of time to shower and change and talk to Benny.*

Richie was still there. His receptionist put me on musical hold, which turned out to be a Muzak version of the Allman Brothers' "Whipping Post"—a truly chilling jolt of cultural dissonance. But then again, what else would I expect from a man who calls himself a "Manilowhead" and claims that his favorite part of the concert is when Barry croons through his repertoire of advertising jingles?

"Rachel?" he said uncertainly.

"Hi, Richie."

"Good news? Bad news?"

"No news. At least not yet. Got a quick question."

"Shoot."

"A baseball-card question."

"You're breaking my heart."

"Lou Brock."

"Okay, what year?"

"1962."

"His rookie card. I'm dying, Rachel."

"You had one?"

"A beauty. Mint condition. Worth at least three hundred dollars."

"How many are out there?"

"In mint condition? Hard to say. Hundreds, probably."

"Could you recognize yours?"

He paused. "I doubt it. The ones in mint condition all look alike. Why?"

"I found one today."

"In mint condition?"

"Not by the time I got there. How did you store yours?"

"In a loose-leaf notebook. In one of those clear plastic sheets with pockets. Nine cards per sheet."

"Could individual cards fall out?"

"Fall out? Well, sure. It happens sometimes."

"Okay. Thanks, Richie."

"Rachel?"

"Yeah?"

He lowered his voice. "How do things look?"

"I have some leads, a few ideas. We just have to keep plugging away." I paused. Although Richie and I never talked about personal matters, I couldn't stop myself. "What about you and Ann?"

"What do you mean?" he said defensively.

"Come on, Richie, you know what I mean."

He didn't respond.

I could feel my anger flare. "Dammit, Richie, why are you still at your office? Can't you see that Ann needs you? Go home. Be with her, for God's sake. Help her, talk to her, be there so she can talk to you, give her someone to lean on." I paused, waiting for a response. There was silence on the other end. "God, Richie," I said, totally exasperated with him, "don't be such a—such a jerk."

I realized, even as I was struggling for the right words, that whatever I said was not going to make a difference, was not going to change him or his relationship with Ann or her relationship with him. Yelling at him served no purpose other than venting my own disappointment. I had enough problems trying to function simultaneously as Ann's sister and her attorney. I surely wasn't about to become Richie's marriage counselor as well.

"Look, Richie," I said with a sigh, "I know it's hard on both of you. I promise I'll call as soon as I have something worth reporting."

Next I dialed Eileen Landau's number. As the phone began to ring I turned in my chair toward the credenza and pulled a fresh legal pad out of the top drawer. I jotted down some quick notes about the Lou Brock rookie card. It didn't sound like a promising lead, but then again, I still didn't know enough to know what was and wasn't promising.

Eileen's answering machine cut in after the fourth ring. I listened to her message, waited for the beep, and said, "Eileen, this is Rachel. I have a question about your Lladro figurine. Is there some way to identify the one that got stolen? A serial number or something? Call when you get a chance." I gave her my office and home phone numbers and hung up.

"Don't tell me you found her fucking ballerina?" said a male voice.

I spun around, startled.

Tommy Landau was standing in the doorway. He was wearing what looked like a safari outfit, right down to the pith helmet.

"What are you doing here?"

He removed his helmet in an exaggerated show of manners and stepped into my office. "It's time we had a chat about my case, Counselor." He smiled, and then he belched. I could smell the alcohol on his breath. His face was moist with perspiration. He settled into the chair facing me across the desk and slowly exhaled. As he did, the animation seemed to drain from his face until I felt like I was staring into the torpid eyes of an alligator. It gave me the creeps.

"That's not the way it works, Tommy," I said, trying to sound more in control than I felt at the moment. "You and I don't 'chat' about your case. We don't talk period. I'm Eileen's lawyer. You've got your own lawyer. If you have something on your mind, tell your lawyer and have him tell me."

He tugged at his walrus mustache. "Relax, Counselor. You want to go get a drink?"

"No."

He nodded slowly, as if he were evaluating my response. "I'm a little hungry. You want to get something to eat?"

"No."

He studied me with hooded eyes. He seemed to be scowling, although it was hard to tell for sure. The structure of the upper half of his heavy face—thick eyebrows joined at the bridge of his nose—gave him a perpetual frown. "My grandfather was a judge," he said.

"I know."

"His father—my great-grandfather—bought him the position," he continued, as if I hadn't spoken, "although I suppose that's the way it usually works." He studied the inside of his pith helmet. "A few years ago I went to the law library at St.

Louis U. I was curious about him. My grandfather, that is. Hizzoner. I read about fifty of his opinions." He looked up from his helmet and stared at me. "You ever done that, Counselor?"

"Read your grandfather's opinions?" I answered, meeting his stare.

"Any judge. Read fifty opinions by any one judge?"

"No."

He snorted with contempt. "Try it sometime. You'll see what's really going on. You'll see that it's all a load of simple-minded, gussied-up bullshit." He leaned back in the chair and stared at the ceiling. He shook his head and lowered his eyes to my level. "My grandfather spent his career shoving messy, fucked-up, real-life situations into tidy little imaginary cubbyholes. That's exactly what law is all about, isn't it?"

He crossed his beefy arms across his chest. It didn't sound like a real question and I didn't feel like giving him a real answer.

"The whole goddam law thing is a confidence game," he continued in his monotone. "A fucking fraud. You know what my grandfather's legal opinions reminded me of? That giant in the Greek myth—the dude with all the iron beds." He belched. "The one who chopped off the feet of his tall victims. Stretched out his short ones. Made sure they all fit into his iron beds after he got through with them. What's his name?"

"Procrustes," I said, watching him carefully.

"Yeah," he said with a snap of his fingers. "You get a gold star, Counselor. Procrustes. That's what the law is, too. Forcing a messed-up piece of reality into one of those iron beds and pretending that it was a perfect fit all along. Total bullshit."

I fought the urge to debate him. Although his eyes were still dead, I could sense his rage.

"That's what you lawyers and judges do for a living, eh?" he said. "You shove real people into imaginary cubbyholes." He paused and gave me a malicious smile. "Well, now someone's trying to shove your sister into one of those cubbyholes. How's she like it in there?"

"What's your point?" I said irritably. I could feel my anger building.

"My point, Counselor," he said, his voice a little louder, "is that I don't like my goddam imaginary cubbyhole any more than your sister likes hers." He pointed a thick forefinger at me. "You don't understand me. You don't understand my marriage. You don't even understand your own goddam client. All you know is your cubbyholes. Well, if Eileen and I have problems, we'll work them out on our own. We don't need a bunch of bloodsucking shysters and dumbshit judges shoving us into cubbyholes."

"Look, Tommy, talk to your lawyer. If it's marriage counseling you—"

"Fuck marriage counseling!" he roared. "That's just more cubbyholes." He took a deep breath and put his hands on his knees as he exhaled. He nodded his head slowly. I could almost see his blood pressure dropping. "Eileen isn't thinking straight," he continued, his voice back to a monotone. "She doesn't want a divorce. Her problem is she doesn't know what she wants. If she ever does decide what she wants, she'll be better off doing it while she's married. I'll take her back. I'll even forgive her for sucking that greaseball's dick. Tell her that. I want you to dismiss the divorce case. You understand?"

"I've had enough." Now I was thoroughly annoyed. "Go talk to your lawyer."

He glared at me. "I'm talking to you."

"I'm not listening. You're going to have to leave now. I have a meeting to get to."

He was breathing audibly through his nose. He studied me, his eyes no longer dull. "I remember you from high school," he said.

"What?" I asked, incredulous.

"I remember you from high school."

"I can't believe this. Leave my office. We'll pretend this meeting never occurred."

"You were a cheerleader."

"What?"

"In high school. I told you I remembered."

"You must be remembering someone else. You went to

Country Day. I went to U City. I'm at least five years younger than you."

"After I got booted out of Mizzou I came back to St. Louis. I started what you might call my own business. I had a few customers in your class. I knew who the great Rachel Gold was." He smiled a crooked smile. "I even went to your homecoming game against Ladue. I watched you cheer on the sidelines. You think I'm shitting you?"

"It's time for you to leave."

"All the cheerleaders wore gold panties under their black skirts. Gold panties with a black U and C on the butt. At least you did. Right?"

"I'm not interested in this."

"I am. I remember that great little ass of yours."

I stood up. "Get out of my office."

He thrust his jaw toward me. "Lady, my point is that you can act as tough and snooty as you want, but to me you're still just another little prick teaser shaking her tits and ass on the sidelines—a little prick teaser who never even got married, for chrissakes. You a dyke? What the fuck do you know about marriage in the first place?"

I reached for the telephone and punched 911, forcing myself to stare into his eyes as the phone rang. It was answered on the second ring.

"Officer, there's a man named Tommy Landau trespassing in my office and he won't leave. I need help immediately." I gave him my address.

Tommy stood up, shaking his head. "You're pretty stupid for a Harvard lawyer," he said as he turned to the door. "I'll just talk directly to Eileen. I'll tell—"

"You keep away from her," I shouted. "You try to threaten her and I'll make sure they shove you into a goddam cubbyhole with iron bars."

He paused at the door, his back still to me, and then he walked out.

I immediately dialed Deb Fletcher's number. I checked my watch as it rang. It was twenty after six. Damn. One of the night secretaries answered on the seventh ring. Mr. Fletcher was gone for the night. "Call him at home," I ordered. "Tell him Tommy Landau tried to threaten me. Tell him he'd better find his client before he ends up in jail."

Then, just to be safe, I called the Ladue police and told them to send a squad car by Eileen's house. I grabbed my briefcase and headed for the door just in time to greet two squad cars responding to my 911 call.

God, I hate divorce cases.

Thanks to Tommy Landau, I set a personal land speed record. In just under twenty minutes I took a shower, put on my perfume, mascara, and blush-on, picked out an outfit, put it on, studied it in the mirror, decided that the neckline was too low and the hemline too high for a business dinner, took it off, returned to the closet, narrowed the choice to two, hesitated, pulled one out, held it at arm's length, frowned, hung it back in the closet, took out the other one and put it on, checked the result in the mirror, nodded, returned to the closet, stared in dismay at my sorry collection of shoes (all is forgiven, Imelda), settled on a pair of silver sandals, found matching pairs of silver bracelets and earrings, grabbed the sandals in one hand and my comb and lipstick in the other, and ran barefoot downstairs.

Benny checked his watch as I came into the kitchen. "Nineteen minutes and forty-seven seconds." He was at the kitchen table with my mother.

"Nineteen minutes and forty-seven seconds?" I repeated with a smile. "Not bad, eh?"

"All depends," he said.

"Come on," I said to Benny as I leaned against the counter to put on the first sandal. "Admit it."

"For getting dressed, not bad," he said. "For having sex, hell, I can probably shave a full eighteen minutes off that time."

"Put on your sandals, Rachel," my mother said, ignoring Benny. She had Gitel on her lap and was gently scratching the cat behind the ears.

"So?" I said to Benny. "Who really owns Firm Ambitions?"

"Now let me see," my mother said when I finished fastening the second sandal.

"Mother," I argued with exasperation.

"Rachel," she parried, ending the debate.

I straightened and turned slowly, as I had been doing for my mother since as far back as I can remember—specifically, all the way back to my first Purim carnival at the Jewish Community Center, which I attended dressed as Queen Esther. I was six years old and wore a costume my mother had made on her old black Singer sewing machine. In the years that followed, she would make all of my Halloween costumes and party dresses. *Turn,* she had ordered in the parking lot. *Let me look at my precious queen.*

"You look gorgeous," she said.

"You think?"

"Think?" She looked down at Gitel and shook her head. " 'Think,' she asks her mother. I don't think. I know."

It was a beautiful dress—French country-style, with a white floral pattern against a navy background. It had a scooped neckline, a button-front fitted bodice, and a long, sweeping skirt—very feminine, very soft, very unlawyerlike.

"Did Ann get it for you?" my mother asked.

"For my birthday last year."

"She has excellent taste." She turned to Benny. "Isn't she beautiful?"

"More than beautiful, Sarah. She looks good enough to— well, to give Richard Nixon a chubbie."

"What an absolutely chilling thought," I said.

"Give Richard Nixon a what?"

"You don't want to know, Mom." I checked my watch. "Come on. He'll be here in ten minutes." I pulled up a chair to the kitchen table. "Start with Firm Ambitions. Give me that ownership arrangement again."

"Okay," Benny said. "As you recall, we had gone up the Capital Investments of Missouri daisy chain until we reached Capital Investments of Vermont."

"Right, and who owns that?"

"Capital Investments, Limited."

I shook my head in amazement. "Which is what?"

"The plot thickens," Benny said with a mysterious grin. "Capital Investments, Limited, is a Cayman Islands corporation."

"No kidding," I said. I leaned back and crossed my arms. "A tax dodge?"

"Maybe," Benny said with a shrug. "We had a few like that at Abbott & Windsor."

"Who are the shareholders?"

Benny shook his head. "Don't know."

"Why not?" I asked.

"They won't tell me. It's one of the reasons people like doing business down there: you can operate incognito."

"There has to be a way to get that information," I said.

"I'm still working on it," he said.

"So what else have you found?"

"I'm still working on the life insurance policy," Benny said. "Large Marge told me to call back tomorrow morning. She should have more info on the change of beneficiary by then."

I leaned over and kissed him on the cheek. "Isn't this guy incredible, Mom?"

My mother nodded without looking up. For the past few minutes she had been studying the information I had copied off the computer terminal screen at the office of Mound City Mini-Storage.

"By the way," Benny said, "score one point for Sarah Gold."

My mother glanced up at Benny. "What?"

He winked at her. "You said I should ask large Marge who the agent on that insurance policy was, remember?"

My mother nodded. "She knew?"

Benny nodded. "The producing agent was none other than Christine Maxwell of Maxwell Associates."

"Interesting," I said.

"She settled out of court," my mother said.

"Settled what?" I asked.

"The lawsuit over that boating accident," my mother answered. "I found the newspaper article on microfilm. She sued the manufacturer of the boat and the manufacturer of the motor. She settled with both out of court."

"How much?" Benny asked.

My mother shrugged. "According to the article, the settlement terms were confidential. I looked up her boyfriend, too.

Remember at lunch I told you I read an article about his company and pollution?" She gave me a self-satisfied smile as she got up and walked over to the kitchen counter. "Read this," she said as she handed me a sheet of slick microfilm copy paper. It was photocopy of an article from the January 27 issue of the *Post-Dispatch*. The headline read:

MIDWEST REFINISHING, INC., NAMED #1
ST. CHARLES POLLUTER FOR 2ND YEAR IN ROW

The article was three paragraphs:

For the second year in a row, one of the area's largest metal refinishers has earned dubious distinction as St. Charles County's top violator of permit limits for the disposal of toxic wastes. According to the annual report issued by the Mississippi Sewage Treatment Plant in St. Charles, Midwest Refinishing, Inc., topped the list of St. Charles water polluters by significantly exceeding its permit limits for the disposal of rinse water containing cyanide and other toxic chemicals.

Efforts to reach Midwest Refinishing's president, Shepherd Sandberg, were unsuccessful.

The Mississippi Sewage Treatment Plant issues its annual report in accordance with regulations promulgated by the Environmental Protection Agency under the Federal Clean Water Act, which requires pretreatment of waste water containing certain toxic substances before it goes to the publicly owned treatment works.

I put the article down and looked at Benny. "Have you read this?"

He nodded.

I glanced down at the article. " 'Rinse water containing cyanide and other toxic chemicals,' " I read aloud. I looked at Benny. "I think it's about time for me to pay a visit to my old friend Chrissy," I said.

"I don't like this," my mother said. She was back to studying the list I had copied off the computer terminal screen at the office of Mound City Mini-Storage.

"What don't you like?" I asked.

"What kind of things do companies put in these storage places?"

"Depends," I said. "A lot of them store old files."

"These don't look like old files."

"Why do you say that?" Benny asked her.

"Look at these times," she said as she slowly moved her finger down the column on the right. I looked over her shoulder at the numbers:

11346780	04-02	12:21
11346782	04-04	02:57
11346781	04-12	22:29
11346781	04-16	03:34
11346780	04-19	12:13
11246780	04-22	21:23
11246782	04-25	03:23
11246781	04-25	23:02
11236780	04-30	01:19

"Except for these two during the lunch hour," my mother said, pointing to the first and fifth row, "the rest are late at night. Three in the morning. Ten-thirty at night. One-thirty in the morning. Three in the morning. Eleven at night. What kind of files are getting stored in there at those hours?"

I looked at Benny. "She's right," I said. "In fact, the guy out there noticed the same thing. Look at the stuff I found in there." I flipped to the next page of my notes, where I had recorded the serial numbers of the speakers, computer terminal, and video cassette recorder. "You'd ordinarily expect to find this kind of stuff in a storage space rented for personal use. Maybe for a family that doesn't have an attic or basement. But not for a business."

"Still," Benny said, "you're talking about a one-man operation. He could have been using the space for personal storage, too."

"If it's a one-man operation," I said, "why were three separate cardkeys issued?"

"His friends?" Benny mused.

"Possibly." I checked my watch. "Tell me about Charles Kimball."

"First let me tell you about Andros and Kimball."

"Okay."

"Andros was a Saudi national who came here for college," Benny said. "He dropped out of St. Louis U after a year and took a job as an aerobics instructor. At some place called, uh—"

"Gateway Health & Racquet Clubs," I said. "Nick Kazankis is one of the owners. He hired him."

"Ah," Benny said, raising his eyebrows. "Connections everywhere. Anyway, before long Andros was Gateway's star attraction. The women loved him. He started doing aerobics workouts at their different clubs each week. But then another plot twist."

"Oh?"

"At eleven o'clock on one balmy night in March four years ago, Andros did two of the dumbest things you can do to a plainclothes cop in a public rest room."

"We're talking about a *male* cop?"

"We are indeed. The scene unfolded with a round of linguistic confusion worthy of an Abbott and Costello routine. Andros tried to offer the cop some cocaine. However, he didn't call it cocaine. According to the police report, Andros asked the officer whether he, quote, wanted some blow. Because Andros had such a thick accent, the officer wasn't quite sure what kind of 'blow' was being offered. It turns out Andros was offering the daily double. First he pulled the cop into one of the stalls and handed him a bag filled with white powder. And then, using universal sign language, our hero offered to, shall we say, play 'Flight of the Bumblebee' on the cop's skin flute."

"Not the kind of behavior designed to get your green card renewed," I said.

"Either crime was enough to get him shipped back to Saudi Arabia. Do you have any idea what happens over there to guys who get caught giving other guys blow jobs? That knucklehead must have been frantic down at the police station. His only hope was to get the charges dropped. Otherwise he spends the rest of his days singing soprano in the Riyadh boys' choir."

"So what happened?"

"His lawyer did a hell of a job. He cut a deal where the case would be nolle prosequied—"

"What?" my mother interrupted.

"Dismissed," I told her.

"Right," Benny said. "The case would be dismissed if Andros stayed clean for twelve months."

"Ah," I said. "And Charles Kimball was his lawyer."

Benny nodded. "Yep. Earned his fee on that one. Nothing on the arrest ever appeared in the newspapers."

"And Andros stayed clean?" I asked.

"I guess. He opened Firm Ambitions four months later."

"With Landau, Mitchell & McCray doing the incorporation work," I added. I leaned back in my chair. "Charles Kimball. You think he's the one who introduced Andros to Harris Landau?"

"Probably," Benny said. "How else does an immigrant health club employee end up represented by someone like Harris Landau?"

"I wonder if Harris knows that his daughter-in-law was involved with Andros," I said, more to myself than anyone else.

"So this man you're going to dinner with," my mother said with an edge in her voice, "represented that pig who was exploiting Ann?"

I shrugged. "Mom, that's what Kimball does for a living. He's even represented Tommy Landau."

"And now you want him to represent your sister?"

I sighed. "I've told you I shouldn't be the one to represent Ann if the case goes to trial. You just can't effectively defend a member of your own family."

"This I still don't understand. Who could possibly do it better? And anyway, you have Benny to help."

"Mom, we're not criminal defense attorneys. You wouldn't want a radiologist performing open-heart surgery on you, and you don't want a commercial litigator handling your murder trial."

"A courtroom's a courtroom," she said with a shake of her head.

"And a sister's a sister, Mom. I'm going crazy on this case. I'm her lawyer, I'm her sister, I'm her lawyer, I'm her sister. One moment I'm the professional evaluating an evidentiary issue, the next moment I'm screaming at her husband for acting like a creep. My head's spinning. This isn't like giving a family member advice on taxes. This is heavy stuff."

My mother shook her head. "I just don't understand, and I certainly don't understand how you can pick a man who would stoop to represent that animal."

"Mom, I'm not picking anyone. I just want to talk to him about the subject. No one but Ann is going to pick her trial lawyer." I turned to Benny with a pleading look. "You want to help me here?"

Benny held up his hands and shook his head. "Me no speaky English. Sorry, mahn."

15

CHAPTER

We were seated in a secluded booth at Dominic's, waiting for the pasta course to arrive. Charles Kimball held his wineglass near mine. "To lawyers with green eyes."

"Hear, hear," I said with a smile as we touched glasses.

The sparkle of the wineglass was reflected in his green eyes. Younger men who wonder why some women their age marry men old enough to be their fathers could learn plenty from watching Charles Kimball, who was, at least for me, the archetypal sexy older man. He was a battered swashbuckler, with a roguish but worldly aura that reminded me of a John Huston or Sean Connery.

"I certainly remember those dazzling green eyes," he said after taking a sip of wine. "And all that dark curly hair. But I must confess, Rachel Gold, that I cannot for the life of me recall the question."

"What question?"

"Back at Harvard. After the lecture. I remember you, but I do not remember your question."

I leaned back in my chair, trying to recall his words. "At the beginning of your lecture you told us that Perry Mason was a buffoon. You said he was a walking malpractice case. But you never told us why. After the lecture I asked you why."

He gave me a puckish smile. "And what did I say?"

"You said that a defense lawyer must never forget that the state has the burden of proof. The accused has nothing to prove."

Kimball nodded in recognition. "Ah, yes. How did I put it? 'A defense lawyer's role is not to state the solution but to cast doubt upon the state's solution.' That remains sound advice, Rachel."

"Maybe so," I said with a sigh, "but it's not always easy to follow."

He nodded. "It is once you realize that a criminal trial is not a multiple-choice test."

I frowned. "I'm not following you."

He paused to refill my wineglass and then his. "The most important element of our criminal system," he continued, "is the presumption of innocence. Among other things, it means that the person standing trial in a criminal case is technically not a 'defendant.' He is the accused." Kimball took a sip of wine. "So long as the accused remains the accused, the jury understands that the state must prove its accusation beyond a reasonable doubt. But as soon as the accused becomes an accuser, as soon as the accused offers his *own* solution to the crime, then the entire dynamics of the trial shift. Suddenly there are two accusers, two competing versions of the truth. In that jury's mind, the trial becomes a multiple-choice test. When that happens"—he paused to snap his fingers—"the presumption of innocence disappears."

"Why?"

He smiled. "Because we are a nation of multiple-choice test takers. We've been taking them since elementary school, and ever since elementary school our teachers have drilled into our heads three rules for picking the right answer when you're not sure. Rule Number One: narrow the choice to two possible answers. Rule Number Two: go with what seems like the better of the two answers. And Rule Number Three: if you still aren't sure, make your best guess. When the accused becomes an accuser—when you offer the jury a *second* solution to the crime—you turn the trial into a multiple-choice test. When you do that, you run the risk that the jury will forget the presumption of innocence and instead choose between two poor answers." He put on his stern lecture-hall face. "So keep it a trial, Counselor, not a multiple-choice test."

"Yes, sir," I said, giving him a salute.

"And just in the nick of time," he added with a smile as our waiter removed the empty salad plates and set down the platters of pasta.

I inhaled deeply through my nose. "Mmmm."

"That does look scrumptious," Kimball said as he watched me take a forkful of linguini with fresh basil and sun-dried tomatoes.

I closed my eyes in bliss as I chewed. "It's heaven."

He chuckled. "With enough garlic to repel Count Dracula."

As he turned his attention to his own pasta, I took a sip of wine and studied him. There comes a point in a man's life— usually, it seems to me, somewhere between his sixtieth and seventieth year—when the gradually accruing scars of time seem to coalesce, and suddenly the robust patriarch becomes an old man. Charles Kimball was still the patriarch, and a sexy one at that, but the scars of time were visible— especially on his face, where up close there were wrinkles and little brown splotches and sags that hadn't been there nine years ago when a dazzled law student—the one with the wild curly hair and green eyes—had hung around the lectern after class.

He'd earned those scars over the past decade, according to Benny. There had been a big malpractice verdict against him after a lawsuit he had filed on behalf of several victims of a toxic chemical spill was dismissed while he was out of the country skiing in the Alps with several politically correct members of the Hollywood rat pack; he failed to learn of the dismissal order until it was too late to get it undone. Then, two years later, just a month after he obtained an acquittal for a man accused of aggravated rape, the same man raped and mutilated his thirteen-year-old niece. Kimball closed his practice and taught law school for a year. When he returned to the courtroom, it was first as a lawyer, then as a defendant, and finally as a Chapter 7 debtor after he lost a $250,000 palimony case brought by his former secretary.

Although he was now back on his feet, professionally and financially, Charles Kimball had long since ended his role as an eloquent champion of underdogs and left-wing causes. Instead, according to Benny, he had settled into the role of an adept, somewhat flamboyant, and rather expensive defender of the bread-and-butter clientele of a successful criminal defense attorney: the alleged drug pushers, pimps, prostitutes, burglars, and thieves, with an occasional murderer; he drew the line at defending accused rapists.

My hopes of having Charles Kimball assist in Ann's defense fizzled on our drive to the restaurant when, in an offhand way, he mentioned his displeasure over the police department's refusal to confirm that it no longer suspected Tommy Landau of any involvement in the death of Andros. I decided he couldn't be Ann's attorney: even if not technically a conflict of interest, it was too awkward to have him represent Ann when he was still representing Tommy Landau and sort of representing Eileen Landau. Nevertheless, I told myself, he could still be a terrific resource. He could recommend some good defense attorneys, and, just as important, help me deal with the multiple-choice-test aspects of Ann's case.

I took another sip of wine. "What about the circumstantial case?" I asked.

He set his fork on his plate and wiped his lips with his cloth napkin. "Such as your sister's?"

I nodded. "How do you cross-examine a can of sodium cyanide?"

He mulled it over. "In a circumstantial case," he said thoughtfully, "the accused is the only eyewitness. I'd put your sister up there on the witness stand and let her deny it."

"But how do I avoid the multiple-choice test?"

He smiled and arched his eyebrows. "Are you proposing to solve the crime?"

"No, but her defense is that someone set her up."

He shook his head forcefully. "No, it isn't," he stressed. "Her defense is that she didn't do it. Period." He paused for emphasis. "Let the jurors conclude on their own that she was set up. Give them the facts to reach it, but don't do it for them. Remember, the state has the burden of proof."

I sighed. "You're right."

We were both silent for a while. "Rachel," he said in a kind voice, "I don't think it's wise for you to represent your sister."

I gave him a resigned smile. "I agree, Charles. I want to turn her over to a good criminal defense attorney well before trial. Frankly, that's why I called you today. I wanted to see whether you could represent her. But with your involvement with Tommy Landau and your prior connection to Andros, it's probably better for Ann to hire someone else."

He nodded. "I tend to agree."

I took a deep breath and exhaled with frustration. "It's a damn shame, though," I said. "You're my first choice."

"I'm flattered. I'll be happy to be a resource. When I get back to town next week we'll sit down and go through my short list of St. Louis defense attorneys. I'll help you select an excellent lawyer for your sister."

"I'd appreciate that."

A moment later the waiter arrived with our entrees and a new bottle of wine.

"Oh, my," I said in awe as I stared at my veal scaloppine with ginger and lime.

The meal was divine. When it was over, I leaned back in the booth and said, with a contented sigh, "Wonderful."

Kimball shook his head and chuckled. "I have rarely seen someone enjoy a meal as thoroughly as you just did."

"I didn't just enjoy it, I was overwhelmed by it. Swept away." I placed my hand over my heart and did a mock swoon. "I'm ready to marry the chef. I'm ready to move to Italy and have his babies and darn his socks and iron his boxers so long as he agrees to cook breakfast, lunch, and dinner for me and still adore me when I weigh two hundred and fifty pounds."

Kimball laughed. "Stop. I'm insanely jealous. Before you run away with him, you must at least sample my veal piccata."

I looked impressed. "You're a chef as well?"

"Absolutely, and not just Italian. My dolmades could be served on Mount Olympus."

"Hmmm," I said, pretending to weigh my options. "Do you wash the dishes when you're done?"

"For you?" He placed his hand over his heart. "But of course."

"Well," I said, suppressing a grin, "I've already pledged myself to one chef, but I suppose a prudent bride should have a backup."

There was a brief awkward moment as we left the restaurant: Kimball suggested that we go back to his place for some cognac. I knew, and he knew I knew, and I knew he knew I knew, that his beverage invitation included not merely an after-dinner drink but also coffee in the morning. *Not yet,* I told myself. *Your life is complicated enough already. First take care of Ann's situation and then you can worry about your own.* So I yawned and I checked my watch and I asked for a rain check. He gave a good-natured shrug, extended the rain check, and picked up the threads of our prior conversation exactly where we had left them.

"Although defense counsel shouldn't try to solve the crime in the courtroom," Kimball said as we pulled onto the highway, "I admit it's hard not to try to solve it before you get in the courtroom. Especially in a circumstantial case."

"I know," I said.

"Do you have any idea who set her up?"

"No."

"Who would have the motive?" he asked as he took the exit ramp off the highway.

"To kill him or to set her up?"

"Both."

I crossed my arms and peered through the windshield. "I suppose there are lots of people who could have a reason to kill him." I debated whether to toss out any names that came to mind but decided against it. If he couldn't represent Ann because of his prior and ongoing attorney-client relationships, it was better to view him as a resource instead of a sounding board. "Kill him, yes," I said. "But who would have a reason to make it look like my sister did it?"

"Do you think Andros had enemies?"

I pondered the question. "Ann was an enemy. She was furious when she found out he was having affairs with other women. She couldn't have been his only conquest who discovered that he was fooling around with others."

"So you think it was one of his lovers or a jealous husband?"

"Perhaps," I said, turning to him, "assuming that the lover was a woman."

Kimball turned to me with raised eyebrows. "A gay lover?"

"It wouldn't be the first, as you certainly remember."

He nodded, his lips pursed. "Your detective skills are impressive, Rachel. That was many years ago, and the file was sealed."

"I'm motivated," I said.

"So I see. Back to your earlier question—why make it look like your sister killed him?"

I said, "If it was a lover, maybe she found out that Ann was 'the other woman' and decided to get revenge on her." Christie Maxwell popped into my mind, and I realized that she had never called me back. I made a mental note to call her first thing in the morning.

"What about the jealous spouse?" he asked.

I shrugged. So far, the only spouse I had found who knew of his wife's infidelity was Nick Kazankis. Notwithstanding his attempts to steer me in other directions, I could still imagine him wanting to kill Andros. But I couldn't imagine him wanting to set up my sister. "I don't know," I said, "assuming, of course, that it was a lover or a jealous spouse."

"And you don't?"

"I can't assume anything, yet."

He nodded. "You're right. Have you found anything else suspicious?"

"I have some other leads to run down."

"Also having to do with sex?"

"I don't think so."

"Drugs?"

"I don't think so."

He shook his head sadly. "If you have other leads, then I fear I have truly misjudged that man's character. I believe he had solved his cocaine problems. His sexual problem, while chronic, was more in the nature of an addiction, regardless of the sex of his partner. But you think there were problems other than sex and drugs?"

We had pulled up in front of my house.

"I don't know yet. I'm just not willing to limit my investigation to his sexual partners and their spouses. Not when there are other question marks out there."

He shut off the engine and turned toward me. "Such as what?"

"Gambling."

"Ah," he said with a smile. "Nick the Greek."

"Don't tell me he's one of your clients?"

"Oh, no," he said with a good-natured chuckle. "Haven't been able to pry him away from the competition. Harry Raven over in Belleville has represented Nick for as long as I can recall."

"What do you know about Nick?"

"Actually, not much more than I read in the papers."

"Then why did you immediately think of him?"

"Nick and Andros go way back together in the exercise business. I believe Andros worked for him at the time I was called upon to represent him."

I nodded. "Nick showed me a ledger book with what he said were Andros's gambling debts."

"Nick showed you a ledger book?" Kimball asked in surprise. "Good heavens, when was this?"

"Today."

Kimball looked at me with admiration. "You must be a persuasive lawyer, Rachel."

I shook my head. "Actually, he sought me out. His ledger book shows total debts of under twenty thousand dollars at the time of his death, and those are spread among four casinos and Nick. He owed Nick a little over five grand."

Kimball rubbed his chin silently. "Not enough," he mused.

"That's what Nick told me."

Kimball thought it over. "How high did those gambling debts get?"

"About fifty grand, combined."

"Still not enough," he said, "unless there was a loan shark or off-the-ledger debts."

"Pardon?"

"There'd have to be a lot of money involved to get him killed. There could be, of course, if there were other gambling debts not shown on the books, or if the real debts were loans used to pay down the gambling debts."

"How would I find that out?"

He gave me a puzzled look. "I have no idea."

"Great," I said in frustration.

"Do you have any other leads besides gambling debts?"

I nodded. "His company."

"Firm Ambitions?"

"I have some questions."

"Such as?"

"I can't find out who owned it."

Kimball looked perplexed. "Didn't he?"

"I don't know. Firm Ambitions is owned by something called Capital Investments of Missouri, Inc."

"Which is what?"

"I can't tell."

"Why not?"

"Because Capital Investments of Missouri is owned by a company in Illinois, which is owned by a company in Vermont, which is owned by a company down in the Cayman Islands."

He raised his eyebrows. "Odd, although it could be a tax-avoidance strategy."

I nodded. "Perhaps."

"Do you know Harris Landau?" he asked.

"I know he's Tommy's father. I haven't met him."

"Call him tomorrow," he said. "His firm helped Andros set his business up back when he started Firm Ambitions. As a matter of fact, I referred Andros to that firm. Harris ought to be familiar with the corporate structure, or be able to put you in touch with someone at his firm who is."

"I'll do that."

"Harris is hard to reach. Use my name."

"Thanks."

We agreed to talk again when he returned from New York next week. I leaned over and kissed him quickly on the lips. "Thank you for a marvelous dinner, Charles Kimball."

"It was my pleasure."

I opened my car door. "I'll talk to you soon."

The lights were out and my mother was asleep when I

walked into the house. I was stuffed from all the food and a little woozy from the wine. I didn't notice the note on my pillow until I leaned over to pull back the covers.

It was a message from Benny, attached to the information I had copied down from the computer terminal screen in the Mound City Mini-Storage office. The message from Benny said: "See what your mother spotted. Call me first thing tomorrow."

I looked at the page of notes it was attached to:

11346780	04-02	12:21
11346782	04-04	02:57
11346781	04-12	22:29
11346781	04-16	03:34
11346780	04-19	12:13
11246780	04-22	21:23
11246782	04-25	03:23
11246781	04-25	23:02
11236780	04-30	01:19

My mother had circled the April 16 entry and had written in the margin: "This was when Ann's house was burglarized."

I sat on the edge of my bed trying to construct a sinister but believable explanation for what otherwise seemed a mere coincidence between Ann's burglary and someone's use of one of the Firm Ambitions cardkeys. I heard a meow. Gitel was seated on the carpet in front of me.

"What?" I asked her.

She stared up at me silently.

I sighed. "Okay, Gitel." I patted the mattress. "Come on." She leaped onto the bed and curled up against my hip. I looked down at her and smiled ruefully. "I shouldn't let you up here," I said with a shake of my head. I rubbed her gently under her chin. "You've been a real bitch to my Ozzie, and you know it. I'm telling you now, Gitel, that once I get Ann's situation straightened out, things are going to change around here. You understand me, young lady?"

She looked at me and purred. I decided to take it for a yes.

"Good," I told her as I turned off the light.

16

CHAPTER

"She just walked in," Ann said. She was calling from her car phone in the parking lot of a Schnuck's supermarket. "If you hurry over she'll still be here."

"How did you spot her?" I asked.

"I went in for some milk and eggs. On my way out I passed her going in with a shopping cart."

"Which Schnuck's?" I asked.

"Ladue Crossing."

I checked my watch. Quarter to ten in the morning. It was a fifteen-minute drive from my office. "Okay, I'm leaving now."

Ann was standing inside the supermarket near the fresh produce when I arrived. "Is she still here?" I asked.

She nodded. "Back in the dairy section. What are you going to do?"

I scanned the checkout lines. "Try to talk to her."

"In here?"

I shook my head. "Out by her car."

"Should we do it together?"

I looked at my sister as I weighed the alternatives. "No. I think it's better for me to talk to her alone."

Ann nodded. "You're probably right. Do you want me to stick around to point her out?"

"Does she still wear her hair the way she had it in the picture?"

"Exactly the same."

"Then I'll be able to recognize her. You should go."

"Okay." Ann paused. "Rachel?"

"Yes?"

"I know Mom's been helping you, and Benny, too. Is there anything more I can do?"

I gave her a sympathetic smile. "Not yet."

"But it's my mess." Her eyes watered. "I want to help."

"I know you do, Ann. But it's not a good idea to get you involved in the investigative side of it. It will just complicate things if there's ever a trial. I don't want anyone to be able to claim that our investigation was somehow tainted by having you work on it."

Her shoulders sagged. "I just feel so useless."

"Don't." I gave her a kiss on the cheek. "You're the client. Go now. Sheila's already in the checkout line."

I was out waiting in the parking lot when Sheila Kazankis came through the sliding doors with a shopping cart filled with bags of groceries. She was wearing dark sunglasses, a white ribbed turtleneck sweater, charcoal stirrup pants with a pleated front and tapered legs, white socks, and brown suede penny loafers. Her long, coal-black hair was parted in the middle and her face was set in a worried frown. I moved slowly toward her as she pushed her shopping cart down a lane to the back of a black Jeep Cherokee. I counted seven bags of groceries and a case of Diet Coke. I waited until she had unloaded four of the bags.

"Sheila?"

She turned toward me with a start. "Yes?" she asked uneasily.

"My name is Rachel Gold. I wondered if we might talk for a few minutes." I gave her what I hoped was a reassuring smile.

She didn't seen reassured. "About what?" she said as she looked back and forth between her half-empty shopping cart and her half-filled vehicle.

"About Andros." At the sound of his name she actually

took a step backward. "You see," I said, moving closer, "I'm Ann's sister. I'm trying to help my sister."

She shook her head tensely. "I can't help. I'm sorry." She reached tentatively toward her shopping cart and withdrew her hand. "I'm sorry. I can't help."

"I saw a picture of you and your husband," I said gently. "You were both in a casino with Andros." Her hand fluttered involuntarily to her mouth as I spoke. "I was wondering," I said, "whether Andros ever talked to you about his gambling, or, for that matter, whether your husband ever did."

She looked down, trying to catch her breath. She was actually shaking. "I'm sorry," she said, her voice quavering. "I don't know about those things. I'm sorry I can't help."

While she was looking down I was able to see behind her sunglasses. The area around her right eye was puffy and discolored. "Is your eye okay?" I asked sympathetically.

She looked up, agitated. "It's nothing. I bumped into something. It was stupid. I'm okay. I have to go now. I'm sorry but I have to go."

"I understand, Sheila. I'll leave you alone." I reached into my purse and removed one of my business cards. "Here," I said, holding it out.

She pressed both hands against her chest.

"Please take my card, Sheila. I'm not trying to upset you. I'm only trying to help my sister. I'm trying to find out who might have killed Andros. If you should remember something you saw or something you heard when you were around Andros—anything, no matter how trivial it may seem—please call me."

I stood there silently, holding out my card. After what seemed a long time, she took it from me and quickly slipped it into her pants pocket.

"Thank you, Sheila."

I turned and moved toward my car. As I walked away I heard the sounds of her frantically putting the rest of her groceries into the car. She was out of the parking lot before I had started my engine.

As I drove toward the exit, the image of Sheila's black eye still vivid in my mind, I debated whether to return to my office or to drop in unannounced on yet another woman who had been avoiding me. I decided that, having already violated one of Miss Manners's rules ("Ladies don't pester strangers in supermarket parking lots"), I might as well go for the daily double.

Twenty minutes later I was cooling my heels (as we hard-boiled detectives say) in the glitzy reception area of Maxwell Associates. The receptionist and I had experienced what the warden in one of my favorite movies described as a "failure to communicate." She had informed me, with an air of finality and just a touch of arrogance, that I didn't have an appointment with Ms. Maxwell.

I answered, "I know that."

"But," she had said, just a tad flustered, "you don't have an appointment."

I leaned forward until our faces were about a foot apart. "So what?"

She had leaned back, apparently unable to fathom my response. I stared at her, expressionless, as her mouth struggled to form a reply. Giving up, she unplugged her telephone headset and ducked through the door to the inner offices of Maxwell Associates. I shrugged, took a seat in the reception area, picked up the current issue of something called *Risk Management,* and idly flipped through the pages.

Although I had needed to question Christine Maxwell, I was not looking forward to our encounter. I had known her briefly back in high school, back when her last name was O'Conner, back when I was a lowly sophomore and she was the great and powerful Chrissy O'Conner, vice-president of the senior class, managing editor of the student newspaper, and chair of the homecoming dance committee. In fact, it was on the homecoming committee that I had my one and only encounter with Chrissy O'Conner. Because ours was a three-year high school, the sophomores served as the grunts on all student council committees. I was a grunt assigned to the decorations subcommittee for the homecoming dance. Chrissy O'Conner issued orders to us all, acting every bit the true monarch even though her physical appearance was too harsh to qualify her for a homecoming queen.

That year, the queen was a blond Barbie doll named Susi Reynolds (and yes, she dotted her "i" with a daisy). Susi's court included the two runners-up, known as the senior maids. Traditionally, the homecoming dance opened with the formal presentation of the queen and her court, each of whom was escorted down the red-carpet aisle to the throne by one of the three co-captains of the varsity football team. That year the co-captains were Rod Thayer, a blond Ken-doll linebacker; Lamar Shelton, a hulking black center whose brutish demeanor belied a gentle heart; and Bobby Hirsch, the Jewish quarterback with dark blue eyes, dimples to die for, and a mezuzah around his neck. (Little did I imagine that night that two weeks later Bobby Hirsch would drop by my locker on the way to class and bashfully ask me out on a date—an event in the life of a sophomore girl equivalent to receiving Divine Grace.)

Anyway, I was helping backstage thirty minutes before the dance started when Chrissy O'Conner came charging by looking for someone or something. "Chrissy!" one of the other senior girls on the committee called.

Chrissy spun around, hands on her hips. "What is it?" she snapped.

"The escorts."

"What about them?" She was tapping her foot impatiently.

"We need to match them up," the other girl said. "Which one's going to escort the queen?"

Chrissy shook her head in vexation. "Use your head. I'm not sending Susi Reynolds down the aisle with a kike and I'm sure as hell not sending her down the aisle with a nigger. Now take care of it! I'm busy." She spun on her heels and stormed off.

I was so upset that I got dizzy and had to sit down. The rest of the homecoming dance passed in a dismal blur.

"Miss Gold?" It was the receptionist. She had returned with some of her composure but none of her chipperness. "This way," she said without a smile.

I followed her down the inner hallway, past about a dozen cubicles, to the large corner office. "Wait here," she ordered in a frosty tone. "Ms. Maxwell will see you when she's ready." She turned on her heel and marched off with an angry shake of her head.

Christine was standing behind her desk issuing instructions

to an older woman holding a shorthand pad. I stood in the doorway and peered around her office. It was hardly the typical insurance agent's office. Although it contained a desk, telephone, and other business equipment, Christine's office had been decorated to look like an elegant but comfortable sitting room. There were fresh flowers and framed prints of nineteenth-century paintings of birds. The furniture was all Queen Anne mahogany; in addition to her table desk there was a console with cabriole legs and lacquered brass handles set against a side wall, two boudoir benches, a library stand on a tripod base, a small writing desk set against the other side wall, and an oval coffee table in front of a traditional skirted sofa that was upholstered in polished chintz. There was a silver tea service on a tea table next to the couch and a vase of fresh flowers on the writing desk. On the console were a chancery clock and a bowl of fresh Granny Smith apples. Propped up on the library stand was a folio-sized volume on flowering herbs opened to a two-page color photograph of blooming foxglove.

"Reschedule that meeting for Friday at ten," Christine told her secretary, who was scribbling furiously. "And tell Frank I want all the numbers on my desk tomorrow morning at eight. *All* of them. No excuses."

Christine's outfit was as imperious as her manner. She was wearing a bottle-green double-breasted jacket edged in navy over a severe knee-length navy dress. The jacket had wide padded shoulders. Her short red hair was parted at the side and brushed back behind her ears, revealing gold dome earrings.

"One more thing," she said to her secretary as she picked up the small portable dictaphone off her desk. Using her thumb, she clicked open the chamber and slipped the microcassette into her palm. "Take this," she said, holding her palm out. "I have about a dozen letters on there, along with several quotes and proposals. I want them typed in draft form and on my desk when I return from lunch at Cardwell's." She dropped the microcassette into her secretary's hand and said, "That'll be all, Dotty."

I stepped back to let the older woman hurry by and then walked into the office. Christine took a seat behind her desk and stared at me as I stood before her. She was strumming her fingers on the desk pad. After a moment, she frowned and said, "You are persistent."

I smiled graciously. "Thank you."

She leaned forward aggressively. "As you *already* know, Rachel, I have a busy day. I told you that yesterday. You shouldn't have come here." She checked her wristwatch. "You have exactly five minutes. What is it you want?"

I remained standing. "Whatever you can tell me about Andros."

She studied me coolly. "Why should I tell you anything?"

I kept my temper under control. "Because my sister didn't kill him. If you killed him, tell me. If you didn't, then something you know might lead me to the person who did."

She gave a short laugh. "I certainly didn't kill him, and I hardly think I know anything that might help you."

"Let me be the judge of that, Christine. You were in his aerobics class, right?"

She rolled her eyes impatiently but nodded. "Yes."

I watched her carefully as I continued. "But you stopped your personal workout sessions with him three months before he died. Why?"

The question clearly caught her off balance. "What do you mean by that?" she asked testily.

"I don't mean a thing. I just want to know why."

"Well, I don't know," she said with an irritated wave of her hand. "I don't remember."

"Did your relationship with him change at that time?"

"No," she snapped. "We weren't like that. I wasn't one of his bimbos. I didn't pose for his album."

"What album?"

She caught her breath, sensing her strategic error. "You know exactly what I mean," she said, pressing on as if I were the one who had originally mentioned the album. "We weren't like that. We were friends." She gave me a proud sneer. "Unlike some women, I tried to keep my relationship with that man on a professional level."

I didn't believe her, but I'd heard enough from her on that subject and needed to move on. Nothing compelled her to talk to me. I'd bluffed my way into her office, and she could order me to leave whenever she wanted. The goal was to find out whatever else I could before she ended the conversation.

"Speaking of professional," I continued, "did you ever provide him with any goods or services?"

She eyed me cagily. "What do you mean?"

"According to the sign in your reception area, you're an insurance agency and a financial consultant. Did you ever do anything for him in those areas?"

She crossed her arms. "Such as what?"

I shrugged. "I don't know. Sell him insurance? Maybe for his car?" I paused. "Maybe on his life?"

She narrowed her eyes. "It's possible. My company is quite successful. We sell thousands of insurance policies every year. I'd have to check my files."

"Nothing comes to mind?"

She sat back in her chair and eyed me with a smirk. "I was in a lawsuit once."

"I know."

She raised her eyebrows. "Oh, you do?"

I nodded.

She paused a beat. "Well," she continued, "the other side took my deposition in that case. Before they did, my attorney gave me marching orders. He told me that if I wasn't sure of the answer to a question, I shouldn't guess and I shouldn't speculate. I should just say I don't know." She unfolded her arms and turned her palms up. "That still seems good advice. Did I sell him a policy?" She shrugged and switched to a helpless maiden voice. "I don't know, Miss Gold."

I could feel my nostrils flare. "But if you did, there'd be a record in your files?"

She shrugged again. "I don't know, Miss Gold." She checked her watch. "My, my, time's up." She stood up, the helpless maiden replaced by the iron one. "You'll have to leave."

I held my ground. "Will you have someone check your files on Andros and let me see what you find?"

She gave me a sarcastic look. "Why should I do that?"

I leaned forward and slowly inhaled. "Because my sister didn't kill him, Christine. And if that's not enough reason, then because I'll say 'pretty please.' And if that's still not

enough, then because you can do it quietly and without a lot
of fanfare now, or you can wait a week and I'll serve you
with a subpoena and show up at your office with a reporter
and a minicam from Channel 5 News."

Her face flushed with anger. "I'll think it over," she said
through clenched teeth.

I nodded. "Don't think about it too long."

"I'll think about it as long as I need to." She pointed toward the door. "Now leave."

"Goodbye, Christine." I turned to go.

"Hey," she said fiercely as I reached the door. I turned. She
was still standing behind her desk, visibly seething.

"What?" I said.

"Don't fuck with me, bitch."

I gave her a perplexed look. "You eat with that mouth?" As
I turned to leave I said over my shoulder, "It's the files or the
six-o'clock news, Christine. Your choice."

By the time I pulled out of the parking lot of Maxwell Associates, it was quarter to twelve. I was supposed to meet Benny
and my mother at my office for lunch so we could bring each
other up to date on the morning's events.

As I got on the highway heading east toward the city I
thought again of Kimmi Buckner, Andros's administrative assistant. I had tried to call her that morning to ask about the
storage space Firm Ambitions leased at Mound City Mini-
Storage. But when I dialed her number, a Southwestern Bell
recording informed me that her phone had been disconnected,
which meant I had to go to her house to make contact. Heading down Highway 40, I decided to swing by her house before my office.

It took fifteen minutes to get there. I rang the doorbell
several times, but she didn't answer. I peered through the
living-room window. Everything looked the same as before:
the framed painting of Jesus Christ rolling his eyes heavenward, the rickety couch upholstered in orange corduroy, the
three empty, crumpled thirty-two-ounce bags of M&M's on
the TV tray next to the La-Z-Boy. But no sign of Kimmi.

I banged on the front door. No answer. Thinking that she
might be working out back, I walked around to the tiny back-

yard. There was a birdbath filled with greenish water, a concrete Madonna, and a rickety clothesline. I knocked loudly on the back door and looked through the window into a dingy little kitchen that was absolutely filthy. There were food-encrusted plates stacked in the sink, dirty pots on the stove, a rusty kitchen knife on the counter. A box of Trix cereal had been knocked over on the table, spilling out its brightly colored contents. For a moment it looked like the table was vibrating. I squinted for a better look and straightened up with a shudder. The table wasn't vibrating; it was seething with black ants feasting on Trix.

I took out one of my business cards, which listed my office and home phone numbers, and scribbled a short note on the back asking her to call me. I came back around to the front of the house and wedged the card into the space between the jamb and the front door just above the knob.

17

CHAPTER

"That's all," I said with a shrug. We were sitting around the conference table in my office—Benny, my mother, and I. I had just finished filling them in on my morning, beginning with the inconclusive encounter with Sheila Kazankis and ending with the inconclusive nonencounter with Kimmi Buckner.

Lunch today was compliments of Benny, the Marco Polo of barbecue, who'd brought us a sampling of hickory-smoked goodies, fried yams, and cole slaw from his latest discovery, a place called Auntie's Rib Shack in north St. Louis. There were ribs, rib tips, burnt ends, homemade smoked sausage, and Benny's latest revolting passion, pig's ears, all smothered in a hot vinegary sauce. With the possible exception of the ears, which neither my mother nor I would taste, the meal was luscious.

I licked my fingers and reached for another rib. "All I'm doing is getting myself more confused," I said. "What do you two have?"

"For starters," Benny said as he took a bite out of the smoked sausage, "more goodies from large Marge."

"Is that the lady at the life insurance company?" my mother asked.

Benny nodded. "She had the information on the change of

beneficiary on the Firm Ambitions key-man policy. Guess who?"

"The Cayman Islands outfit?" I said.

"Bingo," he answered with a wink.

I sat back and mulled it over. "If Tommy Landau's father's firm formed the Missouri company, there's a good chance they'll know who owns the Cayman Islands company."

"But will they tell you?" Benny asked.

"There's only one way to find out," I said. "I'll call after lunch." I turned to my mother. "You have any luck, Mom?"

She nodded. The plan had been for her to spend the morning reading through police reports of burglaries over the past six months in the more affluent suburbs of St. Louis.

"How many?" I asked.

She smiled triumphantly. "Six."

"Whoa!" Benny exclaimed. "Way to go, Sarah."

"Six counting Ann?" I asked.

"Six *plus* Ann *plus* Eileen."

"Eight," Benny said. "Shit, that's got to be more than just a coincidence."

She took us through her notes, which showed what she had been able to piece together by comparing the police burglary reports with the appointment calendar I had printed off the Firm Ambitions computer. Including Ann and Eileen, during the past six months burglars had hit the homes of eight women who had been personal fitness clients of Andros during the same period.

"Eight out of how many clients during that period?" I asked.

My mother counted the names on the appointment calendar. "Sixty-four," she said.

"More than one in ten," Benny said as he wiped a glob of barbecue sauce off his chin.

"How many burglaries in all during that period?" I asked.

"I didn't count," she said. "More than a hundred."

I looked at Benny. He shrugged as he stuffed two slices of fried yam into his mouth. "Sounds suspicious," he said.

I nodded. "Very suspicious," I said. "I'm going to call Poncho after lunch. I want him to go look at the stuff out at that mini-storage place."

"You really think this guy was breaking into the homes of his clients?" Benny asked me.

"It's possible. That's why I want the police to look at that place. So what about the parent companies?" I asked him. "What else did you find out?"

"Interesting," Benny said. "I had the Missouri secretary of state's office do a records search back to the origins of the Missouri company. It's been around for almost ten years."

"So it predates Firm Ambitions?" I said.

He nodded. "Definitely. It's apparently owned two other companies over the years. The first was a company called Arch Alarm Systems."

"What's that?"

"No idea. According to the corporate filings, the president of Arch Alarm was a man named George McGee. I checked the phone books. No listing for the company or McGee."

"You said there was another company," my mother asked.

"Six years ago," Benny said. "Coulter Designs, Inc."

"Which is what?" I asked.

"Don't know that one, either," he said. "No listing in the phone book."

"Coulter," my mother repeated.

"What, Mom?"

"I remember a big-shot designer named Coulter."

"Really?" I said.

She rubbed her forehead in concentration. "He was an interior decorator, I think. It was a real *shanda*." *Shanda* is Yiddish for "disgrace."

"What was a real *shanda*?" Benny asked.

"I think he killed himself," my mother said.

"A decorator?" Benny asked.

"I think it was him."

"That's a good explanation for why he isn't in the phone book," Benny said.

My mother frowned. "I remember hearing about it on the radio, or maybe I read it in the papers."

"His suicide?" Benny asked.

My mother nodded. "In fact, I'm going to go to the library to make sure." She turned to me. "You want to go with me?"

"Let me call Detective Israel first," I told her. "I want to see if he can meet me out at that mini-storage place."

I cleaned my hands and face enough to pick up the phone. The police dispatcher told me Detective Israel was out for a few days. "That's right," I said, remembering his fishing trip with his son. "Let me talk to Detective Green."

"Detective Green isn't in."

"Is he out of town, too?"

"Oh, no. He's just out of the office at a meeting."

"In St. Louis?"

"Well, actually at the airport."

"Perfect."

I explained who I was. "I need to show him something out near there," I told her. "If you could get in touch with him now it would save him from having to drive all the way back out there again."

She took my name and telephone number. Ten minutes later, while I was telling Benny and my mother about Charles Kimball's theory on defending a circumstantial case, the phone started ringing.

"Miss Rachel Gold?" the man asked when I answered.

"Yes. Detective Green?"

"You got him, ma'am. What can I do you for?"

He confirmed that he was in charge of the Andros homicide while Detective Israel was out of town. I explained what I had seen yesterday at the Firm Ambitions storage space at Mound City Mini-Storage.

There was a pause. "So?" he said.

"So he could have been running an illegal operation out there."

"And exactly what kind of operation would that be, Miss Gold?" There was an edge in his voice. I couldn't tell whether it was impatience or sarcasm.

"Burglary," I said.

"I'm in homicide, ma'am."

"This involves a homicide, Detective." I explained the pattern that my mother had pieced together from the burglary reports. "Eight of his clients had their homes burglarized."

"Which tells you what, Miss Gold?" Definitely sarcasm.

"It tells me that maybe what I saw in that storage space is

connected to some of those burglaries. One of the homes that was burglarized was my sister's, Detective. She's the person you've charged with his murder."

I heard him sigh. "Miss Gold, just because you can match eight burglaries to the homes of eight of that man's customers doesn't suggest much. You can find those kind of patterns everywhere. I could take the customer list for a lawn service or a pool service or a fancy hairdresser or a dry cleaning delivery service in that area and I bet I would come up with at least as many matches. These are wealthy people, Miss Gold, and for wealthy people this is a small town. They all shop at the same stores, get their BMW's serviced at the same place, belong to the same clubs, and get ripped off by the same burglars."

"Come on, Detective, you're five minutes from there. I can be there in fifteen minutes. What's the harm? If some of the stuff in there is from one or more of these women's houses, then you have something worth pursuing. If it turns out to be a dry well, all it will cost you is thirty minutes."

Another pause. "Well, I don't know."

"You people have charged my sister with murder. All I'm asking for is a half hour of your time. A half hour to let *you* make sure *you* charged the right person."

He gave an exasperated grunt. "What's this place called?"

"Mound City Mini-Storage." I gave him directions from the airport.

"I still have no idea how this storage space is supposed to have anything to do with that homicide, Miss Gold, but I'll meet you there in fifteen minutes."

Detective Curt Green crossed his arms and turned to me with an aggravated expression. I could see my reflection in his aviator sunglasses. "This little peckerhead is right on target."

Dan-not-Dan nodded his head rapidly. "I am most displeased with you, lady. My boss was quite extremely displeased at myself because of your talking me into this access that I permitted to you. No one without a warrant are his strict orders to me." He turned to Detective Green. "I am sorry to report that this injunctive includes you, Your Highness."

Detective Green and I were at the entrance to Mound City

Mini-Storage. Dan-not-Dan was on the other side of the gate. He adamantly refused to let us in without a warrant.

"Sorry to bother you, little buddy." Detective Green looked over at me and shook his head. "I'm out of here, lady."

I followed him back to his unmarked car. He went around to the driver's side while I stood on the passenger side.

"Let's get a search warrant," I said.

He turned to me and took off his sunglasses. He was of medium height, with sleepy green eyes and a one-sided smirk, which he was giving me. "Pardon?" he said deadpan as he brushed back his thick brown hair. He looked like one of the upperclassmen you'd find on a beautiful Sunday afternoon holed up with a couple buddies in the darkened TV room of the fraternity house, sipping his sixth beer and uttering an occasional wisecrack as they watched a golf tournament.

This time I said it louder and slower. "A warrant, Detective."

"A warrant?" he repeated incredulously. "Based on what?"

"On what I've told you."

"Look, lady—"

"My name is Rachel Gold, Detective Green."

He forced a smile. "Look, *Miss Gold,* all you've told me is that (A) you've got eight gals—excuse me, eight women—who were personal fitness customers of the decedent and whose places of residence were burglarized, and (B) you happened to see some stereo speakers, a personal computer, a VCR, and a broken figurine in the storage space rented by the decedent's company. I already told you what I think of the first, quote, pattern, close quote. As for part B, I bet half the goddam storage spaces in that goddam facility have old goddam consumer electronic equipment in them. That's not enough for a goddam warrant, *Miss* Gold." He yanked open his door.

I banged my hand on the hood. "Wait a minute, Detective. Quit jerking me around. Look, I wrote down serial numbers for the speakers, the VCR, and the computer. Why don't you at least call them in? See whether any of the stuff has been reported as stolen. How long can that take? If you get a match, you'll be a hero. If you don't, well, you can get your rocks off yanking my chain."

I glared at him across the hood of his car. A hint of a smile formed in the corners of his lips. He looked heavenward and shook his head. "You have that information with you?" he said at last.

I nodded. "In my car."

"Well, go get it. I'll call in. If there's a match, we'll get a warrant. If not, you can save your goofy theories for when Poncho gets back."

It took close to two hours to find a judge to issue the search warrant, and then, on the way back to Mound City Mini-Storage, we got stuck in the early wave of rush hour, which added another half hour to what would otherwise have been a twenty-minute ride. By the time we pulled up to the computerized entrance gate, I could almost see the smoke curling out of Detective Green's ears. Dan-not-Dan actually saw the smoke when Detective Green thrust the search warrant into his face. He read the warrant quickly, pressed the button to open the gate, and actually bowed when he said, "This way, Your Highness."

"Well, this has to be a first," I said as we followed Dan-not-Dan out to the storage space rented by Firm Ambitions.

"What?" Detective Green growled.

"This time both of us hope I'm wrong."

He grunted. "Maybe."

The search warrant was premised primarily on the likelihood that I had made a mistake in copying down the serial number of the VCR. Although there were Bose speakers or Macintosh computers on several police reports over the past year, none of the burglary victims had had the foresight to record the serial numbers of their stolen items, and none had given the police any unique identifying characteristics of their items, such as a decal or a prominent dent. However, two of the five burglary victims who had lost the same Panasonic VCR model that I had seen in the Firm Ambitions storage space had been able to give the police the serial numbers of their VCRs. One of those serial numbers appeared on the police report of the burglary of the Zemel home in Creve Coeur. It so happened that Barbie Zemel was one of Andros's personal fitness clients. Moreover, her VCR serial number was—

with the exception of the seventh digit—identical to the one I had copied down: 3475GARW6344. My notes had R as the seventh digit while the Zemel VCR had B as the seventh digit. I could have miscopied the B as an R or the Zemels could have made the converse mistake when they copied the serial number, or at least that's what we argued to the judge. In any event, the search warrant authorized Detective Green to seize the VCR; that way, even if I had correctly copied the serial number, the Zemels might still be able to identify it as theirs.

We stopped in front of the garage door to the Firm Ambitions storage space. Dan-not-Dan punched the combination into the electronic keypad one number at a time, checking it each time against the combination he had scribbled onto an index card. "Okay," he said as he turned the lever and slid up the door.

Shit, I silently groaned.

Detective Green put his fists on his hips as he stared. "Jesus Christ," he said as he shook his head in exasperation. He turned to me. "This is the perfect end to a perfectly fucked-up afternoon."

The storage room was completely empty.

"I guess they came back and cleaned it out," I said.

"They?" he said incredulously. "Who are they?"

"According to Dan here—"

"Not 'Dan,' missy," the Pakistani interrupted. " 'Dan,' not 'Dan.' "

"Right," I said. "According to him, there are three separate access cards for this space. That means that one of his accomplices must have come back—"

"For chrissakes!" Detective Green said in disgust. "Accomplices? It's probably some poor guy storing his stereo speakers and computer in here until he moved to a bigger apartment. Maybe a buddy of the stiff. They probably have some other spaces in here with three access cards. Isn't that right?"

Dan-not-Dan nodded his head. "I am not completely familiar with these numbers—"

Detective Green dismissed him with a wave of his hand. "I've wasted enough time on this crap already. Do me a favor, lady. Next time you get one of these brilliant ideas, write it down and send it in to one of those police shows on TV. They love crazy shit like that. I don't." He turned to Dan-not-Dan. "Sorry we had to bother you with this, little buddy."

Dan-not-Dan raised his hands and smiled obsequiously. "Really it is not in the least amount to me a bother, Your Highness."

Detective Green shook hands with him and then turned and walked off without even a glance at me. I watched him get into his car and drive off.

I turned to Dan-not-Dan. He frowned and shook his head at me. Although I was fed up with him, I still felt bad for getting him in trouble with his boss. He had believed me, and I had taken advantage of him.

He waggled his finger at me. "I am saying again to you that I am most displeased with you, missy." He pointed toward my car. "You now must leave."

As I walked back to my car, I tried to summon up some pluck from the reserve tanks. I checked my watch. Earlier that afternoon I had called Harris Landau from the police station while waiting for Detective Green to prepare the warrant papers. He hadn't been in at the time. When I nonchalantly suggested to his secretary that Charles Kimball had assured me that Mr. Landau would have a few minutes for me, she admitted that his appointment calendar showed a meeting in the office at four o'clock, another one at six, and nothing in between. I asked her to pencil me in for a short visit at five o'clock. She couldn't agree to schedule a meeting without his permission, but she did agree to leave him a message with my request.

If I called now to confirm the appointment, he would probably use my call as an opportunity to have his secretary blow me off. It was 4:40 P.M. As I headed north and approached Highway 70 I could see that the traffic heading east was flowing swiftly. I could be downtown in twenty minutes—thirty tops. There was a sign up ahead with an arrow pointing the way to the entrance to I-70 East. I slowed. The worst that could happen was that he'd refuse to see me. He would hardly be my first rejection of the day. I put on my right-turn blinker and pressed on the accelerator.

18

CHAPTER

The law firm of Landau, Mitchell & McCray occupied the thirty-seventh floor of the Metropolitan Tower in downtown St. Louis. The firm's lobby decor was a *tour de force* of Anglophilia: framed English hunting prints on the walls; built-in bookcases filled with leather-bound sets of Dickens, Thackeray, Trollope, and Blackstone; a receptionist with a British accent; a fake fireplace with an ornately carved oak mantel; heavy dark leather chairs and couches; three English butler tables of varying heights and widths, each with hinged leaves and polished brass hardware. It looked like the sort of place where Kentish country gentlemen gathered after supper for port and cigars—a facade that worked until you realized that the "fireplace" was on the thirty-seventh floor of a sixty-story steel-and-glass skyscraper.

On the drive downtown I had prepared myself for Harris Landau refusing to see me. But to my surprise, no more than five minutes elapsed between the time I gave my name to the receptionist and the time Landau's secretary appeared to greet me in the lobby and usher me back to his corner office. She told me he would be in in a moment.

It was an enormous office. The initial east wall was glass and looked out on a dramatic view of the Old Courthouse, the Arch, the Mississippi River, and the riverboats moored to the cobblestone levees along the St. Louis shoreline. A tug pushing four barges moved slowly under the Eads Bridge on its journey upriver.

"Hello, Rachel. I'm Harris Landau."

I turned, expecting to see an older version of Tommy— heavyset, thick eyebrows, angry eyes. Instead, I saw a slender, debonair gentleman—a dark-haired version of David Niven in *The Bishop's Wife*, except that under his conservative three-button suit there was a crisp white shirt and a dark striped tie instead of a clerical collar. He had a white handkerchief poking neatly out of the breast pocket of his suit.

All we had time for was a handshake and an advance apology for a telephone call he was expecting from Washington, D.C. "Senator Bond's office left word earlier today that he wanted to have a word with me at five-fifteen," he explained. "If he does call, I'm afraid I will have to take it."

Just then the phone rang. We both paused, waiting for his secretary to answer it. She did, and buzzed him ten seconds later. "Senator Bond on line one, Mr. Landau."

"Please have a seat, Rachel," he told me as he reached for the phone. "This won't take long." He lifted the receiver. "Hello, Kit," he said in a friendly, low-key voice.

If I was supposed to be impressed, I was.

Senator Bond seemed to do most of the talking. Other than an occasional "I understand, Kit" or "I certainly agree," Harris Landau listened.

So as not to seem an eavesdropper, I stood up and went over to look at the awards and memorabilia on the wall. In addition to his diplomas from Princeton and the University of Chicago School of Law, there were plaques commemorating his service on various local and national organizations and a framed picture of Landau and his thin blond wife posed on the deck of a large sailboat. The remainder of the wall space was devoted to Landau family history. There was a mounted display case containing the gavel his father had used on the Missouri Court of Appeals and a signed copy of his opinion in an appellate decision that I was not familiar with. Next to the display case was a formal portrait photograph of the Honorable Bernard Landau in his judicial robes. His Honor had an austere look, close to a scowl. With his dark straight hair cut blunt above the ears and brushed to the side, he bore a striking resemblance to his grandson Tommy. Given Tommy's dark view of his grandfather's *corpus juris,* the strong family resemblance was ironic.

Next to the Judge Landau tableau was a display devoted to Abram Landau, the founding father and by far the most interesting member of the Landau clan. Shortly after I had agreed to represent Eileen Landau in her divorce proceedings, I spent an hour on the telephone with Muriel Goldenhersh, a friend of my mother's who is a walking, talking almanac of juicy gossip on prominent members of the St. Louis Jewish community, living and dead, especially the Briarcliff Country Club crowd. If you want to know when, where, and how the late Harold Blumberg met his lovely second wife Cynthia, Muriel has the answers: the when was 1975, the where was in his Reno hotel suite, and the how involved the payment of $500 for the performance by Cynthia of an act that Harold's first wife, Helene, had steadfastly refused him for all twenty-seven years of their marriage. If you want to know whether the settlement of all partnership dissolution issues between Robert Rothberg and Donald Stein (né Rothberg-Stein Realty) included any undisclosed terms, Muriel will be delighted to tell you that it did indeed: Rothberg, who was on the membership committee of the exclusive Briarcliff Country Club, agreed not to blackball Stein, whose membership application was pending at the time. That one-sentence covenant in the settlement agreement cost Donald Stein at least $1 million, a fair price in the eyes of his socially ambitious wife.

Naturally, I had assumed Muriel would have plenty of information on the Landau family, and she did. Abram was the star of the story, and what she told me was enough to lure me into the Missouri Historical Society a few days later over what became a three-hour lunch break.

I studied the three framed black-and-white photographs of Abram Landau on Harris Landau's wall: a wedding portrait, a shot of him in his fifties on a golf course, and a newspaper photo on his seventieth birthday scooping the first shovel of dirt at the ground-breaking ceremony for the Abram Landau Elementary School in north St. Louis. None offered any clue to the real man, whose American story began on July 3, 1886, the day the paddle wheeler *City of Louisville* docked at the port of St. Louis just south of the Eads Bridge and a twenty-eight-year-old German immigrant named Abram Landau walked down the gangway onto the cobblestone levee of what was then the fourth-largest city in America. He had come to America seven years earlier and settled in Louisville, where he became an itinerant linen peddler in the small villages along the steamboat route down the Ohio River to the Mississippi. Sensing that the emerging railroad industry would soon eclipse the steamboat era, he waited for the right moment, sold his route to a less perceptive immigrant, and bought a one-way passage on the paddle wheeler bound for St. Louis.

Within a few years, the Landau Linen Supply Co. was providing clean linens and towels to a growing list of downtown St. Louis hotels. Before long, he expanded the business into a related industry and became the principal supplier of clean bedsheets and towels to several of the St. Louis brothels. Shortly thereafter, Abram Landau vertically integrated this newest division of his operations by inducing Miss Eloise Hampton to transfer title to Eloise's Dance Salon, which at the time was the city's most popular whorehouse. By 1895, he owned the three finest "dance salons" in St. Louis and his patrons included the financial, social, and political power elites of St. Louis, along with visiting dignitaries from throughout the nation and the world. He became a fixture in booth one at Faust's Restaurant on South Broadway, then the most popular dining place in St. Louis. On any given night, he might be seen dining with Joseph Pulitzer (publisher of the *St. Louis Post-Dispatch*), Chris von der Ahe (owner of the St. Louis Browns), Sam M. Kennard (founder of the powerful St. Louis Business Men's League), or even William McKinley (who had come to St. Louis for the 1896 Republican Convention, which nominated him for the presidency).

In 1897, Abram Landau married Malka Iskowitz, the daughter of a Russian immigrant, in a small ceremony at Temple Shaare Emeth—the first and only time Abram Landau set foot in a Jewish house of worship in America. At his insistence, Malka changed her name to Mary a year later, just before the birth of their only child, Bernard. Forty-five years later, when the Honorable Bernard Landau delivered the eulogy at Abram's funeral service at the Ethical Society, he

spoke of accompanying his father to the opening ceremonies
of the Louisiana Purchase Exposition, a/k/a the St. Louis
World's Fair of 1904. He recalled his father's joy at those ceremonies. Bernard was only six at the time—far too young to
understand the economic basis for that joy: the lure of a
world's fair *and* the Olympic Games *and* the Democratic National Convention (all in St. Louis that year) held the promise
of a financial bonanza for the proprietor of the three largest
brothels in the city. The promise was kept. Indeed, on opening
night alone the guests at Eloise's Dance Salon included Pierre
Chouteau (great-grandnephew of St. Louis founding father
Auguste Chouteau), ex-governor David R. Francis (president
of the Exposition), and John Philip Sousa (whose band had
opened the festivities earlier that evening by playing "Hymn
of the West," the official song of the fair).

But the story of Abram Landau grows murkier after the
World's Fair. By 1910, he no longer owned any brothels, at
least according to the official records, and his involvement in
the business of Landau Linen Supply seemed diminished. It
was no longer clear just who or what Abram Landau was.
Under one version (put forward by Dr. Taylor Armstrong in
an essay published in a 1941 issue of the *St. Louis Historical
Review* under the title "The St. Louis Underworld: 1880 to
1930"), Abram Landau controlled all racketeering activity on
the north side of St. Louis, recruiting Jewish immigrants from
Eastern Europe to serve as enforcers. Under the other version
(favored by the newspaper editors of his era), he was a savvy,
well-connected entrepreneur who had the good sense to close
his linen supply business before the mob squeezed out all
competitors in St. Louis. Whichever version was true, from
the end of World War I until his death in 1943 at the age of
eighty-seven, the public Abram Landau was untouched by
scandal and increasingly touched by the sorts of honors and
amnesia that big money can purchase. At the age of eighty-
two, he received an honorary doctorate of law from Washington University in recognition of generous contributions over
the years.

Gangster or Horatio Alger, or both? The three framed pictures left the mystery unanswered. His wedding portrait was
stiff and serious—strong nose, dark hair, piercing eyes, han-

dlebar mustache. By the time of the golf shot, most of the hair and the stiffness were gone. All remaining sharp edges had disappeared by the time of the ground-breaking for the Abram Landau Elementary School. Indeed, in the last shot he looked like a sweet old man, which, by all accounts, was the one thing Abram Landau definitely was not. No hint in any of the pictures of the former whoremaster and rumored racketeer, nothing to taint Harris Landau's careful efforts to present himself as possessing the Jewish equivalent of *Mayflower* roots.

I returned to my chair as the telephone conversation came to a close. "I'll be there on Thursday," Landau said. "We'll talk then. Goodbye, Kit." He hung up and turned to me with a penitent expression. "I apologize for that discourtesy, Rachel. The senator and I have been missing one another all day, and he is departing for Europe this evening. Now, where were we?"

I smiled. "Nowhere, yet."

"Ah, yes. Well, first, I am delighted that you came here today. As a matter of fact, it was just this morning that I decided to contact you." He steepled his hands in front of him, elbows on the desk. In an earlier era he would have removed a cigarette from a gold case, inserted it in a long silver holder, and lighted it with an elegant flick of his Dunhill lighter. "As you may imagine," he continued, "Mrs. Landau and I are deeply saddened."

I wasn't sure what he was talking about.

"Mrs. Landau had hoped it would never reach this stage," he continued. "By contrast, I have always been the family pessimist. For the past few years the question for me has not been if but when."

I nodded my head sagely, as if I understood what he was saying.

"But," he continued with a sad shake of his head, "I had never suspected the addition of this last lurid detail."

"Which detail is that?"

"Her tawdry affair with that slimy little Casanova."

I stiffened as I simultaneously realized what he was talking about and took offense on behalf of my client, Eileen. I fought the urge to suggest that perhaps a wife trapped in an empty marriage with his creepy son might seek the physical intimacy of an affair as a substitute for the emotional intimacy she'd been deprived of at home. But I kept quiet. He obviously had his own agenda for this meeting, and, as usual, I could learn more by listening than talking.

He sighed. "My son has already had enough adverse publicity in his lifetime, Rachel."

"He has had some bad press," I acknowledged.

He nodded solemnly. "This time it would be far worse, for this time there are the children to consider as well. Innocent children. And your client, of course. Eileen is a woman with powerful social ambitions. To paraphrase William Herndon's description of his former law partner, Abraham Lincoln: her social ambition is a little engine that never quits. Unfortunately for Eileen, her ambition outstrips her sophistication. Understandable, I suppose. After all, she is still new at all this. She may not yet grasp the full implications of her indiscretion. When one is climbing up the social ladder, one simply does not sleep with the help. Should her faux pas become generally known, Eileen will discover that her new friends consider that sort of liaison tacky, and in that circle to which she aspires, tackiness is fatal."

"Hold on, Mr. Landau," I said, making the "time out" signal with my hands. "I'm lost."

He smiled good-naturedly. "Then I shall back up. To understand my stance you need to understand my view of the media. They operate contemporary America's freak show. The publishers are the proprietors, the reporters are the barkers and the guides. Unfortunately, my son has been on display inside that tent before. Your sister and Andros have become the newest attractions. She has my deep sympathy. However," and here he suddenly became intense and precisely stated each word, "I will not allow the press to put my family inside the tent again." He paused, and his face relaxed into a pleasant smile. "This is good news for you, Rachel. It means that I do not want a messy divorce."

"Neither do I," I said with a shrug, "but I don't control your son."

He gazed at me in silence for a long moment. "I do," he finally said. He looked down at his desktop, which was bare except for a leather-edged blotter, a portable dictation recorder, and an antique brass inkwell and quill pen. "At least on this matter," he added softly as he lined the portable recorder even with the edge of the blotter. "I have discussed my concerns with Thomas. In addition, I have explained certain facts of life and economics to Mr. Debevoise Fletcher. I have informed both of them precisely what I am prepared to do." He opened the top drawer of his desk and lifted out a sheet of paper. "As your financial expert will soon conclude," he continued as he glanced at the information on the sheet, "my son is cash-poor. He is dangerously overleveraged in more than a half-dozen strip shopping centers, all of which are presently incapable of generating sufficient revenue to service the debt. There is little, if any, equity in any of the properties, and the lenders have wall-to-wall liens on all the assets. In addition, they hold personal guarantees signed not only by my son but also by your client." He looked up from the sheet of paper, his eyes narrowing. "That means that, as things presently stand, your client will most assuredly be forced to sell her house, get a job, and lose her precious membership in my country club."

"Okay," I said. Actually, my financial expert had already reached the same conclusion.

"I offer an attractive alternative."

"I'm all ears."

"I will acquire one of my son's shopping centers at a price that is seven hundred and fifty thousand dollars above the existing debt. Your client will receive that seven hundred and fifty thousand dollars, *plus* the home, in full settlement of all marital rights *if* the divorce remains confidential."

I was taken aback. It was an extraordinary offer, given the present state of Tommy's assets. "And what if the divorce doesn't remain confidential?" I asked.

He crossed his arms over his chest and firmly shook his head. "Then the offer is withdrawn. Totally. The entire transaction will be expressly conditioned upon entry of a final divorce decree without any mention of the dissolution proceeding in any newspaper or magazine of general circulation or any radio or television station in metropolitan St. Louis. If the divorce receives any publicity whatsoever, the sale is off and my proposal terminates."

It was a harsh condition, but given Eileen's alternatives, Harris Landau's proposal was far better than she could hope to obtain at trial. "It's an interesting idea, Harris. I'll explain it to my client and get back to you with our response."

"I'd prefer that you convey your response directly to Mr. Fletcher. From this point forward you should deal with my son's attorney on all matters pertaining to his divorce."

"Fine."

He started to get up. "Rachel, I am quite pleased that we had this opportunity to—"

I raised my hand. "Hold on a minute."

He stopped and looked at me with an amiably quizzical expression.

"Actually, Mr. Landau, I came here to see you on a different matter."

"Good heavens, how rude of me." He sat back down with a self-deprecating smile. "Please proceed."

"This other matter," I said, "happens to involve the guy you called a 'slimy little Casanova.' But not his affair with Eileen."

Harris Landau nodded soberly.

"I believe he was a client of yours," I said.

He looked mildly surprised. "Andros?"

"Or his company, Firm Ambitions."

He leaned back in his chair and glanced up at the ceiling. He pursed his lips and pressed his index finger against his chin. "You are absolutely correct," he said after a moment. "As I recall, he came to us several years ago. We helped him set up his company."

I couldn't tell whether he had actually dredged that information from somewhere deep in his memory or had just pretended to. He was smooth and controlled, the perfect corporate attorney. I watched him closely as I asked, "How did he end up with you as his attorney?"

Harris Landau was far too masterly to give away anything in his face or body language. "As I recall, he came to us on a recommendation."

"From Charles Kimball?"

Landau seemed to ponder the question. "I don't believe I should answer that, Rachel."

"I know about Andros's prior criminal problems," I prompted.

He raised his eyebrows. "If so, Rachel, you have not learned of them from me. Call me old-fashioned, but I should think that any such problems would fall within the attorney-client privilege."

"Fair enough. Actually, I wanted to ask you a few questions about the corporate structure you set up for Firm Ambitions."

"That was several years ago, Rachel, and, at least compared to the usual corporate matters my firm handles, it was a somewhat inconsequential matter. Frankly, I doubt whether I did any of the actual work on that matter."

"I'm not a corporate lawyer, but the whole structure seems way too elaborate for a little exercise company."

He gave me a look of ignorance, or a superb impression of a look of ignorance. "Too elaborate?" he said. "In what way?"

"All the holding companies."

"When you get to be my age," he said with a chagrined smile, "your memory isn't always up to snuff. Help refresh it for me."

I briefly sketched out the Firm Ambitions corporate family. Then I asked, "Did your firm set up all those holding companies?"

"Good question, Rachel. I don't know. You have made me quite curious, though." He rubbed his chin thoughtfully. "Why the elaborate corporate structure, eh?"

"Exactly. Some of those companies predate Firm Ambitions, which tells me that there must be other investors out there."

He nodded pensively. "Possibly. That kind of corporate structure could have been designed for tax reasons, or perhaps for a specific regulatory purpose."

"Could you find that out for me? Along with the names of the investors or owners?"

"Well, it may not be that simple. If my firm did handle the formation of the other companies, I should be able to find out the tax or regulatory purpose behind that corporate structure as early as tomorrow. But if the information you're seeking isn't generally available to the public, or, in the alternative, if we have an ongoing relationship with any of these entities, I may not be able to share much if anything with you."

"I'll call you tomorrow."

He nodded. "Try after lunch. I should know something further by then."

On the way out of the offices of Landau, Mitchell & McCray I stopped in the lobby to call my office. Although my secretary was already gone (it was close to six o'clock), she knows that if I'm out of the office when she goes home she is supposed to record my messages on the answering machine. There were five of them—two from opposing attorneys in lawsuits, one from a headhunter calling about "an exciting position at a large law firm" (an oxymoron), one from a court reporter (with "a couple questions about the spellings of a few names in Mr. Conrad's deposition"), and one from my mother (with "some surprising news for you").

I called my mother and got her answering machine. I looked through the rest of the messages, asked myself whether I felt like returning any of the calls, answered my questions with a definite no, and headed for my car.

19

CHAPTER

My mother must have been in the shower when I called from Landau, Mitchell & McCray, because when I walked in the front door she was moving around in the kitchen wearing her robe.

"Hi, Mom." I gave her a kiss. "So surprise me."

"What?"

"Your phone message. You said you had some surprising news."

The microwave dinged.

"Ah, I do. Just a sec."

She opened the microwave and removed a serving bowl covered with plastic wrap. I noticed the table was set for one.

"Who's not eating here tonight?" I asked.

"Me," she said. "I'm going to dinner with Maury."

"The judge?" I glanced down and noticed she had on stockings and low pumps.

"Of course the judge. How many Mauries do we know? Listen, doll baby, I warmed up some pesto pasta." She gestured toward the covered bowl. "Be careful. It's hot. I made a nice salad for you. It's in the fridge."

"Thanks. So where are you and Maury going tonight?"

"Some sort of dinner for judges. It's down at the Hyatt. I won't be late."

"You can be late," I said with a wink.

She blushed. "One step at a time, please." She checked her watch. "He'll be here any minute. Let me tell you what I found."

"Okay."

"It turns out he wasn't the only one dead. They're both dead."

"Who are both dead?"

"Both men."

"Which men?"

"The designer and that other guy."

I lifted the plastic wrap off the bowl of pasta and leaned away from the steam. "Mom, what are you talking about?"

"Don't forget your salad. Those men who ran those companies, that's what."

I looked up. "Really? How'd you find out?"

"Just how I told you I would. I read the old newspapers on microfilm at the library. I copied the articles. They're on the dining-room table."

"Great. Did you tell Benny?"

"I put a set in his mailbox. He wasn't there."

"Oh, that's right," I said. "He has a faculty dinner meeting. He'll be home later."

The doorbell rang. My mother and I looked at each other. She patted her hair. "Should I get it?" I asked as I got up.

She hesitated and then shook her head. "I'm not sweet sixteen anymore. I'll get it." She loosened her robe and slipped it off. "How do I look?" she asked as I took the robe from her. She was wearing a black knit jersey dress with a pearl choker and matching earrings.

I kissed her gently on the cheek. "Like a dream."

"Come on," she said, slipping her arm around mine. "Say hi to Maury."

Tex Bernstein arrived bearing smiles and gifts. He had a big bouquet of flowers for my mother and a box of Bissinger chocolates for me. I noted with approval that he was freshly shaven. Tex might not be Robert Redford, but any man who takes the trouble of shaving twice in one day for his second date with your mother deserves a little slack. Even if he was one of the goofier judges in St. Louis County, Tex Bernstein was starting to worm his way into my heart. I wished them a good time and returned to the kitchen with a smile.

The sound of munching was unmistakable, even through the telephone line.

"Didn't you just have dinner?" I asked Benny.

"So?"

"That sounds like eating to me."

"I am engaging in a bit of postprandial mastication in the privacy of my own apartment. I believe that that remains legal even within the reactionary confines of the Show-Me State, which, by the way, is truly the strangest state nickname in the country."

There was the sound of coal tumbling down a chute, and then the sound of stones inside a rock crusher.

"Benny, what in the world are you eating?"

"Actually, Miss Smarty-Pants Communist, you'll be pleased to know that I happen to be consuming a high-fiber selection from one of the four basic food groups."

"Cracker Jacks?"

"Score one for the girl with the All-World Tush. Frankly, I view some Cracker Jacks before bedtime as a special gift to my large intestine. It's my way of saying thanks to Mr. Colon."

"You're such a considerate guy."

"You know I'm a hopeless romantic."

"I know you're hopeless. So did you read the articles?"

"Yep."

I was at the kitchen table, staring at the photocopies of the two newspaper articles. The first had appeared in the *St. Louis Post-Dispatch* eight years ago:

ST. LOUIS BUSINESSMAN KILLED IN SOUTHERN ILLINOIS HUNTING INCIDENT

The president of a St. Louis area burglar alarm company died yesterday of a gunshot wound as a result of what Illinois officials have tentatively labeled a hunting accident. Two Belleville men on a hunting trip discovered the body of George L. McGee, president of Arch Alarm Systems of St.

Charles County, yesterday afternoon in a wooded area near Cartersboro, Illinois. McGee, of Hazelwood, was 54 years old.

According to Jackson County Deputy Coroner Bobby Ray Vinton, McGee had been dead for approximately twenty-four hours when his body was discovered. He was wearing hunting attire. A rifle later identified as his was found near his body. According to Cartersboro Sheriff Harvey Young, the rifle had not been fired. McGee's automobile was discovered parked on the side of Illinois Highway 149 three miles from where his body was found. The area, located near the eastern edge of the Shawnee National Forest, has been a popular deer-hunting site for years.

The preliminary autopsy report showed that McGee died as a result of massive hemorrhaging and blood loss caused by a rifle-caliber bullet that apparently entered through the back of his neck and shattered his spinal cord, according to Vinton.

Sheriff Young stated that his office is treating the fatality as an accidental death. He made a plea for the person responsible for the death to come forward.

"I'm sure he feels just awful," Young stated. "But he shouldn't be afraid. We're not looking to press charges. We just want to talk to the man and close the books on this one."

McGee's death marks the third time in five years that a hunter has been accidentally killed during the opening week of the deer-hunting season in southern Illinois.

The second article had appeared in the *Post-Dispatch* four years later:

WELL-KNOWN INTERIOR DECORATOR FOUND DEAD; APPARENT SUICIDE

Laurence Coulter, president and founder of Coulter Designs, was found dead in his Central West End townhouse yesterday. The popular interior decorator, whose clients included members of many prominent St. Louis families, died of a single gunshot wound to the head, apparently self-inflicted. He was 44 years old.

Police entered Coulter's townhouse and discovered the body after his longtime personal secretary reported him missing. Coulter had failed to show up at his office that morning and then missed several appointments in the homes of his clients, according to St. Louis Police Lt. James Moran. Coulter's personal secretary, Harry Amber, told police that Coulter had been despondent for several weeks for no apparent reason, according to Moran.

Two years ago Coulter formed his own interior design company after more than a decade with Gateway Designs. In a cover-story profile that appeared last year in *St. Louis Magazine,* Coulter was described as "the hottest interior designer in St. Louis, with a waiting list of names from the rolls of the most exclusive country clubs in town."

He is survived by his mother, Anna, 78, and a sister, Blair, 56, both of Indianapolis.

"Did your mom find anything else on them?" Benny asked between crunches.

"All she found on McGee was his obituary."

"Was he married?"

"Nope. On Coulter, all she found was an article on his estate sale. It was about a month after he died, with all the proceeds going to his personal secretary."

"Harry Amber?"

"Right. He's dead, too," I said.

"No shit?"

"Mom tried to track him down. He moved to Memphis right after Coulter killed himself. He died of AIDS two years ago. The *Post-Dispatch* ran his obituary."

"Your mom's a goddam bloodhound."

"She's on another date with Tex," I said.

"Good for her."

"I'm still trying to get used to a dating mom."

"Hey, she's got a lot of life ahead of her."

"I know."

There was a pause followed by the sound of cardboard tearing. Then coal tumbling down the chute, then stones getting crushed.

"Not another box, Benny."

"Helps me concentrate. So did Harris Landau agree to see you?"

"He sure did." I filled him in on my meeting.

When I finished, Benny asked, "What's he like?"

"Nothing like his son. Nothing at all. He's smooth and polished and elegant."

"Sounds dangerous."

"I can't get a read on him," I said. "I'll wait to see whether he comes across with the information on the corporate structure of those holding companies."

"Hey, how was your second visit to that storage outfit?"

"Oh, Benny, a total disaster. I felt like the star of *Nancy Drew Gets A Frontal Lobotomy*."

He was laughing. "What happened?"

I told him the whole sorry tale.

"Hey," he said, "nothing ventured, nothing gained."

"I guess," I said glumly as I noticed that Gitel's food bowl was empty.

"So where are we?" he asked. "Give me some of that women's intuition."

I walked over to the cabinet and pulled out the box of Cat Chow. "For starters, call your friend at the insurance company tomorrow."

"Why? Ah . . . you really think?"

I poured some Cat Chow into Gitel's food bowl and put the box back in the cabinet. I realized that I hadn't seen her the whole night. She probably was prowling around outside. Before long she would be meowing at the back door. Her internal food clock brought her home every evening around nine-thirty.

"Someone killed Andros," I said. "The police think a jilted lover is the link. But maybe the real connection is somewhere up there in that parent company. The company that owned Firm Ambitions also owned Arch Alarm Systems and Coulter Designs. All three were essentially one-man operations. Take out the main guy and the business collapses. What if Capital Investments had a key-man life insurance policy on those two other guys?"

"That's not necessarily sinister, Rachel. You said yourself these were essentially one-man operations. If that's the case, you could argue that a prudent investor would insist on an insurance policy to protect his investment."

"I know. You sound just like Harris Landau. Just see what your girlfriend can find out for us. And if she does turn up a policy on one of them, be sure to have her find out who the insurance agent was."

"Good point. Damn, wouldn't that be something? Hey, you're getting good at this, Rachel."

"I'm getting lost at this," I groaned. "By the way, my mom is going to ask Tex to help out."

"Tex? Oh, brother, how the hell is he going to help?"

"Benny, he's a state court judge. He can get access to records that we might never be able to get at." I paused. "He'd better treat her right."

"Rachel, your mom's a class act. For chrissakes, it's not like she's going out on a date with Richard Speck."

"I know. Wait a minute."

"What?"

"She's home. His car just pulled into the driveway."

"At nine forty-five?"

"He's an early riser. I'll talk to you tomorrow. Kiss Ozzie good night for me."

I hadn't run in three days and was starting to get antsy. When Benny called I was actually putting on my jogging outfit and was lacing up my Nikes. So after checking in with my mother—who confirmed that she and Tex were going to start digging into the police records on George McGee and Laurence Coulter beginning tomorrow during the lunch hour—I kissed her good night and stepped out into the dark.

Our house is close enough to a busy street to make jogging after dark not as reckless as it sounds. Nevertheless, as I passed under each lamppost and watched my shadow appear, swing from back to front, and disappear, I realized again how much more relaxing a nighttime jog can be when you are running alongside a big, healthy, vigorous, and fiercely protective golden retriever. I resolved again to get this cat-versus-dog problem straightened out. Either Gitel the cat was going to learn to put up with Ozzie or I was going to have to do what

I had been putting off, namely, move out of my mother's house.

The second option no longer seemed as difficult to implement. We had both viewed my moving in as a temporary arrangement when I returned to St. Louis, but my mother's depression during the first months after my father's death made the prospect of moving out of the house seem an act of abandonment. That had changed, thank goodness. She was getting back into the swing of things, and even had a boyfriend, which was more than I could say for myself.

Charles Kimball popped into my head. *Maybe,* I said. *Maybe. First get Ann's situation straightened out. Then you can think about dating an older man.*

As I made the turn at the three-mile point, I went over tomorrow's schedule. I needed to talk to Eileen about Harris Landau's settlement proposal. If she decided to accept it, I would have to arrange a meeting with Tommy Landau's obnoxious divorce lawyer to try to close the deal. I also needed to check back with Harris Landau to see if he had learned anything about the investors in Capital Investments of Missouri and whether he would disclose what he had learned. If he stonewalled me, as I suspected he would, I'd have to consider trying to persuade a court to order him to disclose that information.

I sprinted the last two hundred yards, pretending it was the gun lap of the fifteen-hundred-meter in the Olympics. The crowd roared as I once again won the gold for the United States.

The house was silent. My mother's bedroom was dark as I climbed the stairs, sweaty and panting and triumphant. I kicked off my running shoes in my bedroom, opened the door to the bathroom, turned on the shower, shed my jogging clothes in a pile on the bathroom floor, closed the bathroom door, and stepped under the hot spray. Thirty minutes later, clean and relaxed and ready for bed, I wrapped a bath towel around my body sarong-style, clicked off the bathroom light, and stepped into my bedroom.

Yawning, I pulled open the top drawer of my dresser to select a pair of pajamas. As I did I glanced at myself in the dresser mirror and noticed the cat in the reflection. She was on the bedspread by the pillow, facing me.

"Hello, Gitel," I said as I sorted through the drawer.

Something must have seemed slightly awry, because I glanced at her again in the mirror. She was studying me with her usual inscrutable stare. I selected a pair of red silk shortie pajamas and loosened my towel.

Red. It clicked.

"God!" I gagged as I spun around, stumbling backward against the dresser. The force of my body knocked over the bottles of perfume and nail polish and deodorant. Several clattered off the dresser and fell to the floor. I pressed my fist against my mouth.

Gitel was studying me through sightless eyes. Sightless eyes in a severed head. She'd been decapitated. Her body was nowhere in sight. The head had been pressed back against the white pillowcase. It was surrounded by a growing stain of red.

I took a step toward the bed, reaching to the floor for my towel, never taking my eyes off the head. Then suddenly I straightened up.

My mother. My God, my mother.

Frantic, I ran down the hall and yanked her door open. The light from the hallway flooded the room. My mother was on her side facing me, her eyes closed. I moved closer, straining to hear the sound of breathing over the pounding inside me. She opened and closed her mouth, frowned in her sleep, and turned onto her other side.

Thank God.

I scanned the room for a sign of the cat's body. Nothing.

And then the full significance hit me. Someone had been in the house.

In my bedroom.

While my mother was sleeping.

While I was in the shower.

There had been an intruder in our house.

Had been? Or still was?

He could be in my mother's closet right now, or in her bathroom, or anywhere in the house.

I had to call the police.

There was a telephone on my mother's nightstand. I lifted it carefully, quietly.

Damn.

It was dead. He'd cut the telephone lines.

Then the other telephones started ringing—the one in the kitchen and the one in my bedroom. The jangling startled me. I moved toward the door and stopped.

My bedroom was down the hallway. I would have to pass two hall closets and another bedroom. He could be waiting in one of those closets, or in that bedroom. He could be waiting in my bedroom.

"Rachel?"

I jumped as I spun around. My mother was sitting up in bed. "Sweetie, why are you naked? Is that the telephone?"

"Ssshh. I think there's someone in the house."

"What?" she said with a frown. "Who's calling at this hour? Plug the phone in." She pointed to the cord by the nightstand. The end of the cord was on the floor near the telephone outlet. Then I remembered: she unplugged the phone every night before she went to bed. I knelt and quickly plugged it in.

"We have to call the police," I hissed as my mother lifted the receiver.

"Hello? No, this is her mother. Who is this? Do you have any idea what time it is? Who is this?" She shook her head. "He won't say."

"Give me it," I said, reaching for the phone. I held it to my ear. There was static on the line. "Hello?" I said.

No response. "Hello?" I said again.

"I guess your pussy isn't feeling so good, huh?" It was a male voice—muffled, disguised.

"What do you want?"

"That was a hint, bitch."

I gripped the telephone. "Who is this?"

"That's what happens to nosy little pussies."

"What's that supposed to mean?"

"Figure it out. Hey, talking about pussies, you got one hell of a bush on yours. Nice titties, too. Too bad I didn't have a camera ready when you dropped your towel. Maybe next time, eh?"

There was a *click*, followed by a dial tone.

20

CHAPTER

"Where did he do it?" my sister asked with a wince.

"In the backyard," I said. "He either caught her back there or he brought her back there to do it."

It was the morning after. Ann and I were drinking coffee in her kitchen. I think I'd had a total of one hour of sleep the night before.

"Was there a lot of blood in the house?" she asked.

I shook my head. "The police think he brought the head upstairs in a plastic bag while I was in the shower. He had enough time to arrange it on the pillow before he left." I closed my eyes for a moment. The image was burned into my brain. "He even made sure her eyes were open."

Ann shuddered. "That is *so* sick. And he was, like, watching you the whole time from the backyard?"

I nodded grimly. "The police found a lot of footprints back there."

Ann pressed her palm against her forehead. "Oh, God, Rachel, I feel so horrible."

"Don't, Ann."

Her eyes were red. "That sicko terrorized you and Mom, killed and mutilated her poor cat, snuck around your house, and ..." She paused, her lips trembling. "And it's all my fault."

"It's not your fault, Ann."

"Of course it is," she said, her voice cracking. "I was the one who had the affair with that creep, I was the—"

"Ann, Ann," I said, "don't punish yourself. You're a victim, too." I reached across the table and grabbed hold of her arm. "You're not to blame for what's happened. Dozens of women had affairs with him."

"Then why's this happening to me?" she demanded. There were tears trickling down both cheeks. "To us?"

"Why?" I said with a shrug. "Why do serial killers kill the people they kill? Just bad luck. There's no reason for any of it. Whoever killed him decided you were a convenient fall guy. It's not some cosmic punishment. There's no one out there balancing the scales of justice. The world doesn't work that way." I stood up. "Let me get you some Kleenex."

After I got her the Kleenex I poured us both a fresh cup of coffee.

"How did he get in the house?" Ann asked after she blew her nose.

I shook my head in resignation. "You know how flimsy that back-door lock is. He just popped it open, probably with a screwdriver."

Ann wiped her eyes with a fresh Kleenex. "Mom's got to get deadbolt locks."

"I called the locksmith at seven this morning. He'll be there before noon."

"Good."

"And," I said with a contented grin, "Ozzie has already moved in."

She smiled through her tears. "That's even better. You two need a big dog around the house." Ann sighed and shook her head. "Mom sounded terrible," she said.

I nodded sadly. "It really freaked her out," I said, "and she's really broken up over Gitel. How old was she?"

"About four, I think."

"Didn't Dad give her Gitel for her birthday?"

Ann nodded miserably.

"Poor Mom," I said softly, my eyes suddenly welling up. I reached for a Kleenex.

We sat together quietly, sipping our coffee.

"You know," Ann finally said, "I didn't realize you can see into your window from the backyard."

"Sure," I said. "Remember we used to watch Mom hang the laundry from up there?"

"God," Ann said with a shudder. "He was out there watching?"

"Judging from the static on the line when he called, the cops think that he may have been standing back there with a cellular phone."

"That is *so* creepy," she said.

I nodded. "You know what was almost as bad?" I said with a grimace.

"What?"

"Having to tell those two cops exactly what he said."

"Were they guys?"

"Yeah. Both in their twenties. Young studs. You know the type."

Ann made a face. "God's gift to women."

"I almost didn't tell them."

"But you did?"

I nodded. "They were okay. The one asking the questions, I looked him right in his eyes and told him exactly what he said to me. Word for word. I swear, if he had looked down even once—at my boobs or lower—I would have kicked both of them out of the house. But he was cool. So was his partner."

"What are they going to do?"

"Probably not much. They're going to send a couple crime-lab guys around this afternoon. I can't wait," I said sardonically. "Believe me, it's not going to be a high priority with them."

"You must be kidding," Ann said in disbelief.

I shook my head. "Think about it. At any given moment they have way more unsolved crimes than detectives to solve them. They have to run a triage operation. When the captain has to choose between assigning one of his detectives to catch a cat killer and assigning that same detective to catch a rapist or murderer or burglar, you know what he's going to do."

She nodded reluctantly. "I guess you're right."

"It's the same with your case. The problem is that the police think they have it solved. They want to leave it that way. Close the file, pass it on to the prosecutor, move to the next case. That's the mentality. That's why it's practically impossible to get them to follow any new leads. They just don't want to hear about it. We're going to have to hand it to them neatly tied up and gift-wrapped before they do anything."

She took a sip of her coffee. "Can you?" she said. I could hear the discouragement in her voice.

"I'm sure going to try." I filled her in on the different leads our mother, Benny, and I were running down. She'd heard most of it before. "Something's going to pan out," I concluded, trying to inject some optimism into my voice. "I just know it."

I poured us both some more coffee.

"Talking about burglars," Ann said between sips, "last night was definitely not a great night for home security."

"What do you mean?"

"Do you remember Holly Embry? She used to be Holly Goodman."

"Sure." Holly Embry was one of Ann's friends from high school—no longer a close friend but someone Ann occasionally saw at parties or in the supermarket.

"What happened?"

"Someone broke into her house."

"Was anyone hurt?" I asked.

"No. Carol Marcus called this morning to tell me. She said it happened while Holly and Chuck were at the hockey game. Their kids were at her parents' house."

"That's good. What was stolen?"

"Carol said the burglars took all of the silver, Holly's fur coat, and several paintings. Fortunately, they're all covered by insurance."

I frowned in concentration. "Holly Embry? I've seen that name somewhere."

"She was in Jerry Berger's column a couple months ago."

"No, it was somewhere else."

Three hours later, I was seated in the office of L. Debevoise Fletcher, waiting for him to get off the damn phone. It was a vintage Ma Bell.

For one creepy moment, I flashed back to my junior-associate days at Abbott & Windsor in Chicago, back to the one act that most partners at most large law firms inflict upon every associate in the firm: they answer every single telephone call that comes in while the associate is in their office. *Every single telephone call.* Dozens of times during my days at Abbott & Windsor—no, hundreds of times—I had been summoned to a partner's office for "a five-minute meeting" only to emerge forty minutes later, having had those five minutes parsed out in sixty-second sound bites sandwiched between five leisurely incoming calls.

At Abbott & Windsor, we called them Ma Bells. Associates at other firms had their own name. At Emerson & Palmer they were known as Your Mamas. The more astute student of hierarchy—such as any ambitious associate at a large law firm—grasps early on that Ma Bells are not restricted to partner-associate relations. Indeed, the pecking order within the intricate power structure of the partnership can be ascertained by a careful charting of partner-to-partner Ma Bells. Figure out which partners are Ma Bell inflictors and which are inflictees, ally yourself with the right inflictor, and someday you may no longer be an inflictee.

Fletcher's Ma Bell, combined with my lack of sleep and general edginess after last night, quickly had me incensed enough to storm out. But I made myself remember that Fletcher's client and Fletcher's client's father were offering Eileen Landau a generous financial settlement. If part of the settlement price was a Ma Bell, so be it.

To calm my jangled nerves, I looked around his office. On the wall above his head was a large wood display plaque—the kind used for displaying the mounted head of an African lion or wildebeest. Fletcher's was empty. Beneath the place for the missing head was a brass plaque that read "MAX FEIGELBAUM (*Homo selachii*)." I had to smile. Max Feigelbaum, a/k/a Max the Knife, had represented Fletcher's wife in their bitter divorce trial. According to an article on divorce lawyers that had appeared in the *National Law Journal,* Max the Knife's victory in the acrimonious case of *In re the Marriage of L. Debevoise and Patricia E. Fletcher* had resulted in a property and alimony award that "resembled a decree by Vlad the

Impaler." When sober, Fletcher refers to his nemesis as the "Fiendish Feigelbaum." After several drinks, according to sources at Abbott & Windsor, the Fiendish Feigelbaum becomes Max the Kike.

I stood up and walked over to the picture window. Fletcher's office had a beautiful view of the Old Courthouse and its shimmering reflection in the Equitable Building. On the wall by the window was a photograph of Fletcher in his Green Beret uniform shaking hands with John Wayne. Next to that photograph was the framed Silver Star awarded to him in Vietnam. One of the unwritten survival rules for any associate assigned to a case with Fletcher was to feign keen interest when, at the end of the day, Fletcher leaned back in his chair to tell one of his repertoire of four interminable Green Beret stories.

At last, Fletcher brought the telephone conversation to an end. "Sorry about that, Rachel," he said unapologetically. "Now where were we?"

I turned to face him just in time to catch his eyes shifting up from my thighs to my face. I held his stare for a moment. "Trying to tie down the loose ends, I believe. We were on point six."

He looked down at the list of settlement demands I had given him. Eileen was willing to accept her father-in-law's divorce settlement proposal, but on my advice had added eight additional points—relatively minor, but proper nevertheless. For example, point five required Tommy to pay the legal and accounting fees Eileen incurred in the divorce. I hoped to prevail on at least four of the eight points. Fletcher and I haggled over the remaining items for another thirty minutes and ended with an agreement in principle.

"You understand, Rachel, that this is all subject to the agreement of my client and his father."

"Then get it, Deb."

"I certainly intend to recommend it."

"Why not call them now? I'll go down the hall and call Eileen from another phone while you talk to Tommy and his father."

"You're certainly in a hurry to get this done."

"So is your client's father, Deb. After I talk to Eileen I'll wait for you in the firm's library."

Eileen was delighted when I told her that Fletcher had agreed to six of the eight points, including the four that we wanted and two of the four we were prepared to give away. Fletcher's door was still closed when I got off the phone, so I walked down the hall to wait for him in the firm's law library. I was on the couch by the periodical stand leafing through the current issue of the *National Law Journal* when Fletcher poked his head in.

"Well, Counselor," he said with a broad grin, "it looks like we have a deal."

"The same deal you and I agreed to?" I asked pointedly, having observed firsthand that Deb Fletcher was the type of attorney who would keep trying to sneak an extra term into the deal up until the time the final papers were signed.

He chuckled. "The very same, Rachel."

"Then I'll draw up the papers and fax you a draft by the end of the week."

"Very good." He grinned as he shook his head. "For a while there I thought you and I were going to be climbing into the ring on this one."

"I'm sure it won't be long before we get that chance in another case."

"Maybe so, but this one would have been a doozy. Especially with those pictures of your client. I'll say one thing about her—"

"Don't," I interrupted.

"My, my, aren't we touchy these days?"

I exhaled slowly. "Deb, unless you want to reopen negotiations, drop it. I won't say anything about your client, you won't say anything about mine. You got it?"

He shrugged and gave a chuckle. "Fair enough, Rachel. I must say, however, that you're getting just a tad hypersensitive as you get older."

I forced a smile. "That's supposed to be clever?"

"Ah, so now we're going to have a battle of the wits."

"I don't think so, Deb. It's against my code of honor to fight an unarmed man."

He gave me a tight smile—the kind that seemed to say that

if I were a man he'd punch my lights out. I returned the sentiment with an equally tight smile that tried to suggest that if I had a Sherman tank at my disposal I would drive it through the side of his house and leave treadmarks across his back. We walked side by side to the front of the offices, exuding that special bonhomie of fellow members of a learned profession.

"I almost forgot," Fletcher said as I waited for the elevator. "Harris Landau told me you had asked for information about some company his firm had done some work for."

"Right. Capital Investments of Missouri."

"Whatever," he said with a dismissive gesture. "He told me to tell you that his firm did some minor work for the company—routine corporate filings and such. However, he found no authority in the files to reveal any information about the company that isn't already in the public record."

"Which means?"

There was a ding as the elevator arrived.

He gave me a smug look. "Which means you aren't going to get the information you asked for."

I stepped onto the elevator and turned to face Fletcher with an impassive expression. "If that's his position, fine. I have to be in criminal courts out in the county in the morning for some pretrial matters on my sister's case. Tell Harris that I'm going to ask the judge to order his firm to disclose that information."

Fletcher gave me a puzzled look. "On what possible ground?"

None came to mind immediately. No matter. I'd have one ready by the time I presented the motion in the morning. "He can find out in court tomorrow," I said as the elevator door slid closed.

On the way back to my office I swung by Kimmi Buckner's house again. She wasn't home, or at least she wasn't answering her doorbell. My business card was still wedged in the front door.

When I got back to my office, I checked my mail and my telephone messages. There were plenty of both, but none from Kimmi Buckner and none from Christine Maxwell.

21

CHAPTER

That peculiar reality known as Anglo-American law contains, indeed requires, certain imaginary creatures known as "legal fictions." For example, the law of torts is built upon the behavior of a phantom known as the Reasonable Man. The Reasonable Man is always careful, always vigilant, always moderate, always sensible, always clearheaded, always prudent. Twenty-four hours a day. The Reasonable Man always stops at railroad crossings, always puts on protective eyewear, always disconnects the cord from the electrical outlet before repairing, and always makes sure he has adequate ventilation. Compared to the Reasonable Man, Ward Cleaver is Evel Knievel.

The corporation is another legal fiction. Under the law, a corporation is a person. Just like you. If you prick it it does bleed, if you tickle it it does laugh, if you poison it it does die, and if you seek confidential information from its attorneys it does invoke the attorney-client privilege, which is exactly what it did the following morning when I appeared in court to present my motion to compel Landau, Mitchell & McCray to disclose the identities of the principals of Capital Investments of Missouri, Inc.

Harris Landau was in court, along with his attorney, L. Debevoise Fletcher. Never one to walk a courtroom tightrope without a net, Fletcher had brought along an intense young associate who had no doubt spent the last hour trying to drive into Fletcher's tiny brain the applicable principles of law. Fortunately for Fletcher and unfortunately for me, the presiding judge was Roman Samuels, a gray-haired GOP stalwart who saw nothing fictional in the legal fiction. Indeed, from the stern look on his face, Judge Samuels seemed to be under the impression that this particular corporation was somehow a blood relative. I got through half of my argument before Judge Samuels ran out of patience.

"Come, come, Counsel," he interrupted, clearly irked. "The purpose of life insurance, as its very name signifies, is to insure a life, i.e., to provide to the beneficiary a fixed sum of money in the event that the named insured should die." He looked at my opponent. "Right?"

Deb Fletcher beamed. "Precisely, Your Honor."

Judge Samuels glared down at me. "Why, I daresay that half the corporations in this city own key-man life insurance policies on their CEOs." He looked over at Harris Landau, who was standing next to Fletcher. "Is that a fair statement, Harris?"

Landau pretended to contemplate that verbal softball as it floated in over the middle of the plate. "*At least* half, Your Honor." You could almost hear the crack of the bat.

Judge Samuels looked down at me. "That's my point, young lady. The mere fact that this company chose to acquire such insurance hardly makes it a murder suspect, and certainly does not constitute a waiver of its attorney-client privilege. Your motion will be denied."

Deb Fletcher and Harris Landau were waiting for me in the hall outside the courtroom. Fletcher was smirking in triumph. "You shouldn't bite the hand that's going to feed one of your clients," he said to me.

I brushed by him without a word and headed toward the lobby. The elevator doors slid open just as I reached them. Fletcher was following, of course, and stepped in with me. He held the door for Landau.

"Rachel," Landau said gently as the elevator started its descent, "please understand that there's no personal animus behind my firm's position. Unless we are specifically authorized to do so, we never disclose facts about our clients or their activities. Our position is based entirely on principle."

I said, "In my experience, Harris, I have yet to come across a position asserted by an attorney in a courtroom that is based entirely on principle."

Three hours later, I handed a filing fee and my Verified Petition to Perpetuate Testimony to the cashier in the Office of the Clerk of the U.S. District Court for the Eastern District of Missouri. As the old cliché goes, there's more than one way to skin a cat. I hoped I'd found one of them. Although there were several procedural hurdles I would have to clear, if I cleared them all I would have a federal court order requiring the law firm of Landau, Mitchell & McCray to disclose the identities of the principals of Capital Investments of Missouri, Inc.

The clerk stamped the petition and handed it to the assignment clerk, who conducted the random draw to determine which judge would be assigned to the matter. As she reached for the drawing cards, two other clerks stepped over to serve as witnesses—a procedure to ensure that the draw is truly random. She lifted the top card toward her and then glanced at one of her fellow clerks. He shook his head and looked up at me with a barely disguised look of pity. The clerk turned the card toward me. It had one word on it: MADIGAN.

"That can't be," I said. "He's on senior status."

She shrugged. "He still handles miscellaneous matters. I'm sorry, Miss Gold."

Stunned, I walked outside the clerk's office and stared at the directory on the wall:

JUDGE KEVIN W. MADIGAN ..... Room 867

I walked over to the elevator and pushed the UP button.

Kevin Wallace "Mad Dog" Madigan embodied the dark side of Article III of the U.S. Constitution, which specifies that federal judges are appointed for life. Lifetime judicial appointments are nice in theory. The problem is, things happen during a long life. Such as senility, which had held Judge Madigan's dance card for the last several years.

But even before senility, Judge Madigan's courtroom had long been known as the Wheel of Justice—a place where the law was dispensed (or dispensed with) in a manner that suggested reliance not on legal precedents but on the entrails of pigeons. A strict constructionist one day, a radical activist the next, Mr. Rogers one morning, Freddy Krueger that afternoon, Judge Madigan might appear on the bench in any one of more than a dozen ill-fitting judicial temperaments selected from the vast walk-in closet of his psyche. As Benny had once quipped, "When E.T. calls home, Mad Dog answers."

Judge Madigan's ancient secretary took my name, disappeared into chambers, and returned a few minutes later. She sat down at her desk without saying a word or even acknowledging my presence. With a shrug, I took a seat and pulled out my copy of *Emma* and comfortably settled in.

Forty minutes later, the judge's secretary announced that he would see me now. Inside his enormous chambers and seated behind a huge desk, Judge Madigan looked even more diminutive than he did in his courtroom. Above him hung a large framed photograph of President Lyndon Baines Johnson. His Honor was holding a yellow highlighter marker in one hand and intently reading a Spiderman comic book that was open on his desk. He looked up briefly, his eyes swimming behind thick eyeglasses, and then returned to his comic, pausing to highlight a balloon of dialogue. His bald head was sprinkled with age spots.

"Good afternoon, Your Honor. Rachel Gold, for the petitioner."

No response. He leaned forward to highlight something in the comic book. His bony hand shook slightly.

I stood up and slid my court papers toward him across the top of his desk. The movement caught his eye. He pushed his comic book to the side and leafed through the court papers.

He looked up and squinted at me. "Who are you?" he snapped.

"Rachel Gold, Your Honor. Counsel for—"

He held up his left hand, shaking his head. "Hold your horses, girlie." He had a high-pitched, nasal twang. "I have to adjust the volume on this damn thing." His right hand fiddled with the knob on his hearing aid. "Say something," he snapped. "Recite the Pledge of Allegiance."

I got as far as and-to-the-republic before Mad Dog held up his hand. "I'm reading you loud and clear." He frowned and held up the court papers. "What the hell is this goddam thing?"

"It's a petition to perpetuate testimony."

"I can see that, young lady. But what the hell is it?"

I got as far as the connection to the Cayman Islands when he cut me off. "This is an outrage!"

"Yes, Your Honor," I said uncertainly.

"What are those dickless wonders at the FBI doing about it?"

"I don't believe they're involved, yet, Your Honor."

"Well, goddammit, get on down there and tell those idiots to drop their cocks, grab their socks, and start pounding the pavement. Jesus Christ, they're just sitting around and letting a pretty little girl like you do all their dirty work. Well, I say shit on that." He gave me a big wink. "I'll tell you one thing, darling: this goddam petition is denied." Using the yellow marker pen, he scrawled the word DENIED across the first page and signed his name. "There," he said proudly, sliding it across the table toward me.

Obviously, I should have read my horoscope before venturing out of the house this morning. *Leo, avoid encounters with older men in positions of authority.* I was 0 for 2 so far today.

"Are you married, young lady?" he snapped as I turned to leave.

"No."

He pointed the yellow marker at me. "You're not a dyke, are you?"

Incredible. "No, Judge." I remained stationary, fearing that any sudden movement could set off one of his legendary gay-bashing tirades.

"Before long," he snorted, "our goddam armed forces will go the way of the Romanians." His eyes flashed behind the thick lenses. He jabbed the highlighter pen at me for emphasis. "You know about the Romanians, don't you?"

"I'm not sure I do," I said, aiming for a soothing tone.

The tendons in his neck were taut, quivering, as if straining to keep his head from popping off. "The second lieutenants in the Romanian army had to wear lipstick and rouge. They were forced by their commanding officers to . . . to commit infamous crimes against nature!"

I said nothing.

He stood up, his eyes darting around the room. I waited, motionless. Eventually, he sat down. He looked puzzled. I tried a docile smile. He stared at me, confused, his eyes blinking rapidly.

"Are you married, young lady?"

"Yes, Your Honor," I gently replied.

He nodded. "Good, good."

His eyes seemed to lose focus. He looked down and spotted his comic book on the edge of his desk. He grabbed his yellow marker and pulled the comic book close to him. I waited a few moments and then, slowly, deliberately, backed out of the room.

22

CHAPTER

Benny snorted in disbelief. "The fucking Romanian army?"

"Just the second lieutenants," I said.

"I'll tell you," Benny said, shaking his head, "we had some spooky goddam federal judges back in Chicago, but Mad Dog is right up there with the worst." He popped the tab on his can of beer. "Someone ought to do the right thing."

"Which is what?" I asked with a grin.

"Haul that goofy motherfucker off to the dog pound and have him put down."

I heard the sound of my mother's car pulling into the driveway. "My mom's home."

"Good. Now where's the pizza?"

I checked my watch. "They have seven more minutes."

The pizza delivery guy arrived with two minutes to spare. The tangy smell of fresh hot pizza filled the kitchen. Is there any combination of scents more mouth-watering than tomato sauce, oregano, basil, garlic, and pepperoni? Benny had brought the beer, my mother had the pantry stocked with diet soda, and I had swung by the supermarket on my way home to pick up some dog treats for Ozzie and two pints of Ben & Jerry's ice cream—Heath Bar Crunch for Benny and Cherry Garcia for me. None for my mother, who had an entire pantry of Nutri-Systems "desserts." During dinner I filled her in on the events of the day.

"So what can you do?" my mother asked when I finished.

"The Cayman Islands angle is worth pursuing," I said. "I'll check my Rolodex tomorrow morning. This guy I used to date in law school became an investment banker at Bear Stearns. Last time we talked he was in one of their international divisions. I'll call him tomorrow."

"Good," my mother said.

"There's also another guy," I said. "I ran into him back at my ten-year reunion. He was in my section first year. He's a partner in the Paris office of one of the Wall Street firms. He might have a contact down in the Cayman Islands."

Benny turned to my mother. "*Nu*, Sarah. What have you and the judge found?"

My mother wiped her lips with a paper napkin. "Plenty," she said. "Starting with George McGee."

"Which one's he?" Benny asked.

"The head of the burglar alarm company?" I said.

She nodded. "Arch Alarm Systems."

"What did you find out?" Benny asked.

My mother raised her eyebrows and slowly shook her head. "That this was a man who definitely understood home security systems." She looked around the table with a knowing smile. "Guess what Mr. McGee was before he was president of that company?"

Benny laughed. "I love it. A burglar?"

She nodded. "Three arrests, one conviction, each time for breaking and entering."

Benny looked at me with a delighted grin. "What a great country, eh?"

"Homes?" I asked my mother.

"Homes," she confirmed.

"But all before he started the alarm company, right?" I asked.

"Right," my mother said. "He was out of jail two years when he opened the company."

"And no arrests after that?" Benny asked.

"Not a thing," my mother said.

"How 'bout the other dude?" Benny asked. "The one who killed himself?"

"Laurence Coulter," my mother said. "Another *mensch.*

You know why he committed suicide? Because he was a real pervert."

"Now hold on, Sarah," Benny said with a grin. "Given present company, you shouldn't be throwing around phrases like 'real pervert' loosely."

"I'm not, believe me," my mother said firmly. "The man was a big fan of child pornography. He got arrested twice. Maury found the records. The first time for taking naked photographs of two little boys. Disgusting."

"What happened?" I asked.

My mother shook her head in displeasure. "Suspended sentence."

"And the second time?"

"Maury read the indictment and the court file. The government said that Coulter ordered a bunch of kiddie porn through the mail and they arrested him when the stuff arrived."

"What happened?" Benny asked.

My mother crossed her arms and frowned. "The judge threw the case out on a technicality. Maury said the judge ruled that there was an unlawful trap or something."

Benny went over to the refrigerator and got himself another beer. "So," he said to my mother when he returned to the kitchen table, "what's the punch line?"

"What punch line?" my mother said.

"You said Coulter killed himself because he was a pervert. How do you know that?"

"Ah, right. Maury got the police file on the suicide. There was a copy of his suicide note. In the note he said that he hated himself, that he couldn't control himself anymore. He said that as long as he lived he'd be a danger to children, so he decided to kill himself."

"When was his second arrest?" I asked.

She checked her notes and gave me the month and the year.

I compared it to the other dates we knew. "So," I mused as I idly drew a circle around the date on my notepad, "he was arrested about a year before he opened his own interior design company."

"Weird, huh?" Benny said. "Seems like a brush with the law is just what these two guys needed to get their entrepreneurial juices flowing."

After dessert, Benny cleared the table and I loaded the dishwasher while my mother went down to the basement to do the laundry. Ozzie was on the floor in the middle of the kitchen, his head resting on his paws. He watched Benny as he moved back and forth between the table and the sink. It was wonderful to have Ozzie back home.

"What are you thinking about?" Benny asked as he handed me two plates to load into the dishwasher.

I rinsed the plates under the faucet. "I'm thinking about coincidences," I said.

"What about them?"

"About the difference between coincidence and design."

"What kind of coincidences are you talking about?"

I slotted the plates in the dishwasher rack. "Common threads among the three companies owned by Capital Investments of Missouri," I said.

"Such as?"

I looked at Benny. "Such as the heads of all three companies are dead."

He squinted in thought. "True," he said, "but three very different deaths."

"None of natural causes."

"Okay," he said. "What else?"

I put the silverware into the dishwasher and straightened up. "All three men had criminal records—or at least all three had been arrested."

Benny handed me the ice cream bowls and spoons. "Which tells you what?" he said.

"If it's a coincidence, nothing. If it isn't a coincidence, well, I'm not sure."

Benny took another beer out of the refrigerator. "It may not even be enough to qualify as a coincidence," he said as he opened the beer. "After all, only one of those guys actually had a criminal record."

"True," I conceded as I closed the dishwasher. I rinsed off my hands under the faucet and dried them on a dish towel. I filled the tea kettle with water. "But," I told him, "there's the one that really bothers me: what's the one common thread for all three businesses?"

He frowned. "I'm drawing a blank."

"Start with the fact that the customers for all three businesses are affluent."

Benny mulled that one over. "Okay. And?"

I joined him at the kitchen table. "For all three businesses, an essential part of the operation requires that the main guy spend time inside the client's home. A burglar alarm company, an interior decorator, and a physical fitness guru who makes house calls. Maybe it really is just a coincidence."

"But maybe not," Benny said, getting more animated. "Take the burglar alarm company. Shit, what a great front for a burglar like McGee. You install the burglar alarm and case the joint at the same time. If the house is worth hitting, you already know everything you need to know about the security system." He stopped with a frown. "But what about the other two?"

"Think about it," I said. "Andros was a foreigner who almost got deported on drug and sodomy charges."

"But he wasn't a burglar. Neither was the other guy."

"But both had a weakness, right? Maybe someone could have used their weakness to get leverage over them. Or maybe they were recruited. Maybe they were just corrupt and got recruited by a real burglar."

Benny leaned back and took a big gulp of beer. He gave me a dubious look. "You really think Andros was breaking into people's homes?"

I shrugged. "I doubt it. But maybe he was connected to those break-ins."

"Well, it's too late to find out now," Benny said. "Even if you're right about him, he sure ain't going to be casing any other homes."

I smiled. "Not necessarily."

Benny paused in mid-sip and lowered his beer with a frown. "What do you mean, 'not necessarily'?"

"It didn't all click until tonight," I explained. "Yesterday Ann told me that her friend Holly Embry had her home burglarized the night before. I knew I'd seen her name somewhere else. I checked my printout of the Firm Ambitions appointment calendar. Guess who happened to be a personal fitness client of Andros?"

Benny raised his eyebrows. "No shit?"

I nodded. "Mondays and Thursdays, nine A.M., at her house."

"But I don't get it," Benny said with a frown. "You said her house was burglarized *two* nights ago."

"Don't you see?" I said. "Andros didn't have to be *alive* at the time of the break-in. If he was only the scouting party, if he didn't personally do the breaking and entering, then Holly Embry's burglary could have been set up *before* he died."

"Maybe," Benny said with a defeated shrug. "But how in the hell are you ever going to be able to prove that?"

The tea kettle started whistling. I turned off the gas and looked back at Benny. "How?" I repeated. "By doing a stake-out."

"A what?"

I smiled sheepishly. "Just like in the movies."

"Wait a minute, Sam Spade. Just what the fuck are you going to stake out?"

"Mound City Mini-Storage."

"I don't get it."

"C'mon, Benny. This isn't nuclear physics. A burglar needs a fence, right? If you steal a bunch of different items, maybe you need a bunch of different fences—one for the art, one for the silver, one for the computers. If it takes a couple days to arrange to unload all the loot, you have to stash the goods somewhere, right?" I took out three mugs. "That's where Mound City comes in," I continued. "It sure seems the most likely candidate. Remember, we know someone was out there *after* my first visit, since they removed everything that was in there. But that was also before Holly Embry's burglary. If that storage space is where they stashed the goods they stole from Holly's house, some of them might still be there."

"Maybe," Benny said with a shake of his head, "but that Pakistani douche bag's never going to let you back in there."

"I know that. The police won't help, either." I smiled and shrugged. "Thus, a stakeout."

My mother closed the basement door as she stepped into the kitchen. "What's this about a stakeout?"

We sat down at the kitchen table for hot tea. Ozzie came over the put his head on my lap. I scratched his head and behind his ears as I explained my idea to my mother. When I finished I said, "All I need is some high-speed film. Dad's camera equipment is still in the basement. He taught me how to use his telephoto lens."

My mother gave me her stern mother look. "And what are you supposed to do, Miss Rambo, if someone really shows up?" she asked.

I shrugged. "Snap his picture. Watch what he does. Try to follow him when he leaves."

My mother blew across the top of her mug to cool the tea. She shook her head at me. "You don't know what you're doing."

"Mom, as long as I just watch, I don't need to know what I'm doing. I can get some film and start tonight. I might get lucky."

"We," my mother corrected me. "We."

"Don't be silly, Mom."

"Shah," she said with an impatient wave of her hand. "This isn't a Hollywood movie, young lady. We'll do this together."

I turned to Benny with an embarrassed smile. "Going on a stakeout with your mother," I said with a roll of my eyes.

"Hold on, Sarah," Benny said and looked at me. "You have that list of times that people entered the storage space. What are the key hours?"

"Late at night," I said. "From around ten at night until three or four in the morning."

"Look," he said to my mother. "I'm a night owl anyway. As long as I'm up, I might as well keep your goofy daughter company out there."

"You?" I said to him.

"Hey, if you're dead set on doing a revival of *The Amateur Hour*, you're going to need a Ted Mack." He checked his watch. "Where's the camera?"

"In the basement," I said.

He followed me down the stairs and through the passageway to the back storeroom.

"I'll take the malpractice claim," Benny said.

"Against who?" I asked, only half listening as I poked around the shelves, looking for the telephoto lens.

"Against the architect who designed this basement," he said.

I looked at him. "What?"

"It's a maze down here."

"Oh." I took down another box and looked inside. It wasn't the one with the telephoto lens. "It's an old house," I said as I put the box back and took down another. "There were three additions. They dug a new foundation each time." I turned to him. "I don't like the idea of my mother staying alone here tonight."

"Didn't the police promise to send a car by the house every half hour?"

"Still," I said doubtfully, "it was really creepy here last night."

"You've got new deadbolt locks. And you've got Ozzie."

"I just don't know. Ah, here it is." I removed the telephoto lens from an old shoebox. "Come on."

As we started up the basement stairs I heard my mother laughing, and then I heard a familiar male voice.

"Look who's here," my mother said when we stepped into the kitchen.

It was Judge Maury "Tex" Bernstein. "Well, hello there, little lady," he said to me. His drawl was just (jes') a little thicker tonight, and he had dressed the part: a Western-style shirt, string tie, blue jeans, and cowboy boots. "Ah," he said as Benny walked into the kitchen, "this feller must be Ben Goldberg." He stuck out his hand toward Benny. "Put it there, pardner."

Benny grinned as they shook hands. "Just call me Slim, Judge."

Tex roared with laughter.

My mother was beaming. "Maury came over to stay with us tonight."

Tex put up his hands assuringly. "Strictly on the up and up," he said and winked at Benny. "I'll sleep downstairs. Brought my own bedroll," he said, gesturing toward the breakfast room, "and some firepower."

I looked toward the breakfast room. On the floor by the table was a neatly rolled sleeping bag. Resting on top of the sleeping bag was a large shotgun and what looked like a box of shells. I looked back at Tex and then over at my mother. She looked radiant.

"Go," she said to me. "We'll be fine. I'll bring you both breakfast."

23

CHAPTER

"Probably because normal people believe that a bowel movement is a private act," I said.

Benny clicked off the flashlight and closed his book. "And sex isn't?"

"Yeah, but sex sells books."

"I'm not just talking hot-sex junk fiction," he said. "I'm talking front page of the *New York Times Book Review* fiction. I'm talking Saul Bellow, Philip Roth, John Updike, Alice Hoffman. You've got people shtupping like crazy in those books. Blow jobs, hand jobs, rim jobs—you name it."

I shrugged. "Maybe the authors think that a sexual encounter is a way to reveal something about a character's personality."

He gave me an astounded look. "And taking a dump isn't?"

"Benny, I'm not a writer," I said with a shrug. "I don't know why no one goes to the bathroom in novels."

We were seated in the front seat of my car, which was parked on an unlit and cracked asphalt lot overlooking the back of Mound City Mini-Storage. We were parked behind what appeared to be an abandoned warehouse. A barely legible EMPLOYEES ONLY sign hung at an angle from a rusted metal pole at the entrance to the parking area. Spikes of grass and clumps of prehistoric weeds grew out of cracks in the crumbling asphalt. My car was pulled up against the chain-link fence of Mound City. From where we sat there was a clear view down the main row of storage facility all the way to the electronic gate at the entrance. The eighteenth garage door on the left was the one rented to Firm Ambitions.

It was a few minutes after midnight. We'd been there for close to two hours. Benny had followed me in his car and parked it out of sight around the side of the warehouse. We had brought both cars, just in case.

Benny shifted in the passenger seat. "I think it's a little strange that no one ever has to take a leak in any of these goddam books."

"I think it's a little strange that you would think that that's a little strange."

"Rachel, this is breakthrough thinking going on here. We're talking literary revolution. Pick a character."

I rolled my eyes. "Forget it."

"Jay Gatsby," he said.

I looked out the window and shook my head. "I can't believe this conversation."

"Bear with me here. I'm on to something. Jay Gatsby. Mr. American Dream himself. Mr. Fresh Green Breast of the New World. Did you ever wonder if he was the type who took the newspaper into the john and spent a half hour on the crapper, grunting and groaning? Or was he one of those strafe bomber types, in and out in two minutes?"

I gave him a look. "Although you may find this difficult to believe, Benny, that particular question has never, ever crossed my mind."

"Watch that tone, lady. They laughed at Sigmund Freud, too. I bet a thorough study of the bathroom habits of world leaders would yield some truly chilling insights."

"I'll tell you what's a truly chilling insight: the impact of four years of undergraduate education at Yale. Is this the kind of question that you philosophy majors were trained to ponder in New Haven?"

"Oh, no. We skipped the little stuff and focused on the biggies, the pivotal questions, the mysteries of the cosmos."

"Such as?"

"Such as what's the story with Jews and four-wheel-drive vehicles?"

I burst into laughter. "What?"

"I'm serious. I mean, have you ever met an American Jew who's had an offroad-driving experience? Other than maybe pulling onto the shoulder of the road to call his broker on the car phone? What exactly is going on here?"

I shook my head, still smiling. "It's not just Jews, Benny."

"Forget about the goyim. They throw everything out of whack. I'm talking Jews. Think about it! You got brain surgeons in Broncos, you got labor lawyers in Land Cruisers, you got exodontists in Explorers. For chrissakes, you got Reform rabbis in Range Rovers! It's nuts. Suburbia is filled with nice Jewish mommies driving Hebrew-school car pools in vehicles designed for chasing wounded rhinos over the African veldt. What the fuck is going on here?"

"Well," I said when I'd stopped laughing, "what did you geniuses at Yale decide?"

Deadpan, he shook his head and sighed. "I'm sorry to report that the juxtaposition of Jews and four-wheel-drive vehicles remains one of the principal enigmas of our generation."

I pretended to mull it over. "I think the key is Reform rabbis in Range Rovers."

"Huh?"

"Jews and Jeeps. Atavism. Buried in our genes is the memory of wandering forty years in the desert."

Benny raised his eyebrows and nodded. "I am impressed, Professor Gold."

I squinted through the windshield. "Here we go."

Headlights were visible at the far end of Mound City Mini-Storage. I took the lens cap off the telephoto lens and zoomed in on the license plate as the gate slid open.

I snapped a picture. "Missouri plates," I said. I read the license number to Benny as the car pulled forward. Benny jotted it down on the note pad.

"Coming our way," Benny said as the car crept forward down the middle aisle.

I lowered the camera and watched. The car stopped four doors shy of the Firm Ambitions space.

I exhaled slowly. "Nope."

Both front doors opened. A chubby guy in a business suit got out on the driver's side. He loosened his tie as he straightened up. A blonde in a miniskirt and heels stepped out of the passenger side.

Benny said, "Hey, it's that babe again."

I raised the camera and focused. Sure enough, it was the same woman we had seen over an hour ago. She had arrived that time in a different car and with a different middle-aged guy.

"You're right," I said to him.

"Definitely a hooker," Benny said as I watched her punch in the combination on the lock. She turned to the guy, who pulled up the garage-type door. A light went on inside the storage space as the door slid down.

They came back out thirty minutes later. She was applying lipstick, he was adjusting his tie. They got in the car, waited at the front gate while it slid open, and drove off into the darkness.

"There's some weird shit going on in here," Benny said.

I nodded.

The weird shit continued. At 1:15 A.M. an older man in a black jumpsuit drove in on a motorcycle. Turns out he had a vintage car—Benny said it was a Packard—parked in one of the storage garages. He pulled the Packard out, along with a lot of cleaning supplies. For forty-five minutes he cleaned and polished his Packard, and then he roared off on his motorcycle. While he was polishing his car, two guys in a pickup arrived and unloaded at least two dozen pink flamingo statues from the back of the truck and put them in one of the storage spaces. They were followed by another two guys in a van, who stopped in front of a different storage space and unloaded what appeared to be several dozen assault rifles. Later, we witnessed what looked like a drug deal take place outside another storage space. At 3:45 A.M., three men in a Ryder truck unloaded two red fifty-five-gallon drums, each of which had the letters K-Y painted on the side—a combination of letters that, naturally, reduced Benny to hysterical laughter.

By the time my mother arrived at 5:15 A.M. with home-made blueberry muffins and a big thermos of fresh coffee, we had watched another half-dozen folks come and go, moving things in and out of their storage spaces. But our hooker didn't return, and no one visited the Firm Ambitions space.

* * *

Later that morning, back in my office, I tried to reach the two law school friends with possible contacts in the Cayman Islands. The guy from my first-year section at Harvard—the one in Paris—was now in Malibu, having left the practice of law two years ago to become a television scriptwriter, a career change that might charitably be described as a lateral move along the evolutionary ladder.

But I had better luck with Bob Ginsburg—a law school boyfriend turned investment banker at Bear Stearns. I tracked Bob down in the New York office. We talked some, mostly reminiscing about our law school days. Bob and I had had a brief romance that, in classic Cambridge style, got derailed over politics. He was a conservative Republican—one of those pro-life, pro-death types—who was, in that absolutely maddening fashion so typical of conservative Republicans, a lot of fun and very sweet and wonderfully thoughtful when not enmeshed in THE CAUSE. We parted friends. Although he was no longer in the Bear Stearns international banking division, he promised to poke around to see what he could find out.

"It could take a while," he warned. "People like doing business down in the Caymans because it's so goddam discreet."

"It's probably a dead end anyway," I told him, "but I want to at least go all the way down the path before I scratch it off the list."

Exhausted, I left the office around noon, went back home, set the alarm for five-thirty, and woke up feeling worse than before. I got to Mound City by seven. Benny showed up thirty minutes later with a Chinese takeout feast. We put out the blanket I had brought and the two of us had a picnic.

"This smells wonderful," I said as I opened the lid on the container of Hunan shredded beef with hot peppers and orange peel and inhaled deeply. In addition to the Hunan shredded beef, Benny had brought fried rice with pork, cold noodles with sesame sauce, smoked chicken with spicy black bean sauce, kung pao squid, General Tso's prawns, spicy sour cabbage, and moo shu pork.

"I swear, Benny," I said as I lifted a portion of Hunan

shredded beef out of the white cardboard container with my chopsticks, "if Chinese takeout was the key to compatibility, you and I could have the marriage of the century."

Our hooker showed up at ten-thirty that night, this time in a Hertz rental car driven by a guy who still had his convention nametag pinned to the lapel of his blue blazer.

Around eleven, I dozed for a while and Benny did some stretching exercises in the parking lot. A few cars came and went, but nothing special. At midnight, Benny started fiddling with the AM radio dial, looking for weird call-in shows. I got out of the car to do a short jog around the warehouse parking lot. I started off at a slow pace but came sprinting back. "Look," I said, panting tensely as I got back in the car.

"What?"

I reached for the camera. "The van."

Benny squinted through the windshield. "At last."

A battered Ford Econoline van had pulled in front of the Firm Ambitions storage space. Its headlights went off and someone got out on the driver's side.

"Go get in your car," I told Benny as I fumbled with the lens cap on the telephoto lens. "This looks for real."

A minute later I had the Illinois license plate in sharp focus.

Click.

Still squinting through the viewfinder, I advanced the film one frame and aimed the camera at the open door of the storage area. He was in there. I couldn't see him, but I did see the beam of his flashlight sweeping back and forth in the darkened storage space.

I heard the crunching of a car approaching across the cracked asphalt. It was Benny. He pulled alongside my car and rolled down the passenger window.

"Is he in there?"

I nodded. "You know the drill?"

"I think so."

"Repeat it." Although we had gone over it several times this shift, I wanted to make sure we knew our roles.

"You'll stay here," Benny said, "and I'll go around the

front. We both follow him. If he meets up with anyone, we split up. I go with the new guy, you stay with the old."

I nodded, still staring at the open storage door through the camera viewfinder. "All we do is follow."

"Right."

"No heroics, Benny."

"Heroics? Don't worry. My colon already feels like it's filled with ready-mix cement." He shifted into reverse. "See you back at the house."

I looked at him. "Be careful, Benny."

"You, too."

Benny backed away with his lights off and pulled out of the parking lot. The sound of his car faded as I lifted the camera back up and pointed it at the open storage space.

A moment later he came out carrying what must have been a large framed picture. It was hard to tell, though, because it was draped with a sheet.

Click.

He was a short, skinny guy with long black hair and a goatee. There was a lit cigarette dangling from the side of his mouth. He had an angular face with a hatchet nose and was wearing a plaid short-sleeved shirt, black jeans with a big silver belt buckle, and cowboy boots.

Click.

I was able to snap off another shot before he disappeared behind the van to load it into the back. I took another when he came back around and flicked the cigarette butt in a high arc beyond the front of the van before stepping back into the storage area.

I took several more pictures as he came out twice more, both times carrying large flat objects shrouded in sheets—two more framed pictures, I assumed. Then he closed the garage door, checked to make sure it was locked, and climbed back into the van. I started my engine as he pulled the van forward, turned it around at the end of the lane, and drove back toward the gate.

I caught up with the van and Benny's Nova as they turned onto the eastbound entrance ramp to Highway 70. We followed the van into the city and then south on Kingshighway to the Central West End. The van turned east on McPherson

Avenue, drove several blocks, and pulled to a stop in front of the Leo Beaumont Gallery. Benny was the second car in the convoy. Wisely, he drove down the block past the van and turned right at the next corner.

The Leo Beaumont Gallery was two doors in from the street corner. So as not to draw attention to my car, I turned at the street corner before the gallery and pulled the car over just beyond the bus stop. I grabbed my camera, jogged back to McPherson, and walked cautiously down the sidewalk along the opposite side of the darkened gallery. Using a parked minivan as a screen, I crouched near its back fender.

I got there just as the skinny driver rang the doorbell to the gallery. I raised the camera and kept the angle wide enough to get the man and the gallery sign.

Click.

A few seconds later a light went on somewhere near the back of the gallery. I could make out the shape of a man moving toward the front of the gallery. I focused on the door just as it was opened by a large man in a white turtleneck and dark slacks.

Click.

He was more than large. He was obese. Everything about him looked oversized—his nose, his bald head, his mouth, his hands. He towered over the skinny guy with the goatee.

Click.

The skinny guy gestured toward the van. The big guy nodded. They both stepped inside the gallery and moved to the back and out of sight.

"What's happened so far?"

I jumped at the sound of his voice, almost losing my balance. "Oh, God, Benny, don't sneak up like that."

"Sorry. What did I miss?"

"The guy from the van is in the gallery."

"What did he take out of the storage space?"

"Three big flat objects covered with sheets. I'd guess framed pictures."

"Here he comes," Benny said.

The skinny guy came out of the gallery with a lit cigarette dangling from his mouth. The big guy waited at the door. I got the camera ready. The skinny guy took the first shrouded object out of the van.

Click.

He walked with it back to the gallery and handed it to the big guy at the doorway.

Click.

The big guy took it into the back of the gallery somewhere.

They repeated it twice more, although the final time the skinny guy paused at the entrance to the gallery and looked back at the van.

Click.

Then he took the sheet-draped object into the gallery himself. Once inside, the big guy had him stop for a moment so that he could lift the sheet up and take a peek.

Click.

It was definitely a painting, although the peek was so brief that I hadn't been able to tell what the painting was. The two men disappeared into the back of the gallery.

"That's all he took out of the Mound City storage area," I said to Benny. "Just those three."

"It's got to be a fencing operation."

"Here they come," I said. "You stay here."

The skinny guy was twirling his car keys as he came out of the gallery. Behind him, the fat guy locked the door.

"See you back home," I whispered to Benny as I turned toward where I had left my car.

Benny touched my shoulder. "Remember what you said. No heroics."

The van sped past the sign on I-64 announcing LAST MISSOURI EXIT. I was in the right lane two cars back of the van, which was in the center lane. My speedometer showed sixty-eight miles per hour. We held that speed as we crossed the Mississippi River on the Poplar Street Bridge. The van moved to the right lane as it passed under the WELCOME TO ILLINOIS sign that marked the halfway point across the river. I was still two cars back.

I gripped the steering wheel as we came off the bridge high above East St. Louis and zoomed through the dizzying lattice-work of merging and branching lanes as the various highways that had squeezed into two lanes to cross the river began veering off to the north or south. Up ahead the van pulled onto an exit ramp on the right. I caught the word "Sauget" on the exit sign as I sped down the ramp. I could see the van turn right onto the undivided state highway.

After less than a mile the van slowed as it approached a lighted sign that pointed the way to P.T.'s Showplace. The van followed the flashing arrows into the immense parking lot. I parked one aisle over from the van and waited inside my car until the skinny guy passed through the front doors of P.T.'s. As I stepped out and approached the entrance to the best-known topless dance bar in metropolitan St. Louis, there was no need to remind myself that I had no idea what I was doing. The two enormous bouncers nodded politely as I walked past. The cover-charge guy waved me past, explaining, "No charge for the ladies, ma'am."

As I walked into the main area, Madonna's "Like a Virgin" was wailing over a sound system so powerful that the walls seemed to vibrate. There were twelve extremely sturdy octagonal tables—mini-stages, actually—strategically placed throughout an area the size of a ballroom. Each table was ringed by eight chairs, and each chair was occupied by a man in heat. There were well over a hundred men in the large room—young and old, T-shirts and Armanis, construction boots and wing-tips, motorcycle jackets and Lacoste shirts. From the odors, most were drinking lots of beer, smoking lots of cigarettes, and sweating lots of sweat.

I counted seventeen other women in the room. Five were barmaids, tarted up in English chambermaid outfits and moving through the room with trays of drinks balanced on one hand over their heads. Twelve were in various stages of undress up on the tables, gyrating to the music, some still with their full costumes on, others down to spike heels, G-strings, and a garter. And then there was female number eighteen: little ole inconspicuous me, way behind in sleep and fresh from several hours cooped up in a car, dressed in faded jeans, a St. Louis Cardinals jersey, and jogging shoes.

I moved slowly through the room, trying to hang back in the shadows beyond the mini-stages as I scanned the faces for the little guy with the goatee. I tried to avoid eye contact, but it wasn't always possible. Some of the men started when they saw me, quickly averting their eyes, as if caught masturbating. Others gave me a big grin and tried to sidle over for some conversation or to buy me a drink. I kept moving.

I spotted my guy at a tableside seat. I arrived just in time to see him take a big swallow of beer, set his beer glass back on the table, and put a dollar bill between his teeth. He was staring up at the dancer, who had her back to him as she entertained the other side of the table. She was a tall black woman in a red G-string. Her garter was festooned with dozens of folded dollar bills. My guy strained upward as she turned to his side of the table, the dollar bill dangling from between his teeth. He had greasy hair and a scraggly goatee. The bright overhead spots highlighted the pockmarks on his cheeks, forehead, and neck. His hands were on the table, each clenched into fists. The letters H-A-T-E were tattooed on the knuckles of his right hand and L-O-V-E on the left.

The black dancer smiled down at him as she rotated her hips in time to the beat. Her large, round breasts moved in syncopated time. Squatting in front of him, she cupped a hand under each breast and let him press his face between them. She squeezed her breasts together and moved away slowly, pulling the dollar bill out of his mouth in the process. Still grinding, she stood up, took the bill, folded it longways, and slid it under the elastic garter belt as she turned to the next guy. He had his hand resting on the table and was holding a ten-dollar bill. When he saw he had her attention, he rolled the bill lengthwise into a tube. Holding the tube pointed upward, he waggled it at her. As she squatted over the money tube and started running her fingers up and down the front of her G-string, my guy took a big gulp of his beer, wiped his mouth with the back of his arm, and jammed another bill between his teeth.

I turned and pushed through the crowd toward the exit. I decided to wait outside in my car for my guy to leave and, presumably, go home. I'd seen enough of P.T.'s action for this lifetime.

The parking lot was brightly lit. Although it was after three in the morning, there were still carloads of men pulling into the lot. I ignored the honks and shouts of "Hey, mama" and

"Yo, baby" as I walked to my car. Are there guys out there who actually think a honk of the horn followed by a "Yo, baby!" has an aphrodisiac effect on women?

I got in my car, locked the door, and turned on the radio. I tried several stations until I came across one of those golden-oldie formats. They were playing "Love Is Like a Heat Wave" by Martha Reeves and the Vandellas, which only happens to be one of the five greatest songs of the twentieth century. I yawned and stretched my arms over my head, pressing my palms against the car ceiling. Bobbing my head in time to the beat, I decided that finding a radio station playing Martha Reeves had to be a good omen. I folded my arms and scrunched back into the corner by the door to wait. I could just see the top of the brown van.

It was exciting at first—arousing, actually. I stood above them, wearing a white wedding dress, white gloves, a white veil, and white spike heels. What none of them knew but would all soon discover was that under that virginal white was a black pushup camisole and matching string bikini. The long white gloves came off first, one at a time. The men cheered and applauded as I slowly unpeeled the second glove, waved it over my head, and tossed it to one of them. Then the dress. I sashayed around the mini-stage in my black camisole, black bikinis, and spike heels.

As the music shifted to Marvin Gaye's "Heard It Through the Grapevine," I suddenly stood still, legs apart, head down. Then my left leg started moving in time to the beat. The men began rooting and pounding the table as I slowly unbuttoned the camisole. There were six buttons. When I reached the fourth one, someone grabbed my leg. I looked up, startled. Nick Kazankis was holding my leg. His face was bright red and his eyes were blazing. He was roaring drunk. "Get over here, pussy!" he shouted. "Sit on my face." Standing directly behind him was Christine Maxwell, dressed as a homecoming queen. She glared up at me, the diamonds in her crown sparkling. "I told you not to fuck with me, bitch," she said with a smirk.

Appalled, I tried to back away. Someone behind grabbed my other thigh. Someone else slid a rough hand up my leg under the back of my panties. I jerked around. Another Nick Kazankis. And another. Stumbling away, I saw eight Kazankis clones, each with a homecoming queen behind him. I spun around. Two of them were climbing onto the table. One had his zipper down and was waggling an enormous half-erect penis at me. There was the scrape of metal as the others started pushing back their chairs. As one of them grabbed my left breast I tried to lurch away.

As I lurched, I banged my head on the window and immediately woke up, completely disoriented. I was alone in my car. I sat up, blinking in the sunlight as "Heard It Through the Grapevine" came to an end. The DJ announced that it was time for the traffic report. I massaged my left side, which was painfully sore from the way I had slept. I looked out the window and scanned the parking lot. There were several dozen cars and trucks, but no brown Ford Econoline van.

I banged my hand against the steering wheel in frustration.

24

CHAPTER

I called home from a gas station pay phone to assure my mother that I was okay.

"Thank God," she said. "Oy, what a night."

"Have you heard from Benny?"

"Heard from him? He's been here for hours. He can't sit still from worrying about you. He's got *spilkes*, poor thing. And you know how he eats when he's nervous."

"How bad?"

"He stopped by Dunkin' Donuts on his way here. He brought a dozen doughnuts."

"Oh, no. How many?"

"Nine so far."

"Is he sick?"

"Sick? Him? He's got the digestive tract of Godzilla."

"Tell him I'll be there soon."

"Listen, Rachel." She lowered her voice. "Don't get upset when you see the front window."

I could feel my heartbeat accelerate. "What happened?"

"What a night," she said with a weary sigh. "Maury was asleep in the living room when Benny got here. Maury got startled and grabbed for his gun. It went off by accident."

"Oh, my God. He shot at Benny?"

"No, no. No one's hurt. Nothing like that. Maury didn't even aim before it went off. The shot blew out the front window. The only damage was the window and the curtain." She paused. "Maury feels terrible, the poor man. He called one of those board-up outfits and he's already been on the phone with the claims adjuster for the insurance company. They'll have someone out this morning."

I couldn't help smiling at the vision of a startled Tex Bernstein blasting out the front window. "Is he still there, Mom?"

"No. He had to go home to change. He's in the middle of that jury trial."

On the way home I dropped the roll of film off at a photo lab that promised to develop it and make prints by noon. When I pulled up to the house there were two men from the board-up company in the front yard taking measurements of the window. They had two sheets of plywood resting against the side of the house. The entire front lawn was sparkling with shards of glass reflecting the morning sun.

Benny and my mother were waiting inside.

"You okay?" I asked him with concern, trying to keep a straight face.

"Me?" Benny said with an ironic chuckle. "Nothing like walking up to your front porch at four-thirty in the morning, the whole world asleep, and suddenly—KA-BOOM!—I'm in the middle of goddamn *Terminator 3*."

Biting my lip, I gave him a hug. "Poor Benny," I said, patting him on his back.

"I'll tell you one thing," he said with a shake of his head. "The explosion seems to have forced my bowels into compression shock."

"I'll get some Ex-Lax," my mother said.

"Ex-Lax," he said with a look of disbelief. "How 'bout a jackhammer, Sarah?" He turned toward me and checked his watch. "Meanwhile . . ." He wagged his finger at me. "Out all night?" he said, slipping into his Desi Arnaz impression. "Lucy, you got some essplaining to do."

I filled them in on the evening's adventures, leaving out only my bad dream at the end. "How 'bout your guy?" I asked Benny when I was finished.

"There is no God," he said glumly. "You end up in a strip joint surrounded by naked babes and I get to spend some quality time watching a fatso stand in front of a filing cabinet in the back office of that gallery. He stood there for close to an hour leafing through the files with one hand while using the other to deal with what appeared to be a massive UD problem."

"What's a UD problem?" my mother asked.

"Underwear displacement," I told her, still looking at Benny. "And then what?" I asked him.

"And then he went home."

"Where's home?"

"Downtown. Mansion House." The Mansion House is an apartment complex overlooking the Mississippi River. "He got there around four-thirty. Parked his car in the building garage. I hung around for another half hour and then headed back here for a run-in with Davy Crockett at the fucking Alamo."

"What's his name?" I asked as I walked over to the telephone.

Benny shrugged. "Leo Beaumont, I assume. The place is called the Leo Beaumont Gallery. Sarah found a listing in the phone book for a Leo Beaumont at the Mansion House."

I looked at Benny. "You and I are going to go see Mr. Leo Beaumont today."

Benny nodded. "When?"

I lifted the receiver. "As soon as those pictures are developed."

"Who are you calling?" my mother asked me.

"Kevin Turelli."

"Kevin?" she said. "Why?"

"He can run a trace on the Illinois license plates."

Kevin Turelli and I met as first-year associates at Abbott & Windsor in Chicago. In fact, we shared an office our first year—a twenty-four-year-old graduate of Harvard Law School and a forty-four-year-old ex-cop from the west side who had worked his way through night school at John Marshall Law School. We hit it off immediately, and remained good pals when, three years later, he left A&W to return to the Chicago Police Department under a fast-track arrangement. These days Kevin was a captain assigned to homicide down at 11th and State, which he called the "smart shop." In a perfect system of government—i.e., not Chicago—he'd be police commissioner someday.

Fortunately, I caught him in the office. He told me all the family news: Kevin Jr. was graduating from college this year, his daughter was pregnant with number three, and his mother had asked him three times whether I was coming to Chicago for Memorial Day.

"Mama's planning one of her feasts," he told me, "and she wants to know if you can come. If you're going to be in town, you'd better plan on coming if you know what's good for you."

I was grinning. "I know what's good for me." I was crazy about Kevin's mother, Katie Turelli (nee O'Donoghue)—a strong-willed Irish immigrant who shocked her family by marrying Mario Turelli, shocked Mario's family by wearing pants back when women didn't wear pants, and eventually won them all back over by bearing eight children named, in descending order, Vito, Patrick, Antonio, Kevin, Megan, Fiorella, Mary Pat, and Gina.

"So what do you need?" Kevin asked.

"I need you to trace an Illinois license plate for me."

"Let me get a pencil." There was a pause while he got it. "Okay," he said.

I gave him the number. "Thanks, Kevin."

"Just a minute," he said, his voice taking on a law enforcement edge. "What's going on?"

"I'm not sure. I think the guy's dealing in stolen goods."

"Uh-huh," he said sternly. "And since when did you join the force?"

"Kevin, all I want to know is who he is and where he lives."

"Rachel, Rachel," he said with exasperation. "Okay, call me in an hour."

I waited an hour and called him back.

"You wanna run this setup by me again?" he asked.

"There is no setup," I told him. "Just some hunches."

"Tell me about these hunches."

I told him about the storage space at Mound City Mini-Storage and the apparent fencing operation I had observed.

"So who is he?" I asked.

"A real scuzzball."

"Define 'scuzzball.' "

"He served four years for burglary."

"Where?"

"Missouri. Moberly. He's got a string of priors in southern Illinois as well. Mostly breaking-and-enterings, one DWI. Word is he does enforcement for a loan shark in Springfield named Zemeckis."

"What's enforcement?"

"Collections, mostly, which includes roughing up the slow pays. Like I say, a scuzzball."

"What's his name?"

"Ricketts. Pete Ricketts. Two t's. He lives in Belleville. His number's unlisted, and I'm not giving you his address. If it's important, you tell the homicide dick on your sister's case to call me and I'll give it to him."

"Kevin, I—"

"Rachel," he interrupted, "we went through something like this once before and you almost got killed. You need more, have that detective call me. Okay?"

"I'll try."

"And promise me you won't contact this scuzzball before then."

I gave him a weary sigh. "Okay, Kevin. Thanks."

If Pete Ricketts was a scuzzball, he certainly looked the part. If Leo Beaumont was also one, he was cast against type.

When greeting a prospective customer in his art gallery, Leo Beaumont was anything but a sweaty fatso with a UD problem. No, he was a portly charmer, a perfumed rotundity. Especially when the prospective customer passing through the front door was none other than Marsha Newman, the recent divorcée back from Palm Beach with money to burn and a new home to decorate, which is how Benny had described me to Beaumont over the phone. With some help from Ann, I tried to dress the part: a gold Matka silk jacket over a navy-and-ivory batik print blouse and matching pleated skirt, a gold beaded necklace and matching drop earrings. I looked *très* elegant, dahling.

Leo Beaumont glided across the floor toward me with surprising grace. With his large bald head and tiny pink ears, he reminded me of one of the hippo ballerinas in Walt Disney's *Fantasia*. There was a red carnation pinned to the lapel of his freshly pressed cream-colored suit. He had matching diamond pinky rings and gleaming black patent-leather shoes. His nostrils seemed to twitch at the scent of a big fee.

"Ah, Miss Newman," he purred with delight as he took my hand in one of his and covered it with the other. His hands were soft and moist. The fingers were as thick as knockwursts. "I am honored to place my modest talents at your disposal."

I nodded and said nothing.

Beaumont turned to Benny and smiled. "And you must be this lovely lady's, uh, personal assistant?"

Benny nodded gravely. He looked more than a little sinister in his dark suit, aviator sunglasses, and slicked-back black hair. His two-day growth added the perfect final touch.

Beaumont pivoted beside me and put a hand gently on my elbow. "Let us withdraw to my office, madame, where we can discuss your decorating concepts without distraction." He had thick lips the color and texture of raw liver.

When we reached the door to the office I turned to Benny. "Gerald, wait for me here."

Benny nodded. "No problema, Miss Newman," he said with an exaggerated version of his natural New Jersey accent. He would have made Central Casting proud.

Beaumont ushered me into his office, which was furnished with chrome-and-glass furniture upholstered with soft white leather. He guided me to a chair beside a coffee table. On the table were three large loose-leaf notebooks filled with 8 × 10 color photographs of the gallery's inventory of art. The walls of his office were hung with framed art posters, mostly from European exhibitions of contemporary artists. The one nearest me was personally autographed by the artist "to Leo B. with admiration."

Beaumont offered mineral water, which I declined, and then he offered white wine, which I also declined. He shrugged good-naturedly. "Very well, Miss Newman. Perhaps you'll develop a thirst once we finish." Chortling with admiration of his little *bon mot,* he pulled a chair alongside me, presumably so that we could look together at the contents of the three notebooks.

"But in order to finish," he said, "we need to know where to begin." Leaning back in his chair, he placed both hands on his left knee and smiled appreciatively at what he no doubt believed was a clever segue into the business at hand. He leaned toward me. "Tell me about your preferences, Miss Newman."

I gave him an arch look. "I beg your pardon."

That triggered another chortle. He was a mouth breather who ended each laugh with what sounded like a gasp. "In art, my dear lady. In art. Some of my clients arrive with a strong predilection, be it for a period or a particular artist. At the other end, some—most, perhaps—look to me to suggest possible additions to their collections." He ended with a tilt of his head, an expectant look, and a gasp through his open mouth.

"I'm the former," I said.

"Excellent, Miss Newman. Excellent. Is your preference for a period or a particular artist?"

"Neither. I'm here for a particular painting."

"I like a woman who knows what she wants." Another chortle, another gasp. "Which one of my works caught your fancy?"

"This one," I said. I opened my purse, removed the photograph, and placed it on the coffee table between Beaumont and me.

Beaumont leaned over to examine it.

It was the shot I had taken of him inside the gallery as he lifted the corner of the sheet to peek at the painting underneath. Pete Ricketts was holding the painting, and his face was visible in the shot.

Beaumont's breath rasped in his throat as he slowly straightened in his seat. He was still staring at the photograph, reluctant to look at me.

I reached into my purse and removed a second photograph. "Or this one," I said as I placed it alongside the first. In this shot Ricketts was removing a shrouded painting from the back of his van. As a result of the foreshortened perspective caused by the telephoto lens, Ricketts was in focus in the lower left quadrant of the photograph while the gallery sign— LEO BEAUMONT GALLERY—and Beaumont himself, standing in the doorway beneath the sign, were clearly visible in the upper half.

Beaumont's eyes darted back and forth from one photograph to the other. Beads of sweat had formed on his upper lip and on his forehead. His breathing seemed to rattle. He still hadn't looked at me.

"You have a problem, Leo," I said in a firm but patient tone. "A big one."

He removed the neatly folded silk handkerchief from his breast pocket and used it to mop his forehead. He stared down at his knees.

"I also have a problem, Leo. A little one."

He continued to stare at his knees.

"I don't really want that picture. I want something else."

He glanced at me with a wince. "What?" he said in a constricted voice.

"I don't know whether you can get it for me or whether the police can. That's a problem for me. Who do I go to? You? The police? I decided to start with you. I have eleven other shots of you, Leo. Some with Pete Ricketts, some just of you. All taken last night. Very nice shots. Clear. In focus. Perfect for a jury, if you catch my drift, Leo. Right now the negatives are being held by my lawyer. He has instructions to give them to the police tomorrow unless I tell him otherwise before then. In a nutshell, that's my problem, Leo."

"What do you want?" he said. His eyes darted toward me and retreated back to his knees.

"I want the name at the top, Leo."

"Of what?"

"Of your little fencing operation."

Beaumont said nothing.

"Pete's obviously not running anything. Neither are you. Who is?"

Beaumont mopped his face again. "I can't tell you that."

I made a tsk-tsk sound. "That's too bad."

"No," he said anxiously, "I don't mean it like that. I can't tell you because I don't know. I thought I knew, but now I don't."

"What do you mean, 'now I don't'?"

He looked around the room furtively. "Because *he's* dead. He's dead, but it's still running."

"Who?"

"That horrid exercise man," he blurted.

"Why did you think he was running it?"

He shook his head, eyes down.

"Why?" I repeated.

"The tapes," he said tensely.

"What tapes?"

"His tapes."

"Andros?"

He nodded.

"What kind of tapes?" I asked.

He mopped his face with the handkerchief. I could smell the sour odor of his sweat.

"What kind of tapes?" I repeated.

He shook his head vigorously. "I can't. You don't understand." He looked up, terror in his eyes. "These people are animals. Carnivores. I've said too much already. I'll never do that kind of thing again. Never." He was starting to plead. "I promise you. The money was easy. I was weak. I'll give the money away. I promise. I'll give it to any charity you name. I'll give it to you." He smiled tentatively at me. "But of course. You can have it all. Please don't give those photos to the police. I'm begging you."

"Then tell me about the tapes," I said evenly.

He banged his thigh with his fist. "I can't!" he cried. His face was collapsing before my eyes, like a Madame Tussaud wax figure under a sunlamp. He moaned. "These are bad people. That man last night—he's a thug. A hyena. He'd kill me in a minute. If I tell you, he'll know. They'll know. They'll kill me."

"Who are they?" I asked.

"Please," he pleaded, his eyes wide with fear. "Just find the tapes. That's all you'll need. But, dear God, please don't give those pictures to the police. It's a death sentence. I implore you."

He started weeping. Head in his hands, sobbing, his entire body heaving. I stood up, staring at him. He was shaking his head from side to side.

I backed out of his office and closed the door.

25

CHAPTER

The police inventory was seventeen pages long. There were twenty-seven CDs and thirty-nine LPs on the list, but no audiotapes. There was duct tape, masking tape, Scotch tape. There were nineteen videotapes, all store-bought, including five workout videos and fifteen titles that sounded distinctly X-rated: *2069: A Sex Odyssey, Rear Entry III, Star Whores, Riders of the Lust Ark.*

Benny and I were at my office studying the police inventory of the contents of Andros's apartment. We had come there after my encounter with Leo Beaumont.

I stood up and walked over to the window. "I don't see how any of those videotapes could have anything to do with a fencing operation," I said. I peered through the blinds. Two women on roller blades zoomed past on the sidewalk.

"Well," Benny said with a shrug, "we could always force ourselves to watch them."

I looked over with a wan smile and shook my head. "Only as a last resort. We'd have to get them from the police. My credibility with them is already lower than ... lower than ..." I shrugged.

"Whale shit."

"Something like that. Look, if I'm actually able to develop something coherent out of this Mound City fencing operation—something that will actually point them somewhere other than Ann—I don't want them to blow me off as some silly snatch, which is exactly what they'll do if I go over there and ask them to let us watch twenty hours of X-rated videos because we think there just might be a clue in one of the movies."

"Actually," Benny said, rubbing his chin judiciously, "*Star Whores* is pretty good for a skin flick."

"Right. And Rudolf Hess is pretty good for a Nazi."

He crossed his arms and raised his eyebrows in an exaggerated manner. "Well, *excuse* me, Phyllis Schlafly."

I put my hands on my hips and shook my head. "For your information, outside the realm of those movies there is no woman in America whose idea of making love includes having the man ejaculate in her face."

"Not an aficionada of the cum shot, eh?"

"Don't get me started. Look, if we can't find any other tapes, then *maybe* I'll ask the police to let us watch them. But not until then."

"What about the Firm Ambitions space?" Benny asked. "You were in there."

"I didn't see any tapes, video or audio. Just CDs."

"So where'd he keep them?"

"*If* he kept them."

"His car?"

I shook my head. "None on the car inventory, either." And then I remembered. "However . . ." I turned toward the safe in the corner.

"What?" Benny asked as I kneeled down and spun the combination dial.

"Wait." I finished the combination, yanked the handle on the safe, and pulled the door open. I removed the Lands' End attaché.

"Who does that belong to?" Benny asked.

"Andros," I said as I placed it on the desk and opened it.

"How the hell did you end up with his briefcase?"

I pushed the Polaroid Impulse camera and the vibrator to one side of the bag and poked around. "This is one of the special little surprises that keep our relationship sizzling." I looked up and gave him a wink.

"What?"

I lifted out three microcassette audiotapes and put them on the desk. Each had a hand-printed title on the stick-on label:

DANCE ROUTINE
LOW-IMPACT WORKOUT
HIGH-IMPACT ROUTINE W/JAZZ STEPS.

Benny looked at me with a dubious frown. "So?"

"These are audiotapes," I said. "Like the kind you use for dictation."

Benny read off the names. "Sound like exercise routines," he said.

"Maybe. Probably. But they're the only homemade tapes we know of." I opened my desk and pulled out my portable dictaphone. "Let's hear one."

I tried to insert the microcassette, but it wouldn't fit.

"Wrong size?" Benny asked.

I nodded, looking at the tape. According to the label, it was a Leuwenhaupt Model 5400. I looked at my dictaphone. It was a Pearlcorder Model 5804, manufactured by the Olympus Optical Co. of Japan. I opened the drawer and took out one of my dictation microcassettes. It was a Model MC-60, also manufactured by the Olympus Optical Company. My microcassette was maybe an eighth of an inch shorter and narrower than the ones that were in Andros's attaché.

"These things aren't standardized," Benny said. "Remember when they switched portable recorders back at Abbott & Windsor? They had to buy a whole new set of tapes to go with them."

I put the three microcassettes into my purse. "Come on," I said. "Let's go to an office supplies store."

"Huh?"

"We'll borrow one of their models and listen to the tapes."

According to the nametag, his name was Bob and he was eager to help. But when he came back from the stockroom carrying a folded slip of paper, all he could do was shake his head.

"I'm sorry, ma'am. We don't carry any Leuwenhaupt products. None of our St. Louis stores does. I don't think they have any retail outlets in town."

"Are they out of business?" I asked.

"No. My boss says they're a specialty electronics manufacturer. Located in Belgium. They market to certain professions, usually at trade shows or through office consultants. They have two U.S. manufacturer's reps, one in Boston and one in Chicago." He handed me the slip of paper. "Here's their Chicago number."

I thanked him and removed one of the microcassettes from my purse. "Do you have any other dictaphones that take this size tape?"

He studied it with a frown. "Well . . ." he said as he looked down at the three rows of portable recorders in the glass case.

He didn't. We tried all twenty-three of them, and none were the right size for a Leuwenhaupt Model 5400.

I dialed the Chicago number from a pay phone outside the store. It was answered on the fifth ring:

"You have reached the Midwest regional office of the Leuwenhaupt Corporation. Our business hours are seventhirty A.M. to three-thirty P.M. Monday through Friday." I checked my watch: 4:12 P.M. "If you are calling from a touchtone phone and would like to receive our current product catalogue, please press one—"

I hung up and turned to Benny. "Closed for the day. I'll try first thing tomorrow. When do you leave for Chicago?"

"Tomorrow around noon."

"I may have a place for you to visit when you're up there."

My mother and I had dinner that night with a much less feisty Tex Bernstein, who'd come back to stand guard with his sleeping bag and shotgun. The boarded-up picture window was visible from the breakfast room, and occasionally during dinner I caught Tex furtively glancing toward it. We gave him an extra slice of cherry pie with a scoop of Cherry Garcia, and that seemed to cheer him up some. The Cardinals were on TV, and that made him even happier. He watched the game as we cleaned up.

"He's a good man," my mother said softly.

I nodded. "It's sort of nice to have him around."

The phone rang and my mother answered it. She looked at me quizzically and held out the receiver.

"Hello?" I said.

"This is Kimmi Buckner. I want you to leave me alone."

I was surprised to hear her voice—and relieved to know she was alive. "Where are you?" I asked.

"I'm not telling you, Miss Gold. I've taken my things and I've left. I didn't like St. Louis anyway. And I want you to stop bothering me."

"I didn't mean to bother you. All I did was leave you my business card."

"Sure," she snorted.

"Really," I said. "That's all I did."

"Well, someone's been looking for me, and I don't like it one bit."

"All I wanted was to ask you one question."

She paused. "What question?"

It took me a moment to recall. "Mound City Mini-Storage. I wanted to ask what you knew about it."

Another pause. "Nothing."

"Nothing?"

"Nothing. Now leave me alone."

"One more thing," I said quickly. "When we talked, you told me that one of your duties was typing letters for Andros."

"So?"

"Did he dictate those letters to you?"

"Some."

"Did he use a machine?"

"Huh?"

"Did he dictate it into a machine, into one of those dicta-phones?"

"No. I take shorthand. He dictated, I took it down, then I typed it up."

"Did you ever see him use a portable dictation re-corder?"

"No."

"You're sure?"

"I don't know nothing about no recorders, okay? You leave

me alone." There was a click at the other end, followed by a dial tone.

I hung up the phone and sat down with a frown.

My mother came over and sat across from me. "Why are you obsessed about those dictation tapes?" She sounded dubious.

"Let me show you," I said as I reached for my briefcase and lifted out the computer printout.

"What's that?"

"It's the Firm Ambitions accounts payable ledger."

"What's an accounts payable ledger?"

"A list of everyone that sent Firm Ambitions a bill. Everyone from the electric company to the outfit that services the copy machine. The printout goes back three years." I flipped to the third page. "Look at this," I said, pointing at the entry for Leuwenhaupt.

My mother leaned over to see.

"That's the company that manufactures the microcassettes," I explained.

"One hundred and twenty-five dollars," my mother read.

"That has to be for more than just a set of microcassettes."

"Of course it is, Rachel, dear. You told me yourself that you have to have one of those dictation machines from that company to record the tapes, right?"

"Right."

"So that must be the bill for the machine."

"That's my assumption, too, Mom."

My mother leaned back and gave me a puzzled look. "And that's what makes you suspicious?"

I nodded. "I have the police inventory for his apartment, for his car, and for Firm Ambitions. And I have the attaché bag that Eileen took from the hotel. Guess what isn't on any inventory and isn't in his bag?"

My mother mulled that over. "So maybe it broke. Maybe it broke and he threw it away."

"Maybe. Or maybe someone else took it when he died. Maybe someone didn't want the police to find it."

"Who?"

"Whoever arranged for that guy to take those paintings

from the Mound City Mini-Storage space to Leo Beaumont's gallery the other night, that's who."

"But why?"

"Mom, assume that there's something incriminating on those tapes. If so, then whoever was involved wanted to make sure that the police never found the tapes or the portable recorder. Presumably, they knew where Andros kept the equipment. When Andros died, they broke into his house or his car or wherever he kept the stuff and took it. They got everything—except, of course, what he was carrying with him in that attaché bag."

My mother frowned in concentration. "You really think so?"

"I don't know what to think, Mom. The fat man at the art gallery said that the tapes were the key. These are the only tapes I've been able to find."

"Did you learn anything from that woman on the phone?"

I shrugged in frustration. "I'm not sure. She took his dictation in shorthand. She said she never saw him use a dictaphone. If he had, she would have needed one of those transcribers, anyway." I gestured toward the printout. "A hundred and twenty-five dollars might be enough for a portable recorder and some microcassettes, but it sure isn't enough for a recorder *and* a transcriber."

My mother shook her head angrily. "Have the police arrest that fat man. Maybe they can make him talk."

"Not after he calls his lawyer. You saw the pictures I took. At best, they're circumstantial evidence of a fencing operation. What do I have so far? Pictures of Pete Ricketts going into the storage space at Mound City and then coming back out with three things shrouded in sheets. Pictures of him carrying those things into Leo Beaumont's gallery at two in the morning. At most, we can say that one of the three things looked like a painting, at least from the corner of it that was visible when Beaumont lifted the sheet. But what paintings? Which paintings? Whose paintings? Those pictures don't even prove that the three things in sheets that Ricketts removed from the Firm Ambitions storage space are the *same* three things in sheets that he brought into the art gallery. Assuming that we could ever convince the police and the prosecuter to file charges in the first place, a good lawyer could get them dismissed." I stood up and walked over to the window. I stared out at the backyard. "We don't have anywhere near enough, yet." I turned to face her. "That's why I'm so obsessed about these tapes."

26

CHAPTER

"Good morning, Miss Gold." He had a gravelly, high-pitched voice that sounded remarkably like Walter Brennan's in *The Real McCoys.* "I'm calling on behalf of Christine Maxwell and Mrs. Maxwell's company."

I was seated at my desk. "Who is this?"

"This is Harry Raven, Miss Gold," he wheezed.

Harry Raven? I repeated to myself. The name was familiar. "What is it you want, Mr. Raven?"

"Welllll," he drawled, "that just happens to be the very question I was hoping to put to you, Miss Gold. I understand you showed up at my client's offices the other day, sort of out of the blue. I understand you started demanding to see any files Mrs. Maxwell might have on that dead exercise fella, threatening to slap subpoenas on that poor widow if she didn't get them files to you lickety-split. I guess that's where I come in." He chuckled and wheezed. "When they been threatened with legal action, most folks, God bless them, hire themselves a lawyer. Welllll, I told Christine maybe it was just a misunderstanding on her part. I told her maybe you were just having one of them bad days. Had a few myself over the years, Miss Gold. I told her I'd give you a call first, see if maybe we could sort of separate the wheat from the chaff. No need to start wrasslin' in the mud if we can work it out, eh?"

"That's fine with me," I said, trying to place his name.

"Which brings me back to my question, Miss Gold: Why do you want them files?"

"I think it's pretty obvious, Harry," I said with a trace of irritation. And suddenly the Harry Raven connection clicked: Nick the Greek. Charles Kimball had said that Nick Kazankis was represented by a Belleville lawyer named Harry Raven.

"Welllll," he said, "maybe what's purty obvious to a Harvard lawyer is still a little fuzzy to a U of I lawyer."

What was a southern Illinois lawyer doing representing a suburban St. Louis woman? I realized Raven had stopped talking. "Pardon?" I said.

"I said maybe you could help me understand what seemed so obvious to you. Why do you want them files?"

"She sold his company a policy insuring his life."

"Okay," he said patiently. "But that don't tell me why you want them files."

"Now he's dead," I said warily, trying to gauge how much I should reveal to Nick Kazankis's attorney.

"Sure can't dispute you there," he said with a wheezy chuckle. "Deader than a doornail, from what I understand. Matter of fact, I'd say it's a purty good thing he had life insurance. Seems to me his beneficiary ought to be purty happy. Seems to me that someone ought to be purty durn grateful to Mrs. Maxwell for selling him that policy. But that still don't answer my question, Miss Gold. That still don't tell me why you want them files."

I'd heard enough to know that this was a one-way street. Harry Raven would pump me for whatever he could get, and when I ran dry he'd give a wheeze and make a puzzled noise and say that he still didn't understand why I wanted them files. I was in no mood to get jerked around.

"Look," I said to him, "I'm just trying to shorten my list of suspects. It's like the song, Harry: I'm making my list, and I'm checking it twice, and I guarantee I'm going to find out who's been naughty or nice." I paused. "If Christine wants to be nice, fine. If not, she stays on the list. Talk it over with her, or with Nick, or with whoever it is you represent this time."

"Welllll, Miss Gold—"

"Goodbye, Harry."

I hung up and stared at the phone, daring him to try to call back. Twenty seconds later, the phone started ringing. I grabbed it before my secretary could answer.

"What?" I demanded.

"Uh, Miss Gold?" It wasn't Harry Raven.

"Yes?"

"This is Bruce Billings up at Leuwenhaupt."

"Oh, excuse me," I said, shifting mental gears. "I thought you were someone else."

I had called Leuwenhaupt's Chicago office first thing that morning, and the operator had connected me with someone named Bruce Billings. I told him I was acting on behalf of a group of small law firms who were in the market for dictation equipment. Bruce told me he'd send down some literature by overnight mail and would love to schedule me for lunch next time he was in St. Louis. That was fine, I told him, but in the meantime I needed to try out some of his dictation products right away because the Sony rep was coming to town the following week. I explained that I was particularly interested in portable equipment, especially recorders that used the Model 5400 microcassettes. Bruce had promised to find someone near my office who was willing to let me try their equipment and call me back with their name and address.

"Any luck?" I asked him.

"You bet," he said. "The Hendin Group. It's a small advertising agency on Euclid." He gave me the street address. It was just three blocks away from my office.

"Perfect," I said.

"Ask for Sheila. They have a portable recorder, a transcriber, and some extra microcassettes. Believe me, you're going to love it."

Before ending the conversation, I found out where his Chicago office was located. Unfortunately, it was out in Naperville, which was an hour's drive from the Loop. Benny had left for Chicago that morning, but it would be tough for him to get out to the boonies during business hours. In his role as expert witness, he'd be spending each day in the Loop, either in the law firm's offices getting prepared to testify or in a federal courtroom playing the role.

Sheila was in when I called the Hendin Group. "No problem, honey. Come on over around one o'clock and you can try them out. We just love the dang things."

My mother arrived at my office around noon with a large takeout bag from the St. Louis Bread Company. Inside were smoked-turkey-on-sourdough sandwiches, potato salad, pickles, two Diet Cokes, two large cups of hot Kona coffee, and—of course—French pastries. For my mother and me, all that comes before French pastries is mere prelude.

While we ate lunch, I brought her up to date, ending with Sheila's invitation. "You want to come hear the tapes?" I said while we were eating the pastries and sipping the Kona coffee.

She checked her watch. "I've got forty-five minutes," she said. "Can we go now?"

I stood up and dropped the empty coffee cup in the bag. "Come on."

I started with "Low-Impact Workout." Nothing. I pressed the FAST FORWARD button for a few seconds and then pressed PLAY again. Nothing. FAST FORWARD again, then PLAY. Nothing.

"Does it work?" my mother asked.

I nodded my head and turned up the volume until we could hear the background hiss. We were in a conference room at the Hendin Group's offices, just my mother and me.

I pressed FAST FORWARD again, held it for the count of five, then PLAY. Still nothing. I kept doing that until we reached the end of Side A. I flipped it over and pressed PLAY. Nothing. Nothing all the way through to the end of Side B. A blank tape.

I removed the microcassette and set it on the table next to the other two, labeled "Dance Routine" and "High-Impact Routine w/Jazz Steps." I picked "High-Impact," slotted it into the portable recorder, and pressed PLAY.

"THIS IS NUMBER—"

The noise was so loud I almost dropped the recorder. I pressed STOP, rewound it, lowered the volume, and pressed PLAY again:

"This is number five uh *click* number five Asbury Way. *click* This house is in Frontenac. *click*."

I stopped it. "That's him," I said. The accent was unmistakable.

"Andros?"

"Definitely."

"What's that clicking noise?"

"When you're dictating, every time you stop or pause the machine it makes that noise when you start up again." I pushed PLAY again:

"There's a door sensor on the front door, with a Telsor combination panel to the right when you come in. *click* There's one in the back. *click* There's one on the side porch, too. All with a Telsor panel on the wall to the right of the door. *click* Ground-floor windows have, uh, *click* magnetic contacts, surface-mounted." Off in the distance a woman's voice called, "Andros." Her voice was followed by a *click*.

"What is he talking about?" my mother asked.

I shrugged. "Sounds like he's describing the home security system."

I pressed the PLAY button.

"The master bedroom is up the stairs and down the hall to the right. *click* Aha. A motion detector. Infrared. Just outside the master bedroom. *click*."

There was background noise on the tape. The sound of water. A shower?

"Jewelry in top drawer of the vanity. *click* Lots of diamonds. *click*." There was the sound of a door opening. "Furs in the closet. *click* A study off the master bedroom. *click* A desk. A notebook computer on the desk. Toshiba T4400SXC. Looks new. *click* A printer on the side table. Hewlett-Packard LaserJet Series II. A little scratched." Then the woman's voice: "Andros, darling. *click*."

I looked at my mother and shook my head in amazement.

"Brilliant."

She nodded. "He's doing an inventory."

"Exactly," I said. "He gets in their houses for his personal workout sessions and his hot little affairs and he brings along his portable recorder. While the lady of the house is distracted—perhaps taking a shower after a workout or after they make love—he pokes around the house and records what he sees, including the security system."

We listened to the rest of the tape. Andros found a stamp collection and a Nikon camera in the study, a Macintosh SE computer with printer in the children's room, silver in the dining room. In the living room he described a Sony stereo system that sounded like it was worth more than my car. He also described several framed paintings in sufficient detail (including artist's name) for someone like Leo Beaumont to determine whether they were worth stealing. Three or four times during the tape we heard that same woman's voice. Once she asked him who he was talking to. We didn't hear the answer.

I looked with amazement at my mother when we reached the end of the tape. "Not bad."

She nodded. "Not bad at all."

The third tape—"Dance Routine"—was blank.

"Jewelry in top drawer of the vanity. *click* Lots of diamonds. *click.*" There was the sound of a door opening. "Furs in the closet. *click* A study off the master bedroom. *click* A desk. A notebook computer on the desk. Toshiba T4400SXC. Looks new. *click* A printer on the side table. Hewlett-Packard LaserJet Series II. A little scratched." Then the woman's voice: "Andros, darling. *click.*"

I turned off the recorder.

"That bastard." Brenda Roberts stood up, hands on her hips. "That son of a bitch." She stormed out of the room.

I was seated at the breakfast table in the huge country kitchen of 5 Asbury Way. It was the home of Dr. and Mrs. Louis Roberts. According to the appointment calendar I had printed off the computer at Firm Ambitions, Andros had had a personal fitness session with Brenda Roberts at 5 Asbury Way at 10:00 A.M. two days before he died. It was his third session at her home that month.

I had called Brenda from my office and arranged to meet with her at four-thirty that afternoon. The people at the Hendin Group had been nice enough to let me borrow the portable recorder for the rest of the afternoon. Brenda met me at the door dressed in heels and a fluorescent exercise outfit. She had frosted hair, a dark tan with sun freckles on her chest and upper arms, and an extra fifteen pounds bunched mostly in her stomach, hips, and thighs. When she opened the front door, I immediately recognized her from Andros's X-rated photo album.

For a moment I had hesitated, realizing that if I was right this woman would have to deal with the additional humiliation of knowing not only that he had used her sexually but that the sexual part was purely incidental to his principal objective. However, I reminded myself, my sister was facing far more than just the bitter knowledge that her lover had betrayed her.

I looked up from my musings as Brenda Roberts returned to the kitchen with her eye makeup smeared. "I'm sorry, Mrs. Roberts," I said gently. "I needed to confirm what was on the tape. I'm sorry about the pain."

She waved her hand dismissively as she wiped her nose with a tissue.

"He was a despicable person," I told her, trying to find words to help cushion her suffering. "He did the same thing to my sister and to many others. It's how con men operate. He conned a lot of good, decent women."

She sat down across the table and looked at me, her eyes blinking back tears. "I went to his funeral. I cried at his funeral. Do you understand what that means? I cried at that bastard's funeral. That fucking goddam piece of shit bastard!" She dropped her head and covered her face with her right hand. Her other hand was still on the table, the fist clenching and unclenching. "Please leave," she said. "Now."

When I turned on the office lights, the first thing I saw was the in-box. It had increasingly come to dominate the landscape of my office. I'd been neglecting my practice ever since Ann's arrest, and the pile of unanswered correspondence and court filings had become an ominous mound. I checked my watch. Six thirty-five. No one but Ozzie was waiting for me at home. My mother was having dinner at Aunt Becky's, Tex Bernstein was in Kansas City for a three-day judicial conference, and Benny was in Chicago. My mother would have fed Ozzie before she left. I glanced again at my in-box. No excuses.

* * *

The house was dark when I pulled up the driveway at nine-thirty. As I got out of the car a police cruiser slowly drove past. Turning to watch it go by, I recalled that Tex Bernstein had told me that morning that he had arranged for the police to send a squad car by our house at least twice an hour for the nights he was gone. The officer waved at me as he drove on.

There was a folded note taped to the front door. Absent-mindedly, I removed it as I unlocked the door. Ozzie was there to greet me. I gave him a hug and rubbed his head and kissed his nose. He followed me into the kitchen. I clicked on the light and dropped my purse and briefcase onto the kitchen table. The red message light on the telephone answering machine was blinking. I pressed the play button on the answering machine and walked back to the breakfast room to check Ozzie's food and water bowls.

The first message was from my mother. "Rachel, I'm calling from Becky's. I fed Ozzie before I left. If you're hungry, there's chicken salad in the fridge and fresh bread in the bread box. I'll be home by nine, sweetie."

There was a beep, and then the second message began:

"Howdy, Sarah. Maury here, calling from the conference. Jes' checking in to see how things are going." He left his hotel telephone number and said he'd be up until eleven.

"Rachel, this is your Aunt Becky. It's about a quarter after nine. Your mother had an accident on her way home after dinner. She's a little banged up, but she'll be fine, darling. We're in the emergency room at Missouri Baptist." She ended the message with the telephone number for the emergency room.

As I grabbed the phone to call the emergency room, I realized I still had the note in my hand. I dialed the number and unfolded the note. It was a four-line poem, printed in red block letters:

> ROSES ARE RED,
> VIOLETS ARE BLUE,
> YOUR PUSSY WAS ONE,
> WHO'LL BE NUMBER TWO?

It was close to midnight when the hospital released my mother. She had a hairline fracture in her left wrist, which the doctors set and immobilized in a cast that ended below her elbow. She also had a red knob on her forehead and the beginnings of two black eyes.

As for the accident, all she knew for sure, and thus all she could tell the police, was that a large van had suddenly swerved in front of her on the highway. She had slammed on the brakes and turned hard to the right. The car skidded off the highway and slid down the embankment. Had it flipped over, my mother would have been in much worse shape.

The police were gone by the time I arrived at the hospital. My first thought had been Pete Ricketts and his battered Ford Econoline van with Illinois plates. But unfortunately, the accident had happened too fast for my mother to notice the make or color of the van or the number or color of the license plate.

On the way home, we talked about the roses-are-red note.

"If it was supposed to be a warning," I said, "I figure we still have at least a day or so for whoever it is to decide whether we've backed off. That's all we need. I'm getting close, Mom, and I'm not going to back off." I told her the outlines of the plan that had been forming in my head ever since the two of us had listened to the microcassettes that afternoon.

"I agree," she said when I finished. "Maury has the police driving by the house all night anyway. See first what you can learn from that man in Chicago."

"By the way," I said nonchalantly, "there was a message from Maury on the machine. He called to see how things are going."

We drove in silence for a while.

"I'm not going to tell him until he gets back," my mother said.

"Maury?"

She nodded. I drove on in silence, waiting.

"He means well," she finally said, "but the answer isn't John Wayne sleeping in our living room." She looked over at me. "I'm an adult. So are you. We're not in the little house on the prairie."

I glanced over at my mother and winked. "Welcome home, Annie Oakley."

A police cruiser was parked across the street from our

house when I pulled up. The officer got out of the cruiser and came over as I helped my mother out of the car.

"Need any help, ma'am?"

"We're okay," I told him.

He walked with us up to the front door. "We'll be keeping a closer watch tonight," he said when we reached the front porch. "After the accident and all. We'll send a car by three or four times an hour."

Knowing that the police were keeping watch outside helped ease our skittishness a little. Nevertheless, my mother and I slept together in her bed with Ozzie asleep on the bedroom carpet. I had a restless night as my emotions shifted from fear to cold rage over what someone had tried to do to my mother. Although it was certainly possible that she had been the victim of a reckless driver, the roses-are-red note had me convinced otherwise.

As I turned in bed, I rearranged the pieces of the puzzle for what seemed like the two hundredth time. If I was as close as I thought, then Leo Beaumont was right: the tapes were the key to Andros's death and the lever for getting Ann cleared. I smiled at the irony. Ann had begged me to represent her best friend in a divorce, and Eileen may have unintentionally repaid that friendship by grabbing the Lands' End bag holding the tapes.

All of which meant that the person unwittingly holding the final piece of the puzzle was Bruce Billings at Leuwenhaupt. The trick was to get him to give it up without realizing what he was doing. To accomplish that, I'd need a convincing sales pitch. When I finally drifted off to sleep around four in the morning, I had my speech roughed out.

27

CHAPTER

Fortunately, my sales pitch worked.

"The problem is," I had explained to Bruce over the phone that morning, "I'm dealing with lawyers and accountants. You know the type: conservative, risk-averse, easily impressed by brand names. The first thing I'm going to hear from each one of them is: 'Leuwenhaupt? What's that?' The second thing is: 'Who else uses them?' Bruce, these guys want to be part of the herd. What's going to sway them is knowing that you have plenty of other customers in St. Louis."

"I understand, Rachel. Let's see." I could hear paper rustling. "Here we are. I'm looking at our brochure on the 6400 Series. Page two. Listen to this. 'With more than ten thousand Model 6400 microrecorders currently in service around the world, Leuwenhaupt—' "

"Bruce, this is St. Louis. In this town, when someone asks where you went to school, he doesn't mean college, he means high school. That's how it works down here. We don't care what people are doing in New York or Chicago. I need St. Louis names, Bruce. In fact, I need the names, addresses, and products sold to each of your St. Louis customers for the past five years."

There was a pause. "Well, I don't know if I can do that. My company is kind of paranoid about its customer lists."

"I understand. Listen, I have to be in Chicago today for a meeting on LaSalle Street at noon. I'll swing by your offices at three o'clock. You show me the list confidentially and that way I'll at least be able to assure my people that I've personally seen it. How's that sound?"

"Well, I don't know if I—"

"Bruce, last month the Panasonic sales rep gave me a complete list of their St. Louis customers—everyone from Peat Marwick to the legal department at Monsanto. Where's the harm in letting me see your names?"

He eventually agreed, and I caught the twelve-thirty flight to Midway.

Unfortunately, as I remembered the moment I pulled the rental car onto the expressway near Midway, the first signs of spring in Chicago are, quite literally, signs. Road signs, that is. CONSTRUCTION AHEAD. MERGE LEFT. RIGHT LANE ENDS 500 FEET. SLOW AHEAD. They had sprouted all along the Eisenhower Expressway and the East-West Tollway. At the pace traffic was crawling, I knew that the seventeen-mile trip from Midway to the Leuwenhaupt offices would take roughly as long as the 287-mile flight from Lambert to Midway. I had a little over an hour to cover the distance, and I would need every minute.

At 3:15 P.M., I pulled into the parking lot of the suburban office complex that housed Leuwenhaupt's Chicago sales group. Bruce greeted me with a wet handshake and a blast of bad breath that would have stunned a charging lion. He had a lopsided Popeye smile in a face that looked like it was pressed up against glass. I assumed he did most of his sales work over the phone. He was wearing an ugly brown suit and had an angry red shaving rash on his neck. To top things off, as I quickly discovered once he ushered me into his little office, he had an irritating habit of staring at my chest while he talked to me. But he did have a copy of the metropolitan St. Louis customer list in his office, which, given the circumstances, went a long way toward transforming him into my Prince Charming.

"These are happy campers, Rachel," he said as he handed me the computer printout of the customer list. "Happy, happy campers." He had a nasal, almost grating voice.

I flipped through the printout, which was twenty-three pages long, with about eight to ten entries on each page. "How is this thing organized?" I asked.

That seemingly innocuous question touched off a ten-minute, eye-glazing disquisition on the industry groupings system used by Leuwenhaupt and how that system differed from the industry groupings used by the last consumer electronics manufacturer he had represented and how the Leuwenhaupt system was based loosely on a proposed system to be used by the Internal Revenue Service and why that was a wise decision, ad nauseam.

"That's interesting," I said when he paused for air.

He started rummaging through his desk. "Ah, here we are." He held up a list. "These are your industry codes. You've got your one hundred series: that's your retail outlets. You've got your one-twenty series: that's your accounting services." Et cetera. He was the world's most boring manufacturer's sales rep. No question.

Finally, mercifully, the telephone rang. Bruce handed me the code sheet as he picked up the phone. He answered it in his hail-fellow-well-met mode, but immediately downshifted. I glanced up and saw him actually cringe as he listened. From the servile tone of his response, he was talking to either an angry boss or an irate and important customer.

While he groveled on the phone, I found Firm Ambitions under the code number for Athletics/Sports. According to the customer list printout, two years ago Firm Ambitions had purchased one Series 5400 microcassette recorder and a box of twenty microcassettes. It had not purchased a microcassette transcriber.

Bruce hung up, clearly agitated. "I have to, uh, go back to the warehouse to check on a few items. It's sort of an emergency. It may take half an hour."

"No problem," I said cheerfully. "I'll wait for you. If I get through the list before you get back, I'll leave it on your desk. We can always talk some more after I talk to my people."

"Uh, sure." He was obviously distracted. "Sure. We'll talk later."

* * *

I don't know if or when Bruce returned. What I do know is that it took me just five minutes to find the name. I found it on page eight of the customer list. It took fifteen more minutes of studying the rest of the list to convince myself, by process of elimination, that the name I found had to be *the* name.

With the customer list in hand, I poked my head out of Bruce's office. No one was in the hallway. Pretending to search for the rest room, I wandered the corridors until I found the copy machine. I made photocopies of two pages from the customer list and hurried back to Bruce's office. I scribbled a short thank-you note, paper-clipped it to the customer list, placed the list in the center of his desk, and left the building.

Like any decent trial lawyer, I immediately started scrutinizing my evidence. It was, after all, an entirely circumstantial case—a chain of facts no stronger than its weakest link. As the plane lifted off for St. Louis, I carefully examined each link, studied it, tapped on it, held it up to the light, tried to pull it apart. Although the chain was still holding when the plane touched down on the runway at Lambert at seven-thirty that evening, several links had me worried.

As I pulled my car out of the airport parking garage and onto the highway, I thought back to the message from Benny that had been waiting on the phone recorder when my mother and I got home from the hospital last night: "Got some interesting news for you two. Called my office after I got to Chicago. Had a message from large Marge at Southwestern Life. Called the Margemeister back. She couldn't find anything on Coulter Designs or Laurence Coulter. However, after she extracted a promise that I would perform acts on her person that may no longer be legal under the Rehnquist Court, she laid the following on me. Check it out. Nine years ago, Arch Alarm Systems of St. Louis took out a nine-hundred-thousand-dollar key-man life insurance policy on one George McGee. Southwestern didn't issue the policy, but had a piece of it through a reinsurance pool. The beneficiary was Capital Investments of Missouri. No word on who the insurance agent was on that one."

His message had not only confirmed my suspicions but reminded my mother of a life insurance scam at the center of a big St. Louis murder trial many years ago. She had decided to spend some time at the library searching for the story on microfilm.

When I got home I showed my mother what I had photocopied from the Leuwenhaupt customer list. She nodded grimly and then showed me the microfilm photocopy of a news story that appeared on the front page of the *St. Louis Globe-Democrat* eighteen years ago on September 12:

SECOND BRANDT MURDER TRIAL ENDS IN SECOND HUNG JURY

Third Trial Unlikely, According to Sources

On the sixth day of jury deliberations, the second trial of insurance broker Arthur L. Brandt on charges of first degree murder and insurance fraud ended in precisely the same way the first trial ended last spring: a frazzled jury announced that it was hopelessly deadlocked and unable to reach a verdict.

Clearly frustrated by the jury's announcement, Circuit Judge Thomas O'Neill declared a mistrial and stormed from the bench into his chambers. O'Neill's frustration was mirrored in the face of Assistant City Attorney William Ramsey, who prosecuted the first trial as well as this one. He silently packed his trial bag and left the courtroom by a rear door, refusing to comment.

By contrast, the defendant's side of the courtroom was a scene of jubilation, as Brandt, 56, embraced his defense attorney, kissed his girlfriend, and triumphantly shook hands with dozens of well-wishers who crowded forward after the verdict was announced.

"We are extremely pleased," said Harry Raven, a Belleville attorney and a longtime friend and adviser of Brandt's. Raven initially represented Brandt in the first trial but was forced to step aside when it became likely that he would testify at the trial, which he did. "Arthur hopes he'll finally be allowed to put this behind him and move on with his life," Raven said.

A more pointed assessment was offered by Brandt's defense attorney in the second trial, Charles Kimball. Referring to his courtroom adversary as the Great Ramses, Kimball stated, "This has gone from prosecution to persecution. The stench of prosecutorial misconduct taints this sorry spectacle. Let us all hope that the Great Ramses allows this ugly chapter in our legal history to come to an end. To paraphrase what a predecessor of mine said to another Great Ramses, 'Let my client go.' "

If this is indeed the last trial, it will close the book on an unusual case that began last November with the indictment of Brandt, a South County insurance broker, on charges of murder and insurance fraud in connection with the shooting death of Herbert Scroggins, an eccentric inventor who had moved to St. Louis sixteen months earlier to head up Ingenuity Ltd., a small company specializing in the development of new products.

Brandt was the sole shareholder of Ingenuity Ltd. and admitted that he had personally recruited Scroggins to move to St. Louis to join the company. Scroggins, a bachelor and self-described loner, was killed in his south St. Louis apartment one year later, apparently the victim of an armed burglary. Brandt was the sole beneficiary of a $1 million "key-man" life insurance policy taken out on Scroggins. The policy was issued by the Royal Assurance Company of Indiana.

In both trials, the key witness for the prosecution was Billy Ray Peterson, 23, of Hillsboro. Peterson claimed that Brandt offered him $1,000 to stage a burglary of Scroggins' apartment and, in the process, kill Scroggins. Brandt denied the accusations and claimed that Peterson made up the story out of spite after Brandt's agency canceled his auto policy.

The Royal Assurance Company had refused to pay the $1 million death benefits to Brandt pending outcome of the trial. Efforts to reach an insurance company official for comment were unsuccessful.

Stapled to that article was a short news story from the *Post-Dispatch* six years later stating that "insurance broker Arthur L. Brandt, 62, of Sunset Hills" had been killed when his automobile rammed into a parked car on Lindell Boulevard at approximately two in the morning.

28

CHAPTER

Twenty-four centuries after it was built, the Parthenon still stands as evidence of the glory of ancient Athens. So, too, the Colosseum remains a stirring reminder of the power and the spectacle of the Roman Empire. But in less than a year after the last of its twenty million visitors had departed, only a skilled archaeologist could have found much evidence that St. Louis had been the site of the Louisiana Purchase Exposition. The huge, ornate palaces celebrating the new gods of progress, the floral clock with a minute hand seventy-four feet long, the Ferris wheel that stood 264 feet high and seated sixty passengers in each of its thirty-six cars, the French Pavilion that included a full-scale reproduction of the Grand Trianon at Versailles, the entire villages of natives imported from South America, Africa, and Asia and plunked down in replica villages on the fairgrounds—all had been quickly dismantled and carted off, with the exception of the gargantuan Ferris wheel, which was literally blown apart with dynamite.

By the spring of 1905, there was little left of the largest single event in the history of St. Louis, a fair that had introduced the world to ice cream cones, frankfurters, and iced tea and would eventually be memorialized in the Judy Garland musical *Meet Me in St. Louis*. Indeed, aside from the occasional chunk of twisted metal unearthed by the grounds crews that maintain the golf course in Forest Park, little today remains of St. Louis's brief turn on the world stage except for the Bird Cage.

The Bird Cage sits along the northern edge of the zoo. Built by the Smithsonian Institution and bequeathed to the city when the fair ended, The Bird Cage is a huge aviary, the largest of its kind ever constructed. Still home to dozens of species of birds, it is a Victorian oasis within the modern world, with a sky of black metal screen suspended over towering iron ribs. Enclosed within are trees, ponds, a stream, and an elevated walkway that allows visitors to move from one end to the other, observing the birds above and below.

While the Jungle of the Apes and the Big Cat Country and the Living World lure the crowds when they first arrive at the zoo, those who spend the day eventually find their way down to the Bird Cage, where almost all succumb to its charm. But the allure it held for me that morning was quite distinct from the attractions it held for the children and young mothers and older couples who were strolling along on the elevated walkway past me. To a lawyer with precious little experience in arranging a potentially dangerous rendezvous, the Bird Cage seemed a uniquely advantageous meeting space. It was an enclosed public space with excellent visibility and nowhere to hide, inside or out. Someone approaching the Bird Cage from any direction would be clearly visible, and anyone approaching me would have to do so along the one elevated walkway. Almost as important, I was clearly visible to anyone outside the Bird Cage—a reassuring thought as I glanced at my mother. She was in her car, which was parked on the street that ran along the northern perimeter of the zoo and thus along the northern side of the Bird Cage. Her videocamera was resting on the car window. The car was idling so that the cellular phone was ready for dialing 911, just in case.

I checked my watch. It was nearly curtain time.

A pair of schoolteachers—both middle-aged women— ushered twenty or so elementary school children into the Bird Cage through the east entrance. The children dashed ahead, laughing and shouting, running down the walkway, pointing at the birds.

A rhythmic grunting noise caught my attention. Below me

in a shallow pond were nine flamingos, standing in a row. Their heads were bobbing slowly in time, nine pairs of beady eyes fixed on me. A hot-pink chorus line. As I watched, the bobbing motions began to accelerate and the grunts grew louder, everything still synchronized. Faster and louder, faster and louder. It peaked in a surreal flamingo climax, and then the tight pattern broke apart as the bobbing slowed and stopped. One by one, the flamingos dunked their heads in the pond water.

"Symbols of the modern world," a familiar voice said at my side.

I turned. Charles Kimball gestured at the flamingos. "They feed upside down."

I looked back at the flamingos. They were standing in shallow water. One swung its head down to water level. Sure enough, its head dipped into the water upside down, the beak pointing toward its feet, its eyes underwater. The anatomical upper beak was underwater, moving up and down against the anatomical lower, which was stationary. The flamingo standing to the right of the feeding one had its head in the air, peering around. I stared at it. The upper jaw—small and narrow—looked like the lower bill of a typical bird. The lower bill was massive and deep and stationary, more like the typical upper jaw.

"Perfectly adapted through evolution," Kimball continued, "and unique among vertebrates. A topsy-turvy animal dressed in Day-Glo colors. Very striking. Very L.A., wouldn't you say?"

"Now that you mention it."

"And speaking of unique, Rachel, this is an unusual meeting place. I assume you have invited me here to discuss more than flamingos."

"I have," I said as I unzipped my briefcase. "But first I want you to listen to something." I removed a Leuwenhaupt microcassette player with lightweight headphones. I handed him the headphones. "The tape is a copy," I explained. "The original is in a safe deposit box."

I waited until he had put on the headphones, then pressed the PLAY button.

"Listen carefully," I said.

The sound of Andros's voice coming through the headphones was faintly audible to me: "This is number five uh *click* number five Asbury Way. *click* This house is in Frontenac. *click* There's a door sensor on the front door, with a Telsor combination panel to the right when you come in. *click*."

I was studying Kimball's face. When the tape first started, with Andros describing the front entrance to 5 Asbury Way, Kimball had glanced at me. As the tape droned on, he frowned in concentration and pursed his lips. I turned it off about halfway through.

"Curious," he said as he removed the headphones and handed it to me. "Where did you find it?"

"With some of his other stuff. It's all in the safe deposit box."

"I fear I may be missing the point of all this."

I gave him a skeptical smile. "I very much doubt that, Charles."

"What's this about a safe deposit box?"

"I call it my key-woman life insurance policy."

"I am still not following you, Rachel."

"The safe deposit box is located inside a major St. Louis financial institution. A trust officer there has a signed and notarized letter from me, witnessed by two other trust officers." I spoke slowly and deliberately. It was important that he understand exactly what I had done. "That letter instructs the trust officer to immediately notify the FBI and give them the contents of that safe deposit box if for any reason whatsoever I should die." I paused. "*Any* reason, Charles, Any cause of death, no matter how innocent."

He nodded gravely. "That must be quite a safe deposit box."

"It is."

"What else is in there besides the audiotape?"

"For starters, the negatives of these prints." I removed the photographs I had taken during our stakeout of Mound City Mini-Storage. "Along with the rap sheet for this upstanding member of the community." I pointed to the picture of Pete Ricketts removing a shrouded painting from the back of his van at the Beaumont Art Gallery. "According to court records, you have had the pleasure of representing Mr. Ricketts on two criminal matters, both involving burglaries."

He nodded his head thoughtfully. "And you have more?"

"Much more."

I laid out the whole scheme. The correlation between personal fitness sessions Andros conducted in certain homes and subsequent burglaries of those homes. The use of Mound City Mini-Storage as a place to store the stolen goods until they could be fenced. The correlation between the dates of certain burglaries and the use of the Firm Ambitions computerized cardkeys at Mound City.

"The conclusion is obvious," I said. "Firm Ambitions was a front for a fully integrated burglary operation. It ran like an assembly line. Andros was the advance scout at the front end, and guys like Leo Beaumont moved the stolen goods at the back end. I assume everyone got their cut along the way."

"Fascinating," Kimball said in a totally noncommittal way. I had assumed at the outset that I would be dealing cards to a grandmaster, so I wasn't surprised by his perfect poker face.

"That kind of operation needs a ringleader," I continued. "It obviously wasn't Andros."

"Why is that obvious?"

"First of all, the burglaries and the rest of the activities continued after he was dead. I took those pictures last week. Second, Andros was strictly small-time before Firm Ambitions. He didn't have a history of that kind of crime. He didn't even have much history in this country. But what he did have was an arrest for criminal conduct that, had he been convicted, would have resulted in deportation to Saudi Arabia. How do they punish homosexuals over there? What's the sentence for cocaine users in Saudi Arabia? He must have been desperate after the arrest. When you got those charges dropped, you literally saved his life, at least in the short term. But it also gave you enormous leverage over him."

He chuckled. "Rachel, this is beginning to sound like a made-for-TV movie plot. Are you suggesting that I somehow forced that young man into a life of crime?"

"No. All I am suggesting is that Andros was someone who could have been forced to take part in the scheme but that he wasn't the ringleader."

He gave me a good-naturedly skeptical look. "And you seriously think I was?"

"I want to be clear on this point, Charles. I am not accusing you of anything. I think of you more as the Hollywood agent of this operation—the guy who could put the right people in touch with each other, keep things rolling."

He gave me an avuncular smile. "All because I've represented a few of these chaps in the past?"

"No. All because of that tape you just heard."

The smile remained, but it was just a little tighter. "I am afraid that you have lost me again."

"Andros didn't break into those homes. Those were professional jobs. All he did was scout each target home. You heard the tape. That was his role. Identify the security system, find the valuables, describe their location. He made those tapes for the pros. The pros came in for the actual burglaries."

"An interesting hypothesis."

"An overwhelmingly likely hypothesis. Otherwise, Charles, why make the tapes? Not for himself. He made them for others."

"Continue."

"But the others had to be able to *listen* to the tapes, or at least read a transcript of them, right?"

"Go on."

"The tape you listened to was recorded on a unique microcassette size. You have to have a special recorder or transcriber to listen to it. That's the key, Charles. There aren't many of those machines in St. Louis. I've seen the manufacturer's records. I even have a photocopy of a key page of those records in the safe deposit box. You own several of those machines, Charles—recorders and transcribers."

"Along with dozens of others in St. Louis, no doubt."

"True. A few of them might even make it onto an initial list of suspects. But you and I both know that all of them will be scratched once the police start investigating. Your name jumps out from the list, Charles. You are the obvious one. You are the only one."

He smiled and shook his head. "Rachel, this is marvelously entertaining—"

"And true," I interrupted.

He chuckled as he turned toward the flamingos. "Let's leave cosmic questions like truth to the philosophers." He inhaled and slowly exhaled as he studied the pink birds below. "I assume you've called me here to talk about your sister's predicament. How does this intricate scheme you claim to have divined bear on the death of Andros?"

"Life insurance."

He turned to me with what passed for a look of confusion. "I beg pardon."

"Key-man life insurance. There was a million-dollar policy on his head. Use him in this scheme for three or four years, then kill him off, and collect the money."

He widened his eyes and smiled. "You are not suggesting that I am the beneficiary of his life insurance policy?"

I pressed on. "The nominal beneficiary is a company down in the Cayman Islands. Someone owns that company—or maybe several someones. Maybe you're one of them." I shrugged indifferently. "Or one of your nominees. Charles, I'm not here to make you prove your innocence. However, I know—and *you* know—that this key-man insurance scam isn't the first one, or even the second. Andros is victim number four."

He frowned. "Now I am totally lost."

"Charles," I said with a patient smile, "I don't believe you've ever been lost."

"Indulge an older man, Rachel. Tell me about the other three."

And so I did. I told him about the two predecessor companies owned by Capital Investments and how their presidents had died. I explained that I had already confirmed a key-man life insurance policy on one and I assumed that the police would be able to find a policy on the other man as well.

Kimball looked fascinated. "And the fourth?"

"Another one of your clients, Charles. Arthur Brandt. Remember? I assume that's where you got the original idea. If a clumsy, greedy fool like Brandt could get away with it, how much easier for someone clever enough to establish a corporate veil between himself and the insurance money."

He smiled appreciatively. "You have a vivid imagination, Rachel."

"I also have copies of everything I've just described. They're in that safe deposit box, along with a videotape of me explaining the evidence against you, Charles. And just for added precaution, I'm having this meeting videotaped." I pointed to the parked car where my mother was filming us. "That's going into a different safe deposit box at another financial institution."

Kimball nodded his head. There was more than a hint of tightness at the corners of his smile. "And the point of all this?"

"The point of all this is cut the crap, Charles."

"Okay." The smile faded, the voice grew more assertive. "Why don't you tell me the purpose of your presentation?"

"My sister."

"Explain."

"Simple. You either had my sister set up or you know who did. Un-set her up. I want all charges against my sister dropped. Period."

"And?"

"No 'and.' That's all."

His confusion seemed genuine this time. "And what about us?" he asked.

I couldn't resist. "We'll always have Paris."

"I am serious, Rachel," he snapped.

"So am I, Charles. When the charges are dropped, our business is concluded."

"I don't understand," he said, clearly off balance.

I let him teeter for a moment. "You don't understand what, Charles?"

"What about all that garbage in the safe deposit box?"

"When all the charges against my sister are dropped, I won't need it anymore."

He squinted at me skeptically. "And that's it?"

"Yep."

"But what about the person who killed Andros?"

I leaned against the railing and looked down at the flamingos. "A wise attorney told me back in law school that only an incompetent defense lawyer tries to solve the crime." I turned to him. "I assume that's still good advice?"

Kimball pursed his lips. "It is."

"I'm not Marshal Dillon, Charles, and I'm not Philip

Marlowe. Someone stole jewelry and fancy toys from some very rich people who no doubt had plenty of insurance coverage for their losses. Let the police catch the burglars if they can. It's their job. Someone killed Andros. He was a slimy, despicable man who exploited a lot of women. Let the police catch his killer if they can. That's their job. Mine is to get the charges against my sister dropped and, in the process, to get whoever has been trying to terrorize my mother and me to back off for good. I know you can make that happen, Charles. But it has to happen fast. I'll give you forty-eight hours. If it hasn't happened by then, I go to the police with what I have, which includes everything in the safe deposit box." I turned to look down at the flamingos, a few of whom were starting to bob their heads again. "I won't ask if we have a deal," I continued in a lower voice, "because I know you won't acknowledge that there's anything to make a deal over." I turned to him and spoke firmly. "But I will ask you if you understand my proposal."

Charles Kimball scratched his neck as he studied the flamingos. He nodded silently, a frown on his face.

The meeting was over, but there was another mystery that had been bothering me. As he started to leave I said, "Charles."

He turned to face me, and I was surprised by his transformation. He had become an old man. Even his shoulders slumped.

"You were one of the reasons I became a lawyer," I said.

He looked at me with weary eyes.

"You were one of my heroes." I shook my head in disbelief. "I even had a photograph of you in my college dorm room."

He leaned against the rail with both hands and peered into the trees near the walkway inside the Bird Cage. An orange-and-black bird fluttered out of the branch directly in front of him and flew past at eye level. He glanced over at me with a wistful expression. "I had three heroes when I was a young man. They all turned out to be charlatans. Heroes are rarely what they appear to be."

"But how did you change from what you once were to what you are now?"

He gestured toward the flamingos with a sad smile. "Just the way Darwin predicted: gradually, and over time."

"But why?" I persisted.

"Why not?"

"That's no answer," I said angrily.

He stared at me. "Why do you believe you are entitled to an answer?"

I took a deep breath and exhaled slowly. "Because you were once my hero, Charles Kimball."

He sighed and shook his head ruefully. "You expect your world to make sense, Rachel. It's one of the fallacies of youth. Let me assure you that the world makes no sense. You expect people's actions to fit into some coherent grand plan, like one of those nineteenth-century English novels. Let me assure you, Rachel, life is not a novel." He leaned against the railing. "Have you read Benjamin Franklin's autobiography?"

"Back in college."

"He became a complete vegetarian in his youth for strictly moral reasons. He believed it was wrong to kill animals for food. Admirable sentiments, I suppose. But young Franklin had a slight problem: he craved seafood. Well, one day, while walking through the city, he found himself overcome by the smell of a fillet of fried cod. As his mouth watered, as his desire for a piece of fish nearly overwhelmed him, he suddenly recalled that when he had seen cod cleaned in the fish market, smaller fish spilled out of their bellies. Ah ha, he reasoned, if fish eat one another, then it isn't immoral for people to eat fish. From that day, Franklin started eating fish again. Just as important," he said as he looked at me with a smile, "he claims that experience taught him an important lesson of life."

"Which is?"

"Which is, as Franklin wryly observes, that it's convenient to be a reasonable creature, since it enables one to come up with a reason for anything one decides to do." He ended the story with a chuckle and a shake of his head.

"So what's yours?"

Kimball shook his head. "Rachel, you are assuming several facts not in evidence."

He was right, of course. Kimball was not prepared to admit to any wrongdoing. Accordingly, special rules governed my line of questioning. To violate those rules would terminate our discussion.

"Fair enough," I said. "What do you think could be a reason for someone to get involved in this kind of scheme?"

"Hypothetically speaking?"

"Of course."

"Well, perhaps this person needed money. That's always a powerful motivator."

"Not enough of a motivator."

He gave me a look of admonition. "Never underestimate the power of greed, Rachel. It is the single greatest motivator in the history of man. But let us assume that greed wasn't enough in this case. Or, taking a lesson from Ben Franklin, let us assume that greed was not an acceptable 'reason.' Perhaps this person, especially if he was a criminal defense lawyer, saw his involvement as a chance to play Robin Hood—especially if he could use his cut to help fund the defense of indigent clients. That's certainly a better reason than greed."

"What's the real reason?" I said persistently. I wasn't going to allow him to wiggle out that easily.

He rubbed his chin. "Hard to say. Perhaps our hypothetical man doesn't even care about reasons anymore. Perhaps he realizes, as Franklin did, that reasons are little fictions we use to sanitize our actions. Maybe he just plain enjoys the risk. Addiction to risk is a common enough personality flaw in trial lawyers. You have a touch of it yourself, Rachel." He seemed to think it over. "Makes sense, eh?" he said with a nod. "After all, the burglary scheme you described is basically a high-stakes rolling crap game with the government as the house."

"But in the end the house always wins."

He laughed and shook his head. "Not in this country, my dear. Not in this country."

We stood in silence as the bobbing flamingos, now all synchronized, did their noisy conga-line routine again. Kimball glanced at his watch as the show ended. "I have certain matters to take care of, Rachel."

"Forty-eight hours, Charles."

"I understand the proposal." Kimball paused and studied me with pursed lips. "Regardless of the eventual outcome, Rachel, I commend you for having the ingenuity to set it up and the sheer brass balls to carry it off."

29

CHAPTER

Charles Kimball left first, which was good, because I don't think I could have kept up my facade much longer. My legs were wobbly as I walked out of the Bird Cage.

If Kimball was innocent, I said to myself, *he would have been outraged, he would have denied everything.* While he obviously wasn't the one who put the cyanide powder into the pills, he hadn't denied anything. Then again, he hadn't admitted anything, either.

Apprehensive, tense, frightened—those words don't even come close to describing the way my mother and I felt on the drive home from the zoo. We checked the locks on all the doors and windows. Benny called from Chicago that night and went ballistic when he found out what I had done.

"Are you fucking nuts?" he shouted at me. He insisted that I go to the police, which I refused.

"Kimball can do it for us," I told him. "He can get Ann off *and* get whoever's hassling us to stop it. I've got to give him his forty-eight hours."

"Kimball? How can you trust that motherfucker?"

We got into a big argument, and I terminated by slamming down the receiver. He called right back.

"What?" I yelled at him.

"Then get out of the goddam house, Rachel," he said, a little calmer this time. "Someone already got in your house to stick a cat's head on your goddam pillow while you were taking a shower. Don't be an idiot. Get the fuck out of there."

Benny's advice began to sound better later that night when my mother and I started getting ready for bed. Although Ozzie was strong, healthy, and loyal, he was only one dog and we were only two women.

"So where can we go?" my mother asked as we both put our clothes back on.

Neither of us knew the answer to that one. We had to improvise. I called an attorney friend who did some work for the Ritz-Carlton, and he put me in touch with the night manager.

If the test of a great hotel is its ability to meet the most unusual needs of its guests, then the Ritz passed the test. By midnight, we were in a suite under assumed names on a restricted floor with an armed security guard posted outside our door. Two floors down, there was another suite—that one empty—registered under the names Rachel and Sarah Gold.

Nevertheless, the only one who slept well that night was Ozzie. At three in the morning I got out of bed and went into the living room to make a stiff gin and tonic. I opened the French doors to the balcony, moved a chair out there, and settled in. I stared east toward the blinking red light on top of the Arch, which was barely visible in the distance. As I sipped my drink, the evidence I had amassed seemed flimsier and flimsier. How could I have seriously hoped to spook a premier criminal defense attorney like Kimball with a trick-or-treat bag of circumstantial evidence? Was he just going to ignore my threat? Call my bluff? Or was he making arrangements for the unfortunate "accident" that would take my life in six hours or six months or six years?

The sun woke me at dawn. The hotel's day manager personally brought up our breakfast and took Ozzie for a walk. I checked in with my office occasionally through the morning, but there was no word from anyone. At twelve-thirty, while taking a shower, I actually hyperventilated and almost passed out. At quarter to five I couldn't stand it anymore. More than thirty hours had elapsed since my meeting with Kimball. What had seemed a daring but powerful gambit two days ago now seemed foolish and impotent.

I felt like Dorothy as she stared at the hourglass, her dread rising as she watched the sand trickle down steadily, implacably. Except that I knew there was no Cowardly Lion or Tin Man coming to the rescue. Just my mother and myself and Ozzie in the role of Toto.

"It's not going to work," I told my mother.

She looked up from her book and sighed. "You don't know that yet, sweetie. Give it time."

I did. And time ran out the following morning.

"Mom," I said, exhausted and frazzled, "it's been forty-eight hours. I'm going to the police. You wait here with Ozzie. I'll call you as soon as I tell them."

At 10:45 A.M., I walked through the entrance to the Clayton police station. The first person I saw inside was Detective Bernie "Poncho" Israel. He broke into a big smile when he saw me.

"Rachel Gold, you must have ESP."

"Why's that?"

"I just called your office. Your secretary said you weren't in." He shook his head in wonder. "We've had a remarkable development in the Andros homicide. It's going to mean more work for us, but your sister's about to become one very happy lady."

I was actually shaking. "What happened?"

"Come on back to my desk. I'll grab you a cup of coffee and tell you all about it."

I joined him and he handed me a Styrofoam cup of black coffee. He took a sip of his coffee and shook his head in wonderment. "You sister owes a special thanks to Charles Kimball," he said.

"Oh?"

"I spent the last hour in an interrogation room with Charles and one of his longtime clients."

"Who?"

He shook his head. "You don't need to know the name, and we don't want it getting out just yet. Let's just say he's a gentleman who's seen the advantages of cooperating with his local law enforcement officials."

"He confessed to the murder?"

Poncho chuckled. "Don't I wish. No, it won't be that easy. But he's given us some vital information that's completely changed the focus and theory of the homicide. Our John Doe is in the drug business. He's a chemist—the guy who tests and cuts and processes the raw materials that come in from South America and East Asia. As such, he has access to a wide variety of chemicals ordinarily available only to licensed professionals."

"Such as cyanide?"

"Exactly."

"He was the one who got the cyanide?"

Poncho nodded. "Not for his own use, though. But the man who had him get it, and the people that man works for—well, these are not the kind of folks your little sister will ever meet in her lifetime. Even if she had wanted to hire someone to kill Andros, she would never have gotten anywhere near these folks."

"The mafia?"

"That's what they call them in Hollywood. Let's just say that the man who had our John Doe obtain the cyanide is an employee of a criminal organization that has a regional head-quarters in Kansas City."

"Why would they kill Andros?"

"Your hunch was the right one."

"I don't understand."

"I talked to Curt Green. He was the detective who met you out at that mini-storage facility while I was on vacation."

"The one who thought I was a dumb broad."

Poncho gave a hearty laugh. "He's had his comeuppance, Rachel. I've seen to that. Anyway, you were right all along. Andros was using that place to store stolen merchandise. Apparently, the Kansas City organization is not a great believer in competition, and Andros's little operation was directly competing with theirs. They had warned him several times, according to what John Doe heard. When Andros refused to back off, they had him killed."

"I thought they got rid of people by shooting them."

"Generally yes, especially when they're dealing with other members of organized crime. This one is a bit unusual, but I've seen ones far kinkier than that."

"So what are you going to do?"

"We're going to talk to other sources, we're going to keep

our ears to the ground. The best we can hope for is an opening somewhere down the line. Could take two weeks. Could take two years."

"And my sister?"

"All charges are being dropped as we speak, Rachel. We've already notified the press. Your sister's been cleared."

"And that's it?" I asked, in thrilled disbelief.

He gave me a broad smile as he reached over to shake my hand. "Rachel, that's it."

We shook hands. "Thank you, Poncho."

"You make sure that sister of yours thanks *you*."

As I stood up to go he said, "One more thing."

He opened his desk drawer and removed an envelope. "Charles Kimball told me to be sure to give you this."

I took it from him. Scrawled on the front of the envelope were the words "For Rachel Gold. Personal and Confidential."

I stopped in the corridor and tore open the envelope. Inside was a folded sheet of paper from a yellow legal pad. I unfolded it and read the handwritten message:

Dear Rachel:
Perry Mason would have been proud. And like any good episode, it was solved just in time. I would be honored to close our deal with a sequel to our last dinner together. As I recall, you still have a rain check. Please call me.

Warmly,
Charles

30

CHAPTER

Detective Israel was true to his word. All charges were dropped, and the official announcement was made in time for the five-o'clock news. My mother, my sister, and I went out to celebrate. It was Girls' Night Out, with Richie staying home to baby-sit.

I awoke the next morning with an all-world hangover and a tongue made of tree bark. The three of us had had way too much to eat and way too much to drink. My last clear memory of the evening was around two in the morning in a smoky, funky dance club somewhere down in the Soulard area: Ann and I had been leaning against each other, laughing and swaying our hips and clapping our hands in time to the reggae music as we watched my mother out on the dance floor getting down with a three-hundred-pound black man in a gold lamé jumpsuit and storm-trooper boots. "Stick with the judge," I told her when she rejoined us after the song ended.

By noon the hangover fog had started to lift from my brain and I struggled into the office. I felt like I could have used one of those aluminum walkers. As I came into my office my secretary told me she had Harry Raven on the phone.

He was charming and somewhat apologetic. "Jes' to tie up any loose ends," he told me, "I got Mrs. Maxwell to make a copy of her files on that dead fella. There ain't much of interest in there, but Mrs. Maxwell's gonna messenger 'em over to you today. Don't want there to be no hard feelings, Miss Gold. You still have questions after looking at them documents, you jes' feel free to give me a call, you hear?"

Later in the afternoon, my mother called from Ann's house, where she had ordered Ann and Richie to go somewhere romantic for the weekend. We agreed that they needed some time alone after all the strain and craziness and hurting—time to start the healing process. The night before I had given Ann the name of a romantic bed-and-breakfast inn an hour's drive outside St. Louis in the Missouri wine country, and she had made reservations for the weekend.

"I told them you and I would take care of the children," my mother said. "I've already packed my bag. I can move in tonight."

"I can, too. After work. It's supposed to be a beautiful weekend. Maybe we can take the kids on a hike in the country."

I spent the rest of the day trying to bring order back to the chaos of my practice before the weekend began. There were letters to answer, court papers to prepare, clients to call, depositions to schedule—two weeks' worth. My secretary stayed late. I signed the last letter at eight-thirty that night. Leaning back in my desk chair, I called my mother at Ann's house.

"I'll be there in a couple hours, Mom. I've got to stop by the house, pack some clothes, get Ozzie—"

"I have Ozzie here. I brought his food, but I forgot his bowls. I left them on the front porch."

"I'll bring them. Kiss the kids for me."

For two weeks I had been running on a high-octane mix of tension, worry, and adrenaline. For the past twenty-four hours, beginning the moment Poncho Israel told me that the charges against Ann were dropped, I had felt myself winding down. The last two hours in my office had been a real struggle. By the time I got out of my car in front of the house, I was almost numb from exhaustion.

Ozzie's two bowls were on the front porch. The house was dark. I clicked on the light in the front hall, hung my purse on the closet doorknob, heaved my briefcase onto the couch in the living room, and walked toward the stairs. Out of habit, I glanced into the breakfast room on my way past. Sure enough, the red light on the telephone answering machine was blinking. I looked up the stairway for a long moment and then back at the blinking red light. It could wait. I clicked on the hall light and trudged up the stairs.

I can usually pack my overnight bag in under five minutes, including toiletries. This time it took almost a half hour. I seemed to keep finding myself shuffling between the bedroom and bathroom, once carrying a toothbrush, the next time carrying one jogging shoe.

As I packed, my mind wandered back again to Charles Kimball and his mystery client, John Doe. The story sounded more credible to the police than to me, but that was because I knew something the police didn't, namely, the key-man life insurance policies. That fact gave others a motive to kill Andros. Then again, it was always possible that the insurance policy was literally that—insurance in case Andros happened to die rather than insurance for when they killed him. If legitimate operations could buy key-man life insurance for entirely prudent reasons, surely illegitimate operations could nevertheless buy key-man life insurance for entirely prudent reasons, too. For all I knew, there was a multimillion-dollar key-man life insurance policy on Don Corleone himself.

I shook my head, trying to clear my thoughts. The charges against Ann had been dropped. She was free. That's what counted. Whether John Doe was telling the police the truth or a story Kimball cooked up didn't really matter as far as Ann was concerned. If and when Kimball and I had our dinner, I could decide whether to push the issue with him. Right now I had barely enough energy to push my closet door closed.

I clicked the lights off one by one as I left my room, came down the stairs, and reached the front door. Then I remembered the blinking red message light. With a weary sigh, I set the overnight bag on the hall floor and walked back to the breakfast room. The answering machine was on the counter that separated the kitchen from the breakfast room. I pushed the replay button and sank into one of the chairs at the breakfast table.

The first message was from my mother: "Rachel, darling,

I forgot my slippers. I'm telling you, if my head wasn't screwed on I'd have left that, too. Thanks, sweetie."

The second was from Benny Goldberg: "Hey, my first day of testimony and now I think these wusses are going to settle. The judge adjourned for the weekend right in the middle of my direct. The lawyers have been talking settlement ever since. You would have been proud of me, Rachel. I was awesome on the stand—a combination of the Shell Answer Man, Mr. Wizard, and Phil fucking Areeda. Call me at the hotel tonight."

There was a beep, and then the next message started: "Ma'am, this is Donny from Ace Thermal Windows. We'll be in your neighborhood this weekend and wondered if we might stop by . . . ."

As Donny rambled on, I noticed that there was light shining through the space at the bottom of the basement door. I had gone down to the basement that morning to get something out of the dryer. Had I forgotten to turn off the light? Maybe my mother had gone down there later and left it on.

I forced myself to stand and walk into the kitchen as the message from Ace Windows came to an end. There was a beep and then another message started as I reached for the basement door:

"Hey, Rachel, Bob Ginsburg at Bear Stearns. I tried calling you at the office, but you were already gone. I'm leaving on vacation tomorrow. I'm going on one of those backwoods fishing trips up in Canada—flown in by plane, Indian guide, no phone, the works."

I opened the basement door. The light at the bottom of the stairs was on. It was the kind with a pull cord. I started down the stairs as the message continued:

"I'll be gone for ten days, and then things'll get hairy when I get back. Anyway, I finally got that information you were looking for. You owe me big-time, woman. We're talking dinner for two at Lutèce, *on you,* next time you're in New York. Don't even ask what I had to do to get this info. I deserve an honorary membership in the CIA."

I was halfway down the basement stairs when the floor creaked above me. I spun around just as Tommy Landau stepped into view at the top of the stairs. He had a large hand-gun and he was pointing it at me.

The voice on the tape continued as we stared at each other:

"Here's the scoop. There are four shareholders of Capital International Limited. Three of them are islanders—a lawyer down there, his secretary, and his paralegal. They each own one share. That's typical. Local corporate laws and all. Anyway, the rest of the ten thousand shares are owned by a guy from St. Louis. His name is Thomas Landau. Hope it means something, Rachel. Give me a buzz next time you're in the city so I can collect on my dinner. Take care."

The tape beeped twice and clicked off.

Tommy Landau shook his head. "Come up to the top stair," he ordered as he backed toward the kitchen counter.

I obeyed.

With the gun still trained on me, he pushed the eject button on the message machine and removed the cassette tape. He was wearing surgeon's latex gloves.

"Took you long enough to spot the basement light," he said with irritation. "I was afraid I might have to do you up here." He slipped the cassette into his front pocket. "Go downstairs," he said.

He followed me down to the basement. I heard him close the door behind him.

"Over there." He gestured with the gun. "By the washer."

I moved to the washer, which was in the corner to the right of the stairs. I stood with my back to the washer. Tommy had stopped at the foot of the stairs. There was a table along the wall between where he stood and I stood. My mother used it to sort and fold clothes from the dryer. The clothes had been pushed to the side to make room for a stack of papers.

Tommy noticed that I was looking at the papers.

"Interesting stuff," he said. "All your notes and papers on your investigation. I found them up in the family room. I read them while I waited for you." He sat on the edge of the table. "Charlie Kimball told me about your meeting at the zoo. He said you needed a fall guy for the murder. He said you've got incriminating evidence on him that gets released if anything happens to you. Is that so?"

I nodded, my mind racing. The sole light was a naked bulb above the table where he sat.

Tommy grinned. "I like that. I like that a lot. All we do is make sure something bad happens to you, and then—abracadabra—poor old Charlie become the perfect fall guy, doesn't he? Case closed, eh?"

"Assuming Kimball doesn't turn on you," I said.

"That's the beauty of it. Charlie Kimball doesn't know enough to turn on me. He's never known the whole story. Shit, you probably know more than he does. This is *my* operation, not his. All he did was put me in contact with some of his clients—the fences, the B-and-E boys. He got a cut of the action, but that's it."

"Did you have them do your own house, too?"

He shook his head. "Pure coincidence, the bastards. But it sure helps point the finger away from me, eh?"

I had to keep him talking. "How far back did Kimball go? All the way to Arch Alarm Systems?"

Landau whistled in admiration. "You have been digging, haven't you? No, he got involved with the second one, after one of my guys got arrested. I asked Charlie for the name of a good B-and-E man. He gave me one of his clients. After that, I started using more and more of his clients. I paid Charlie a commission on each job. A couple years after I finally got rid of that fag interior decorator, Charlie brought me Andros. Talk about the perfect candidate. I had leverage out the wazoo on that camel jockey. He was scared shitless. Anyway, by then, Charlie was almost a full partner."

"Including the insurance end?"

He smiled and shook his head. "No way. He didn't know dick about that."

A plan was forming in my head. It might work. "So the mob didn't kill Andros?"

Tommy laughed. "Hell no. Charlie fed them that bullshit and they swallowed it whole."

"I don't get it," I said. "Why did you do it? You didn't need the money."

He gave a snort of disbelief. "After you and my wife finished carving up my estate in divorce court? Deb Fletcher filled me in on you. I knew exactly what kind of bloodsucker you are. You'd have squeezed me for every penny."

"I still don't get it. You made enough the first time. Why do it three times?"

He thrust his chin forward defiantly. "Because I'm not a chump. My father's a chump, and so was my grandfather—a pair of social-climbing schmucks. The only one who ever knew the score was my great-grandfather. He was one nasty motherfucker. But guess what? They named a grade school after him, for chrissakes. Treated him like one of the goddam founding fathers." He stood up, his brows furrowed. "All the time my father spends brown-nosing important people, and you know what? I'll be the one people remember."

"For killing Andros?"

He laughed. "Like the world is any worse off without that piece of camel shit walking around."

"Why my sister?"

He gave me a puzzled look. "What?"

"Why pick on my sister?"

He chuckled and shook his head. "Bad timing on her part. Her letter was perfect. I had them plant the cyanide and take those pages from her magazines during the burglary. Her letter was the icing on the cake."

Darkness was the key. It was the only way to even the odds. I knew the basement and he didn't. I glanced around. There was a mop leaning against the wall to my right. It was long enough to reach the light bulb over his head. I needed to distract him long enough to get to the bulb.

"Why me?" I asked suddenly.

"Why you? You did it to yourself, you dumb bitch. You set Charlie up, and then you set yourself up. Nice going."

"Not this," I said. "I mean back when he died. He was supposed to die with me, wasn't he?"

Tommy Landau's stare turned icy. "What are you talking about?"

I gave him a look of disgust. "You're really twisted. You ordered him to schedule one of his home workouts with me, right? Even told him to set the appointment for three in the afternoon, didn't you?"

He feigned indifference. "So what?"

"The session would last for forty-five minutes. Then he would take his vitamin pills. Every day at four o'clock, right?"

Tommy said nothing.

I shook my head, trying to seem cocky. "Andros didn't have a clue, did he? He must have thought you actually wanted him to scope out my house, as if my parents had ever owned *anything* worth stealing. Why me, Tommy? Because I was your wife's lawyer? That was your idea of revenge?"

He grinned. "This is even better."

"Let me ask you something," I said, improvising as I went along, trying to figure out a way to distract him long enough. "Who had the last laugh, you or Andros?"

"What are you talking about?"

"He was supposed to be with *me* when he died, right? But he was with your wife instead. Did you even know about them before that?"

"It's none of your goddam business, you cunt." He took two steps toward me and raised the gun. "I'm going to enjoy this."

"Cunt?" I repeated, refusing to flinch. Time to bait the hook. "Nice, Tommy. So Andros had the last laugh with your money *and* your wife."

"My money? What the fuck's that supposed to mean?"

"It's right there in those papers you found."

"Where?"

I gave him a look of disbelief. "You haven't figured it out?"

"What are you talking about?"

"It's a two-step process. Start with three entries in the check ledger files I printed out of the computer."

"What are they?"

I paused. "Why should I tell you?"

"Because I'll kill you if you don't."

"You'll kill me if I do."

He took a step closer. "Maybe not. Believe me, cunt, you got no downside here."

I pretended to mull that over. "Okay. Start with the entry for Vogel Productions."

"And then what?"

"Find that entry first. It's easier to explain once you're looking at it."

He frowned and then turned toward the table. I quickly glanced to my left. The closest cover was the water heater, which was just beyond the dryer. There was a foot or so of space between the water heater and the wall. He was looking down as he sorted through the papers with his left hand. The gun was still in his right hand.

The mop was upside down, leaning against the wall. "I think it's back in March," I said as I slowly reached for the mop. "Or maybe April."

I bent slightly and grabbed the mop midway down the handle. Then I took a quick step forward and jammed the mop head into the light bulb. The bulb shattered before Tommy Landau was able to react. He was still looking down when the basement went black.

I stumbled backward and squeezed behind the water heater as he spun and fired at the sound. The gun roared. The bullet punched into the water heater waist-high. My ears were ringing. I couldn't see a thing.

"That was real stupid, cunt."

I could barely hear him over the reverberations in my ears. I scrunched down low behind the water heater, blind and still partially deaf from the gun blast. My only reality was the curve of the steel against my hands.

I heard a gurgling noise close by. My hearing was coming back. Water. Hot water from the water heater was gurgling through the bullet hole and splattering onto the cement floor. It was absolutely pitch-black. I couldn't even detect any outlines.

"I thought you were smart," he said. "There's no other way out of this basement. Come out. You show me that stuff in his papers and maybe we'll talk."

It was too dark to pinpoint Tommy's location other than by sound. His voice had come from somewhere near the stairs. He probably hadn't moved since the light went out. He probably was still standing against that table.

Get to the back, I told myself as I crouched down. I reached around in the darkness, trying to find something, anything. My hand bumped a plastic water bucket. The splatter of the water masked the noise.

My eyes had adjusted just a little. I could barely make out the shape of the stairway. I lifted the bucket as I slowly stood up behind the water heater.

Get to the back. Get away from him.

I inched to the left along the wall, holding the bucket in my left hand, using the noise of the splashing water as cover. When I was clear of the water heater I slowly took a deep breath and heaved the bucket toward the stairs. I tensed, waiting for it to hit, trying to visualize my path toward the back of the basement.

The bucket hit the ground with a clonk. There was a startled grunt and then a spark of light and a thunderous roar as I scrambled toward the passageway that led into the back rooms of the basement.

I leaned my back against the passageway hall, temporarily deaf from the gun blast. I tried to keep my breathing slow and quiet. I strained my ears, waiting for the ringing to subside, waiting for my hearing to return.

I couldn't see anything. I couldn't hear anything. Every few seconds I winced involuntarily, expecting another spark of light and another thunderous roar.

Despite the pitch darkness, Tommy still had the crucial advantage: he had the gun. He also knew that my only avenue of escape was up the wooden staircase. The only two basement windows had been boarded up for years. Even if I were able to reach the staircase, how would I ever make it up alive? There was just enough light over there and the wooden steps creaked just enough to turn the staircase into an easy target range.

My mind was racing as I edged slowly, slowly, down the passageway, toward the rear storage room. I didn't realize my hearing had returned until there was a sudden scraping noise followed by a "Shit." I stopped, trying to get my bearings. The sounds put him beyond the water heater. He must have been moving slowly along the wall, perhaps searching for a light switch. There wasn't any, thank God. All the lights in the basement had pull cords.

I continued down the passageway. With my back against

the wall, I inched all the way to the last storage room and stepped inside. Using memory and touch as guides, I found the bag of softball equipment on the concrete floor. I paused, straining my ears, trying to hear over the hammering of my heart. Nothing but the distant splashing of water.

Kneeling, I slowly, carefully unzipped the bag, slid my hand inside, found the bat handle. I was drenched in sweat. My arms were shaking as I carefully removed the aluminum bat, making sure not to scrape anything. I turned, still on my knees. He could be anywhere. He could be upstairs searching for a flashlight. He could be right outside this storage room waiting for me.

"Hey!" His voice came from somewhere down the passageway back in the main area of the basement. "You wanna play, we can play. Just like that movie, eh? This is cool. Except you forgot your gun." He snickered. "Clarice," he crooned. "Clarice."

I got to my feet and stepped out of the storage area. When I reached the end of the passageway, I stopped against the wall and tried to scan the main basement area. My eyes had adjusted to the dark as much as they were likely to. All I could make out was vague outlines—the shape of the water heater located at a diagonal across the basement to my right, the shape of the washing machine and dryer beyond that, the slant of the stairway ahead on the left.

I strained my eyes. I couldn't detect a human shape anywhere. He could be under the stairs. He could be crouching by the table at the foot of the stairs. He could be standing behind the bags of winter coats hanging from the pipes somewhere on my left. He could be anywhere.

Water was still splattering onto the floor. The stairway was my only option. The only option. I had to somehow get over there, and then charge up and pray he couldn't hit a moving target. At least I had a chance that way. Otherwise it was only a matter of time. I had to reach the stairway.

Gripping the bat with both hands, I edged forward and to my right.

Little goals.

One at a time.

The first goal was the side wall. Then the water heater. If

I made it that far, then I could worry about getting psyched for a dash up the stairs.

I took one step and waited. Nothing. A step, a pause, a step, a pause.

I winced. Any moment I expected to feel the jab of a cold, hard muzzle against my temple.

I reached the wall. I strained my eyes. The outline of the water heater was barely visible ten feet away. That meant the metal tub sink had to be directly in front of me. I moved forward. My thigh made silent contact with the sink. I turned so that my backside was against the sink. Keeping myself in that position, the bat cocked in my hands, I worked my way around the rim of the sink until I was pressed back against the wall.

My arms were shaking. The bat felt like a lead pipe. I lowered it. My entire body was slick with perspiration. Beads of sweat kept running into my eyes.

The water heater was to my right. I held my breath. Creeping along the wall toward the sound of splashing water, I slid in behind the water heater.

Yes.

Slowly, I exhaled. The foot of the stairs was fifteen feet away. The distance seemed like the length of a football field. There was enough light from upstairs to faintly illuminate the top few stairs. I strained my eyes. There was no body shape near the stairs.

He's out there, I told myself. *Be ready for him.*

I pressed the end of the bat against the top of my shoe. I didn't want to let an accidental scrape of the bat give away my position.

I stared at the foot of the stairs.

You can do it.

I took a deep breath, held it for a moment, and slowly exhaled.

You can do it. Fly. Just fly.

"Here, pussy, pussy."

Startled, I jerked my head back, thonking it against the cement wall. I grimaced, holding my breath. He was standing out front to my left, perhaps six feet away from the wall, somewhere between the tub sink to the left and the water heater.

I peered into the dark. I couldn't see a thing.

He chuckled. "Come out, little pussy. Come out."

He was closer, moving toward the water heater. I took a deep breath and held it.

"Here, pussy."

He was just a few feet away, on the other side of the water heater, moving slowly toward the stairs. He would pass in front of the water heater. Gripping the bat, I moved slowly to the right until I was standing in the clear, between the water heater and the dryer. I held the bat up, as if I were in the batter's box.

The gurgling and splattering water masked any sound.

I could smell him. I could sense his position.

Now, I told myself as I cocked the bat.

Please, God, please.

I aimed blind at what I hoped was knee level.

Now, I said, and I swung as hard as I could.

Thunk.

The bat whacked into the side of his leg. I could hear the bone crack.

He screamed in pain as he crumpled at my feet.

Still moving blind, my ears buzzing, I raised the bat over my head like a club and swung down hard. It hit the cement floor. The metal vibrations through the bat handle felt like an electric shock.

Gasping for breath, I raised the bat and swung down again. This time I made contact. The bat crunched into a soft part of his body. He howled. I swung again. Another howl.

The world suddenly shifted into fast forward. Nearly hysterical, I dropped the bat and stumbled toward the staircase, lunging for the handrail. I bolted up the stairs, sobbing for breath. I slipped. There was a roar of gunfire as I grasped for the rail. A stair splintered behind me. I grabbed for the door handle and burst into the kitchen, slamming the door behind me.

Moaning and wheezing, I grabbed the telephone with one hand and opened the knife drawer with the other. I punched in 911 and pulled out my mother's meat cleaver. I backed out of the kitchen as far as the cord would stretch. I stared at the basement door, mumbling, "Answer it, goddammit. Come on come on come on come on."

A policewoman answered on the third ring.

"There's a killer in my basement," I said, struggling to keep my voice coherent, remembering that these calls were taped. *Give them enough.* "His name is Tommy Landau. He's killed others. He has a gun. He tried to kill me. I'm Rachel Gold. He's Tommy Landau." I gave her my address. "Hurry, goddammit! Hurry! Hurry!"

I didn't hang up. I stood there staring at the basement door, gasping for breath. Waiting. Waiting

She came back on the line. "They're on their way, ma'am. Get out of the house."

"Right," I said mechanically, eyes on the basement door. I gripped the meat cleaver.

"The police are coming!" I shouted at the door.

In the silence that followed, the bedlam inside me seemed to recede. The ringing in my ears stopped. My heartbeat slowed. Everything became almost microscopically focused. I could hear the electric hum of the kitchen clock, the distant drip of the bathroom sink.

I took two steps closer to the basement door. His leg was broken. Had to be. He wasn't going anywhere.

Here pussy. That's what he'd said. Here, pussy? And then he laughed.

The cat.

The rush of anger blurred my vision—zero to warp speed in a flash. "You bastard!" I screamed at the closed door.

In the distance I could hear the wail of police sirens. I moved closer, until I was pressed against the wall near the basement door. I strained my ears. I heard a groan of pain. It came from down in the basement.

"It's over, Tommy," I shouted. "The police are here."

I listened for movement below. I heard nothing. I waited. The police sirens were getting louder.

I reached for the door handle, as fear struggled against rage. But then I remembered Gitel and my mother's broken arm. I opened the door a crack. I inched my head along the wall toward the doorway.

"Tommy," I said. I quickly peeked around the edge of the doorway as light from the kitchen illuminated the scene. "You said you—" I stopped.

He was seated on the bottom stair, his back to me. His right leg was bent at a horrible angle. It was dark down there, too dark to make out details. He seemed to be hunched forward.

"It's over," I said angrily. "You said you'd be the one they'd remember. You'd better hope they'll give you enough time to write your memoirs on death row."

Outside there were the sounds of arriving police cars— screeching brakes, skidding tires, doors slamming. As I glanced around, flashing red lights strobed through the front windows and into the kitchen.

As I turned back toward the basement, Tommy leaned forward, and suddenly the back of his head exploded. There was a concussive boom, a micro-second of silence, and then splats and thunks all around me. I stared in horror at the shuddering body. Clots of blood spurted rhythmically into the air from the pulpy stump on his shoulders. His body reared back for a long moment, the arms flailing, and then pitched forward onto the floor.

I heard the police running up the front walk toward the house, their walkie-talkies crackling. I turned away from the basement and leaned back against the kitchen wall, staring up at the ceiling. I slid down to a sitting position and hugged my knees to my chest. As the police came charging into the kitchen, I rested my chin on my knees and closed my eyes.

EPILOGUE

"Really?" Benny said with a big grin. "What happened?"

I shrugged, amused. "Farmer Bob's been born again."

"Come on," Benny scoffed.

"That's what he claims. Big Sal died about a week ago. Two nights later, while Bob was still in mourning, Jesus appeared in his bedroom."

"With another collie?"

I shook my head. "With some celestial marital advice. As soon as Jesus left, Bob hopped in his pickup, drove over to June's place, got down on his knees, and begged for forgiveness."

"She fell for it?"

"Yep," I said with a smile. "They were in yesterday to sign the court dismissal papers. You should have seen them. Like a pair of newlyweds. In fact, as soon as the crops are in, they're heading off to Orlando for a second honeymoon."

Benny reached for another bottle of Sam Adams and removed the cap with a bottle opener. He had showed up at my office late that afternoon on his way home from a law school faculty meeting. Happy Hour, he had announced as he walked in with a chilled six-pack of Sam Adams and a bag of peanuts.

Benny sat back and shook his head in wonder. "That was one kinky divorce case."

"And," I reminded him as I reached for another handful of peanuts, "my last divorce case."

He took a long sip of beer. "Turns out Charles Kimball was serious."

"Really?"

"Yep. He's leaving town. One of the guys on the faculty is friends with the dean of the law school at North Carolina. He confirmed that Kimball's going to run their trial practice program."

I leaned back in my chair and shook my head wearily. "Some month."

"No kidding."

Thirty days ago, I'd watched Tommy Landau die at the foot of my basement stairs. Although he'd killed himself at approximately 10:30 P.M., the official time of death, as recorded in the police report, was 1:30 A.M. His final metamorphosis began somewhere in that gap and was complete two days later, which is when the first account of his death appeared in the *Post-Dispatch*.

The initial hint came in the wee hours that first night, during a break in the police interrogation. I was alone in the room when Harris Landau came in. "Hello, Rachel," he said quietly. He looked haggard but resolute. We talked for a few moments, and then he said, "My son was a monster, but now that he's dead, there's nothing to be gained by telling the world. Allow me to bury him without a freak show."

I did, without even having to try.

By the time Harris Landau's spin doctors were through, the late Tommy Landau was just another victim of the real estate slump. Despondent over a failed marriage that had been strained to the breaking point by his financial woes, he took a gun and ended his life in an undisclosed location. Although he hadn't left a suicide note, he did call his father earlier that night.

"Tommy told me to tell his wife that he was sorry," Harris Landau said. "He told me to tell his children that he loved them. I was worried. He sounded down. I asked him if there was anything wrong, but he hung up."

That's the exact quote, as published in the third paragraph of a four-paragraph story that appeared on page five of the second section of the *Post-Dispatch* under a small headline that read, *Real Estate Developer Dies from Gunshot Wound.*

Ironically, the story fit the police department's ready-made theory about Tommy, which was shaped by the recent spree of angry men attacking their ex-wives' divorce attorneys. From the cops' perspective, Tommy neatly fit that cubbyhole, especially given his prior conduct, which included my 911 call to get him out of my office and (and as revealed in the billing records for his portable phone) his thirty-seven-second telephone call to my home telephone number late on the night that Gitel was decapitated. They essentially closed his file without looking beyond the divorce. As for the murder of Andros, the bogus leads supplied by Charles Kimball's source continued to guide the police investigation.

Eileen Landau no longer needed a divorce lawyer. I found her a good workout specialist with plenty of real estate experience. In our last meeting, I explained the Cayman Islands situation to Eileen. As sole heir under Tommy's will, she now owned Capital Investments, Ltd. That meant she also owned a Grand Cayman bank account containing the proceeds of at least one key-man life insurance policy. In death, the two men in her life had placed her in a far better financial position than she would have been in if either had lived.

"You talked to your sister lately?" Benny asked.

I nodded. "She's doing okay. Richie's never going to become Rudolph Valentino, but he's better than before. They seem happier."

He took another sip of beer and gave me an impish grin. "And look at you. Going on a double date tonight with your mom."

"It's not really a double date."

"Oh? You've got a date, she's got a date, and all four of you are going to the same place in one car."

I felt my cheeks redden. "Okay, it's a double date."

My mother and I met our dates ten days ago when I took her to the orthopedist to get her cast removed. We had both known Dr. Seymour Feldman for years. In fact, he had put a cast on me when I was ten years old and broke my wrist falling out of a tree. It so happened that his son, Mark, was now in the practice as well, and he joined us while we were in his father's office. Seymour was recently divorced, Mark had never married, both had good senses of humor, Mark had gentle eyes, and between them they had four mezzanine seats to the evening performance of *Les Misérables*. If you're going to double-date with your mom, I can think of worse ways.

"What about poor old Tex?" Benny asked.

"She still likes him. But it's not like they're going steady or anything."

Our Happy Hour came to an end. As I was closing up the office, the phone rang. I glanced over at Benny.

He shrugged. "Take it," he said. "It could be General Motors with a big case."

I reached for the telephone on my secretary's desk.

"Please hold for Mr. Max Feigelbaum," his secretary cooed.

I turned to Benny, covering the mouthpiece with my hand. "Max Feigelbaum," I whispered in surprise. Benny raised his eyebrows, intrigued.

Although I'd never met Max, I knew him by reputation and had seen him more than once in the hallways of the Circuit Court of Cook County back in my Chicago days. He was a tanned and ruthless little ferret who wore dark glasses and Italian suits and was one of the most feared divorce lawyers in Chicago. His principal victims were the men of the Chicago ruling class who had had the misfortune (literally) of marrying one of Max's future clients.

"Rachel, Max Fiegelbaum in Chicago." He had a classic Chicago accent ("Chi-cawgo") and spoke in a slow, raspy tone that reminded me of Jack Nicholson.

"Hello, Max," I said cautiously.

"I need you to handle a domestic matter down there."

"Well," I said as I looked over at Benny and shook my head, "I'm getting out of divorce work."

"You'll want to make an exception for this one. It's a beaut. Lady's name is Tricia Fletcher. Her ex-husband's a putz named Deb Fletcher. You used to work at his firm back in Chicago."

"I know him," I said, intrigued in spite of myself. I could feel those litigator juices starting to flow.

"He's screwed up big-time," Feigelbaum continued. "Trying to hide assets, crap like that. I've decided it's time to drill Mr. L. Debevoise Fletcher, Esquire, a brand-new asshole. I'll need a St. Louis firm to help out. I hear you got brass balls. You want in?"

I could feel my pulse quicken. Asking a trial lawyer if she wants to take part in a good courtroom battle is like asking a ballplayer if he wants to take part in a World Series.

"By the way," he continued before I could answer, "you'll need some help on this one. Money's no object. You got a reliable associate?"

I looked over at Benny and grinned.

"What?" Benny asked eagerly.

I covered the mouthpiece. "Trust me," I whispered back.

"Well?" Feigelbaum asked.

"I've got the perfect associate," I said with a wink at Benny, "and I'm sure he'd love a shot at Deb Fletcher."

"Fletcher?" Benny said, his eyes widening with delight. "Yes!" he hissed as he pumped his fist.

"Good," Feigelbaum grunted. "I'll have my girl ship you the documents."

"Excuse me," I said, with feigned indignance. "Your *what*?"

"Aw, shit. No offense. I meant the woman who is my secretary. So you'll do the case, huh?"

"Maxie," I said with a smile, "I think this is the beginning of a beautiful friendship."

Don't miss the next Rachel Gold mystery,
Due Diligence,
available at bookstores now
in a Dutton hardcover edition

DUE DILIGENCE

PROLOGUE

Down in the darkness it waits. Down in the subbasement of the Gateway Corporate Tower. From its open maw comes the stench of rotting flesh. Its single eye glows red.

The tenants of the Gateway Corporate Tower include lawyers and accountants, architects and insurance agents, advertising executives and business consultants. None has ever ventured down to the subbasement. None has ever imagined what is down there, waiting silently.

The trash chute of the Gateway Corporate Tower is essentially a 240-foot stainless steel tube that runs from the subbasement to the top floor, eighteen stories above Olive Street. It drops through fifteen floors in a straight perpendicular near the north elevator shaft, veers north at a 45° angle through two levels of the aboveground parking garage and then makes a final, two-story descent, emerging at a steep angle through the ceiling of the subbasement near the northeast corner of the building.

Motionless, it waits beneath the open end of the trash chute. By any standard, it is huge. Twenty-four feet from end to end, nearly eight feet wide, just shy of seven feet at its tallest point. It weighs at least fourteen tons, although, for obvious reasons, no one has ever tried to maneuver it onto a scale for a more precise measurement.

The night cleaning crews cherished that chute. There was

access to it on every floor, usually in a utility closet around
the corner from the elevators. Better yet, the building's de-
signers had specified access doors large enough to accommo-
date just about any form, shape, or quantity of trash that the
office tenants and the ground-level restaurant and newsstand
were likely to produce during a busy day. As a result, there
was never need for a time-consuming trip down the freight elevator from the upper floors to the subbasement to unload a
cumbersome cloth hamper. Just shove the trash down the
chute and get on to the next office.

It is squat and massive, with all that weight resting upon
four small legs. Those legs seem almost dainty in contrast to
the bulk they support.

The eight-person night crew from Ace Office Maintenance
arrived each weekday shortly after 5 P.M., started on the lower
floors and gradually worked their way up, usually reaching
the top floor a little after midnight.

The consulting firm of Smilow & Sullivan, Ltd. occupied
the entire ninth floor. Those at the firm who regularly worked
late knew that the cleaning crew reached their floor around
nine o'clock and left before ten. The pattern held that night.
The first two members of the night crew (Darlene Washington
and LaTisha Forest) got off the elevator on the ninth floor at
9:06 P.M. The last departing member of the night crew (Yao-
Wen Hsieh) boarded the elevator for the tenth floor at 9:45
P.M.

The police eventually interviewed all eight members of the
crew. All remembered seeing him up there, as did Cynthia
O'Malley (who saw him in the hall) and Mr. Sullivan (who
poked his head in his office on his way out). According to the
night crew, he was definitely alive and hard at work when
they left, and by then Cynthia and Mr. Sullivan were definitely gone. Yao-Wen Hsieh was in the firm's lobby vacu-
uming the carpet at 9:15 P.M. when Cynthia boarded the down
elevator carrying her purse and jacket. Three members of the
crew saw Mr. Sullivan. He arrived in his tuxedo straight from
the Barnes Hospital fundraiser around 9:30 P.M., picked up a
few papers from his desk, and left ten minutes later. The time
of Cynthia's departure and Mr. Sullivan's brief visit were both

confirmed by the guard downstairs, who saw Cynthia sign out when she left and watched Mr. Sullivan sign in and out.

In short, according to the eyewitness and the sign-in sheet, there should have been only one person left on the ninth floor at quarter to ten that night. He was definitely up there.

Unfortunately, he was just as definitely not alone.

Although it has stirred only once in the last twenty hours, it is ready. Day or night, summer or winter, it's always ready. It is, quite literally, programmed for vigilance. Its single red eye, hard-wired into its tiny brain, never closes. And that brain—assuming that something so limited can still be called a brain—is primed to issue the one command that defines its existence.

The command—like the command issued from any brain—is just a weak electronic blip that travels quickly from brain to receptor. Here, that blip means "GO!" And here, the receptor is a crushing jaw, technically known as a power wedge. The power wedge is hidden within the open maw and aptly named; it can exert more than 122,000 pounds of force. Under that kind of pressure, a man's skull will crumple like a soft-boiled egg beneath a tractor wheel.

He often worked late. It had been his style ever since joining the firm as the hotshot boy wonder out of Purdue seven years ago. His promotion to manager last winter had not diminished his capacity for long hours. He typically stayed down late two or three nights each week. On Saturdays—true to his nickname FILO—he was usually first in and last out.

Looking back, Mr. Sullivan told the police, the young man had seemed a tad jumpy that night, although, he cautioned, his observation was based on a conversation that lasted less than sixty seconds. Nevertheless, Mr. Sullivan was on target. The young man had been a tad jumpy. More than just a tad. Distressed was a better word.

At 10:20 P.M. he was standing at the worktable just outside the copy room collating a stack of documents to make a working copy to take home with him that night. The hallway was carpeted, he was agitated, he hadn't been sleeping well, and the document on top of the pile was clearly the most troubling one—all of which may explain why he didn't hear the approach. The attack was swift, professional and nearly painless—a powerful arm grabbing him from behind, a sharp pressure on the side of his neck, and then fade-out.

Echoing down the steel tube comes the sound of an access door opening.

It doesn't hear the sound.

It doesn't hear a thing. Unable to hear, or to even detect the presence of sound waves, it remains unaware of the noise above, unaware that something is about to come sliding down the tube.

But that doesn't matter. It's programmed for vigilance. It simply waits. Patiently.

Unconscious, he plummeted down the chute in total darkness. The medical examiner surmised that he may have stiffened just before his body hit the 45° bend, which would have made it even worse. The impact shattered both ankles and splintered his right tibia, jamming shards of bone through the skin of his lower leg. If he was unfortunate enough to regain consciousness during that descent, he surely lost it upon impact.

It took a full five minutes for his limp body to work its way through the bend in the tube. The blood helped lubricate the passage. Once through the bend, his body started sliding, feet first, down the tube, which passed at an angle through the two levels of the aboveground parking garage. His body gradually accelerated as it approached the final drop-off. Unconscious, he slid over the edge and plunged the final fifteen feet, landing facedown on top of several large bags of trash.

The single red eye detected motion. The falling body briefly broke the narrow beam of red light when it dropped into the open maw—barely a flicker, far too quick to trigger the countdown.

Perhaps it was the stench. Perhaps it was the pain. Perhaps it was the thud of yet another bag of trash landing on his back. Whatever the cause, he regained consciousness inside the chamber, according to the medical examiner.

It was pitch black, the air heavy with the stench of putrefaction. The large bags beneath him felt like bunchy, crinkly cushions. When he opened his eyes, he saw the eye. It was directly in front of him, about two feet above his head. There was a thin beam of red light emanating from the eye.

He would have been confused, of course. In the total darkness, the red beam would have seemed almost unearthly. He may have reached up to pass his hand through the beam. It would have made a fuzzy red dot on his palm.

The interruption is long enough to trigger the countdown: Ten . . . Nine . . . Eight—He let his hand fall forward onto the bag of trash—*Seven. The countdown stops. The timer resets.*

Somehow, despite the excruciating pain, he managed to pull himself into a sitting position. It took a long time, and the effort left him shaking and drenched with sweat.

The sensor triggered the countdown: Ten . . . Nine . . . Eight . . . Seven . . . Six—As he waited for his jagged breathing to return to normal, his body and mind on the verge of shock, the intense pain muddling his thoughts, perhaps he looked down at the beam. The red dot would have been centered on his chest—*Five . . . Four . . . Three*—According to the medical examiner, he probably lunged toward the front wall, toward the single red eye—*Two . . . One . . . Zero.*

The brain fires its one command: GO!

Exactly 2.5 seconds later, the power wedge system responds, precisely in accordance with the manufacturer's specs.

He was leaning against the wall when the 35-horsepower engine kicked on with an electric growl. The noises came from somewhere just beyond the wall. At first he would not have realized the deadly relevance of the sound.

And then the lurch.

It would have seemed as if part of the wall was moving toward him—which is precisely what was happening. The lower half of the wall was actually the business end of the power wedge ram system, pressing toward him at the rate of two inches per second.

As the power wedge slowly shoved him backwards into the bags of trash, he must have strained for the answer. The stench, the bags of trash, his plunge down the metal chute. *Where was he? What the hell was happening?*

Based on his final body position, he had tried to shove the power wedge back, grunting and gasping, struggling to hold it at arm's length. The trash behind him began to compress, to solidify. His arms strained against the advancing metal. Perhaps he screamed for help. The increasing pressure would have constrained his voice.

Eventually, his arms buckled.

As designed by the mechanical engineers at the Vanguard Trashpacker Corporation, the compacting cycle on the Model 7800 lasts 42 seconds. The power wedge ram is designed to push forward 84 inches into the receiving chamber without stopping. That distance, in the industry jargon, is known as the "ram stroke." With 122,000 pounds of pressure supplied by the latest in hydraulic cylinder technology, the Model 7800's ram stroke is as close to unstoppable as modern engineering techniques can achieve.

On this occasion, the power wedge performs as designed. When it completes the 84-inch journey forward into the chamber, the gears shift and it slowly retracts until flush again with the rest of the front wall. The electric motor shuts off with a metallic shudder.

Other than the occasional crinkling sound of a bag of compressed trash expanding, there is no motion and there is no sound inside the compactor.

Bags of trash continued to plunge down the chute from higher and ever-higher elevations within the Gateway Corporate Tower. The mound grew closer and closer to red beam until, around 12:30 A.M., a falling bag came to rest in the middle of the beam, triggering one last compacting cycle for the night.

The cleaning crew left the building at 1:05 A.M.

Down in the darkness it waits. Down in the subbasement of the Gateway Corporate Tower. From its open maw comes the stench of rotting flesh. Its single eye glows red.

Ⓢ SIGNET   Ⓞ ONYX   (0451)

SUPER SLEUTHS

☐ **HEIR CONDITION** *A Schuyler Ridgway Mystery* by Tierney McClellan. Schuyler Ridgway works as a real estate agent and watches videos at home alone on Saturday nights. She is definitely not having an illicit affair with a rich, elderly Louisville businessman, and she certainly hasn't murdered him. She's never even met Ephraim Benjamin Cross. So why has he left her a small fortune in his will? Now the Cross clan believes she's his mistress, and the police think she's his killer.   (181441—$3.99)

☐ **FOLLOWING JANE** *A Barrett Lake Mystery* by Shelly Singer. Teenager Jane Wahlman had witnessed the brutal stabbing of a high school teacher in a local supermarket and then suddenly vanished. Berkeley teacher Barrett Lake will follow Jane's trail in return for a break into the private eye business—the toughest task she's ever faced.   (175239—$4.50)

☐ **FINAL ATONEMENT** *A Doug Orlando Mystery* by Steve Johnson. Detective Doug Orlando must catch the murderer of Rabbi Avraham Rabowitz, in a case that moves from the depths of the ghetto to the highrise office of a glamor-boy real estate tycoon.   (403320—$3.99)

☐ **THE HANGMAN'S BEAUTIFUL DAUGHTER** by Sharyn McCrumb. The grisly case of murder was supposed to be "open and shut," but it bothered Sheriff Spencer Arrowood. He had the worried feeling that the bad things were far from over. "A haunting novel of suspense with a fresh new voice ... Sharyn McCrumb is a born storyteller!"—Mary Higgins Clark   (403703—$5.50)

Prices slightly higher in Canada

Buy them at your local bookstore or use this convenient coupon for ordering.

PENGUIN USA
P.O. Box 999 — Dept. #17109
Bergenfield, New Jersey 07621

Please send me the books I have checked above.
I am enclosing $_____ (please add $2.00 to cover postage and handling). Send check or money order (no cash or C.O.D.'s) or charge by Mastercard or VISA (with a $15.00 minimum). Prices and numbers are subject to change without notice.

Card #_____ Exp. Date _____
Signature_____
Name_____
Address_____
City _____ State _____ Zip Code _____

For faster service when ordering by credit card call **1-800-253-6476**

Allow a minimum of 4-6 weeks for delivery. This offer is subject to change without notice.

Get a $1.00 rebate on
FIRM AMBITIONS!

To get your $1.00 rebate, mail:

- Original sales receipt for FIRM AMBITIONS
  with price circled
- This rebate certificate or photocopy of certificate
- Write in book UPC number_____

To: FIRM AMBITIONS REBATE
P.O. Box 8146
Grand Rapids, MN 55745-8146

Name_____
Address_____
City_____ State_____ Zip_____

⬛ Onyx

This certificate or photocopy of certificate must accompany your request. Void where prohibited, taxed, or restricted. Allow 4-6 weeks for shipment of rebate in U.S. funds. Offer good only in U.S. and its territories and Canada. Offer expires 11/30/95. Mail received until 12/15/95.

PENGUIN USA

Printed in the USA

Plan your summer dream vacation with the
⓪ Signet/Onyx ⊛
BOOKS THAT TAKE YOU ANYWHERE
YOU WANT TO GO Contest

GRAND PRIZE $5,000 in CASH!
3 – 1st Prizes $1,000 in CASH!
25 – 2nd Prizes $100 in CASH!

To enter:

1. Answer the following question: **WHY WAS THIS BOOK THE IDEAL SUMMER READ?**
2. Write your answer on a separate piece of paper (in 25 words or less)
3. Include your name and address (street, city, state, zip code)
4. Send to: **BOOKS THAT TAKE YOU ANYWHERE YOU WANT TO GO** Contest P.O. Box 844, Medford, NY 11763

Official Rules:

1. To enter, hand print your name and complete address on a piece of paper (no larger than 8-1/2" x 11") and in 25 words or less complete the following statement: "Why Was This Book The Ideal Summer Read?" Staple this form to your entry and mail to: BOOKS THAT TAKE YOU ANYWHERE YOU WANT TO GO Contest, P.O. Box 844, Medford, NY 11763. Entries must be received by December 15, 1995 to be eligible. Not responsible for late, lost, misdirected mail or printing errors.

2. Entries will be judged by Marden-Kane, Inc. an independent judging organization in conjunction with Penguin USA based upon the following criteria: Originality 35%, Content 35%, Sincerity 20%, and Clarity 10%. By entering this contest entrants accept and agree to be bound by these rules and the decision of the judges which shall be final and binding. All entries become the property of the sponsor and will not be acknowledged or returned. Each entry must be the original work of the entrant.

3. PRIZES: Grand Prize (1) $5,000.00 cash; First Prize (3) each winner receives $1,000.00 cash; Second Prize (25) each winner receives $100.00 cash. Total prize value $10,500.00.

4. Contest open to residents of the United States 18 years of age and older, except employees and the immediate families of Penguin USA, its affiliates, subsidiaries, advertising agencies, and Marden-Kane, Inc. Void in FL, VT, MD, AZ, and wherever else prohibited by law. All Federal, state, and local laws and regulations apply. Winners will be notified by mail and may be required to execute an affidavit of eligibility and release which must be completed and returned within 14 days of receipt, or an alternate winner will be selected. Taxes, if any, are the sole responsibility of the prize winners. All prizes will be awarded. Limit one prize per contestant. Winners consent to the use of their name and/or photograph or likeness for advertising/publicity purposes without additional compensation (except where prohibited).

5. For a list of winners available after January 31, 1996 include a self-addressed stamped envelope with your entry.

Be sure to read all the ideal summer books from Signet/Onyx:

INSOMNIA
Stephen King

BLESSING IN DISGUISE
Eileen Goudge

THE BURGLAR WHO TRADED TED WILLIAMS
Lawrence Block

DEADLY PURSUIT
Brian Harper

NIGHT SHALL OVERTAKE US
Kate Saunders

FIRST OFFENSE
Nancy Taylor Rosenberg

JUSTICE DENIED
Robert K. Tanenbaum

ONLY YOU
Cynthia Victor

THICKER THAN WATER
Linda Barlow and
William G. Tapply

FIRM AMBITIONS
Michael A. Kahn

Signet Ⓞ Onyx®
Printed in the USA